ALSO BY JEFFREY A. CARVER

DRAGON RIGGER

JEFFREY A. CARVER

A TOM DOHERTY ASSOCIATES BOOK
NEW YORK

DRAGON RIGGER

Copyright © 1993 by Jeffrey A. Carver

Cover art by Boris Vallejo

Edited by James R. Frenkel

A Tor Book
Published by Tom Doherty Associates, Inc.
175 Fifth Avenue
New York, N.Y. 10010

Tor® is a registered trademark of Tom Doherty Associates, Inc.

ISBN: 0-812-53323-2

First edition: June 1993
First mass market edition: September 1994

Printed in the United States of America

0 9 8 7 6 5 4 3 2

For all my friends at Pilgrim,
wherever the winds may take you . . .

*

. . . and for Sam,
dragon among dogs.
See you in the Final Dream Mountain.

Jael's first arrival, Dragons in the Stars

Site of Highwing's Garden

Farsight's cavern

Windrush's cavern

Valley of Fallen Light

...un ...agon ...mpment

...ile ...sion

Amethyst Cliffs

Jael's second arrival, Dragons in the Stars

the Edge of the Realm

Deep Caverns

The Held Land

Grotto Garden

Forest Mountains

...n of ...irits

beneath the Realm

Cavern of Clouds Below

Sawtoothed Ridge

Pool of Visions

Point of arrival of Jael's ship in Dragon Rigger

ELISA MITCHELL 1992

PART ONE
THE DRAGONS

PROLOGUE

"Now you all know—" the lanky ex-rigger paused to gulp from his ale—*ahhhh!*—"just how dangerous star travel can be." He peered out across the spaceport bar, studying the faces looking back at him—mostly young star-riggers who *thought* they knew a lot more than they did. "You all know that much, right?" he asked rhetorically. "Well, I'm *tellin'* you, it's a lot more dangerous than you ever imagined. Swear t'God!"

He burped and made a sweeping gesture with his mug. He reeled a little from the movement. His unkempt hair fell across his eyes, and he swept it back in annoyance. He had a story to tell, and the audience was volatile. Mustn't keep them waiting. "Y'see—"

"Just tell us the frickin' story, will you?" a fat man complained, from across the room.

"I *am* tellin' ya, dammit!" he said with a glare. He ticked off on his fingers the events that had occurred seven years ago this month. "*One!* We flew into the mountain region, cocky as all hell, thinking—there ain't nothing that can hurt *us.* We're two topflight, cream-of-the-crop, stay-out-of-our way, kick-ass riggers! Right? Besides, everyone knows there are no dragons really *there.*" He snorted at his own words. He glanced up, and twitched as a rigger in the back of the bar, not a human but some kind of horse-headed Swert, inhaled something from a chrome cylinder and blew an enormous, billowing neon bubble into the air above the barroom patrons.

He continued quickly, before anyone could get distracted. "*Two!* It wasn't more'n ten minutes before a whole flight of dragons appeared—and I don't mean some kinda cute lizards. I mean *dragons*. Huge things! We tried to make contact with them. *Friendly* contact." He barked out a bitter laugh, which seemed to have an odd effect on his audience. Some looked cynical, others looked puzzled. At least he was getting through to somebody.

A sword-wielding knight sprang up from the top of someone's head about three tables back and stabbed a few times with its blade, before winking out. The ex-rigger glared at the kid with the holo, a scrawny-looking, red-haired misfit who didn't even look old enough to be at a bar. The kid snickered nervously.

"*Three!*" the rigger roared, trying to overcome the interruption. "The bastards set on us like a pack of Alsepian blood wolves!"

"A real dogfight, eh?" someone called helpfully.

"It *was* a dogfight!" the rigger snapped. "Just like in prespace times. Except there was just the two of us in our ship, and at least four of them, flyin' around like crazy, blowing fire and smoke and tryin' to knock us out of the sky! You wouldn't've known we were in space, it looked so much like real mountains and sky. Never *seen* anything so real in the Flux. We couldn't do a thing to change the image, except turn our ship into a fighter-flyer and pray for the best." He shook his head, lost in his own story. "But our best wasn't much. There we were, twistin' and turnin' in the air, tryin' to scoot away from 'em. But—" and his voice caught as the fear rolled back up his spine, as though it had happened yesterday.

"They beat you, is that what you're trying to say?" snickered the red-haired kid.

The rigger leveled a drunken gaze at his taunter, so cocky and naive. Another holo erupted from the kid's head—a cartoonish figure of a man reeling and spinning before falling over with a sword hilt sticking out of his stomach. That evoked a few sardonic titters, which was clearly the reaction the kid wanted. The older rigger shook his head. He hated whiny, false bravado.

"Yeah, they beat us, you little punk. Four dragons, each

one the size of this room, beat us in combat. Can you imagine that? We musta been weaklings."

He was answered with a restless stirring, and he continued at once. "They didn't kill us right off, though. They boxed us in and forced us down on a plateau. *Full-stop landing.*" He paused for emphasis. The Flux never stopped moving in its endless course among the stars; everyone knew that. Only this time it had.

"They started lookin' us over," he said more softly. "Four fire-breathin' dragons, about to flame us to cinders right there in the net—and two scared-as-piss riggers, I don't mind admittin' it." He paused and gulped his ale. "I didn't think I'd ever see home again. And I wouldn't've, either, if it hadn't been for the iffit, I mean if'ing . . ." He struggled with the memory, teetering, even with one elbow propped on the wooden bartop to support himself. "If that thing hadn't've showed up and told the dragons—" A belch erupted without warning from his throat, interrupting him.

"Let me guess! A prophecy?" someone shouted.

He stared in the general direction of the shout. He had at least some of them listening, even if they didn't want to admit it. "Well, you're getting a little ahead of the story, but yes, it told them the proph—*buurp!*—ecy." He put his fist over his mouth in embarrassment.

"Which of course *you're* going to tell *us!*" called a whip-bodied humanoid, who maybe didn't know human rules of etiquette, or maybe couldn't help speaking in such a sneering tone of voice.

"Unless you don't remember it!" called a shrill-voiced woman. Derisive laughter echoed after her.

"I remember it!" he said hotly. "Better than you remember your own name! Just give me a second to collect myself." He was trying not to become angry.

"Canteen, we've given you too much time already!" yelled a man just down the stand-up bar from him. "Tell us another one, will you? Of course—" and the drinker guffawed—"we won't believe that one, either. We don't even believe you when you're sober!"

"Oh, no?" The rigger drew himself up in an effort to maintain some dignity. "Well, this partic'lar story happens to be true, you half-witted imbecile. And my name is *Kan-Kon*, if you don't mind." He ignored the answering cackles and continued, heedless of the momentum that was clearly building against him. "So you don't think I'm tellin' the truth? Let me tell you something—I was out there flyin' the stars before most of *you* was in *potty* training, much less rigger training! I'm telling you the dragons are out there, and they killed my shipmate and they damn near killed me! You're all so smug here, you don't—"

"The prophecy, Canton!"

"Tell us and be done with it!"

Kan-Kon took another gulp, slopping ale on his sleeve. His fingers brushed uselessly at the spill. "Gah! Don't you know that stories—*true stories*—have to be savored like—"

"Kan-coon," shouted one of the veteran riggers, "either tell the damn story or shut up about it! We can't even have a conversation over here, with everyone laughing at you!"

"All right, Whitie," Kan-Kon said good-naturedly. "You've paid your dues. You've earned the right to nudge me a little, mebbe. As for the rest of you—*ahhhhh.*" He snorted and upended his mug, draining the last of the ale. Gasping, he cried, "All right, then! Here's what they told me—*after* they killed my partner, and before they threw me and my spaceship back into civilized space." He slammed the mug onto the bar with a crash that brought near silence to the barroom. "*Listen to the words!*"

The only sound now was the whir of the drinks dispensers. He gazed over the crowd and cleared his throat. "*From beyond life will come one! From beyond . . . ahh, hope . . . will come one . . .*" He hesitated. "Let's see, now—"

Someone slid a fresh mug of ale in front of him.

He nodded, frowning, then raised his voice again. "*Without friend will come one. And the realm . . . and the realm . . .*" And suddenly the words would not come. The words that were practically branded on his heart.

"Come on, you can do it! 'And the realm'—?"

Kan-Kon sweated, trying to dispel the fog that was clouding his brain. "*And the realm shall tremble!*" he shouted.

The murmur from the crowd was not entirely sympathetic.

"Great! Is that it?" his encourager asked.

"No, there's more. I have it right on the tip o' my tongue. *Speaking her name will come one*—hey!" Someone was jostling his arm.

"Hey, Rangoon!"

He turned.

"Come on, Can-can!"

Someone or something tripped him, and his legs went out from under him like rubber. He crashed to the floor in a gush of ale. The other riggers shouted and jumped out of the way. "Jeez, I hope his *dragons* hold their ale better than he does!" one of them cried. "Hey, Ashcan," complained the whiny red-haired kid. "I think one of your dragons just *peed* on me! Can't you keep 'em on a leash?" Brightly colored holos danced in the air as someone helped Kan-Kon to his feet.

"Sorry, there. Just lost my—lost my—ah hell!" Kan-Kon moaned, peering with chagrin into his now-empty mug.

"I think you've had a little too much to drink, old man," said the one who was supporting him. "You tell enough of those stories, and sooner or later you're going to start believing them."

Kan-Kon grunted, wounded. "Yeah, I guess so. Hey, wait a minute! *Hey, what do you think you're doin'?*"

The hand supporting him wasn't just holding him up; it was propelling him toward the exit. A rising tide of hoots seemed to add impetus to the movement, and before he could fight back, he felt more hands pushing him toward the back door.

"Hey! Listen, you miserable—" he squawked, struggling to dig in his heels. But there was no stopping the movement now. The crowd surged and flowed like the currents of the Flux, making room for his passage.

"Good night, Tin Can!" someone yelled as the door opened before him. He felt a final shove at his back, and he stumbled out the door and fell to his hands and knees in the alleyway.

He raised his head and looked back indignantly. The door slammed shut, muffling the sounds of laughter. He hadn't exactly played the crowd tonight, had he? The stupid drunken sots. Didn't they know he was telling them the truth, and it was important? Were they too blind to see?

He sighed and lowered his head again, praying that the spinning would stop. Maybe he'd had a little too much to drink. But so what? He felt tears begin to well in his eyes, and the rest of the words rose suddenly, unbidden, in his throat, and he croaked them into the empty alleyway:

> *"From that one*
> *comes a beginning!*
>
> *From that one*
> *comes an ending!"*

He raised his voice to a shout.

> *"And you can bet your ass the realm will tremble!"*

Sighing in bitter triumph, he pushed himself back onto his feet and staggered away into the night.

Chapter 1
DRAGONS IN THE REALM

LIGHTNING FLASHED in the sky like a demon's breath, splitting the night air with great jagged thrusts, hammering the vale with thunder. It was unnatural, WingTouch thought—that lightning, driven by a power no dragon could comprehend. All the dragons had felt its sting. Those who confronted it directly were burned from the sky. Those who lacked the courage, or perhaps the foolhardiness to stay in the battle, had already fled.

WingTouch fought to remain airborne in the tossing winds. Even here at the edge of the skirmish, the very air had become an adversary, turned against them by the devilish power of the Enemy. How could he fight a storm like this? All he could do was tumble through the maelstrom of wind, ignoring all else but the need to destroy the creatures who were attacking the valley.

Something blacker than the night passed before him, and he instinctively flexed his wings in pursuit. Gaining on the shadowy thing, he exhaled a lance of flame. His aim was perfect. The fire struck the fleeing creature, and he heard its wail of pain. WingTouch roared in triumph, but his victory was fleeting. The blackness rippled and veered and fled into the night. He had hurt it, but it was still alive and now he had lost it.

So it had gone for half the night, since WingTouch's patrol had responded to a cry for help from the guardians of this grove. WingTouch had watched strong and faithful dragons being driven back from the flashing storm clouds, back from these *undragon drahls* of the Enemy that filled the sky with their trills of laughter. Dragon in shape, but not in substance, the drahls were the Enemy's most hated warriors, the leaders of his army of destruction, delusion, and fear.

But the drahls were not the only sorcery in the skies tonight. The Enemy had turned the very elements of nature against them. Amidst the lightning, it was hard even to see his fellow dragons. There were many in the sky, but fewer than at the start of battle. How many had died? How many had fled? WingTouch had felt death all around him, and dragons passing to the Final Dream Mountain, but mostly he had felt terror reigning in the sky. The valley below, with its precious *lumenis* groves, was being pummeled by lightning; and the dragons themselves by withering attacks of freezing fire from the drahls. So far, the dragons had held the defense in the air, and the guardian spells had held below. But for how much longer?

As if in answer to his thought, an explosion of lightning and thunder rocked the air. WingTouch shuddered, and felt something change in the air below. He glimpsed a pair of drahls flickering like shadows low across the basin. How had they gotten so low? Had the guardian spells failed? He thought he heard a roar of anger from the spell-wielding dragons on the ground.

Bucking the winds, Windrush dove to give chase. He passed harmlessly through the layer where he should have encountered a challenging spell-barrier. He felt nothing; the spells of protection *had* failed. He bellowed his rage; he gathered fire in his throat. But before he could catch the drahls he saw cold flames ripple across the ground ahead of him, pouring from the speeding creatures. His heart cried out—and *he* cried out to his fellow dragons for help, but his cry was lost on the wind. The others were occupied in battle high overhead. From the ground, he heard the wail of dying guardian dragons.

Speeding low over the valley, too far behind the drahls to stop them, WingTouch saw their freezing bursts of fire exploding in a long line, where the lumenis and the garden of power were being blasted into ruin. Within moments, one more living garden was gone, one more source of strength against the darkness. WingTouch beat his wings with impotent fury as he climbed back toward the others. There was nothing left to fight for here.

"DRAGONS, GATHER!" he thundered. His voice was nearly lost in the crashing of the storm. But some of the dragons heard, and they repeated his words in trumpeting cries. Three dragons fell in beside him. The rest gathered slowly, giving up the battle. When he was satisfied that all who still lived had joined him, WingTouch bellowed, "DRAGONS, AWAY!" and they banked away from the wind and fled eastward into the night.

As they crossed the Scarred Mount Ridge, WingTouch wondered what he could say to Windrush and to the others back at the camp. With another lumenis grove lost to the Enemy, the outlook for the realm was bleaker than ever.

No, it would not make for a joyful report to his brother, the leader of the dragons. He could only hope that Windrush had fared better tonight than had his own patrol.

Chapter 2
WINDRUSH

THE WIND sighed through the mountain pass like a restless spirit. The tall, silver dragon Windrush felt like such a spirit himself, just now. He smelled the wind and squinted into the fading sun. It was cold on the outcropping where he was perched, but it wasn't the cold that troubled the dragon. It was what he smelled, and didn't smell.

Windrush was probing not just the outer air, but also the air of the underrealm—the insubstantial world that lay beneath the one that his eyes beheld. He was searching for clues to an invisible path, a path lost now for many seasons. He was searching for the Dream Mountain, where the female dragons lived. He grunted throatily to himself. There was no sign, no hint at all. The Dream Mountain, once a day's flight away, was now simply gone as though it had never existed. The air blew cold and empty in his nostrils, except for the faint but ubiquitous smell of the Enemy, Tar-skel. It was the same all through the realm—here in the south borderlands, as well as in the north where the male dragons lived.

Windrush would not admit discouragement. He could not explain *how* the Dream Mountain could have vanished, or where it might have gone. It all seemed so impossible. But he had already flown far in search of it, and he would fly as far as he had to, to find the place where the draconae lived. *The draconae.* How he wished he had valued them properly when they'd still graced the realm with their singing and teaching! But who could have guessed that they would vanish without a trace?

The sparks from Windrush's breath glowed briefly in the air. Gazing out over the tumbled landscape, he felt a deep sorrow. This was a changed place, even from a season ago. The land here was called the Forest Mountains; but the forests, once green and dark and vibrant, were now brittle and lifeless. The trees were stunted, the wild lumenis virtually nonexistent. He sensed no small animals. It was a part of the desolation that afflicted the whole realm. Even near the dragon strongholds, the long-woven spells of protection were weakening, as if the land itself were being bled of life. Bled by the sorcery of Tar-skel.

It had not always been so. While Tar-skel's influence had been growing in the realm far longer than any of them liked to believe, Windrush remembered well the victory of just a few seasons ago, when the Enemy had been dealt the most serious defeat in the history of this generation of dragons. It had been a magical moment: Jael, the outsider from another world, with her friends, riding on Windrush's back to the aid of his father Highwing. Sentenced to death in the Black Peak, Highwing had been the one dragon to actively resist the rising tide of evil in the land. The one dragon with courage, the one dragon to keep faith with the Words of Prophecy by befriending an outsider. The one dragon . . . until, at Jael's urging, Windrush himself had flown against all hope to challenge the darkness, to free his father.

They had saved Highwing—Jael had, really—in an astonishing rescue, bringing him back from the brink of a fiery death in an alien realm. They had not been able to save him from death itself, but they had allowed him to die with a dragon's honor and peace. And with that act, they had broken the power of the Black Peak and freed many of their fellow dragons from the ensnarement of the Enemy. For a time afterward, the realm had enjoyed a renewal of life, a renewal of hope.

But it had not brought back the Dream Mountain. And now, in the face of new losses, that victory seemed long removed.

Windrush blinked, bringing his thoughts back to the present. Southward, toward the Sawtoothed Ridge, which ran east and west dividing the Forest Mountains from the harsher Stone Peaks of the far south, he caught sight of an odd-looking, puckered cloud formation that was moving in a peculiar corkscrew fashion. It was probably nothing; but still . . . if Enemy sorceries were at work there, he probably ought to investigate. He hesitated, because there were many old places of magic in the far south, and he had little knowledge of what he might find. It would be wiser to travel in company. But the nearest companions were far to the north.

Finally he launched himself into the south wind, wondering at his own decision. It had been almost as if he had heard a voice whispering in the back of his mind, urging him on. But if so, whose voice? The spirit of Highwing, whose leadership he had assumed? He didn't think so. Perhaps it was one of those enigmatic ifflings who appeared at the oddest times, bearing news or counsel. He shook his head, scanning the land below.

Windrush?

Startled, he glanced to his left and glimpsed a shimmer of light in the air. A reflection off a distant peak, a trick of sunlight? Now it was gone. But he *had* heard a voice. A moment later he caught another sparkle of light in the corner of his eye, and he looked again.

Flying alongside him was an airy being of light. It seemed to have no substance; it expanded and contracted as it flew, like a slow-moving flame. "Iffling!" Windrush murmured.

The iffling made no response. Windrush was accustomed to this behavior from ifflings, though he sometimes found it irritating. He flew on, letting the iffling follow in formation.

When it finally spoke, he almost missed its whisper. *Where you are bound, dragon, you might well find one who can help.*

Windrush rolled slightly toward the iffling, peering at its intangible form. "Did you speak?" he rumbled.

With a chime of laughter, the iffling transformed itself into a dragon-shaped flame. *Am I so difficult to hear? You must listen to me, dragon-leader!*

Windrush flicked his gaze ahead to his course. "I am listening."

Very well. Do you fly in search of the Dream Mountain?

"Of course! What do you imagine?"

Then perhaps I can help.

"Indeed!" Windrush whispered, with more frustration than relief. "How often have I called out to you, asking the way? But your kind would not come to tell me."

The iffling flickered as it glided alongside him. It answered, sadly it seemed, *It is not that we would not, dragon, but that we could not. Do we know the way? Not any way that we could tell you.*

Windrush let his anger erupt in spite of himself. "You always *act* as if you know such things!"

Dragon! Do we travel on the winds? Do you travel as the ifflings do? What good to spin images of airs and currents that you could never know—that we cannot even travel ourselves?

Windrush flew in silence, absorbing the iffling's words. "Perhaps," he muttered. "But couldn't you have just said so? Why must you always speak in riddles?" He already regretted his outburst. He had no quarrel with the iffling. "Still," he sighed, beating his wings, "I suppose I would rather hear your riddles than nothing at all."

If the iffling had taken offense, it gave no sign. *You must search for a cavern,* it murmured.

"A cavern?"

In the ridge ahead, in a place of forgotten magic.

Windrush cleared his great throat.

There you may find one like a demon, a changeling spirit.

The dragon coughed a small flame into the wind. A demon? A changeling spirit? That sounded more like a drahl than a friend. Still, his friend Jael had once been likened to a demon, and he would have given almost anything to see her again. But his friend Jael was a human.

The iffling seemed to recognize his thought. *I doubt that it is anyone you know—or who will welcome you. Nevertheless, if you speak to it with care, you may gain useful knowledge.*

"Knowledge?" Windrush asked. "What sort of knowledge?"

The iffling did not answer. Windrush beat his wings, scanning the peaks ahead. That odd storm cloud had risen and dissipated. Perhaps, he thought, it had merely been a coincidence of nature; or perhaps a perfectly ordinary cloud had passed close to a place of power. When he glanced sideways again, his companion seemed to have disappeared. "Iffling?"

Then he saw its twinkle in the air, a little behind him. It was dropping away, and its words sounded tired, as though it were having trouble maintaining its presence here. *You must pass into the range. Look for a cavern within. Use all your senses to locate the entrance. But beware of treachery!* And with that, the iffling vanished.

Windrush clenched and unclenched his talons, exhaling slowly as he soared onward. Beware of treachery? It seemed to him that advice from an iffling always carried some warning of danger. But their advice also generally turned out to be perceptive and true, and he had never regretted following it. And given his present need, what choice did he have?

He flew high over the range. The sharp summits of the mountains passed beneath him, icy grey claws reaching toward the sky. The wind currents felt hostile and unpredictable, lifting and buffeting him. He felt a brooding presence in the air. Beneath him were rock formations cracked and broken from some age-old convulsion of the land. He searched, riding the treacherous air currents, feeling the fires of impatience in the back of his throat. What had the iffling said? *You must pass into the range.* "Into," not "over." Was there some passage hidden in the spine of the mountains?

He banked back toward the north side of the ridge and skimmed low over the slopes. Soon he felt a faint tingle in his undersense. Dropping close to the withered scrub, he spotted a thin line of shadow, a vertical crevice in the face of the slope. He flared to a landing and peered into the opening. It was too small for him to enter; but his undersense continued to tingle, and he thought he sensed a magic woven into the stone. Possibly the crevice was open to anyone, of any size, who wished to enter. Possibly it was also a trap.

Sniffing, he looked around. The wind sighed, filling his nostrils with a tang of dust and barren stone. Nothing else moved. Muttering to himself, Windrush drew back and breathed a short tongue of flame along one side of the crevice. The flame didn't touch the stone, but passed straight into it, undeflected. With a rumble of satisfaction, he thrust his head in and stepped through the stone wall.

Blinking his eyes as the entry spell quivered over him, he half expected to find himself standing in a cavern. Instead he stood in a long passageway that looked exactly like the same crevice, but vastly enlarged. It looked deep, but wide and high enough for him to fly in.

Spreading his wings, he glided cautiously down the passageway, slow-flying between its twisting walls. There was a certain comfort in being surrounded by stone, even unfamiliar stone. As deeply as he loved the wind and sky, he also loved the feeling of solid mountain around him. It reminded him of his own cavern, with its weavings of protection. But here, he knew, he must keep his senses sharp for danger.

The walls gradually closed inward and at last forced him to land. Ahead, the dark passage constricted sharply and crooked to the left. Windrush drew a slow breath, smelling for treachery. There was a dank mustiness here, and a cobwebbing of old magic, but nothing he could identify as a danger. The thought of squeezing through a tight passage did not much appeal to him, but if this was the passage the iffling had referred to, he saw little choice.

Still, he was vulnerable here; he could no longer fly away. He sank his thoughts into the underweb of the world, probing to see if he could craft an escape spell if he had to. What he found was an astonishing murkiness in the underrealm; he could not probe far at all. But he felt a distinct tingle; he was approaching a change in the passage spell. It felt like an old-magic spell, not specifically familiar to him. But he suspected that it might lead him, through a twist of the underrealm, into a cavern deep within the mountain—

and thus, perhaps, to the one he was looking for, a demon who possessed knowledge of the Dream Mountain.

He crept forward into the constriction, his nails rasping on the stone. As he craned his neck around the bend, he felt the new spell wrinkling open. "Someone inviting me in?" he rumbled aloud. There was no answer.

He squeezed past the bend, and felt a shiver from head to tail as he pulled his massive body out of the constriction. He blinked in confusion, gazing suddenly into a dazzling, unnatural-seeming yellow light. With a hiss, he stepped forward.

"WELL, DRAGON," boomed a voice that seemed to reverberate from an enormous space. "HAVE YOU COME BACK TO CHALLENGE AGAIN THE ONE YOU ABANDONED?"

Chapter 3
DEMON IN A CAVE

Blinking slowly, Windrush tried to focus through the hazy glow. Gradually he became able to discern the outlines of a large cavern. He still could not identify the source of the light, or of the voice. But the smell of magic was strong, ancient, and unmistakable. "To whom," he rumbled, "might I be speaking? Do I know you?" What had the voice meant by, ". . . *challenge the one you abandoned*"?

He was answered by harsh, reverberating laughter, then a sound like a claw being drawn across stone. Windrush squinted and saw movement. Something was dancing, just out of focus. Something enormous. Some great enemy warrior? Or perhaps merely a shadow.

He shrugged. He had not come here to be intimidated, and he didn't care if the thing outsized him. He probed again in the underrealm and, to his surprise, found a recognizable tangle of a simple spell of obscuration. He tugged the threads apart with his thoughts.

The haze of light abruptly shrank; and a small, glowing, crystal-faceted thing became visible, floating in the air directly in front of him. It looked alive; it pulsed and changed shape with a fluid movement, growing tall and slender with only a few glowing facets, then collapsing and billowing out to the sides with a great many facets. Inside it, a much smaller thing moved—a thing of dark, dancing fire. Windrush thought he recognized that shadow-fire. It looked exactly like the moving shape that, just moments ago, had appeared so huge and menacing.

"So. You are not without powers." The dark fire spoke in a smaller, but not friendlier, voice. "To answer your question—*you* I might not know, but I know your *kind* well enough."

"I see," the dragon murmured. He knew now what he was facing. It was a spirit jar. It was a cell containing a consciousness that had been stripped from its original body. Dragons in past times had used them for the capture of demons, or those believed to be demons. Though Windrush had never actually seen a spirit jar before, he recognized its appearance from tales told over the years. It was not a physical vessel of any sort, but rather a powerful confinement spell. He probed briefly, but could not make out the precise weaving in the underrealm; it was a highly complex crafting, far beyond his skills. Probably it was beyond the skills of anyone left in the realm—anyone on the side of the true dragons, anyway.

How did one deal with a spirit in a jar? He had no idea—nor did he know how dangerous it might be. He didn't think he could free it by accident, but then again he wasn't sure. He assumed there was a good reason for its imprisonment.

"Have you come to release me?" the thing asked curtly, as though reading his thoughts.

"I hardly think so," Windrush answered. "I don't know who you are, or why you are here. Perhaps you would like to tell me."

The being hissed and danced violently in its squirming prison. "Why should I tell you, dragon?"

Windrush cocked his head, blinking first one eye, then the other.

"You don't answer," the thing said.

"I won't answer," Windrush said, "until I have an answer to give." The dragon peered again around the enormous cavern, which was lit only dimly now by the glow of the spirit jar. It had the look of a dragon stronghold, but one musty and long abandoned. There were many forgotten holds scattered through the southern parts of the realm, but he had heard of none so large. Windrush felt dwarfed by it, and that made him uneasy.

With a rumble, he asked the spirit, "Have you done some wrong, that you are imprisoned——?"

"*I have done nothing wrong!*" the being cried, interrupting him. "It is *your* kind that holds me here! Imprisoning me and then abandoning me!"

Windrush deliberately opened one eye wider than the other. "You have done nothing wrong? You are an innocent captive?"

"That's what I just said! If you wish to challenge me, then first free me!"

The dragon drew a silent breath and studied the demon. "Allow me to pose a question. I have been told that there is a creature living here who is possessed of . . . certain knowledge and wisdom. I was wondering if you might *know* of this creature."

"Who told you that?"

"A being of my acquaintance. An iffling."

The spirit hissed. "Iffling! If that is supposed to be a recommendation, I hardly think—" It shuddered with rage, then suddenly calmed. "Still. A being of knowledge and wisdom? It may be that *I* . . . could be described as such a one as you mention. But you have not told me who *you* are."

"That is true," Windrush said. Nor did he have any intention of giving his name, at least not yet. Sharing one's name was a risky proposition. It *could* lead to a sharing of enormous trust, as he had learned once, when he'd shared his name with the human Jael. But he had no reason to trust this being. "It appears," Windrush noted, "that you have been alone here for some time. And that you do not often have the benefit of civilized company."

"I have all the company I need," the spirit retorted bitterly. "If your only purpose in coming here is to quote ifflings at me, then you can leave now, thank you very much."

Windrush wondered at the bitterness, and wondered if he didn't detect an air of false bravado in them. "I would guess," he hazarded, "that my departure would leave you quite alone."

The being shivered.

"And I would guess that I could learn what I wish to know in other ways."

"Oh? How is that?"

"By peering into the binding spell that holds you. I would guess that your secrets cannot withstand my gaze."

The being danced nervously in its prison of light.

Windrush stepped closer to the glowing jar. He cocked his head, searching for the best angle. Within the shifting facets of the jar, he thought he might find doorways into the being's mind. The jar's glow flickered as he narrowed his focus into one facet, exactly as if he were searching the gaze of another dragon. The demon hissed with alarm. Windrush searched the layers of the binding spell, and eased them apart just enough to touch the glinting threads of knowledge on the inside.

The demon reacted with blinding rage, *waves* of rage. Heedless, Windrush continued to probe, seeking the memories of the being. He soon realized that the rage was not a deliberate defense, but a rush of pent-up anger that had grown during long years of captivity in this cavern.

Windrush found himself moved almost to pity. But he reminded himself: Is it so terrible to keep a demon in isolation, where it can't work evil upon the realm?

Certainly not. *If it is a demon of evil . . .*

Doubt rose in his mind like groundwaters in a subterranean cavern. *If it is a demon . . .*

The spirit lashed futilely, trying to resist his probes.

Beyond the pain and rage, in the misty reaches of the spirit's mind, images began to form: memories of long years of lonely emptiness, of humiliation, of hatred toward all things dragon. Still they did not reveal who this being *was*. Windrush probed deeper, further back in time. The mists parted, and Windrush glimpsed movement, the quick movement of dragons in the air, the slower movement of something that glimmered silver and gold, large as a dragon, but undragonlike in form. He heard the sounds of a challenge and knew that he had found the memory of a duel.

He recalled the rush of another's memories, shared seasons ago. There was scant resemblance between his friend Jael and this wretched creature in the jar. And yet . . .

The outcome of the duel was clear. Windrush ignored it and peered deeper. It was difficult not to recoil from the touch of the alien thought, the touch of hostility and anguish. But Windrush wanted to know the nature of this being. He glimpsed fluttering memories that preceded the duel: boredom and careless flight into danger. Threaded through these memories were others, dark and incomprehensible, which seemed to arise from hidden lusts and emotions. Probing deeper, the dragon found a group of clearly focused images.

He was so stunned he almost broke the link with the creature's mind.

He saw it in its physical form. He saw it in its own mind's eye, as it flew into the dragon realm. *The being was a rigger—a human!* The similarity of body shape was unmistakable, and so were the glimpses of the ship in which it flew. Glimpses were all Windrush had ever gotten of his friend Jael's ship, but it was impossible not to see that the gleaming surfaces, the silvery sheen of the ghostly shapes, the sparkle of that magical thing that Jael had called a *net*, were very much like what he saw now in this being's memory.

This thing before him was a *rigger*—or had been, until its duel with the dragons. Windrush tried to look again at the duel, to see what had happened, to see why the dragons had imprisoned the human's spirit; but those images had receded out of sight now. Had the dragons considered the rigger an invading demon? Many dragons would, but especially Tar-skel dragons. Windrush could not discern any hostile intent in this rigger's memory; neither could he tell whether the dragons who had captured him had been true dragons or Tar-skel dragons.

But he did glimpse one thing that he hoped might help him coax the being into talking. He caught, in a stray flash of memory, its name.

The spirit thrashed violently. *Get out!* it hissed. *You have no right!* It was trying frantically to close off its thought to him. Windrush shrugged inwardly; with a wordless mutter, he released the spirit from his gaze.

The figure sputtered with rage in its jar of light, mouthing incomprehensible words. Windrush regarded it silently. After a few moments he murmured, "I note your anger. But you would do well to control it, one named Hodakai."

The sounds of rage cut off, and the cavern was filled with silence. Then, softly: "So, you know my name. What good do you think it will do you? Your friends who imprisoned me knew my name, and I gave them nothing. I will give nothing to you, either." The voice was stiff with defiance.

"I know who you are," Windrush said. "And I know the realm from which you come. I know your people." That last statement was an exaggeration to be sure. He knew only three riggers, and only one of them human; but they were friends, and not just to him. The entire realm owed them a debt beyond measure. Without them and the breath of life and strength they had brought to this world, the realm would have fallen long ago.

Hodakai laughed flatly. "You know my people, do you? Do you think that they can't still come get me out? Perhaps it's what you *don't* know that should worry you. Do you think I did not see *your* thoughts, lizard?"

Windrush studied the shadow-in-light. Quite possibly Hodakai *had* learned something of Windrush's thoughts while they were joined. If the spirit knew enough to look, there was probably no avoiding it.

Hodakai chuckled. "I know what you're looking for."

"Oh? What do you think I am looking for?"

"Answers, answers . . ." the thing said in a crafty tone. The dragon snorted.

"Keepers of the Words, and those who make the realm tremble," Hodakai said, dancing defiantly.

The dragon's blood chilled. *Keepers of the Words.* So Hodakai knew about the Dream Mountain. And the draconae. "Do not toy with me, one named Hodakai," he murmured softly.

The shadow capered in the light. "You know my name,

you think you own me. But I am not yours. I have not *given* you my name. You may command my life, but not my thoughts."

Windrush exhaled steam. Hodakai clearly understood much—and not just of spells. Did he know and understand the ancient prophecies? Windrush faced a delicate choice. Whatever risks he might be taking with Hodakai, it could well be worth it. But it was going to be difficult to gain the being's trust.

The spirit interrupted his thoughts. "Dragon, I tire of your presence. You are no longer welcome here." The shadow seemed to leer at him out of its jar. It made stabbing motions toward him.

Windrush exhaled smoke. "I have come intending no harm. But I might say that it would not hurt you to learn some respect, rigger-spirit. I am many times your size and power."

Laughter echoed in a ring around the cavern. "You might be many times my size on the outside—but in here, all sizes are made equal, dragon. Take a good look around."

Windrush glanced warily out of the corner of his eye. Sizes made equal? Certainly the cavern dwarfed both of them. Several boulders stood nearby, and he realized that there was something unusual about them. They were streaked with large veins of malinor crystal—stunningly large veins. Unless those rocks weren't really the boulders they seemed. Windrush touched them with his undersense and felt something odd.

"Note the lumenis branch to your right," Hodakai said.

The dragon shifted his gaze. A large branch from a dead lumenis plant lay on the stone. An enormous branch . . . unless it was actually a twig, as the size of the desiccated blossom-nub at its tip seemed to indicate. Windrush recalled the entry spells that had brought him into this place—the crack on the outside, and the way that the inner passage had seemed much larger, but otherwise identical.

Suppose the passageway had *not* been made larger. Suppose *he* had been made *smaller*.

The shadow-spirit crowed and made little cackling sounds, delighting in the dragon's discomfiture.

Windrush tugged with his undersense, hoping to unravel any remaining spells of illusion. Nothing changed that he could see: not his size, nor the size of the jar, nor the lumenis branch. How could this have happened, without his even noticing it? Had his wisdom fallen so far? The spell must have been left here by the departed guardians of this vault; and if so, its makers might return to discover whom they had ensnared. And if they were Tar-skel dragons, or drahls, or other beings sympathetic to the Enemy . . .

Windrush slowly scanned the area, trying not to betray his alarm. Was someone else watching him? The cavern walls were full of shadows, shifting in the light of the spirit jar. For an instant he thought he spied a moving gleam in a far corner, and he swung his head, flame hot in his throat. But he saw nothing.

"Feeling edgy, all of a sudden?" the spirit asked.

The dragon checked an urge to flame the jar. "Spirit-named-Hodakai, you play a dangerous game, toying with matters that you little understand."

"Oh. Tsk, tsk. Do you intend to stop me?"

"I have no need to stop you. But your life could perhaps be pleasanter if you chose your enemies more wisely—and your friends."

"Ah—you know so much of my life, then. Perhaps you would have me choose a *dragon* as a friend. You, perhaps?"

"I have no need of your friendship," Windrush answered coldly. "I merely remind you of the difference between choosing well and choosing poorly."

He shifted his gaze. There were clear signs of dragonwork here: faceted surfaces that spoke of artisan spells, and surfaces burnished by dragon fire or scarred by dragon claws. Everywhere was the rubble and dust of long neglect. Why had Hodakai's captors abandoned him here? Had they planned to return, and forgotten? Servants of the Enemy might well do such a thing.

"Perhaps indeed you were wronged," Windrush said

offhandedly. "Tell me, what do you know of the Keepers of the Words? Were you imprisoned by their enemies?"

There was no answer.

The spirit's shadow was no longer visible in the jar. Windrush cocked his head, puzzled. It seemed unlikely that the spirit had escaped; more likely, it was busy sending a message out through the underrealm.

"Dragon!" he heard—a soft, whispery voice, not at all like Hodakai's. Where had that come from?

"Dragon!"

This time he glimpsed movement, in the gloom off to his left—just a shimmer in the air, like an iffling. But he did not feel any sense of the presence of an iffling. And yet *something* was nearby. Perhaps a simple cavern sprite.

"It is a stubborn one that you speak to, dragon," whispered a different voice. He glimpsed another shimmer. Yes—*sprites*, he thought. "There are others who seek to win him over, as well." There was high, tinkling laughter, then a third voice. "Of course, *they* won't give him what he wants, either."

Windrush asked softly: "Others?"

"Silence!" shouted Hodakai, his shadow-form reappearing in the spirit jar, expanding and contracting angrily. "You pests, you meddlers, you flies upon the earth!" He was answered by tiny peals of laughter, which made him angrier still.

Windrush blinked slowly. "So, Hodakai—what others do you speak to? Perhaps you are not so isolated here, after all! Is this some treachery of yours, to make me think otherwise?"

Hodakai hissed.

Windrush angled his head, searching for the sprites as he called out to them. "You say, creatures in the shadows, that there are others with whom I must contest?"

"Quiet! Silence!" shouted Hodakai, even more furiously than before.

Windrush heard more laughter, then silence. He glanced back at Hodakai. "Well now, it would seem that we both seek something. Are you so certain that you wish to oppose me? Would you not prefer civility between us?" He recalled that the last time he and a rigger had met, it had been the rigger who had proposed civility.

Hodakai didn't answer; but Windrush felt something shifting in the underrealm. He heard a rumbling sound and glimpsed flashes of light at the edges of his vision, just out of focus. Deep in the underweb, some tightly wound sorcery had just been released. Instinctively, he crouched in readiness; a shiver passed through his body.

Hodakai cackled.

Windrush spat fire at the demon, but his own hot breath washed back at him. The spirit jar was shrinking. He couldn't tell what was happening in the confused twistings of this new sorcery. But one thing was certain—another trap was springing. His muscles coiled for a leap.

He caught himself. The ceiling loomed low over his head, much lower than before. A leap would have sent him smashing into it.

Was the ceiling dropping? *No—he was growing!* He was about to be crushed against the rock. To his left, a visual distortion was unkinking, and he glimpsed a much larger space there. He lunged sideways, keeping his head low. His wing pinions scraped the ceiling, but then the floor dropped away and the ceiling vanished—and he leaped out into a vast open space. He landed with a roar and swung his head back and forth, shocked at the extent to which he had been deceived. Surely these spells were the work of the Enemy! He probed again at the underrealm, trying to shake free any further folds of illusion.

At the sound of laughter, he turned to face Hodakai.

The laughs came from a jar that was no larger than one of Windrush's foreclaws. It sat in a small alcove carved into the side of the cavern. It was in that space that the shrunken dragon had been standing—and nearly crushed—when the spell had been released. Hodakai's laughs sounded thin and reedy now, as Windrush peered in at the jar. "So! Your true stature is shown!" he muttered, wishing he could be more triumphant. "I grant you your skill in the use of the spells, spirit—even if you stole them."

"Stole them?" Hodakai squawked.

"Come, these spells are hardly your working."

The spirit responded wordlessly and angrily. The dragon felt a sudden draft in the underrealm, as though another opening spell had been triggered deep in the mountain. Was some new power coming into the cavern?

He glimpsed a movement in the shadows to his left and jerked his head, catching the smell of drahls. Fool! he thought. He should not have remained here so long, in a place where he was disadvantaged in a fight. Now it was too late to slip away.

Three drahls abruptly appeared—dragonlike shadows, above and to either side of him. Hot fire rose in his throat. He raised his head and blew flame at the drahl overhead, then swung side to side, breathing fire at the other two. The flames crackled and lit the cavern. The drahls vanished in the fire, but reappeared a moment later, farther away. They hissed in unison: "*You are a trespasser here, and trespassers die!*"

Windrush breathed fire again. It passed through the drahls as they darted in and out of the shadows of the cavern. Smoke and dust billowed, clouding everything. The drahls were a deadly threat here, where he could not fly and fight properly.

The drahls flashed overhead, sputtering freezing fire. He snapped at them, but they were fast, and hard to follow. He felt a chill. Where were they now?

Craning his neck, he spotted them close to the ceiling, their cold fire flickering over the stone. That was puzzling; they seemed to have forgotten him. "Hodakai!" he hissed—but there was no answer from the spirit. Keeping a wary eye on the drahls, he extended half his awareness into the underrealm, trying urgently to understand the sorcery he was facing.

He heard a crack of splintering stone, and suddenly understood. A spell was unraveling: the spell that held the cavern intact! Could drahls have such power? He was in peril if they could destroy the cavern. It would be one thing if he knew the weaving that bound it together, to defend it.

But he didn't, and there was no time now to explore it. The cracking sounds were growing louder.

He had to get out. He probed feverishly in the underweb, through the murk that the drahls had stirred up, searching out the entry and exit spells. The way he had come in was closed, but there had to be other ways out of this dragon stronghold!

Rocks were falling deafeningly around him; he tried to ignore them as he traced pathways through the fog of the underweb. He heard the drahls keening, preparing to attack, and he ignored even that. And then he found it: a fold in the underweb where an opening was concealed. It was all he needed. Finding the thread that would pull it open, he exclaimed, *"Gharkeei!"*—and opened his eyes, spread his wings, and leaped toward the fracturing ceiling, past the startled drahls.

The way was clear. But even as he passed into the spell-opening, he glimpsed another spell collapsing—and the drahls flickering out of sight. He heard raucous laughter. His last glimpse behind was of a completely intact cavern, with no sign of drahls at all.

Before he could react, dizziness hit him, then a blast of cold. His wings bit into a freezing nighttime air, and before he could even focus his eyes, he knew that he was high above the mountains in the dead of night. And he knew, too, that something had just gone shockingly wrong. The drahls had been works of illusion, smells and all, and so was the falling ceiling! Only his own exit spell had collapsed the image.

He had been tricked by Hodakai—tricked into leaving. Whether it was ancient dragon magic or the Enemy's sorcery that the spirit had commanded, he had used it diabolically well.

Windrush banked and turned, fuming. An angry fire burned deep in his throat, and he vented it at the mountain he had just left. The peak was a jagged, sullen presence in the night, and his flame an impotent protest. He could probably force his way back in, but for what? To take revenge for the humiliation? No, the demon wielded surprising powers, and it would be pointless to engage in a contest with it now. When Windrush returned to speak with Hodakai, it would be on his own terms.

His pride stinging, he climbed higher in the night air to find his bearings for the long journey home.

Chapter 4
RENT

HODAKAI LAUGHED long and hard. He laughed until his laughter became hollow, his triumph cold and lifeless. He had humiliated the intruder with his trickery, but that dragon was the first real visitor he had had in a very long time. He hated dragons, to be sure. But that one seemed less arrogant than his captors, even if it had refused to free him. And now, it had fled to freedom while Hodakai remained trapped here in a demonic bath of light in the emptiness of the cavern. He knew perfectly well that the dragon had merely been caught off guard by a sophisticated illusion. If it returned bent on vengeance, there was little he could do to stop it.

Still, he knew something that the dragon wanted to know. He had glimpsed the need in its mind. *Dream Mountain*. Hodakai didn't actually know the way to the place; but he knew how, or at least by whom, the way had been hidden. And that knowledge was his only possible weapon against the despised race of creatures who had imprisoned him.

But the trouble with savoring any feeling of victory here was that the feeling never lasted. The passage of time in this spirit-prison was something beyond his comprehension. Moments of pleasure were like birds on wing, rare and fleeting; but the rest of his hours clung to him like a smoky pall, broken only by flights of fantasy, and memories of rigging. Never until his capture by the dragons had he believed in an eternal life, but he was living one now. He envied his shipmate, who had died in the duel with the dragons.

Still, he was not totally alone here. He had company in

the sprites that lived in the cavern, emerging from time to time to dance about and tease him. He didn't really understand them, or their purpose in the scheme of this world. They spoke intelligibly, but in other ways seemed more like pigeons in the rafters than meaningful companions. They seemed to have no real understanding of him, or of his pain. What did they know of the realm of the Flux, or the universe of humanity?

Come to that, what did Hodakai know of humanity anymore? For all he knew, centuries had passed in his absence, sweeping away all that he had once been a part of. Not that it mattered; he could never return. He would forever regret his folly in venturing into the dragon realm in the first place, but regrets could not change what had happened.

He blinked, and for a moment slipped back into memory . . . felt the streams of the galactic Flux moving past his fingers like golden rays of light as he piloted his ship in wondrous freedom . . .

The image collapsed quickly. *Mustn't get lost in that now,* he muttered to himself. *Too much to think about. Can't keep this to myself.*

He did have one other place to turn for conversation, one other person to share his thoughts with. It wasn't someone he *trusted,* exactly, but it was someone who at least understood him—understood what it was like to be torn from his body and exiled from his own universe. This someone knew the experience—and furthermore, claimed to have a way out, a way to something better.

Hodakai wasn't so sure about that last part, but he did have a feeling that Rent might be interested in hearing of the dragon's visit. The trouble was that Rent was on the side of the drahls and the drahls' Master, and that made Hodakai most uneasy. He had no interest in becoming embroiled in this world's conflict. There were dragons on both sides, and things far worse than dragons, and Hodakai wanted no part of either side. But there was one certain enticement that Rent kept dangling before him . . .

Without actually being aware of making a decision, Hodakai murmured the words of the spell that Rent had left in place, that twisted space and opened the connection to Rent's hideaway. Hodakai had no idea where, in space, the other rigger-spirit was; but with this spell-weaving, his thoughts passed easily through the vastness of the under-realm, tracing their way along the wispy strands that led to Rent's inner sanctum. Hodakai felt the guarding spells of the other's territory; he paused and gave a little hoot to let Rent know he was here.

The guarding spells shifted and opened. *Yes? Why, my dear friend Hodakai—is that your voice I hear? Let me look upon your face!* cried the faraway spirit.

Why not? Hodakai replied, with a flash of annoyance. If they were such good friends, why wouldn't Rent reveal his real and full name? Hodakai had revealed *his* name to Rent early on, and he'd wondered ever since whether in doing so he had given Rent some subtle and indefinable power over him.

The only "face" he had to show was his dancing-shadow self. Rent, on the other hand, appeared in full body, a human figure walking through the aura of light that was the underrealm connection between them. Rent was a tall and iron-featured man. His expression was flinty and arrogant; he walked with a casual bluster and wore a smile that, far from being disarming, made Hodakai tighten his guard.

It is always so good to see you, Hodakai! To what do I owe the rare privilege?

Hodakai hesitated. Now that he was here, he wasn't sure what he wanted to say. *I've been thinking,* he said finally.

Rent cocked his head. *Dangerous habit. Are you calling to ask my permission?*

Hodakai twitched with anger. All right, so it was Rent who had taught him all that he knew of underrealm magic—and for that matter, most of what he knew about the realm, period, from the fate of his shipmate to the concealment of the dragons' Dream Mountain. But Rent had also withheld much, and it was clear that he would continue to do so until Hodakai accepted servanthood to him, and to the one whom Rent served.

Hodakai decided to ignore Rent's jibe. *I've been thinking about those flying serpents you call friends,* he said finally.

Oh? And what have you been thinking about them? I presume it is true dragons you are speaking of, yes? There was a pinch in the center of Rent's forehead, and it deepened as he spoke.

Well . . . What Rent called "true" dragons were those loyal to Rent's Master—the one called Tar-skel, the "Nail of Strength." Hodakai, frankly, didn't know if there was much difference between the Tar-skel dragons and any others, except for their allegiance in the war. But he knew this: it had been Tar-skel dragons who had captured him.

Hodakai, Hodakai! Rent chided, apparently reading his mind. *Can you not be the master of your own outrage? How can you be counted in the coming victory if you cling to your petty grudges? Accept what has happened and move on!*

Hodakai didn't answer. This was Rent's way of asking what he never tired of asking, which was: when would Hodakai give up and declare his allegiance to Tar-skel, and of course, to Rent? Not that Tar-skel himself gave a flying finger at the moon, Hodakai was sure. Probably the Nail had never even heard of him.

But Hodakai's hatred of the Nail's dragons ran deep in his soul. He couldn't understand why Rent didn't hate them equally. Rent too was a rigger who had fallen prey to dragons in the Flux. But unlike Hodakai, Rent had parlayed his captivity into power and influence, into both servant-hood and mastery. The trouble was, whether Hodakai liked him or not, Rent was the only human he was likely ever to see again in his life.

Are you planning to tell me what you've been thinking? Rent asked sharply. *Or did you call just to announce to me that you had been thinking? Some of us do that every day, you know.*

Hodakai seethed at the sarcasm, but tried not to show it. *I called, actually, to tell you of an interesting visitor I've just sent away.*

Rent's expression narrowed. *Visitor? Why didn't you tell me that in the first place?*

I was trying to. Anyway, it was a dragon.

One of your captors, coming to see if you had decided—

No—not one of those. One of the others. One not . . . aligned with you.

Rent's eyes shone with a fervor that made Hodakai nervous. *Do tell! And to what did you owe this visit from the enemy?*

How would I know? I'd never seen him or heard of him before. And I sent him packing, if that's what you're driving at.

I should hope so. But did you get any information out of him first? Every encounter with the enemy should be used to good purpose.

Your enemy, you mean—not mine. Or no more than any other dragon.

Hodakai, Hodakai—

And I wish you'd stop doing that.

Doing what?

I think you know. It was just one more way Rent had of pressuring him, by presuming that he and Hodakai had the same notion as to what constituted "the enemy." Hodakai wished now that he hadn't told Rent about the dragon.

No, Hodakai. What is it you want from me?

I want you to stop pushing me. I don't like it when you push me. I can make up my own mind.

Rent stared at him silently. His eyes shone with a power that seemed to penetrate every facet of Hodakai's being. *You're taking a very long time to decide where you stand, my friend.*

To that Hodakai had no answer, because it was true. When he replied, he chose his words carefully. *I sent him away, telling him nothing that would help him. But I suspect that he will be back. He seemed very interested in me. Seemed to want to offer some kind of . . . dragon friendship.* Hodakai stared at Rent, leaving his words hanging. It seemed just possible that, for the first time since he had become a captive in this land, he might actually have some bargaining power. Though he was hardly interested in any sort of friendship with the dragon, it might not hurt to have Rent believe that someone else was offering him enticements. And he had heard rumor of at least one other rigger who had formed such a friendship, so it was not a wholly empty threat.

It was impossible to judge the success of his tactic. Rent smiled inscrutably. *Tell me, Hodakai. Can this dragon, with its friendship, give you back your body? Can this dragon let you walk as a man?* Rent's underrealm figure executed a little tap dance for Hodakai, to emphasize the point.

Hodakai could not answer. In the end, it always came back to this. Rent, like Hodakai, had lost his physical body. But Rent, who not only served Tar-skel but also wielded his sorcery, now walked again as a man. Hodakai, Rent had promised, could do the same—if only he would swear allegiance to the Nail of Strength.

If only.

If only Tar-skel didn't give him such a bad case of . . . he didn't know what, exactly, but just the mention of the invisible sorcerer's name made Hodakai tremble. He couldn't say why. He just had a feeling that there was nothing good about this being, who was not a human or a dragon or anything else he had ever heard of.

Still, he couldn't say that to Rent. *I was only telling you what happened. I didn't say I was planning to throw in with the blasted dragon.*

But Rent persisted. He made a stabbing gesture with his finger. *Can the false dragons let you walk as a man, Hodakai? Can they?*

Hodakai shook his head; the gesture appeared as a slight tremor in his shadow. *No,* he whispered.

I can't hear you, Hodakai! Rent cupped a hand to his ear. *Can they?*

No, he repeated, a little louder.

No, Rent agreed. *They can't.*

And you of course can, Hodakai thought glumly. Or could, if you wanted to. But your price is high. I wish I could end this conversation.

The burden is light, Hodakai, and the pleasures are many. Think of that, before you do anything foolish.

I wasn't planning to do anything at all, Hodakai muttered.

I'm glad to hear that. I truly am. You will let me know if this dragon visits again?

Hodakai nodded reluctantly.

Splendid. Then I must be tending to other business. If there was nothing else—? Rent held his hands out in question.

Hodakai made a slight bowing movement, not quite in supplication but acknowledging the dismissal. He hated himself for doing it.

Then we shall speak later, Rent said and vanished, along with the window into his domain. Hodakai was left holding open the threads of a nonexistent connection in the under-realm.

Hodakai let the nimbus of his own world close back around him. He was trembling with anger and frustration. It seemed that every conversation with Rent ended this way. Around him he heard the chittering sounds of the sprites. He didn't have it in him to engage in their banter, or even to tell them to shut up. He couldn't keep his thoughts off Rent's offer; and he wept, as his world shimmered with the dark crimson heat of his trapped emotion.

Soon it was more than he could take. Thoughts of the Flux opened up before him and he drifted back into memories of Hodakai the rigger, fingers and hands stretching the net, crossing the gulfs between the stars, slipping the surly bonds of human space and time. . . .

But in time he found himself, to his own surprise, coming out of the memory and thinking again of the dragon that had come to see him.

Wishing that it would come again.

Wishing to hear the voice of the dragon.

"DREAM MOUNTAIN! That is Windrush's obsession—not mine!" hissed the black dragon SearSky. His back was turned as Windrush landed in the main encampment. "We should be going after the Enemy to destroy him! Forget the underrealm! Forget the Mountain! Win back the lumenis, that's what I say!" The powerful dragon snorted fire.

At least a dozen pairs of glowing, faceted dragon eyes turned to follow Windrush as he strode to the center of the gathering, where the complaining dragon held forth. "SearSky! You wish to command us to victory—is that it?" Windrush asked. His mood was dark; he was still stinging from his encounter with the rigger-spirit.

SearSky turned, flared his nostrils, and fixed Windrush with a red-eyed stare. "At least I would command us into *battle*, Windrush—not into some endless search for something that is gone, probably forever! Why don't we take the fight where it belongs? To the Enemy!"

For a moment, Windrush said nothing, but he let the flame in the back of his throat produce a small flurry of sparks with each outgoing breath. "That is your wisdom, then?" he said at last.

He was answered, not by SearSky, but by mutters from many of the others gathered around. There was a good deal of sympathy for SearSky's opinion here. And these were many of Windrush's best leaders.

"I expect you heard about the defeat in the Valley Between last night?" SearSky said acidly.

Windrush swung his head in alarm, looking for his younger brother, WingTouch. WingTouch had been the leader of that patrol. He found the grey-green dragon standing among the others. "Is this true?" he asked.

WingTouch's eyes flickered the color of a sun-drenched sea, then darkened with sorrow. He flexed his wings restlessly. "We lost a lumenis grove and six dragons. I am sorry, Windrush. The Enemy's sorcery was stronger than ever."

Windrush exhaled a cold breath. Another grove lost. How many more could they lose? The Enemy was destroying the grounds that fed the dragons' bodies, even as it destroyed their spirit by hiding the Dream Mountain, the very source of life and beauty in the realm. "I see," Windrush said.

"Do you?" asked SearSky. "We are wasting time on this foolish search of yours, on your efforts to regain the past. Let us move on and win the future!"

Windrush was weary beyond words, but as their leader he could not let this pass. "You believe," he said, "that we are clinging to a forgotten past? Have *you* forgotten what the Enemy has taken?" He shifted his gaze from one dragon to another, letting the fire in his eyes speak his anger.

"Have you forgotten that without the Dream Mountain, this realm would not *exist*? That our gardens would be lifeless valleys? That lumenis would not grow? Have you forgotten that without the draconae, *there will be no more dragons*? Are you so blind that you have forgotten?"

He was answered by a muttering near silence. He heard raspy breathing, and the movement of claws on stone. Then a sullen voice—Stonebinder's?—protested, "What of the dracona in the Grotto Garden? There is an egg there!"

"One dracona, huddling in our protection!" Windrush roared. "An egg that will probably never hatch, away from the Mountain! Do you think *that* is our future?"

SearSky, eyes glowing red, turned his craggy head. "That has ever been your argument, Windrush. But we have been following your way, and we are losing. The Enemy seems to create life well enough without the Dream Mountain. Perhaps it is not so vital as you think. Perhaps you should think about another way. Unless—you have come to tell us of some new victory in your travels, eh?"

Windrush thought of the humiliation he had suffered in the cavern earlier tonight. "No," he said softly. "No victory." He vented sparks, trying to dredge some encouragement from his thoughts. "No victory, but perhaps a hope. Perhaps one who knows something of value to us."

He described to the others what he had found in the cavern, but he could see that most of them were only puzzled by it. What was wrong with them? he thought. Could they not see the potential value of the knowledge they might gain from the captive spirit? As he told how the episode had ended, he was answered with rumbles of disbelief. He hissed sparks of frustration.

"Windrush! We thought you were the master of underrealm skills!" This was Stronghold, the tan dragon to his left. "If *you* can't see through the Enemy's deceptions, how do you propose for *us* to defeat them?"

Windrush blinked slowly. He hoped that this was not turning into a challenge to his leadership; if it was, it could not come at a worse time. While they argued among themselves, the Enemy tightened his grip around their territory; and more importantly, around their hope and belief in themselves. This encampment stank of anger and hopelessness, and he had to answer it.

But he was having trouble focusing his gaze upon Stronghold, and he let out a breath of steam as he gathered his thoughts. "I have some skills in the underrealm," he said, his voice rising in volume. "But *never* have I claimed mastery of the arts of deception. That is the work of the Enemy. Those who admire such skills should give credit where it belongs—to their Master, the one who destroys! SearSky, you spoke of the Enemy creating life. Well, he might *twist* life to his purposes, but I do not believe that he can create it. You almost sound as if you believe his lies!"

His words sent a murmur of displeasure through the assembly. SearSky growled, "I have never believed the lies of the Enemy!"

Windrush glared back at him, and finally grunted in

acknowledgment. It was true, SearSky had never been a servant of Tar-skel. But many of those gathered here, including his own brothers, *had* once been under the Enemy's sway—until Jael's victory at the Black Peak had freed them. They knew Tar-skel's dark mastery firsthand, but it was not something of which any of them boasted. Nevertheless, Windrush could not deny their right to question him. He had been foolishly unwary, and his encounter with Hodakai had been a minor display of the Enemy's powers.

Fire burned uselessly in his throat as he regarded the unhappy dragons. He was their leader, and somehow he had to find not just greater wisdom, but greater skill and cunning. At this moment, though, his thoughts were like a slow landslide of stones in his head.

He heard the low sigh of Farsight, the younger of his two living brothers. Farsight swung his head from side to side as he spoke, his silvery-clear eyes twinkling. "My brother, your scales and your eyes are as dull as a moon behind a storm cloud. When did you last take of lumenis?"

Windrush exhaled smoke. "Well, I—"

He felt a gentle shove on his right flank. WingTouch was staring at him with eyes that glowed like lanterns in the sea. Even in the face of defeat, WingTouch never seemed to tire or grow discouraged. "Fly, brother—fly and feed, before you fade away. We need you. Do you hear?"

A rumble of agreement rose among the others. Windrush realized suddenly how right his brothers were. He had not fed in many days, and he needed the restorative power of lumenis before he could think clearly. "Very well," he murmured. He raised his voice. "All who need lumenis, rise with me and fly!"

"*Fly now!*" called Treetooth, a dark green dragon.

"Fly and feed!" "Fly and feed!" The cry rose quickly, even among those who had questioned him. Most of the dragons present took to the air with a thunder of beating wings.

The Valley of Fallen Light lay eastward, just over the ridge from the main encampment. It was the largest lumenis reserve in the realm, and so far it had been kept safe from the Enemy. As the dragons passed over the ridge, they encountered the guardian spell, one that would pass only dragons whose inner twists of true being, *garkkon-rakh*, matched its pattern. The weary Windrush was a beat slow in preparing for it, and it struck him like an invisible sheet of flame. *Foe! Foe!* it cried, as it wrapped its underweb sinews around him. Stunned by the spell's hot flash, he reached out with dragon thought to trace the grooves and twists of the spell. It required, not great skill, but an aware and true dragon presence. He touched the fire with his thought, and the heat vanished and he passed unharmed.

Followed by his two brothers and the rest, Windrush flew past the watchful guard dragons who maintained the spell-barriers, and descended into the Valley of Fallen Light. Even in darkness, the place glowed as though alive with fire. It boasted not just lumenis, but plants of all kinds, nourished by the fire of the lumenis. Even from the air, especially at night, the lumenis stems could be seen reaching skyward like silent branches of glittering, fiery ice.

Windrush dropped a wing and plummeted, murmuring under his breath the ancient words of beckoning: "Living fire, give breath to my wings! To my heart! To my eyes!"

A heartbeat later, he glimpsed one branch of lumenis that seemed to rise up beckoning to him alone. He felt its touch in the underweb, its energy flowing up to meet him. He reached down with his talons, caught the branch, and swooped back upward, pulling it from the ground. The plant sputtered with light as it broke free. All around him he saw sparkles in the night as other dragons caught up branches. Beating his wings, he climbed back into the sky before lifting the lumenis to his powerful jaws.

"Strength from fire!" trumpeted a dragon. The vale echoed with the sounds of dragons bellowing.

Windrush was too famished to celebrate. With a silent thought of gratitude, he crushed the lumenis like glass. The plant erupted between his teeth, melting into pure sunlight. It streamed in all directions; it coursed through his body like an elixir, filling him until he began to feel himself glow from the inside out. All around him, starbursts were exploding, and dragons were pulsing with inner light.

Fragments of lumenis flew across the sky like exploding embers, droplets of light raining down over the grove. Where they fell onto soaring dragons, the particles vanished with a sparkle into the dragons' scales. But fragments that fell to the ground exploded softly, each explosion the beginning of a new lumenis plant.

Windrush gladly let droplets of light spill from his mouth, seeding the grove. Energy flowed into his body and his mind together, driving out fatigue and burning the fog from his thoughts. Lumenis flame danced in his brain like an elemental; it had no thought, but it was the energy that fed life, fed all dragon thought and dragon being, all garkkon-rakh. He felt strength flowing into his wings, his eyes, and his claws. He might be unrested, but he no longer felt weary. Anyone who dared to attack him now would be destroyed by claw and flame. He bellowed his fury into the night air, and heard his cry echoed.

He was not just feeding; he was growing intoxicated with the power of the lumenis. He ground the remaining fragments between his teeth, squeezing the light from them. His spirits soared with every splash of light; he felt as though he could fly the breadth of the realm in the time it would take to shape the thought. He felt an overpowering urge to fly higher than a dragon could fly—to soar to the uppermost limits of the realm, to challenge the emptiness, the winds and the darkness beyond. His wings labored to carry him higher.

The cries of the others receded below him, an echo in his ears, a fading din. The threads of the underweb began to glow in his thoughts, and he felt an impulse rising in his mind: Why not challenge Tar-skel directly? Why not just reach out through all that was dragon and real and *garkkon-doh*, and challenge the Enemy's magic, and defeat it once and forever? It was a dizzying thought. Enough wisdom remained in him to let it spin harmless into the night air—but the intoxication was still growing. And something else was happening . . .

A voice, somewhere, was calling out to him. It was a silent voice, and yet it reminded him of a dracona singing to him as of old, singing out a story, a vision of the realm as it was, or as it might be. Someone calling to him . . . but who?

Even in the euphoric glow, he recognized that something extraordinary was happening. This was not the usual lumenis intoxication. A power was coursing in his veins that he did not understand. Through the dizziness and strangeness, he felt a connection opening in the underrealm, and it was not under his control.

The realm was changing.

The darkness of the night grew deeper, and the points of light in the sky gleamed with a strangely cold intensity. They looked very far away. And yet, as he watched them, it seemed that they were being transformed into something different—not warm, distant lights, but rather tiny *points of ice*. And they were not isolated from each other, but were joined together by a pale, gossamer *web* that somehow stretched out of the underrealm into the outer world, and encircled the sky.

Windrush was so astonished that he stilled his wings and glided in the thin, high air, staring at the web. He could still see the dark outline of the mountain range, but the strands of the web were growing brighter, and the mountains were receding. What was this? He felt that he was seeing illusion, and yet not illusion. He smelled the power of an enchantment, but could not discern its nature, whether good or evil, nor could he tell its source. Perhaps if he flew higher . . .

He was far above the other dragons already, but still he beat the air, climbing toward the roof of the sky. The valley, with its popping lumenis, dwindled below. He was in danger of climbing out of the spells of protection; but still he climbed, hoping to make the vision come clear.

The web grew stark against the night sky. It seemed a peculiarly geometric thing—like the underrealm with its strands and connections, and yet hard and cool; and he thought suddenly that it was a vision of the realm bound together in power, and he felt an electric excitement. Was this a vision of dragon power—of the dragons' final victory, of the realm restored to unity?

No . . .

He smelled a tang of steel—and the web suddenly began to shrink, its points of light growing inward like daggers of sharpened ice. He felt his breath hissing, his link with the underrealm being choked off. This was no weaving of beauty; it was a thing of malice, of imprisonment.

And yet he sensed movement beyond the web. He heard the sound of chimes, the sounds of draconae, the sounds of the dreaming ones. For an instant he thought he glimpsed the Dream Mountain itself, rosy and translucent, and hope sprang into his heart. But it was locked far out of reach, beyond the web of ice.

Closer, in the web, he saw dragons caught, struggling; and the harder they struggled, the harder the ice became. Some fought with each other, and that made the ice grow thicker. It filled half the sky, closing around him. And now, beyond the web, the sky began to shiver and crack . . . and beyond *that* he glimpsed a different sky, the sky of another world. The ice crystals stretched, like clawed fingers, out of this realm to take hold in the next.

He shuddered, circling helplessly in the center of the vision. He glimpsed a new figure, not dragon yet glowing with dragon magic, climbing its way up the web. And he heard words drifting through the air:

> From beyond hope
> will come one . . .
>
> Innocent of our ways
> will come one . . .

The sound of the words faded, but not his memory of them. They were the Words of the ancient prophecy, passed on through his father from his mother, the dracona Skytouch.

As Windrush pondered the Words, the new figure became clearer. He could see its form now: neither dragon nor beast, it was human. *Rigger.* His breath rushed out in a silent exclamation. Where the rigger touched it, the ice was melting. The glow of the Dream Mountain began to shine through more strongly.

The human turned her head. It was Jael.

But in that moment of recognition, she became transparent and disappeared. The Dream Mountain faded, and the icicle prison walled him in on all sides. It stretched out forever, through the fractured sky to the skies beyond.

Windrush could do nothing except circle angrily. Finally he roared and flew straight toward the wall of ice, his hot breath boiling the air before him. Better to die than to let this terrible work go unchallenged! But when his fiery breath touched the wall, it vanished. The shattered sky vanished, and the web; everything vanished except the night air whispering over his wings. He cried in protest, but his voice faded on the wind.

He looked down at the other dragons, a swarm of fiery insects in the valley below. He heard his name floating up on the air. Without answering, he searched the night sky one more time, looking for the source of that vision. Finally he gave up and spiraled downward.

As he rejoined the windmilling flight, he saw that the flush of the lumenis seemed to be wearing off most of the other dragons. "Did you see what I saw?" he rumbled.

"We saw you trying to fly to the summit of the world," answered Farsight. "What else was there to see?"

"A vision," Windrush murmured. "I'd hoped you might have seen it, too."

"A *vision*," crowed SearSky, flying up from behind. "Another work of your trickster friend?"

Windrush waited until the other dragon came alongside. "Whose work it was, I cannot say," he answered. "It could have been a taunt from the Enemy—but I think not. I believe it may have come from the Dream Mountain. It had a smell of prophecy about it."

As his words carried on the wind, a murmur passed through the flight of dragons. But SearSky was unimpressed. His eyes blazed like coals of fire beneath his knobby brow. "How can you judge it a work of the Dream Mountain, if you cannot tell a false vision from a true one?"

Windrush snorted sparks, not dignifying the insult with an answer. He peered around at all of the dragons. "What I saw was a great web encircling the world! A web of ice— ice as hard as stone, a trap of the Enemy. It stank of despair. I saw the Dream Mountain beyond it, out of reach. And then . . ."

He described what he had seen: the small human figure climbing and melting the web. And the Words. His voice became husky, rasping his own words into the air. "It was Jael!" he said, breathing a soft, billowing flame. "Jael, friend of Highwing, friend of the realm. She was undoing the work of the Enemy, which the rest of us were powerless to fight."

His words hung on the night air for a dozen heartbeats, before he admitted that Jael had vanished before winning against the ice and darkness.

"We heard your outcry," Farsight whispered, his diamond eyes flashing.

"My rage broke the vision. But it could not break what was *in* the vision. It was a power greater than our own." He let loose an angry flame and veered off into silence.

The others began to debate what he had told them, but Windrush stayed outside the circle. The air was soon filled with questions, not just about the vision, but about the past, about the truth of the Words, about Jael. "Do you doubt," Farsight said caustically to one questioner, "that Jael broke the Enemy's sorcery against Highwing? And against us?"

"So we have heard," came a rumbling reply. "We know that the enchantment was broken. But by whom? Who can say?"

Farsight snorted in disgust.

And on it went. Windrush had come to expect it. He had observed that few dragons seemed to remember sacrifices made on their behalf, unless they were direct witnesses to the acts. There were many here whose spirits had been freed from the Enemy's influence—but perhaps not so completely as they would have liked. Despair and discord were powerful weapons of the Enemy, and they were present in good measure here.

Windrush circled silently, until he heard SearSky again question the source of the vision. SearSky was one who worried him. A formidable warrior, SearSky commanded considerable respect among the dragons; but not all of his followers were clear thinkers, in Windrush's view. It would be unwise, he thought, to let SearSky's words go unanswered. He veered back into the circle. "Whatever the source," he snapped, "the *vision* was real. And surely it had a meaning, which we must try to understand."

"And what, Windrush, do you take its meaning to be?" asked Longtail, cutting off a rejoinder from SearSky.

Windrush answered soberly. "I do not know for certain. Perhaps it was intended to frighten, or perhaps to warn. But its roots lie deep in the underrealm, that I know." He sighed and was suddenly aware of a great need for solitude, and for rest. "My brothers, I am weary—and so must many of you be. We will speak more of this later. But I will say this: What I have seen, I believe to be a thing of prophecy. I believe it bears upon the meaning of the Words."

He could hear the unspoken questions hanging in the air. Despite the terrible war with Tar-skel, few among the dragons spoke openly of the Words of the draconae—perhaps because the prophecy was so frighteningly ambiguous about the outcome of the struggle.

"And why should Windrush son of Highwing be granted a prophecy?" SearSky asked.

"Perhaps because I am also Windrush friend of Jael the rigger," Windrush retorted, punctuating his words with a blast of fire. "If you forgotten who broke the power of the Black Peak, I have not. If I have received a prophecy, it is not because I asked for it. Nevertheless, it was given; and if there is any wisdom left in this realm, we will consider it well." He exhaled a long, steamy sigh. "My brothers, I must take my leave. Are the night patrols ready?"

WingTouch flew close, bobbing in the air. "They are ready."

"Then farewell until the light of day."

Windrush soared away, departing the vale for the mountains to the north. His thoughts were deeply troubled as he flew, and he had the feeling that they would grow no quieter before this night was over.

Chapter 6
BATTLE AND BETRAYAL

Once his older brother was gone, WingTouch departed also—to the west, back to the main encampment. These days, this was the most populous part of the realm. The air seemed full of dragons flying in one direction or another, and yet the realm was far from normal. The war had so overshadowed life that it was hard to remember what it had been like to fly freely in the night, seeking fast winds and adventure without wondering if the eye of the Enemy would fall upon you, or the wings of his drahls. The jumbled slopes were a windswept remnant of a land that had once borne countless varieties of flora and fauna—life that had mattered, not because it was of any particular use to the dragons, but because it was a gift from the fires of the Dream Mountain. Now, most of the life that had not been stolen or transformed by the Enemy was stunted or destroyed.

WingTouch was aware of this, but did not allow himself to dwell upon it as he flew. He had a patrol to lead, and he was determined that the defeat of the previous night would not be repeated.

The camp came into view over the ridge, marked by scattered fires and embers. WingTouch floated down through rising plumes of smoke and landed at the northern corner of the camp. He tramped through the grounds, calling out for his night patrol. As always, many dozens of dragons were asleep, or muttering in conversation around piles of blazing deadwood or burning *draxis* bushes, the poor cousin of lumenis.

Any number of dragons raised their craggy heads and peered at him with eyes glowing in the night like stars, but no one answered his call. WingTouch sighed, knowing that his dragons were undoubtedly somewhere in the camp, lost in conversation. Draconic discussions, especially when they turned upon the war and upon the powers and designs of the Enemy, could drone on throughout the night. Wing-Touch regarded most such talk as foolishness, and had little patience with it. Still, when he reached the far perimeter, he was not surprised to find two members of his patrol, Rocktooth and FireEye, perched on stone outcroppings, part of a small gathering absorbed in just such a conversation.

Rocktooth hailed him with a plume of smoke. "Wing-Touch! They are saying that the Enemy has been capturing shadow-cats from the valley and turning them into spirits that can move right through the earth!"

"Why not?" cried another dragon, behind Rocktooth. "If he can create drahls out of smoke, and cause the moon itself to spy upon us, I see no reason why he couldn't do that, too."

WingTouch answered with an impatient snort. "If you believe every story about the Enemy's powers, you'll make a sorry excuse for a warrior!"

"Then tell us what you believe!" said Rocktooth. "Stonebinder said he *saw* a shadow-cat come right out of the ground!"

WingTouch inspected his talons, dismissing the story with his silence. "What the Enemy is doing," he said finally, "I can't guess. But what *we're* doing is flying a patrol. Stretch out your wings and let's go."

Rocktooth grumbled, opening his jaws in a tooth-glittering yawn. "All right—but if we don't think of these things now, we might wish we had, later."

"We might," WingTouch acknowledged. "FireEye! You too."

FireEye slowly stirred, as though waking from a stupor, and blinked his red eyes. A stout dragon with thick, leathery wings, he was a good fighter—once aroused. Another dragon, hunched down in front of him, muttered, "I've heard that some of the *sweepers* are not to be trusted, either.

Who knows about *their* sympathies?" FireEye, still only half alert, cocked his head and blinked his ruby eyes again as though ready to join in.

WingTouch was determined to let this go no further. He snapped, "*FireEye*—where are the others? Where are Loudcry and Longnail?"

"They're in the sleeping warrens," said the dragon who had spoken of the sweepers.

"Summon them," WingTouch commanded. "It is time to take to the air." As FireEye and Rocktooth rose to obey, WingTouch surveyed the camp, shaking his head. Even his friend Loudcry was sleeping when he should have been ready to fly. In a state of war, how could they be so unwatchful? WingTouch flexed his wings and considered reproving the others here, but decided that it was not his place. They were, after all, off duty. Nonetheless, he was troubled by the idle chatter. When the four of his patrol appeared, he breathed a few dark words about unpreparedness, then they took off and left the matter behind them.

The early hours of the patrol passed quietly, as they soared southward over the eastern face of the Scarred Mount Ridge. Beyond the ridge, some distance to their right, lay a sparsely inhabited plain known as the Valley Between, where they had fought for and lost the wild lumenis grove the other night. Neither the dragons nor the Enemy actively controlled the plain, but both flew there at times, and both claimed friends among the small winged flyers and shadow-cats that lived there. The known strongholds of the Enemy were much farther to the west, across the Valley Between and over yet another range known as the Borderland Mountains.

The night was calm but cloudy, without a hint of trouble. As it wore on, with endless gliding flight over dark, silent slopes, the temptation to relax grew almost irresistible. WingTouch found himself wishing, on patrols like this, that he had Windrush's gift for undersensing. He had at best a blurry awareness of the underrealm, and he had to depend upon sharp eyes and quick reflexes to detect and avoid danger.

Still, giftedness in the underrealm was a mixed blessing. Their father Highwing had been so blessed, and even Farsight, to a lesser degree. But none of them could have matched their youngest brother, FullSky—and that was warning enough. FullSky's underrealm gifts had led him to foolish temptations, and ultimately to his succumbing to the Enemy's sorceries. Even in that dark time when WingTouch and Farsight had lived shadow lives under the influence of Tar-skel, they had lost all track of FullSky. He had vanished long before the victory at Black Peak, and by now, his brothers were certain that he was dead.

WingTouch knew that he himself was not much suited to thoughts of the underrealm. Even now, he was sure, there were many dragons awake discussing Windrush's claim to a prophetic vision. He himself had wasted little thought on the matter. He had no idea what Windrush's vision *meant*, but he believed in it and was content to let others wrestle with the subtleties of its meaning. His only duty right now was to remain alert until dawn and the end of his patrol.

It was only a little later, while winging over lowlands on the flank of the ridge, that he caught sight of something a less alert dragon might have missed: just a movement of shadow upon shadow, low in the foothills, barely enough to catch his eye. He swooped for a better view. He didn't call out to the others, because he wasn't sure he had really seen anything.

An instant later, the shadow suddenly loomed before him, with eyes and teeth. WingTouch banked sharply, barely evading the thing's claws. Turning, he spotted it fleeing to the west, close to the ground. "FOE IN THE TERRITORY!" he bellowed and dove after it.

The shadow was a drahl—fast and elusive, but not so fast that he couldn't catch it, WingTouch thought. He gathered fire in his throat, prepared to dispatch the abomination. But before he could do so, four more drahls climbed suddenly into the air to join the first. They turned to attack.

WingTouch swerved. His own comrades suddenly seemed far, far away.

* * *

Many mountains to the north, Farsight had just crossed a low ridge, winging his way homeward to his cavern. Over the sigh of the night wind, he thought he heard voices—voices that didn't quite sound as if they belonged in this area. He was flying opposite to the direction his brother WingTouch's patrol had taken, a northwesterly course over the Scarred Mount Ridge. Far ahead, the Black Peak glowed sullenly over the northwest horizon. Listening carefully, Farsight veered into the west wind, scrutinizing the landscape below. It was a patch of thin, bedraggled meadowland, where in a better time wild lumenis had grown. Bordering it on the west was an undulating cliff where voices could easily echo for some distance.

Farsight swung his head from side to side, listening. There was nothing now, except the wind on the cliff. Could that have been what he had heard? He didn't think so; there was a smell in the air, an undersense of a presence that didn't belong here. Still, he couldn't quite identify it—except that it had a vaguely malevolent quality, and he was unwilling to leave without investigating more closely.

Employing a trick that Windrush had taught him, he drew a simple spellweb of silence about himself. He banked and glided, following the tingle in his awareness, until he felt the presence growing stronger. He dropped low over the meadow and landed, hoping to lose himself in the gloom. Then he gazed upward along the face of the cliff wall.

His ears found it before his eyes—voices whispering across the air. He peered up at an inky patch of shadow halfway up the face of the cliff. It was probably a ledge, a perfect place for someone to hide in the night, a perfect place for a secret meeting. Farsight realized suddenly that he heard both a dragon voice—and another, a voice at once husky and smooth, chillingly lilting, a voice shaped by magic. *Drahl.*

A drahl and a dragon talking together, almost inaudibly. He dared not move closer. For all he knew, there was a small army hidden nearby, preparing for an attack. Or had he stumbled across a pair of spies? He strained to listen.

The drahl's voice drifted, forming half-connected words: ". . . finest lumenis . . . those with courage . . ." There was a rustling sound. The dragon spoke inaudibly, and the drahl answered, ". . . for *those*, servitude . . . little time left . . ."

The dragon's words were louder this time. ". . . they talk and complain . . . but haven't the courage to move . . ."

The drahl answered, ". . . no use . . . let them serve *us* . . ."

The dragon pleaded, "Let me speak again . . . close to persuading . . ."

Farsight realized what he was hearing—a drahl seducing dragons to the Enemy's side. He trembled with cold fury. He knew how reasonable, how persuasive a drahl's voice could be! Oh yes, he knew! It was nothing more than a dragon's voice twisted by sorcery, evil and yet beguilingly beautiful. He knew all too personally the power of the Enemy's seduction. But that had been a long time ago, before the Enemy's true nature had been revealed, before the drahls had begun to wage war upon the realm—killing dragons, destroying gardens and lumenis groves, destroying the very source of life to dragons. What was Tar-skel promising now, treasured lumenis for those who followed him?

If only he could identify that dragon's voice! If only he had his brother's undersense! Farsight strained, but the wind was rising again, rustling the grass of the meadow, carrying the voices away. Finally he decided that he had to move against the two, whatever the risk. He could not allow such treachery to go unchallenged. He sprang, and beat the air silently, climbing in the shadow of the cliff.

He had nearly reached the height of the ledge when reason overcame his rage. He was outnumbered. It was senseless to die and lose the knowledge he had just gained. He veered and glided back down into concealment, praying that he had not been seen. His heart burned with shame. It was un*garkkondoh* to retreat from a battle that deserved to be fought. But it was far better that he return to warn Windrush, to let him know of traitors in their midst.

The breeze over the meadow floor was dying down, and as he landed softly near the bottom of the cliff, the voice of the drahl reached him again: *"Speak no more! Someone is here!"* Then all was silent, except for the faint scratching of the dragon on the ledge.

Farsight kept utterly still, his eyes closed to slits. He heard a rustle of wings. Fire burned in the back of his throat. Find me and die, he thought, even knowing the advantage that an airborne adversary would have. It galled him to crouch like an animal in the grass. He hoped that the knowledge he'd gained was worth the sacrifice of dignity.

A pair of dragon wings caught the air with a snap, in insolent disdain for silence. He heard another flutter: the drahl taking flight. He craned his neck to watch the sky. He glimpsed a dragon's silhouette, flying southward, but the drahl he didn't see at all. When the sounds had faded, he took to the air.

He flew in search of the dragon for a time, but it had already vanished into the night. He thought of returning to the main camp to report, but instead finally turned northward again, back toward his own cavern. He wanted to discuss this with Windrush. His brother would be sleeping now, and badly needed the rest. But at dawn's light, Farsight would seek his counsel.

As he flew, he listened to the wind over the mountains and thought: What you must have to tell, Wind, if only I could understand your voice. And he thought of Wing-Touch on patrol, and hoped for the sake of the realm that his brother was having better luck tonight.

WingTouch had only an instant to decide whether to flee from the five drahls, or to fight. His reflexes decided for him. He banked right and climbed with powerful wing thrusts. When he glanced back, he saw the treacherous shadows in pursuit. The drahls were half a dozen lengths behind, and gaining.

Very well, he thought. He was still strong from the feeding; perhaps it was time to unleash some of that power. He climbed into the wind, faster and higher—then abruptly pitched up and over into inverted flight, and plummeted back upon the drahls. The ground loomed crazily over his head as he dove, breathing crackling flame into the enemies' midst. The drahls answered with freezing fire, but he scarcely felt the chill before they scattered from his mad assault.

He rolled upright and climbed again. He glimpsed his patrol above him, their breaths flickering in the night. "FOES BEHIND!" he cried. "FIVE DRAHLS, AT LEAST!"

He wheeled once more as his companions passed over him, and the five dragons joined in formation. The odds were evened; it was time to do battle.

The drahls were climbing quickly toward the dragons. They were not easy targets. The dragons dived, exhaling fire. The drahls wavered and darted, shadows in the darkness. The movements of shadow and dragon intersected, and suddenly all was chaos. The air reverberated with battle cries; the night flared with fire.

The dragons were stronger, the drahls more elusive. The dragons cried warning after warning to each other as they wheeled in the air, glimpsing one drahl here and losing sight of another there. WingTouch heard the sound of a drahl screeching in its death throes, but he could not tell who had made the kill. The battle was spreading out over the foothills, and he was dodging an attacker of his own. Shaking free of it finally, he turned back toward the others.

He spotted Loudcry grappling with a drahl—but above and behind Loudcry, another creature was dropping for a kill. WingTouch thundered a warning and sped to intercept the attacker. Before he could reach the drahl, he saw cold fire ripple along Loudcry's wings and heard the dragon bellow with pain. Loudcry stalled in midair, caught squarely by the terrible cold of the drahl's breath. The drahl he'd had in his grasp slipped away, as the one behind him billowed another freezing breath. WingTouch shot toward them, trumpeting his outrage. He dared not use his fire so close to Loudcry; instead, he caught the attacking drahl in his claws and, banking steeply, hauled the loath-some thing away from his friend.

The shadow squirmed in his grasp, trying to bite. He sank his nails into its body. At first, it felt like nothing *but* shadow; then it turned suddenly into a repulsive, shivering thing. It continued to change, metamorphosing into the form of a dragon, an innocent fledgling. WingTouch felt sickened, knowing that it had once *been* a fledgling. He could not avoid a shiver of compassion and an urge to release it. As it arched its neck, he caught a glimpse of glowing eyes and an imploring gaze. But he knew its inner nature as it was now, no matter what it once had been. It was a servant of the Enemy, and it killed dragons. With a shudder, he drove his talons deep and ripped the thing's throat apart. Its death cry was hideous, but brief. It turned back into a shadow, a lifeless one.

WingTouch released it and looked for Loudcry. His friend was below him, cartwheeling downward—alive, but unable to fly. WingTouch dove after him.

The drahl that Loudcry had been grappling with earlier was slipping through the air toward him. WingTouch called in warning, but again the drahl was too close to his friend. Loudcry's eyes flashed as he spun, struggling to move his wings. He cried out: "Ki-i-ill it for me—kill them all! I'll be all ri—!" His words were strangled off as another icy flame washed over him. The dragon tumbled out of control, close to death. He was beyond WingTouch's help, falling toward the rocks below.

It took WingTouch several heartbeats to reach the drahl as it turned upward, screaming in triumph. It saw Wing-Touch in the instant the dragon's fiery breath enveloped it. Its cry turned to a screech of agony. It tried to squirm out of the flame, but WingTouch was upon it, and he caught its head and body with his claws and ripped it apart, flinging the pieces away in rage.

WingTouch looked frantically downward, where he had last seen Loudcry falling—and then up to where the rest of his patrol were fighting. He saw Rocktooth and FireEye close together, and heard Longnail's shout. Reassured, he dove toward the spot where he had last seen Loudcry. He boomed out a call, but there was no answering cry.

It came inside his mind—the sharp, final pain. He saw a glimmer down on the rocks, a dragon turning to crystal glass in the instant of death, before vanishing from the realm. Loudcry had just taken flight to the Final Dream Mountain.

WingTouch climbed back toward the remaining battle. He heard a screech as another drahl died, and Longnail's trumpet of victory. It gave him some consolation. A good dragon and friend had died, but the enemy were almost all disposed of. Just one more remained.

Perhaps it was the shock of Loudcry's death that dulled his alertness. When he felt the stab of pain in the center of his back, he was stunned senseless. He glanced back and saw the drahl's eyes gleaming over his shoulder in triumph. He drew a breath to shout, and the pain lanced up through the crown of his head. The drahl had slipped its claws between his scales and driven them deep between his wing joints. Its breath was close on the back of his neck. What was stopping it from freezing him? It was not breathing fire, but soft, vicious laughter.

WingTouch jerked his head around to try to vent his own breath on the thing; but it was well positioned, out of reach. It tightened its grip—and fire flashed through his body. "Brothers—!" he started to cry out, but he felt a freezing flame on his neck and heard, *"Die now if you make a sound!"*

He choked off his words, and tucked forward into a rolling dive, trying desperately to shake the thing loose. The drahl's nails held tenaciously, and its whispered voice cut through the wind. *"Descend . . . slowly . . . and silently . . . if you would live."*

If you would live, WingTouch thought, the voice of the drahl chilling him as bitterly as its breath. What was it intending?

Its nails had found a nerve that commanded excruciating pain. Gasping, WingTouch descended in a glide, scarcely moving his wings at all. The torment eased a little. He hoped, with faint hope, that his fellows would see him and come to his aid. He strained to call silently: Come. Help. Quickly. But he felt no answering thought. If he could just snap out a quick cry. He began very slowly to draw a deeper breath—but the drahl's nail tightened on his nerve, driving the wind from him. He wheezed, barely able to draw breath at all.

He heard the others calling in the night, for him and for Loudcry. But Loudcry was dead, and now he was as good as dead, too.

"We may let you live, if you do as we say," the drahl whispered, behind his head. *"You who have killed so many of ours."* Its voice was soft and measured, almost a chuckle.

I will kill many more of you before I finish, WingTouch vowed furiously, irrationally. The drahl laughed behind him. Had it heard his thoughts, or had he spoken aloud?

Through the haze in his mind, WingTouch thought how his brothers would grieve, and how badly they needed his help. The whole realm needed help, now more than ever. It needed all dragons who could fly against the Enemy.

"Fly to those shadows at the base of the ridge," the drahl whispered. WingTouch turned as he was told. He could still hear his comrades calling. Come, he thought. Help. Quickly. Their voices were growing fainter. They were flying in the wrong direction. If Windrush were here, he would know better; he would use his undersense. But Windrush was not here.

"Fly along the base of the hills, and turn west through the break. Let us hope that you are strong, dragon. You have a long journey ahead." The drahl laughed cruelly.

Come. Help. Quickly. The thought was dying in his heart. The shouts of his comrades were distant now. He was alone here, with a drahl who commanded his life and death. Should he end it now and try to take the enemy with him? That might be the better way.

But if he waited, there was always the chance that he would find an opening. Always the chance to learn something useful. Always the chance to escape.

It was a faint hope, but it was all the hope he had.

That last spark of hope died when he saw a new cluster of drahls rise from the shadows and climb to join them in westward flight. In flight toward the home of the Enemy.

Chapter 7
TRACKS IN THE UNDERREALM

BACK IN his cavern, Windrush found sleep eluding him. The lumenis vision had left him far too restless. He peered about the stone-and-spell confines of his cavern, noting that the sweepers had been busy in his absence, gathering up his fallen scales. The tiny creatures had left the ledges around the cavern adorned with their jewellike sculptures, his fallen scales twisted together into silvery shapes that balanced and pointed in odd ways, glinting in the gloom. Windrush had never attached any meaning to those decorations, and yet, in some way he could never quite fathom, they seemed tantalizingly suggestive of some deeper intent. Tomorrow they would be gone, carried into the dim crevices of the cavern to line the sweepers' nests.

Sighing, he sharpened his nails, raking them on the stone floor. It felt too cold in the cavern, too dark. A few patches of luminescent moss provided the only light. He peered into the hearth where a draxis bush stood and focused his thoughts there, until he had coaxed from the bush a burst of flames tinted with amber and ruby. The flames pleased him; they were the colors of distant suns.

It was only after he had stared at it for a time that the dragon understood his desire for the flame. A memory flashed through his mind: three small figures pacing before just such a fire, in this very spot. The rigger Jael, with her friends Ar and Ed, had visited this cavern one eventful night, far too long ago.

Jael. Human, rigger, friend. It was his father who had first befriended her. Highwing had recognized in a frightened young rigger the possible fulfillment of the Words—barely remembered by most male dragons, but held at the very heart's center of the song and history of the draconae. "*From beyond life will come one . . . without friend will come one . . . and surely the realm shall tremble.*" Jael, an outsider, had accepted Highwing's friendship; and soon thereafter, the silent corruption of Tar-skel had erupted into an open reign of terror. In punishment for trusting an outsider, Highwing was sentenced to exile and death in the static realm.

It was on the morning following the night in this cavern—the night when Jael had questioned a reluctant Windrush until he thought he would go mad, questioned him until he changed his mind and agreed to challenge the darkness—that they had flown together to the Black Peak to save Highwing. It stirred his blood to remember it—the trumpeting dragon cries, the fire and smoke, the flash of sorcery that hurled Highwing out of the realm with Jael in fast pursuit. And then . . . the anguish of waiting, fighting off Tar-skel's followers, until the riggers reappeared with the dying dragon. In the end, Windrush bore his great father on his own back, giving Highwing the precious moments he needed to die in triumph, with peace and dignity. . . .

The hearth fire danced before Windrush, throwing shadows about the cavern, shadows that jumped up to tower over him. Windrush gazed into the flames, mesmerized. He wished that the fire could help him unravel the knots of the day, or somehow transport him back to more fathomable times. He recalled the strange little parrot rigger, Ed, who had accompanied Jael—and he wished he could laugh at the memory. But laughter would not come to him, not from this fire. The flames danced bright and warm, but they seemed only to replay the puzzles of the day. What had it all meant: the demon, the vision? Even an iffling's explanation would seem clear compared to today's bewildering events.

He was scarcely aware that he was drifting in and out of sleep. It seemed as a dream to him when he first saw a small, silken-furred creature loping out of the cavern's shadows. The creature sat up on its hindquarters, peering up at him with huge, dark eyes. Windrush blinked, flexing his talons unconsciously as he tried to decide whether he was awake or asleep. "Iffling?"

"Dragon," whispered the iffling.

Windrush drew his thoughts together. "Did you hear me wish that you would come?"

The iffling blinked its dark eyes and shivered, its silvery fur rippling down its back. "We felt a need."

Windrush exhaled steam. "I hope you've come to explain the mysteries of the past day. Were they your doing?"

The being cocked its head. "My doing? Dragon, you would give us powers that are not ours. What is it that you wish to know?"

Windrush eyed the iffling. "You have to ask? I saw a vision tonight, a most disturbing vision. I hoped you would know where it came from. I also spoke with a demon who was once a rigger—and I wonder how I might gain its trust. Or should I? What can you tell me, iffling?"

The creature did not answer at once. It cocked its head the other way, its eyes half closed as though it were listening to some distant voice. It began to sway from side to side. It seemed to have forgotten the dragon's presence.

Suddenly it spoke, very softly. "I do not know all of the answers that you seek. But I can show you something. Follow me." It sprang toward the hearth and vanished into the air.

Puzzled, Windrush searched with his eyes, then probed with his thoughts down into the underrealm. He felt the quiver of an unfamiliar spell and was startled to discover that the underrealm surrounding the cavern had changed dramatically. A glow filled the cavern, penetrating into corners that had long lain in darkness. Where his own guardian spell had tightly closed the underweb against intruders, he now saw a doorway out of his cavern, leading to a place of sunshine. Sitting in the doorway, silhouetted in the sunlight, was the *kuutekka*, or spirit-presence, of the iffling. Behind the iffling was a vast green meadow. *What is this?* Windrush whispered, amazed.

The iffling's answer came soundlessly. *It is our memory of the place where the Dream Mountain stood before the Enemy stole it away. I know your question—but we cannot tell you where the draconae have gone, or even if they have truly moved at all. The Enemy obscures our sight of that place, and makes the way impossible to find. But . . . there may be other ways to find it.*

Windrush muttered, *If there were a way in the outer world, I would have found it by now! If you know some other way, I would be grateful if you told me!* He narrowed his undersight, trying to see more clearly the meadow beyond the doorway. He thought he heard faint singing, draconae singing. It felt more like a memory than an actual sound.

The iffling flickered in the sunlight. *Dragon, I am sharing with you our own vision, our memory, as clearly as I can. Unfortunately this is not a doorway through which you can pass.*

Windrush scowled. *If you can, why not I?*

Dragon, my undersight is not your undersight. I walk where you cannot; and where you go with strength and pride, I may go with great peril.

The creature paused. *You must find your own way. Not on wing, but in the underrealm. But take comfort in what I have come to say: You have more friends than you know.*

Windrush stared at the iffling, puzzled by its words. He recalled the lumenis vision, in which the realm had been lost to the Enemy. Who had created that vision? Was it a warning from the ifflings? A warning to act quickly?

You say I must search the underrealm, he replied at last. *I doubt that my skills are sufficient to the need.*

Windrush, your skills are the greatest of any dragon flying free in the realm today. And tonight, when you ate the lumenis, your skills grew.

Windrush blinked. *If you mean the vision . . . will you explain it to me?*

It was not from us, but from another. Know this: there is one who is trying to help. You must seek in the windows he has left you here. Find him, before it is too late! Start tonight! With those words, the iffling suddenly turned and bounded through the doorway and was gone. The doorway vanished as well.

Windrush stared after the being, blinking in bewilderment at its parting words. What exactly did it want him to do? As he peered again about his cavern, his bewilderment grew. His haven was a changed place. There were openings in the weave of the underrealm, passages out of his cavern that did not exist in the outer world, that had not existed here before. Someone had cleverly penetrated his protective spells—someone who knew his mind and his thoughts. This was truly *rakhandroh*—astonishing, and most unnerving.

The passages were dark; he could not guess where they led, or what lay beyond them. But he sensed that they were windows onto other places in the underrealm. Rakhandroh! He caught hints of smells from them: salt and tree, sulfur and fire, wind and dust. As he sat and studied this puzzle, he came to realize that the passages might open further in response to his active touch.

After a long hesitation, he stretched out his thought to one dark passage. With a shimmer, the weave in the underrealm became an open window. Peering through it he glimpsed a barren land, a sun low and red in its sky. It looked remote, and oppressively empty and desolate. He pulled back, uncertain what sort of spell this was. Could his thoughts, his kuutekka, actually come and go through these windows? It darkened as he drew away.

He touched the next one with his thought. It opened to a view from a great aerie, high over a woodland. Yellow sunlight glinted from the tops of the trees, and shone from within the forest. He smelled a distant ocean, mingled with the forest smell. It was not a place he recognized. Most strange. He let the window close.

The next opened onto darkness, a subterranean gloom lit by a red flicker of distant fire, volcanic fire. He could not see much, but he sensed a labyrinth of underground passageways. He smelled sulfur; he sensed, though at a great distance, the presence of the enemy. He pulled back with a shudder and made certain that the window drew itself tightly closed again.

The fourth window opened onto darkness, also. But it

was a kind of darkness he understood; it was the natural gloom of the underrealm. He could see connecting threads rippling outward, twisting and joining and stretching off in various directions. He was surprised by the clarity of the view. One thread seemed particularly bright and promising, and he thought he heard a faint tinkle of laughter from it. He sniffed cautiously—and thought he caught the smell of a demon-spirit. He was startled to realize that he recognized the smell. *Start tonight*, the iffling had said. *Find your way in the underrealm.*

Sighing, he stretched his kuutekka cautiously outward through the window, into the underrealm beyond his cavern. His thoughts ranged down the thread, searching and testing every knot he encountered, taking note of each change in direction. The laughter grew louder, but came to sound more like crying than laughter. In time, there was a faint yellow glow ahead, and the demon smell became stronger. Windrush sniffed the underrealm for treachery. He heard a faint metallic jangle of protection spells, but easily swept them aside. A moment later, a lazily dancing figure of light came into view. When he had last seen it, it had been a figure of shadow-fire, but there was no mistaking who it was.

Hodakai, he called.

There was no answer. The figure seemed to be stretching its arms and turning about, as though pretending to be soaring—diving and banking and climbing. He was muttering words that Windrush couldn't understand. "*. . . Vela Oasis off the port bow . . . let's take her straight on through, and leave the spiral arm behind . . .*"

Hodakai! Windrush shouted.

Gaaahhh! cried the demon, jumping and twisting around. *Who's there?*

The dragon hesitated. Surely Hodakai should have been able to see him—unless he was not manifesting his kuutekka visibly here. *Do you not recognize the presence of a dragon?* he inquired.

Dragon—it's you! Yes—of course I do! Hodakai gulped. *I was just—ahhh, testing your honesty!*

Ah, said Windrush. *That is a good thing to do . . . Hodakai.* He repeated the demon's name deliberately—not that there was any real power in doing so. The demon, after all, had not *given* his name, and it was the willingness to be known that gave a name actual power. But there was no harm in reminding the spirit of how much he knew.

Hodakai seemed a little unnerved. *If you wish me to judge your honesty favorably,* he grumbled, *perhaps you wouldn't mind showing yourself.*

Windrush wasn't sure why he was invisible, but he didn't want to say that. He cleared his throat. *Considering your treatment of me when we last spoke, wouldn't you say—?*

The spirit twisted in space. *You come here interrupting my peace with your sorcery, and now you wish to discuss old grievances? Let me tell you—!*

I did NOT come to discuss old grievances! Windrush snapped, cutting him off.

There was an uncomfortable silence. Windrush didn't want Hodakai to regard him as a foe, if he could help it. However much the rigger-spirit hated the dragons who had captured him, it was Windrush's impression that Hodakai was not a committed ally of Tar-skel. *Perhaps,* he rumbled, *we can agree that your little trick on me was very clever, if not very hospitable.*

The figure of light danced, bending toward him. *So why have you returned to hide in the shadows harassing me?*

Windrush sighed, allowing his breath to escape in a plume that materialized before him in the underweb. The spirit pulled back, growling, *Don't try sorcery on me, dragon!*

I am not using sorcery on you, Windrush said in irritation. He didn't remember the rigger being so jumpy the last time they'd met. But if the plume of steam had become visible with his unconscious thought, then perhaps he could materialize an image of himself, as well. He recalled his own face as it appeared to him in the surface of a still pool. He felt his kuutekka become solid, a craggy, silver-scaled head with faceted green eyes, glowing nostrils, and enormous jaws. *There,* he said. *Is that nonthreatening enough?*

Hodakai twitched and danced wordlessly.

Can you see me all right now?

Is that supposed to be funny? Hodakai snapped.

I would not presume to attempt humor with you, one called Hodakai. From your reaction, I will assume that you can see me.

Okay, I can see you. Why are you here?

I have come . . . Windrush paused and thought a moment *. . . to ask whether you are in service to the one who is called Nail of Strength.*

Hodakai snorted. It sounded like a flame sputtering in the wind. *I am in service to no one.*

But you are held captive by those who are in service to the Nail of Strength.

I am the captive of dragons! Hodakai screamed. *Don't talk to me of the Nail of Strength! I am imprisoned by dragons! It was DRAGONS that took my body from me!*

But—Windrush pointed out—*dragons in service to the Enemy, not to the realm.*

It took a moment for Hodakai to calm down enough to reply. *So you say. I only know that those who imprison or threaten me are my enemies.*

Including me, I suppose?

What have you done to make me think otherwise?

Windrush thought about that for a moment. He supposed what the spirit meant was that he hadn't set it free. But in truth, he doubted that he could break the spell of the spirit jar even if he wanted to—and if he could, it would only end the spirit's miserable life. Was that what Hodakai wanted? *I have learned your name, and not used it against you,* Windrush pointed out.

You took my name. I never offered it, nor did you offer me yours.

That was true enough. It had briefly occurred to him to offer his name, but he had no reason to expect Hodakai to respond in friendship. Still, *something* made him feel that Hodakai might be turned to the cause of the realm. He needed to offer some gesture of peace.

He cleared his throat. *I'll not deny your words, spirit. But remember—whatever the harm done you, it was done by those who are my enemies, as well. If you would strike back at your captors, you could do so by joining those who stand with me. You would not be the first . . . rigger . . . to do so.*

The spirit's flame turned reddish orange. *Help you? You're mad, dragon! Can you give me my body back? Do you think I don't know what you want? You search for your precious Dream Mountain, and you think when you have it you'll cast me aside. But you'll have no help from me! Not for you or your kind! Now, go away and leave me to my peace!*

Is there nothing that would change your mind?

Nothing, dragon. Go away!

Windrush stared at the spirit, his weariness returning. He was wasting time here. Hodakai was too bitter. And yet, he was sure that Hodakai could help them if he chose to. *Very well. But perhaps, Hodakai, we will speak again.*

The spirit flickered toward him, as though to issue a lashing retort. But its voice sounded almost wistful. *Perhaps, dragon. I do not foretell the future. Now, good night.*

Windrush nodded. Hodakai, and then Windrush's own image, vanished as he drew away through the underrealm.

In the darkness of his cavern, Windrush gathered his thoughts. Surely he had done enough today! But he knew he would not be able to rest. Three other windows beckoned. And he remembered the urgency of the iffling.

He chose the window that had opened onto a barren wilderness. Something there seemed to call to him, something beneath his conscious awareness. Drawing a deep breath, he slipped his kuutekka through that window.

He tasted aridness. Hot wind sighed over stone. Heat clamped around him like a mantle, and he felt the grit of dust and the hardness of rock beneath him. A sun was low and smoky red in the sky. He was in the underrealm, but it felt like the outer world, though a place unfamiliar to him. What had called him to this forsaken place? He stretched out his senses for any track of friend or foe, any sign of magic or sorcery. He felt nothing.

He moved cautiously through the broken landscape, shards of a land that felt as if it had once harbored life and abundance. Was this another place that had been ruined by the Enemy? Or was it simply a land where life had been spent and time had moved on? It was impossible to tell.

He chose no particular direction, but allowed the land to lead him on. It was a place of tumbled and carved stone, a maze of ravines that even a tracker-dragon would find confusing. And yet, he felt that he might find treasure in this maze, if he followed the feelings that were coursing in his veins—as he had followed the urge that led to the lumenis vision.

He caught a hint of a memory-smell, the faintest whiff on the air. Was it the beginning of a track? Perhaps. For some reason, he found himself imagining Highwing whispering silently to him from the Final Dream Mountain, urging him onward. He shook his head. There was too much peril here to be dreaming of those who had fallen before him.

The landscape deepened and began to seem like a terrain of *thought*, runneled and carved, not by wind and water, but by years of pain. Once, he thought he heard angry laughter echoing over the tops of the ravines. It faded, but later he thought he heard music, the music of the draconae, and this time he was sure that it was an echo from long ago, somehow carried on the wind. That too faded. Other whispering sounds of memory seemed to rise and fall, never quite catching hold in his thoughts. He began to feel that he was creeping along beneath the winds of the past, the winds of time.

A little later, those winds brought him something new—a *presence* that felt, somehow, familiar. It made him think again of Highwing. Since his father's death, he had often thought that he'd felt his father's spirit with him, encouraging him in the struggle. And yet this was different: it was as though his father, or someone who reminded him of his father, were actually nearby.

Are you there? he whispered softly, not wanting to awaken the wrong presence.

In answer, he heard the sighing of the wind. But the wind seemed to speak. *I am here*, it whispered. *Trying . . .* And then the words faded back into a lifeless sigh. Was that all it had been—the sound of the wind? Windrush felt flame tingle in the back of his throat.

Trying?

The wind gusted suddenly, and a cloud of dust whirled up from the ravine ahead of him. As the dust spun, the air slowly cleared and in the place of the dust he saw a face— the face of a dragon. He gasped in recognition. It was a male face, but shimmering and near-crystalline, almost like a dracona's. The eyes were dark, like wells of emptiness.

FullSky? he whispered in shock. *FULLSKY?*

It seemed an eternity ago that FullSky had vanished. Windrush's heart trembled at the thought that his brother might still be alive. He rushed forward, sure that the apparition must be unreal.

Stay! the dragon's dark eyes seemed to warn. Come no closer!

Is it you—my brother? Windrush asked, barely able to contain his grief and wonder. *We thought you were dead.*

The other dragon gazed at him with what seemed an expression of exquisite pain. He shook his glassy head. Not yet, his eyes said. Not yet.

You're alive! Windrush breathed. *But you cannot speak?*

There was no answer, but the eyes agreed. FullSky glanced meaningfully up into the sky.

Danger near? Windrush drew a sharp breath. *Dream Mountain?* he whispered. *Can you help us find the Dream Mountain?* His brother nodded slightly. Windrush felt dizzy with astonishment. But he remembered as if it were yesterday—FullSky's powers of the underrealm were like no other living dragon's. He thought suddenly of the lumenis feeding. *The vision! Was that your doing?*

His brother's eyes met his, but were unreadable now, and somehow unutterably distant. With a pang, he realized how much he had missed that annoying trait in his brother. He had never been able to tell what FullSky was thinking. He would give anything to know now. *Was it a message from you?* he breathed.

His brother's kuutekka rose large before him, those dark, bottomless eyes seemingly focused in another realm entirely. Yes, they seemed to say, he had had a hand in the creation of the vision. Was it a message? What did Windrush think?

Windrush remembered suddenly the iffling telling him of one who was trying to help. Had it meant FullSky?

FullSky's eyes shifted and grew wide with alarm. *Go!* his gaze cried almost audibly in Windrush's mind. *You must seek help from beyond the realm!*

Wait! Windrush protested. *We have to find the Dream Mountain; we are lost without it! Can you help? Where are you? How can I find you again?*

His brother's gaze was like the fire of lumenis. *Go!* it cried. *Seek help!* Then, without any perceptible change in the underweb, he was gone. The ravine was empty.

Windrush hissed in dismay. He crept forward, looking for any remaining sign of his brother's presence. But FullSky's kuutekka was gone without a trace. Had he not actually seen FullSky, seen those eyes . . . But Windrush had no doubt he had just seen his brother alive—no more than he'd doubted the lumenis vision.

Looking skyward, he saw a formation of dark clouds coiling strangely. There was a terrifying sensation in the air now, the underrealm ringing soundlessly, as though a great change were coming, a power moving nearby, approaching from beyond the ravine. Some servant of the Enemy—or perhaps the Enemy himself? Windrush sensed that it was looking for him and knew that he was here, but perhaps did not yet know precisely where. And perhaps it did not yet know his name. FullSky's command echoed in his mind: *Go!*

Windrush turned and fled the way he had come, with the speed and silence of thought. Within moments he had left that place behind—and the underrealm as well. Emerging in the outer world, he stared in hissing astonishment at his own cavern, glowing redly about him in the light and silence of the hearth.

Chapter 8
CHILDREN OF THE IFFLING

FOR A long time afterward, the dragon lay staring at the draxis burning in his hearth. It seemed that the more he learned, the less he understood. First the demon. Then the vision. Now the strange paths of the underrealm, and his lost brother. FullSky! Still alive! But where was he, and what was he doing, and why? *Seek help from beyond.* Clearly FullSky was aware of the struggle, and was on the side of his brothers. Had *he* created those pathways?

Windrush sensed footsteps nearby. "Iffling," he murmured, shifting his eyes. "Have you observed my efforts since we last spoke?"

"We know that you moved in the underrealm," the iffling answered. "Did you learn anything helpful?"

Windrush rumbled thoughtfully. "Helpful? Who can say? I met my brother FullSky, whom I had thought dead! The lumenis vision was his work. He seems to want to help us, but is hindered somehow."

"Ah," whispered the iffling, dark animal-eyes blinking. "Indeed!"

"And he said that I must seek help." The dragon hesitated. "From beyond the realm."

The iffling seemed to tremble.

"That is what he said," Windrush repeated, suddenly thinking: *From beyond life will come one. Jael!*

"Did you learn . . . anything . . . of the Dream Mountain?" the iffling whispered.

Windrush shook his heavy head. He dug with a foreclaw at the stone floor of his cavern. He knew now whose help he must seek. But he didn't know how. The iffling swayed, waiting for him to speak. Windrush drew a breath. "I cannot tell you how terribly I miss my friend Jael—how often I have wished that she could return to aid us, as she aided my father!" Windrush's breath whistled in and out as he jabbed at the unyielding stone with his talon. "And now the vision, the Words, FullSky—everything says to me that she *must* return, if we are to have any hope. Perhaps she can find the draconae, where we cannot. Perhaps she could appeal to the rigger-spirit, Hodakai, to share his knowledge with us. Perhaps," and his voice became husky, "she could unite us, as we cannot seem to unite ourselves."

When he looked at the iffling, he was surprised to see its dark, oversized eyes moist as though with grief. It was blinking slowly and repeatedly, in apparent distress. "Dragon Windrush . . . what you seek *may* be possible. But we dared not try . . . without knowing."

Windrush cocked one eye down at the creature. How much *rakhandroh* could he experience in one night? "*Iffling!* You know a way to reach Jael? Why haven't you said this before?"

The iffling craned its neck to peer back up at him. "Dragon, please—we seek the Dream Mountain as much as you do."

"That is not what I asked."

The iffling trembled. "It is far from sure. There are grave risks. I cannot say for certain. I cannot say."

"Do not toy with me!" the dragon roared.

The iffling flickered, losing its solidity for a moment. Windrush flared his nostrils angrily. The iffling seemed to regain its strength. "There is one way that we might be able to reach out to her world. But it could cost us dearly, dragon—more than you can know. I must return to speak with the others."

Windrush squinted. "What is this cost that you speak of?"

The creature became transparent, then a thin flame dancing in the air. "That," it whispered, "must be our concern alone. Dragon, what we can do, we will. But do not abandon your search! It may yet be the thing that will save the realm!"

"But—" The flame was gone, before Windrush could complete his question. He stared at the spot where the iffling had stood. Rakhandroh! But as exasperating as the ifflings were, he knew he would hate not to have them as allies.

At last he vented steam from his nostrils. I hope the cost is not *too* great, he thought. Farewell, iffling.

The draxis-fire was burning low. This night had drawn on long already. He closed his eyes, thinking of the under-realm windows that awaited him. Before the thought was finished in his mind, he had drifted into an unquiet sleep.

The ifflings spoke softly but urgently together, their thoughts murmuring in the flickeringly luminous place that was their home in exile. There was a great disturbance among them. Whatever they decided, there must be no delay.

The path to the Dream Mountain must be found, or it would not be just the dragons who faced the choice of dwindling and dying, or being transformed by the Enemy into something ungarkkondoh. The ifflings too would fade from existence if the Mountain were not found, if they did not rejoin the heartfires from which they had sprung. But even if they succeeded, even if they brought the One of the prophecies back to the realm, the sacrifice required could threaten their own survival. They had so little strength left before their own fires were exhausted!

And yet, if they refused, the future seemed clear. The dragons were foundering in the struggle. The dragons' strength, already failing, would die as their deeper vision and wisdom grew clouded, as the prophecies were lost. Too many of the draconi had already forgotten their history and their knowledge of why the draconae were important, beyond reproduction of their kind. And even for that last, many had already lost their concern. They cared now only for some hollow notion of victory, as their numbers dwindled and lumenis was destroyed by the Enemy. The draconae *were* their wisdom; without the draconae, they were missing the heart of what made them dragon, garkkondoh.

Even the ifflings missed the songs and tales of the draconae!

Nor was it just the dragons and ifflings who were endangered. From the tiny cavern sweepers to the trees and shadow-cats and flyers of the forests, to the distant denizens of the seas, all creatures of the realm were falling under the shadow of the Nail—and not just the creatures, but the realm itself. It could survive without ifflings, maybe, but never without the dragons to defend it. And if the realm fell, the Enemy would gain complete control of the underrealm—and more than that. The ifflings had glimpsed the vast web of power that the Enemy was spinning, a web that could reach across the twists and layers and folds of reality into entirely different realms, perhaps even the static realm of Jael and her people. That was what the ifflings had seen in Windrush's vision—FullSky's vision. Not until this night had they truly understood the Enemy's avarice, or the reach of his claw. It seemed that more of creation than they had imagined might be threatened by the one who called himself Tar-skel, the Nail of Strength.

Therefore, they must do what they must. They might even die as a result—but if they did not die now, what would life under Tar-skel be, if not a living death? Should they not therefore act as they could, in keeping with the Words, to bring life to the ancient prophecies?

The discussion seemed to go on for a very long time, flame mingling with flame, the glow flickering around them, brighter and dimmer. As might have been measured by any others, the debate took hardly any time at all. The voices whispered:

—*to touch the static realm with our thought*—

—*to be* HEARD *there*—

—*we must send the children*—

—*the* LAST!—

—*but only* born *into that place can they seek out and speak to the One, where she dwells*—

—*and if they fail, there will be no others, none to seek out the Dream Mountain*—

—*and without its fires, there can never be others*—

—*no other children*—

*—but if we do not send them, the Nail will triumph. Shall we
save them, only to be the last to search and struggle in vain?—*
  —they must go—
  *—but first let us reach out with our thought to listen, to find
the One!—*
  —we have listened—
  —we sense her dreams and her longings for this place—
  —then let us begin—
  —without fear—
  —to prepare the children for their perilous path—
  —to send them out alone—
  *—if only there were a way to go with them, to protect and
guide—*
  —there is none—
  *—we must teach them in their very conception, and then trust
them—*
  —there is no other way—

And in the end, they began the process, as they had
feared all along that they would, turning inward the last of
their strength toward the one great task still within their
power . . . the creation of the last children who could ever
be spawned, the last new ifflings—until the day came, if it
ever did, when their life energy could be regenerated in the
dreamfires of the Mountain.

The creation of the children was a thing of mystery, only
partially under their control. The forces of space and time
responded to their urgings, twisting and curling and knit-
ting together in new and sometimes unexpected ways,
piercing through the layers and boundaries that separated
realm from realm, underrealm from underrealm. Only in
this creation-act were the realms brought so close to one
another, made so intimate, one to another. As the iffling-
children took shape in that ephemeral boundary-realm,
they were blessed—or burdened—by a gift of knowledge
from their elders, an awareness and a terrible need im-
pressed upon the very core of their being.

In the final moments of creation and birth, the ifflings, in
an agonizing act of will, turned their children out—dis-
patching them not to a place of security where they might

safely grow to fullness, but rather across a fleeting opening into the static realm, into the strange cold universe where the rigger Jael lived. . . .

They were born like winks of light in a universe to which they were strangers, even in the deep memory of their heritage. They were five in number, dancing and twinkling in the darkness of the void. For a time there was no understanding among them: life came first, and then sight and hearing and thought, and only gradually memory and dawning consciousness, and finally an uncertain kind of understanding.

They grew and matured, floating in the darkness, drinking the radiance of the nearby (distant!) sun. There was a cooler world close by, and in time they were drawn toward it as though toward home. There was one they must find and meet there, one to whom they must speak, though they did not yet comprehend exactly what it was they would say.

They skated on space and time like water-skimmers over a pond. They would find their way, and deliver their message.

Their message was crucial. Nothing must stop them, nothing living or dead.

* Accursed ifflings. *
Far across the realm and the underrealm, another felt the stirrings in the space-time boundaries, felt the sudden emergence of new life in the iffling-children, felt the ripples of their breakthrough into the static realm. This one's heart and being were as closely tied to the fabric of the underrealm as the ifflings', and it knew instantly that it had just felt a shift in power, a shift that it recognized as the genesis of a profoundly important event. It felt the stirring and rippling of the iffling-births as a movement toward the long-awaited, long-dreaded fulfillment of the prophecies:

> *From that one*
> *comes a beginning*

From that one
comes an ending

And most surely the realm shall tremble.

No one knew better the Words as they had been born, ages ago, in a vision from the Dream Mountain. No one had pondered more deeply upon their truth and ambiguity.

The one will fall
as the battle is fought

Upon her death
is the ending wrought.

No one had thought harder, with more fear or more hateful hope, upon the reappearance of the One from beyond the realm. That reappearance was to be the crisis point about which the ending, for better or worse, would turn. In no way did the Nail intend to leave the summoning and the arrival of the One in the care of iffling-children.

* **Rent! I require you!** *

There were ways to take control of a situation even when it had passed out of the realm itself. The ifflings were not the only creatures who could, at need, project their presence into the static realm.

As dragonlings had been twisted into drahls, so could other beings be transmuted to suit the needs of the one called the Nail. It was time that the near-ifflings, the cavern sprites, be put to use in the life to which they had been born. Rent could perform the actual work, under the Nail's supervision. The sprites would be altered, strengthened, made shrewder and more cunning and ferocious. They would be reborn into a life of long journey—a journey of pursuit, and deception, and if need be, destruction. They would become false-ifflings, warriors of fire—transformed in the turbulence of the underrealm, molded by the one who would soon control not just the underrealm, but *all* of the realms.

They would follow the iffling-children, and the result

would be most satisfying. The demon Jael would come, yes. But not to the fulfillment of the Words as the dragons clung to them.

The Dream Mountain would be kept safe from the dragons and the ifflings. And the realms would be his.

* Rent, I require your assistance NOW. *

In the cold darkness of the void, the warriors of fire took form and grew quickly to the fullness of their strength. Led by one called Jarvorus, the strongest and shrewdest of them, the false-ifflings shone like icy diamonds in the dark as they drew their given memories from hidden places within, and searched for their direction in this strange realm into which they had been born. They sensed somehow that they were different from their forebears, that their heritage had been changed for them; they were special creations under the command of one who was never to be challenged. This was good and proper and right. It was the destiny for which they had been born.

Casting their senses outward, they soon discovered the nearby others, the ones they were instructed to defeat. They did not move against these others yet, but observed them, biding their time. Like the iffling-children, the warriors would search for their quarry, the one about whom victory and defeat would soon dance like a spirit in a jar.

Shadowing the unsuspecting iffling-children, they learned the skills of movement with their bodies of light, and they dreamed of the new bodies into which they might transform themselves when the need arose. Skating on space and time, they followed the iffling-children, moving toward a world that floated blue and innocent against the eternal night.

It was sometime during the night—he was not sure precisely when—that Windrush stirred in his sleep and felt a presence close by. He opened one eye, without lifting his mind from the dreamland of sleep.

It came as a flame this time, and it flickered, as though in weariness. It danced with a sense of urgency that caused him to awaken enough to speak. "Iffling?" he whispered.

Dragon. It has been done, all that we can do. She will come, or not. We can only hope, and trust. The iffling's flame dimmed, then flickered a little stronger.

Windrush regarded the being in silence. "Will you not tell me what you have done?" he murmured finally. "Will you not tell me, so that I may hope?"

There was an almost imperceptible sound, a mournful sound. The iffling shimmered, trying to become a soft, sleek animal; but it was unable to hold the form. As a flame, it whispered, *Messengers have been sent—at great cost, dragon. If they succeed, value their work well! Much has been sacrificed that they might do so. And much will yet be sacrificed—and by none more than by your friend Jael.*

Windrush peered at the iffling, uncertain how to respond.

Do you not know the Words? the iffling asked, sensing his uncertainty. *"The One will fall as the battle is fought; upon her death is the ending wrought."* Do you not know these words? The iffling dimmed with the question.

Windrush stared at the iffling, dumb with horror. If he had heard those Words, he had long ago forgotten them. Had he called for his friend to come to their aid, only that she might die? For an instant, as he stared at the iffling flame, he felt its spirit touch his with something like understanding, as though it were a dragon and their gazes had met. He felt in the iffling a fathomless loss, and low keening grief, and a terrible fear for its own kind. And yet, beneath all that, deep within the well of its soul, he glimpsed a ray of hope.

If the iffling could have hope, he thought, then so too could he. The dragon drew a breath and the connection was broken. He said very softly, "For the dragons, I thank you. Go and rest, as will I. Iffling, farewell."

Farewell, Windrush. The iffling darkened and was gone.

Windrush stared into the emptiness of the cavern where the creature had been, and despite his words, he knew he would have no more rest this night.

PART TWO
THE RIGGERS

PROLOGUE

IT WAS a memory that sparkled with life in the deeps of the mountain. The refrains rang like chimes as the draconae sang the ancient memories, keeping them strong and intact. It was a memory of days long departed, of a time before their imprisonment. Without such memories, the draconae would surely have withered and died. The crafting of the images was their only remaining defense against the Enemy's sorceries, against the darkness that sought to control this place of power; and so the draconae sang the memories ceaselessly, preserving that which was beautiful and good in the history of the realm.

At this moment, a handful of draconae were gathered near the fire at the heart of the mountain. They sang in a soft choir:

> *Suns sunk low, moons risen high,*
> *The joining ones spiral in a deepening sky*
> *Creating fronds of living pearl,*
> *Living glass where dreams may swirl,*
> *In a barren vale where life ebbed low*
> *Until the mountain's breath might blow . . .*

As the draconae sang, motionless except for the quivering of their wings of glass, the image formed like a perfect crystal in the air:

Two dragons in flight—the dracona Clearsong, her wings shining of amber and sapphire and her eyes of golden flame, and her mate FlareTip, a male of pewter scales and red-tipped wings. The memory caught them over a vale of stone and parched earth, under a sky of brooding twilight.

They sang and flew, surveying the vale that was soon to be transformed.

Their flight was a dance, their song a throaty hum. Their voices floated in the wind, and the wind flowed over their wings, as they banked and soared in unison. Their eyes shone golden and crimson, and their gazes joined as they flew, not touching and yet spiraling downward as one into the vale. It was a dance of weaving, a crafting-dance upon the currents of the air, but reaching down into the under-realm, as well—a spinning of threads of power.

Below them, the land was changing.

Light glimmered through cracks in the rocks, a light that seemed to seep out as though a sun lay deep within the rock of the vale. It was the light of the Dream Mountain, streaming out of the underrealm. The dragons were creating, and yet not by their own power. Wielding the power of the mountain, coaxed here through the underrealm, they were weaving the threads that would nurture a new creation.

The cracks in the rock widened and the light blossomed. It grew in richness and color as it touched the barren rocks, splintering into hues of crimson and gold and emerald and amethyst. Everywhere, it blurred the angularity of the surfaces, until shape itself slowly disappeared in the radiance. Splinters of color burst into flame here, and pulsing beads of light there. As the crafting grew, the light billowed upward until even the air overhead seemed shot through with living flame.

The dragons blew their own fire in joyful chorus. Even in flight, they stroked at the threads of the underrealm. They spun and wove, dancing in midair, wingtip-to-wingtip; and beneath them flowers and shrubs and lantern-trees emerged in the bathing light.

When it was done, the light faded away as quickly as it had come.

The dragons circled over the new garden and landed. The light was receding into the rock; but it left behind a treasure trove of living color, plantlife sparkling and blushing. Even the rock seemed alive, charged by the radiance of the underrealm.

The two dragons furled their wings and surveyed the crafting. They found stout trees glimmering with fire-crystal, and translucent broadleafed bushes, and lantern-trees with slender arching branches tipped with the very first ruby-colored lanterns. Here were tiny spikes of lumenis, and there shrubs made of gossamer, twinkling with starlight. It was indeed a garden, truly garkkondoh, fully dragon, and alive with magic—a perfect place for their hearts to dwell, a place to bring the fledglings soon to hatch in the Dream Mountain. . . .

> *And so created*
> *A garden of light*
> *A thing of life*
> *A gathering of stars*
> *Against the night* . . .

whispered the draconae choir, as the image grew still and garkkondoh, as it etched itself clear and shining in the memory of those who tended the Dream Mountain. Clearsong and FlareTip were long gone from the outer world now—their spirits lofted in death to the soulfires of the Final Dream Mountain—but their song and their creation would never be gone.

Not as long as the draconae sang their creation and kept the memory alive. Not as long as they denied the Enemy what he most wanted: power over their hearts and minds and souls. Not as long as they remained faithful in their wielding of the Dream Mountain, whatever the cost might be, now and forever.

Chapter 9
TALES RETOLD

In the spaceport bar, the spectacle of a drunken ex-rigger proclaiming his duel with dragons was watched by a young woman seated as far from the shouting and jeering as one could be in the confines of the tavern. Jael LeBrae rose from her seat—astonished, delighted, dismayed—unable to speak, and scarcely able to breathe. Could she have just heard what she thought she'd heard?

"—hope his *dragons* hold their ale better than he does—"

"—think one of your dragons just peed on me—"

She craned her neck to get a better look, but there were too many people standing between her and the speakers at the bar. At her table, the young man she'd been talking to was waving, trying to recapture her attention. She squeezed out from her seat, past two other crowded tables. *Damn*, she thought. She hated these crowded bars; she didn't know why she even came to them. *Don't let that man get away!*

"—you okay?" she heard the young rigger shout after her.

She glanced back. "Excuse me—I have to go!" At that moment a space opened up and she pushed her way through the crowd, determined to reach that drunken man who had just been spouting nonsense to the whole room, nonsense about a world of dragons, a world that he claimed was as real as this one.

The bar crowd seemed to have swallowed him up. By the time she reached the spot where he'd been, he was gone, and the people were laughing and jeering about something else altogether. Only a puddle of beer where the man had fallen remained as evidence of the commotion he had created, and already a janitor was clicking and whirring its way through the crowd, coming to clean up the spill. Jael rose up on her tiptoes and looked around to try to see where he had gone. An elbow caught her in the side and she smacked it away in annoyance. "Scuse *me*," someone grunted irritably.

Jael started to snap a reply, then shook off the impulse and instead asked a blue-tinted fellow whom she thought she'd seen near the storyteller, "Do you know where that guy went?"

The blue rigger peered at her over the top of his glass. "Who?"

"The guy who was telling the story. Just now."

Blue took a swallow before lowering his glass. "Rangoon? They tossed him out the back door. Why?" He looked her up and down appraisingly.

Jael stretched up on her tiptoes again, trying to see over the crowd. "Where's the back way?" she demanded, ignoring his expression. Blue hooked a thumb over his shoulder, past the end of the bar.

Jael squeezed urgently through the crowd. She passed a doorway to a smoky hallucinogen room, then found the rear exit behind a knotted group of bar patrons. Shoving past them, she stepped outside into the warm night air.

The back door opened onto an alley, which was lit with a shadowy twilight glow. Jael peered left down the alley, then right. She heard someone grumbling, and thought she heard the words, "From that one comes a beginning . . ."

Her heart raced. Where was that voice coming from?

The voice continued, more forcefully, "From that one comes an ending. And you can *bet your ass* the realm will tremble!" Then the voice broke into what sounded like tears.

At last she caught sight of a tall figure picking himself up out of the shadows close to the building. He staggered down the alley away from her. She ran after him, out onto the main street. "Wait! Hey, excuse me—!"

The man turned, peering back at her through half-lidded eyes. "Huh? D'I know you?" His brow was furrowed, and his long hair fell across his eyes. He drew himself upright in an attempt to display some dignity, but the effort failed as he staggered sideways.

"My name is Jael," she said breathlessly. "I heard you back there. Your story—"

He pressed his lips together angrily. "Now, what story would that be?"

"About the dragons."

His laugh was harsh and bitter as he rubbed his scraped elbows. "I don' know nothin' about no dragons! Now, leave me alone." He hiccuped and started to turn away.

"Rangoon—wait!" Jael cried.

The man drew himself up with a great effort. "My name," he said, with great deliberation, "is *Kan-Kon*."

She blushed. "I'm sorry—someone told me—" She cut herself off with a gesture of agitation. "Never mind that. I have to talk to you about the dragons!"

"I told you." Kan-Kon shook his head vigorously. "Don' know nothin' about no dragons."

"That's not what you said back there."

"Ahhhhhh . . ." He snorted, shifting his gaze away. His face was illuminated by the strange twilight from the sky. It was spillover light from an orbiting farm sat, an array of mirrors reflecting sunlight onto some round-the-clock farmlands not far outside the city. He looked back. "That was just storytellin'. You can't go believin' what some old lush says in a bar, girl!"

Jael stared at him. "You said it. And you meant it."

His voice was harsh. "Now, how would you—"

"Because of *this*," she snapped. She mimicked his voice: " 'From beyond hope will come one. Speaking her name will come one. And the realm shall . . . *tremble*.' " Her voice started to quaver as memories of another time, another world, rushed back to her. She forced herself to continue the familiar words of dragon prophecy. " 'From this one comes a beginning. From this one comes an ending. And surely—' "

"*And surely the realm shall tremble!*" Kan-Kon hissed. He squeezed his eyes shut and mouthed the words again, silently. He opened his eyes slowly and stared at her with an anguished gaze. "How do you know those words?" he whispered. "How do you know them?" He stared at Jael as if he were standing in the presence of a ghost.

How do I know those words? Jael's heart ached at the memory of those words, ached until she thought it would burst. It was two years since she had heard that prophecy spoken—and not a day had passed that she hadn't thought of the realm, of the dragon Highwing, of his sons. Of the struggle that she had left behind. And just lately, hardly a night had passed without new and disturbing dreams . . .

"*Miss?*" the man whispered. "Talk to me!"

She came back to the present with a start. She had accosted a drunkard. A drunkard who knew dragons. A drunkard who knew the prophecy. Never had she met another human who actually had set eyes upon the dragons, or would believe her if she said that she had. "The words?" she murmured, in a voice so low that the man leaned forward, his beery breath in her face as he cupped his ears to hear. "How do I know the words?" she repeated. She shook her head, full of cobwebs—then suddenly blurted, "What are you doing? *Hey! Stop that! What are you doing?*"

Kan-Kon had dropped to his knees, his head bowed. He was shaking, clutching her leg. As she struggled to pull away, she realized that he was weeping, sobs racking his body. "Oh, miss—*miss!*"

"What? What's wrong?" Her hand went out hesitantly, but she drew it back without touching him. She tried to tug her leg from his grasp.

"Don't be doing this to me!" Kan-Kon moaned. "Don't be lying to me!"

"I'm not lying to you! Stand up, will you? Will you let go of me? *I'm not lying to you!*"

With painful slowness, Kan-Kon released her and sat back on his haunches, gazing up at her like a lost dog. Embarrassed for him, she gestured to him to stand up. With great clumsiness, he rose to his feet. His cheeks were streaked with tears, and his lips were trembling. "Have you . . . been there?" he whispered. "Have you? Is that where you . . . heard those words?"

Jael hesitated, then nodded dizzily. She'd told no one of her experience, had talked of it with no one except her Clendornan friend and shipmate Ar. And even Ar, though he'd gone through much of it with her, had put it behind him in a way that she'd found impossible. And now here was someone literally crying to hear her story. Someone who knew.

A drunkard, outside a bar.

No, she reminded herself—a rigger. Former rigger, anyway. He might be a drunkard, as well—but first he was a rigger. And she could well understand how someone who had been with dragons, and been unable to make anyone believe it, might turn to drink.

He was still waiting, his eyes imploring her to speak. "I—" she began, and choked on the words that would have followed. She didn't know what to say. Several people, walking by in the night, stared at them oddly. She couldn't just spill out the whole story in public. But as she hesitated, she could see the hope fading from Kan-Kon's eyes. She *had* to tell him. "I—I was there," she stammered, her voice rasping. "Twice. I know . . . the realm. I know what you heard. I made friends with a—with a—" With Highwing! *Highwing, why did you have to die?* She gulped. "With a dragon."

The man's eyes widened. "Made friends?" he croaked. "Made *friends?* They tried to kill me, they did! Tried to kill me! But the iff—the iff—" His voice caught, as he struggled to shape the word.

"Iffling," she sighed.

"*Yes!* Yes, the *iffling!* That's what saved me. Talked 'em out of it. One of them, anyway. Said I wasn't 'the one.' " He gulped, as though remembering his relief. "Did you . . . did you meet . . . an iffling, too?"

Jael was dizzy with memories. "Yes," she whispered. It was an iffling who in the darkest hour of the night in Windrush's cavern had told her to go to Highwing, had told her of his impending sentence of exile, had urged her to try to save him. And even before that, when she'd first met High-wing, it was an iffling who had appeared to Highwing and urged him to accept her, and not to kill her.

"Oh jeez . . . oh jeez!" Kan-Kon wept again. It took him a few moments, gasping, to compose himself enough to say anything more. Finally he caught her arm and gazed straight at her and said, "Please, you must tell me of these things. You must come with me and tell me!" He began to propel her down the street.

"Wait!" she protested.

"No, please—you must!" His strength was astonishing, considering how much trouble he had in just standing. He would have none of her protests, and she wondered frantically if she would have to scream to avoid being forcibly abducted.

But he apparently had no such thing in mind. He steered her to a bench on the edge of a small park, set back a little from pedestrian traffic on the street. He begged her to sit with him. She hesitated—but the park was well-enough lit by farmsat light spilling down through the trees, and his only interest seemed to be in hearing her story.

"Well, I—" She sighed, and thought of her agreement with Ar that they would not discuss the dragons with out-siders. This was different, she thought. They hadn't imag-ined actually meeting someone else who had encountered the dragons. She tried again. "I first flew into dragon space against the wishes of my ship's captain. But that's really . . . another story." A terrifying story: of an abusive ship-owner who had tried to enslave her psychologically, and failing that, to physically dominate and rape her. She had killed him in self-defense—ejected him from an airlock into the Flux of interstellar space.

"Yes, yes," Kan-Kon urged. "When did you go there?"

"Two years ago, standard."

"Ah!" His eyes burned. "It was seven years ago for me. But my God, it seems like yesterday! I can't get it out of my mind! What an astonishing, terrifying place! And dragons now make friends of riggers!" he whispered in disbelief.

"Yes." Jael cleared her throat. "Or some do, I should say. It is a realm at war. Or was, when I left."

Kan-Kon shook his head. "War. Dragon against dragon?" Jael nodded. "Then not all dragons are . . ." His expression darkened.

"There are dragons of greater kindness and honor than you would believe," Jael said, guessing at his thoughts.

The ex-rigger stared at her. "The ones I met damn near killed me. They—they did kill my shipmate." He swallowed, clearly struggling to control old emotions.

Jael shuddered. "How did they—do that?" Heaven knew she had seen enough dragons that had wanted to kill her.

Kan-Kon's breath went out, and something seemed to release, and he said, "They reached right into the net. Did something with his eyes—something terrible. Took his spirit, they said." Kan-Kon stopped and laboriously cleared his throat. "But they just plain killed him, as far as I'm concerned. Right through the net. There was his, his b-body in the r-rigger-station, and—" Kan-Kon began trembling, and turned to gaze across the park. This was a part of his story that he did not tell in the bars, apparently. "They—they were going to do the same to me, too. But this other thing came along and stopped them. The iff'ing—"

"Iffling," Jael corrected.

"Iffling, right. It came and, and, and—"

Jael touched his sleeve gently. "What did it do?"

"It—it talked to them. Didn't like what they were doing. Said they shouldn't mess with beings from outside the . . . realm. Because of that prophecy. The one I told you— the one you know. Except that no one believes me."

"I do."

He coughed and nodded, his chest rattling. "Anyway, that seemed to scare them somehow—spooked 'em good. So they let me go. Told me never to come dueling again, or the next time they would kill me. And I didn't—never went there again. Quit rigging pretty soon after that, too." He took a deep, shuddering breath. "Damn those dragons. But I just can't . . . It was such a beautiful place, it . . . haunts me. And the iff, the iffling—it looked like—a flame, or an angel, or something. It was just . . . wonderful . . . like some kind of miracle."

Jael nodded. "I know," she said huskily, remembering the shimmering being that had appeared, urging her to go to Highwing's aid. It had spoken to her one last time—after she had saved Highwing from burning to death in a sun, only to see him die in the Flux—reassuring her that she had not failed. A shiver went up her spine. She knew that her dragon-friend had died well, and she felt that his spirit lived on even now in some way she didn't understand; and yet she could not stop mourning his death.

"You met them, the ifflings," Kan-Kon said.

Jael nodded and took a breath, and told him the whole story—how she had met the dragon, and instead of dueling him, had given him her name. And how, in the end, he had befriended her and taken her to secret places and shown her things about herself that she had never known. And how she had returned later, with her new rigger-friend Ar and their parrot, Ed, only to find the realm a changed place, and Highwing a condemned dragon for what he had done. Kan-Kon sat silent and astounded beside her, as she described how she had saved Highwing from exile, then lost him again, gaining in the process the friendship of his sons.

"I guess," she said, "a lot was changing in the realm. I don't know *that* much about those prophecies, but it seemed as if they were starting to come true. All those beautiful places, wrecked by this . . . *Tar-skel*." Her voice trembled with that name, the name of the one who had killed Highwing. "And when we left, there was going to be a terrible war—between those who were like Highwing and those who served . . . that other one. I've . . . been dreaming about it lately. At night, I mean."

Kan-Kon opened his mouth. He seemed to be staring at the trees across from the bench. The light from the farmsat made his forehead glisten beneath the strands of sweaty hair.

Jael peered up through the treetops at the dazzling satellite that turned this port city's night into twilight. Fifty kilometers to the west was the farm sector that was being lit almost as bright as day. "I hate those things," she muttered. "Why can't they let night be night? That's how the world's supposed to be. I don't see why they have to go and not let any of us have night here, just so they can grow a little more feed."

Kan-Kon squinted. "Their all-night tribarley makes good ale," he said.

Jael frowned back at him—seeing him again for the pitiful mess of a human being that he was. "Is that what made you . . . drink like this? You couldn't forget the dragons, so you just—"

He interrupted her with a fit of coughing. "Don't you—" *cough* "—don't you go—" *cough* "—lecturin' me about drinkin', young lady!" He sounded more drunk than ever before. "You try leavin' a dead shipmate in th' Flux, then losin' your whole damn career!" *Cough.* "You jus' try it an' see how good *your* life is!"

Jael sat back, suddenly ashamed of herself. Who was she to judge? "I'm sorry," she whispered. "Was he a good friend, your shipmate?" Kan-Kon grunted. "What was his name?"

Kan-Kon grunted again. "Hoddy."

"Hoddy," Jael repeated.

Kan-Kon nodded. "I sometimes wonder if he really . . . could still be alive there. Somewhere. I know it's crazy, but I can't help it."

Jael stared at him, then shrugged helplessly.

Kan-Kon sighed. "You were the one, then," he murmured.

"What?"

"The *One*. You were the one the prophecy talked about." Kan-Kon's gaze suddenly seemed very sober, probing her face. "You were, weren't you?"

Jael stared at him, unable to answer.

He pushed his cheek out with his tongue, nodding slowly. "That's all right. You don't have to say it. It's plain obvious. You and that dragon and everything you just told me." He sat back, crossing his arms. "Well, I'll be damned. I'll be *damned*."

They sat without talking for a while. The crowd was dispersing noisily from the Green Tap, where chance had brought Jael and the ex-rigger together. Finally Jael murmured that it was time for her to return to her quarters. Kan-Kon raised his hand in farewell. "Where do you stay?" she asked.

Kan-Kon shrugged. "Here and there. Around."

She frowned. "Well, where can I find you?"

He grinned, showing teeth. "Why, right here," he said, hooking a thumb over his shoulder. "At the Tap. If you don't see me, just ask!"

Jael tried not to let her wince show. She tried to smile as she said, "Good night, then. I'll look for you here. Take care, Kan-Kon."

"Likewise, little lady." The former rigger gave a showy wave and walked away, stumbling only a little, in the opposite direction.

Jael breathed deeply and hurried through the late, eternal twilight back to the rigger dorms.

Chapter 10
IFFLING DREAMS

FOR THE iffling-children, the knowledge of their purpose emerged gradually, filtering up through their consciousness like deep memories in time, memories far older than their own being. As they stretched out their undersenses to search the world that curved away before them, they knew, with an instinctive certainty, who it was they were searching for and what they were to say. They were to find the One, a human named Jael, and they were to call her to return with them. Their purpose in life, and the totality of their being, were dedicated to that task. If anything came between it and them, their own existence was secondary.

As they swept downward into the misty atmosphere of their destination, they noted other beings bobbing and darting in space just like them, moving as they moved, perhaps even following in their wake. But the iffling-children gave no thought to whether the beings might be friend or foe; the distinction never occurred to them. They focused all of their thought upon the faint but brightening glow before them, the underglow that stood out from all the spirit-presences on this world, the glow of the one called Jael. As they drew closer, the urgency of their mission buzzed ever louder in their souls, drowning out all else.

Dropping across space-time toward Jael, they were nearly close enough to call out. And that was when the beings that so resembled them abruptly reappeared, speeding into their paths like blazing sparks of fire. They had no time to think.

—*Veer away!*—
—*But they are like us*—

—*No!*—
The new beings swerved and flew at the iffling-children
with a flaming fury that sent the ifflings reeling in shock and
confusion.

What was happening?
—*Flee!*—
—*Find safety!*—
They flashed outward in retreat, circling to reunite. But
one of them was slow—and it was taken from behind by
something that swooped and hissed and collided with the
iffling with a blaze of orange fire. As the two separated, the
iffling-child cried out, once, then flickered and vanished
into darkness. The others called out:
—*Come back!*—
—*Do not*—
—*leave us!*—
But it was gone. Stunned, the ifflings fled from their
attackers, from the ones that looked like ifflings but were
not. There were only four true-ifflings now. Bewildered,
they flickered with sorrow and fear and mourning. They
peered back at their goal, blocked from them by the cluster
of false-ones.
—*Killers!*—
—*Killers!*—
—*Killers!*—
—*Do not let them close*—
—*Keep sight of the One*—
As they watched from afar, the false-ifflings seemed to
forget them, turning instead to spiral inward toward the
glow of the human, Jael. They too were seeking the One,
then! And they were calling out to her now, calling in
voices that made the true-children tremble with fear as they
listened—not quite able to distinguish the words of their
adversaries, but hearing in the undertexture of the voices
the untruth that was in them.
The ifflings cried ahead to the human, their undervoices
wailing. They tried to call to her from a safe distance, but
they were too far away, and the false-ones had begun circling the One possessively. The human's glow pulsed, as if

she felt the false-ones' presence with her undersense, but only dimly, perhaps not consciously. If she heard or recognized the true-ifflings' cry, she didn't answer. They had to do something—but what? One of them was gone, and their goal had been taken from them.

The need was clear.

—*We must*—
—*Cannot retreat*—
—*Our duty*—
—*Our lives*—

They must risk everything to reach her, to fulfill their purpose. They must challenge the false-ones, silence their lies . . . perhaps even deny them life altogether. *Kill them.* The iffling-children barely knew how to grasp the thought of killing. But they had just witnessed the extinguishing of one of their own, and it appeared that the same thing might have to happen to the false-ifflings.

The false-ones glowed hot and combative between them and the one called Jael. They surrounded Jael, their light and energy turned in toward her, their voices whispering lies and betrayal: *"Windrush . . . traitor to your work . . . to your deeds. . . ."* The true-ones did not understand all of the words they heard, but they felt their rage grow. The enemies were a daunting force, but the ifflings were not to be deterred.

They spun about one another, gathering energy and determination, until their presence burned even hotter and whiter than the flames of the false-ones. They drew themselves together—and dove straight toward Jael.

Jael woke up rubbing her eyes. The soft amber light of the clock told her that it was the middle of the night. She heard a quiet snoring sound. It was Ed the parrot, asleep in the holographic stondai plant in the center of a tiny rainforest holo in the corner of the room. The whole display had been turned down for the night, and glowed just brightly enough to be visible.

What had awakened her? It was the damn nightmares. Dreams of dragons, dreams of pain and need. But why now, after so much time? It felt almost as if a voice were calling to her. She had dreamed often of the dragons since leaving their realm, and it had taken her a long time to accept that it was just her subconscious looking for excuses to return. But lately, a new and somehow different sort of dream had been tormenting her.

She blinked in the darkness, remembering the man she had met just hours ago at the bar. That conversation might explain tonight's dreams. But it didn't explain the past week of them: dreams of strange beings dancing in the air, calling out to her, dreams filled with whispers of heart-breaking betrayal, and helpless need.

The details of tonight's nightmare were already vanishing into the murk of forgetfulness. But she knew it had been more vivid, more violent than any before it—as if there were some kind of life-and-death struggle going on around her, and yet not around her at all. It was extremely disturbing. Worse, it had felt real to her in a way that no ordinary dream ever did.

She lay back in bed and stared at the ceiling, glowing faintly in the light of the holotrees. A dream, real? She knew better than to dismiss the possibility.

Some would have said that she plied her trade in a dreamland—and in a sense that was true. The Flux that carried rigger-ships among the stars was a realm in which real topographies were mapped and given form by the imagination of the rigger-pilot. It was dream and reality, woven inseparably into one. But it was different from the dream of sleep; the rigger-dream had real form, and the power to physically transport its bearer, and the power to kill.

The nightmare from which she had just awakened had felt more like a stirring of the Flux than a construct of the subconscious. It had felt like something with the power of reality. But . . . she was not in the Flux. She was in a dorm room. Without the rigger-net of the starship, there was no way for the dream-images of the Flux to become real.

So it was just a bad dream, after all.

She stared up into the gloom of the dorm room that for

the past eleven weeks had been her home. She listened to Ed's soft breathing and thought that in a way, Ed was just a dream, too; and yet, in another way, he was real as her hand in front of her face.

If only she had someone else to talk to about it! If only Ar were here! But Ar wouldn't be back for another week at best, if his flight stayed on schedule. She almost wished she hadn't remained here on Cargeeling while he'd accompanied another rigger to Benree, Vela Oasis, and back. But Ar had been restless to fly, and their employer, Mariella Flaire, had required someone she could trust to make the trip. Jael had wanted some time off—from flying, and even from Ar. In two years they had logged thousands of hours together in the net; and while it had been vastly rewarding, and she prized their friendship, they'd reached a point of needing a vacation from each other. But now she missed him terribly.

Of course, if she hadn't stayed behind, she would never have met that strange and interesting man Kan-Kon. She was burning to tell Ar about him.

She sighed deeply, desiring sleep most of all. She gazed past the foot of her bed at the faintly glowing stondai, the holographic parrot perched motionless in one of its lower branches. The bird's breathing was soothing, and Jael thought that what she ought to do was follow Ed's example. She nodded to herself and closed her eyes.

Images flickered up at once in her mind—images of dragons and strange landscapes, and ifflings. *Please*, she thought. *Please give me peace.*

Her plea was not answered; but eventually she did drop off to sleep, with the images dancing vividly before her.

For Jarvorus, it was all happening so beautifully that success seemed certain. The goal was close now; he could not conceive of failure. The iffling-children had been easy to sweep aside. He was aware of them flitting about on the outside now, seeking a way past his warriors, but they were so meek as to pose no threat. Jarvorus himself was already within reach of the spirit-presence of "the One"—whispering his message, the words given to him by his master, the one whose voice had sent them all on their way. Jarvorus was delivering his master's message, the one that would transform the One into the One-Who-Would-Fail.

His voice whispered like the wind. *Windrush has abandoned . . . betrayed . . . all that was good. All that you hoped to accomplish . . . was in vain.*

Was she hearing his words?

You have no friends in the realm . . . all have failed . . . will fail.

The glow of her presence flickered and trembled. His words were slipping beneath the surface of her thoughts, causing ripples of disturbance. He was confident that she would believe them. Together with his fellow warriors, he had only to persevere, spiraling ever closer, murmuring, until a perfect fabric of disbelief was woven, a skein of distrust and despair. And in that way, the warriors would gain the approval of their master.

The assault came as a swarm of fire, taking Jarvorus completely by surprise.

The iffling-children blazed into the warriors' midst, scattering them and turning their whispers to cries of alarm. Jarvorus cursed and veered away from the human, fearful of letting the delicate web of deception be ruined by a struggle with the iffling-children. He swept back around to fight, calling upon his fellows to join him in battle. But the ifflings shot past them, toward the human, crying out urgently. They seemed not to care for subtlety or web-weaving. Whatever deception they were planning, it was apparently so simpleminded that subtlety didn't matter.

Jarvorus arced across the slippery slope of space-time, pursuing the iffling-children toward their quarry. He could not allow them to succeed. His fire burned hot, as he called to the warriors to join him.

This time they would defeat the ifflings utterly. This time the battle would be to the death.

Jael woke with a cry and sat up. She felt a pain in her chest; her face was on fire; her vision swam and her ears rang.

Something terrible had awakened her, something more than just the pain. Another nightmare. She remembered a terrible feeling of despair.

She glimpsed a movement near the foot of her bed, near the holographic rainforest. *"Who's there?"* she cried.

Ed flapped awake in the stondai, sputtering as he hopped to a higher branch. "Hawwwk! What is it? Hawwk!"

"I don't—" . . . *know*, she meant to say, but her breath was cut off by a sudden glimmer of light near a tree at the edge of the forest. It wasn't Ed, and it wasn't the tree holo. A malfunction in the projector? Then why was she suddenly gasping again, unable to move her head or lift a hand to shield herself?

The dream . . .

There had been a struggle, a terrible struggle between two glimmering forces, between hope and despair.

Through the blur of her confusion, she glimpsed something moving in the air—like a shadow, or a light—like neither, and both. Ed was flapping his wings in alarm. But she couldn't tell what she was seeing.

"Rawk! *Jayl!* What is it?" The parrot's voice drew her to full consciousness.

She answered without taking her eyes off the moving forms. "I don't know, Ed," she whispered. "Do you see it?" It was clearer now; it was like watching two ghosts of flame and shadow twisting around one another, in a tortuous ballet. They shifted and interchanged, the movement too quick, too intense to follow.

The parrot's voice dropped to a low gargle. Out of the corner of her eye, she was aware of the parrot hopping back and forth on the branch, clucking and muttering, "Urrr, see it . . . but what . . . what?"

Jael couldn't answer. She was transfixed. The ghostly dancers moved closer. She heard voices, as though from a great distance. She heard hissing, as of water touching flame. She heard a groan, and a dim, distant screeching. She leaned forward, straining to hear the voices, to hear any recognizable sound. *Who are you?* she mouthed. *What do you want?* She could not force the words from her throat.

The air itself seemed to murmur, and she caught the words, "N-needs-s-s you-u-u . . ."

What? she mouthed. *Who?*

There was a moan, and out of it, the words rose: "Go-o-o to-o-o him-m-m."

"Go to whom?" she whispered, barely making the words audible.

"W-wind-d-d-d-rushhhh—"

Her breath went out as though she'd been punched.

"—n-needs-s-s youuuu . . ." And then the air stirred oddly, and she caught a sharp, familiar tang; and then the voices were lost in a cacophony of groans. She thought she heard a cry, and the words, "Windrush-h betray-y-y-s . . ." and then the voice faded, and silence and darkness swallowed her, and she was alone in the gloom of her room.

She could not move or breathe. It was as though, for an instant, the air before her had opened up, offering her a breath of another world, the *smell* of another world. If she had not heard the name Windrush, she still would have recognized that tang in the air.

Dear God! she thought. *What just happened?*

The darkness of her room surrounded her like a cloak, closing in upon her. An instant later it seemed to open up with a great wrench, not a suffocating darkness, but a vast and endless space. Her lungs were burning. She took a sharp breath, panting in desperate lungfuls of air. Had she really just seen . . . and heard . . . ?

Windrush needs you . . .

She shuddered, feeling two years' grief and worry welling up in her. Was this another nightmare—or was Windrush really, somehow, calling out to her? Could this be another astonishing dragon magic, her friend crying to her across the gulfs of time and space? "Windrush!" she whispered, clutching her bed sheet around her. "Highwing! Windrush!"

But where had those voices come from? Had she really heard them, or had she dreamed the whole thing, in a terrible fever? She was sweating, her heart pounding in her ears. Could she have imagined it all?

But I heard it. *Windrush needs you* . . .

She was aware suddenly of Ed's voice, rasping across the room. "Jayl—rawwk!—what was it? What was it? Rawwwwwwk . . . Jayyyl . . . what's wronnnnng?"

Letting her breath out with a sigh, she turned to Ed. The holoparrot was jumping from branch to branch in agitation, a flutter of scarlet and green. Her voice came out as a dry croak as she said, "I don't know, Ed! I don't know!"

The parrot folded his wings and settled down on a branch, listening to the air. "No more, Jayl. It's gone. Gone."

She nodded wearily. Then, with a jolt, she realized what Ed had just said. It was not her imagination. He had heard it, too. "Ed—" she whispered, "what exactly did you hear?"

"Awk?"

"What did you hear? You heard it, didn't you?"

"Urr—something—"

Jael patted the blanket beside her. "Come here, Ed." The ghostly parrot fluttered across to her, landing on her shoulder. She patted the blanket more insistently. With a mutter, Ed hopped down beside her. "Listen, Ed, I need your help. Now. I need you to tell me exactly what you saw. And what you heard."

"Urk!" The bird clacked his beak, looking around. "Saw—Jayl sit up, not happy. Saw—not sure, not sure." He shook his head violently.

"But you saw—"

"*Something*—rawwwwwk. Not sure what."

"And you heard—"

"Scrawwwww. Voices. Someone. Urrk." The parrot cocked his head, fixing Jael with a stare. "Who, Jayl?"

She drew a breath. "I'm . . . not sure. Tell me everything you can remember, Ed."

"Rawk." The bird pranced in agitation on the blanket.

"Did you hear . . . any words? Any words you recognized?" She wanted to plead with him. She wanted to grab him and shake him until he either confirmed what she had heard or told her she was crazy. "*Please*, Ed?"

The bird cocked his head one way, then the other, then sputtered for a moment. "Not sure. Thought I . . . *urk.*" Jael's heart pounded as he paused. "Someone . . . needs you. Sounded like . . . someone needs you. Urk." Ed shook his wing feathers.

Jael stared at him. "What'd you just say?"

"Not sure," Ed croaked. "Sounded like . . . *need.* Heard *need*, maybe. Not sure. *Go*, they said. *Go to him.*"

Jael began to shake somewhere deep inside, and then to weep. Ed hopped frantically beside her, cawing and murmuring, asking what was wrong. She could not answer; she didn't even know if her tears came from sadness or joy, or both. A terrible loneliness and pain was welling up inside her. A friend needed her, and she was too far away to do anything except weep for his need.

Eventually, the tears subsided and she sat back, snuffling and telling Ed that it was okay, he could stop worrying. She took a deep breath and began to review what had happened. Windrush, somehow, had reached out to her. How, she could not imagine—nor could she imagine the need that might impel the dragon to do that. Even Highwing, imprisoned and facing death, had not reached into her universe to tell her. She would never have dreamed that such a thing was possible.

And yet it had happened.

But what could she do about it? What could she do?

She thought long and fruitlessly, and finally sighed. Ar would be back in a week or two. Perhaps he would have an idea. *Please, Ar!* The only way to go to Windrush was to get a ship. And how could she possibly get a ship? Hijack one to the mountain route, to the dragon realm? Surely Ar would have a better idea. Surely.

And just as surely, this was going to be the longest night of her life—the longest *week* of her life.

Chapter 11
"WINDRUSH NEEDS YOU . . ."

In the terrifying swirl of light and dark, the iffling-children tried to strike back at the false-ones, to hurl them away, to extinguish their flame; but the true-ones had no experience in killing, no knowledge of fighting. In sheer desperation they had penetrated the false-ones' gauntlet and cried out their message to Jael. One of the enemy had flickered out in the storm of their passage, a fortuitous accident that showed them how their foes might be killed. But now the others boiled toward them in a rage. They had to fight or flee.

—*Escape!*—

—*Where? Where?*—

—*The false-ones block us*—

—*Release your fire!*—

Driven by stark terror, they caught one of the false-ones and burned it to silent darkness. But an instant later another loomed blazing, and this time an iffling cried out and died. The surviving ifflings, in a panic, surrounded the foe and crushed the fire from it before the rest of the false-ones could intervene.

—*Opening*—

—*That way!*—

The three ifflings darted away, fleeing across the underrealm. The enemy gave chase. The living flames, all of them, burned bright in this strange arid underrealm. But in the darkness behind them, the ifflings sensed the human alone once more, temporarily abandoned by the false-ones.

—*Make contact again!*—

—*She must be led!*—

The ifflings swept back in a great arc. But the two remaining enemies flew quickly to block the way. The ifflings veered. Before the false-ones could intercept them, they skated around the human and flanked it from the opposite side. Now three true-ifflings and two false-ifflings surrounded the human. The ifflings darted and jockeyed; but they could not approach closer without drawing a new attack. The false-ones were equally wary.

Hovering in an uneasy truce, they waited and watched, calling out, hoping that even from a distance, the human might hear their voices and follow.

Jarvorus watched his adversaries with gnawing apprehension. No longer was he so certain of his ability to sweep them away! Three of his fellows were gone, destroyed! He had been too confident. But no more. He would not drop his vigil even for an instant. And if the chance came, he would crush the ifflings once and for all.

At the same time, he felt drawn to the shimmering presence of the human. Her awareness in the underrealm was a flickering and uncertain thing. The ifflings had gotten through to her briefly; but now neither they nor he could get close enough to speak directly. He would call out to her in the underrealm anyway—call from a distance. That way might not be so subtle as he wished, but his message would be heard.

She would know: Windrush was a traitor who sought only to entrap her. Jarvorus' mission was clear and he would see to it that he was heard.

Jael got no more sleep that night. Voices seemed to keep calling to her in the night, voices that she could not quite make out, voices that would give her no peace.

She spent the following day in solitude, overcome by feelings of déjà vu. She remembered her feelings two years ago, between her first encounter in the dragon realm—the trip that culminated in her killing her own captain in self-defense—and her first meeting with Ar in the port of Lexis, a meeting that ultimately led her back to Highwing's mountains. Then, as now, she'd been alone on a world that was not home, waiting and hoping the impossible hope, for circumstances that would permit her to return to those harsh, alien, beautiful mountains.

Now she could only await Ar's arrival. She could not conceive of returning to the dragon realm without him. In the meantime, she desperately wished she had someone she could talk to about it. There was Ed, of course. But Ed, her beloved cyberparrot, was not human and not what she needed now. She felt terribly alone.

It helped a little to get out and walk around. The port of Krakow on Cargeeling was more a town than a city, with a large park at its center, surrounding a lake. She walked in the park in the afternoon, watching the birds and recording images of them for Ed, who accompanied her in a small memory-device hung on her neck chain. She slowly began to be able to think.

How could she get a ship so that she might go to Windrush? There was no doubt in her mind that she must go. The question was how. And how would she find the dragon, if he was in trouble? She had an unsettling feeling that someone meant to lead her.

Her thoughts returned, as well, to last night and that strange man Kan-Kon. He was a sad case, perhaps, but he knew of the dragons and believed in them. That was more than anyone else here could offer.

That night she returned to the Green Tap, but to her disappointment, there was no sign of Kan-Kon. She approached some people who had the look of regulars. A polite query brought only shrugs, and a muttered deprecation about Kan-Kon. Sitting down at a table, she sat drumming her fingers, wondering what time Kan-Kon was likely to come in. Finally she sought out the human manager and asked him. He told her that Kan-Kon had been in the 'lucie room earlier. He hooked a thumb toward the rear of the bar.

Jael frowned and hesitated at the entrance to the 'lucie room, wrinkling her nose at the stale, smoky smells coming through the curtained doorway. She took a deep breath of fresh air and ducked in. It was a close, dim room, the air stifling with incense, tobacco, and God knew what other substances. Colored lights and holos danced in her eyes, making it hard to focus. There was a grumbling undertone of music, leaking from the headsets worn by the half dozen or so patrons, all of whom were under 'lucie wires or tabs. None of them, with the exception of a horse-headed Swert, paid her the slightest attention. The Swert's large-eyed, penetrating gaze caused her to shiver and look away.

Kan-Kon was sitting cross-legged in the far corner, looking even more disheveled than he had the night before. Synaptic auggie wires streamed from his head, and he was smoking a hookah from which a sweet, greenish white smoke curled into the already thick air. She exhaled with a cough and took another dizzying lungful. She picked her way past the other motionless bodies, stepping carefully over the bare stick-legs of a sallow-faced man who was puffing energetically in and out through a seemingly empty glass cylinder. Jael didn't even want to know what he was doing. She reached the ex-rigger and crouched in front of him. "Hey," she said. "Kan-Kon!"

He sighed, rocking his head from side to side. He looked as though a deep fog lay about his brain.

"Kan-Kon!" she said sharply. She hesitated, then reached out, wondering if she could just remove the wires from his head.

"It is not permitted to touch the wires of another patron," said a voice from overhead. "Please respect the privacy of others and do not disturb their sessions."

She craned her neck to look up. The voice was coming from a speaker in the ceiling. A long plastic robot arm, also attached to the ceiling, was shaking a finger at her. She flushed, feeling foolish. Was she going to argue with a robot? She dropped her hands to her sides.

"Thank you, ma'am."

Kan-Kon was still oblivious to her presence. Clearly she could give up on him tonight. She turned away in distaste and fled from the room, trying not to breathe, until she escaped from the bar by the rear exit.

In the alley, panting to clear her lungs, she walked out

toward the street and then into the park where she and Kan-Kon had sat last night. She wanted both to cry and to scream. Resting on a bench, she inhaled the night air, smelling the lake and the dark-cedars and spider-blossoms. She leaned her head back and closed her eyes, wishing she could blot the farmsat's light from the sky so that she could see the stars.

She felt a profound loneliness, and she wept silently for her friends who needed her, who were so far away. Eventually she dozed off. When she awoke, the town was quiet, the clubs were mostly dark, and she had a terrific neckache. She trudged back to the dorm, got a sandwich from a dispenser, and returned to her room, where she ate one bite before falling into a deep and dreamless sleep.

She spent the next day in the rigger nav library, running sims of various routes to the mountain region of Aeregian space. Later, she again went looking for Kan-Kon, hoping to find him before he could lose himself in drink, drugs, or wires. But her search was fruitless; no one in any of the clubs had seen him all evening. One woman told Jael that she'd seen him sitting in the park that morning and he'd looked . . . *scared*, she'd thought. But where he'd gone, the woman had no idea.

Jael gave up. On an impulse, she went to the depot and caught a night train out of Krakow to one of the small tourist towns out beyond the radius of the farmsat's light. She took a room, but spent most of the night sitting out under the stars, watching the rotation of the sky until it brought the constellations of Aeregian space blazing high over the horizon. Somewhere out there, among the stars scattered like motes of glowing dust in the sky, was the mountain route leading to the port of Lexis. Somewhere in that region, dipping into the Flux, one could find the realm of dragons. She gazed for a long time, and felt her hopes and fears rise and fall like an invisible tide.

The feeling persisted that someone, or some spirit, not of this world, lingered nearby—trying to speak to her across an unbreachable barrier. When she finally slept that night, she dreamed of voices booming and rushing about her, like water in a stream pounding down a carved channel. She dreamed that someone was calling Windrush a traitor to the realm. She dreamed that Windrush was calling out to her in his sleep. She dreamed of someone calling: *They are trying to entrap you!* and she woke up with those words echoing in her mind.

Returning to Krakow, she renewed her search for Kan-Kon. No one seemed to think it unusual for him to drop out of sight. Who could predict the habits of a rigger turned lush—and who cared, besides Jael? She began to wonder if she had imagined her conversation with the man. She checked with registry and verified that Ar had not yet returned. She fumed and went to the nav library and ran another sim. She went to a holoshow and left in the middle. Finally she went to a bar and, uncharacteristically, got stinking drunk, telling at least three potential suitors to drop dead.

The next morning, waking with ringing ears and a splitting headache, she could remember nothing of the previous night's dreams. She decided that perhaps it would be smart to forget Kan-Kon, as well. She spent the day in the park, thinking through various options for getting back into space. The most obvious was to seek an assignment on an unaccompanied single-rigger to Lexis. But her memories of begging work alone in the rigger halls were as vivid today as ever—and anyway, she didn't seriously intend to go anywhere without Ar. And yet, she feared waiting too long.

They are trying to entrap you! The words swirled in her mind. *Windrush needs you.*

She reviewed her finances. She was no longer poor, by the standards of her profession. Flying with Ar, she had saved most of her earnings, and she could add to that the settlement she had received from the estate of her late former captain, Mogurn—not just flight pay, but damages for Mogurn's coercive abuse. Still, that hardly put her in the category of being able to acquire a ship. She thought of appealing directly to Mariella Flaire. But it seemed absurd to think that Flaire would divert a starship for Jael's personal needs.

That only seemed to leave . . . stealing Flaire's ship the next time she and Ar were sent out together. And that was almost unthinkable.

And yet . . .

What was she willing to do to help her friend? She had already once risked Flaire's ship, and her own life and her shipmates' lives, to help Highwing when he was in need. She had no regrets about that. But that had not been a premeditated theft.

She rubbed her eyes, staring hopelessly. The lake seemed almost incongruously peaceful as she gazed out over its waters, thinking.

"Miss—"

She started, and looked up into the craggy face of Kan-Kon.

"I've—I've forgotten your name," the man stammered. "But you know—I have this feeling we talked some, a day or two ago." He scratched his stubbly chin.

Jael gulped and nodded, and gestured to the grass beside her. The retired rigger eyed her for a moment, then carefully lowered himself to the ground, like some ungainly, spindly bird.

"I've been looking for you," she said. "Where have you been?"

Kan-Kon shrugged. "Here—there—no place special." He was silent for a moment, then grunted. "*You* were looking for *me?*"

Jael frowned. She was sure that he remembered perfectly well what they had talked about the other night. Why else would he be here? "I wanted to talk to you about the . . . dragons. I thought maybe—"

His voice shook as he interrupted her. "About—?"

"*Dragons,*" Jael snapped. "Remember them?"

"Well—" He swallowed and glanced away. "No, I—don't think I really know anything about that, miss—"

"Jael. My name is Jael. And yes you do." She took a sharp breath. "Are you telling me you don't remember losing your shipmate there? And you don't remember the ifflings? And their prophecy? You don't remember—?"

"Okay!" he hissed. "Okay, miss—Jael. You don't have to be—" And he suddenly turned his back to her, and trembled as though crying.

Jael felt sorry for him, but not sorry enough to let go. "Kan-Kon," she said, hardening her voice. *Damn you,* she thought, *what are you afraid of?* "Kan-Kon, listen to me! We may be the only two people on this planet who know the dragons are real. And the ifflings." And it suddenly hit her, like a bolt—how could she not have seen it before? The creatures who had spoken to her in the middle of the night—were they *ifflings?*

"Ifflin's," Kan-Kon whispered. "Saved my life." He slowly turned back to face her.

"I think—I saw some ifflings—a few nights ago," she said. "They spoke to me."

"It scared me," he said, seeming not to hear her words—"talkin' to you and knowin' that you been there, too. I been—tryin' to forget, ever since."

"Why? Because you lost your friend there?"

For a moment, she thought he was going to cry again. His face tightened up, and twisted, and he nodded. "I'm just—always wonderin'—if he might be—" He looked away, suddenly, and stared out over the water. Then his chin jerked, and he gazed back at her. "Did you jus' say you saw ifflings—*here?*"

Jael nodded.

"Damn," he whispered. "*Damn.* I've been feelin' like I've been hearin' voices lately. That same night we talked was the worst—didn't sleep a wink, not a damn wink. I—I just figgered it was the booze, the damn booze makin' me hear things."

Jael strained toward him. "You've heard them, too? What did they say to you?"

Kan-Kon snorted. "To me? Nothing. It was more like I dreamed they was there, hoverin' around, watchin' something that had nothing to do with me, and talkin' to each other." He hesitated, stroking his chin. "Mebbe I 'magined the whole thing. I dunno."

Electrified, Jael stared at Kan-Kon. But when she spoke, it was as much to herself as to him. "I have to go back there," she said. "They need me."

"*Shuuuuu*—WHAT?"

"I have to go back. To help my friends."

Kan-Kon's eyebrows quivered in disbelief, or horror.

Jael looked away, remembering the iffling's words . . . remembering how much had gone before, to draw her and the dragons together in friendship. It had not merely been her rescue of Highwing from a fiery exile, or even Highwing's help in freeing her from the bondage of the shipowner Mogurn. Those acts had grown out of another— Highwing's freeing her from the bondage of her own past, from the bondage of a lifetime of bitterness against her father. That was what the dragon had done for her, which no human had been able to do—and it was not only because he had recognized in her the embodiment of an ancient dragon prophecy. It was done, she believed, out of genuine friendship. And that was why she would never abandon Highwing's son, any more than she would have abandoned Highwing himself. She nodded, looking back at Kan-Kon. "I don't have a ship yet. But I'll find a way. Somehow."

Kan-Kon looked as though he would pop a vein in his forehead. "You're going back," he whispered.

She nodded again.

"Ship. You need a ship." He was squinting now, as though every fiber of his body were concentrated in thought.

"Do you know where I can get one?" She didn't really expect an answer.

Kan-Kon angled his face up into the sun as though contemplating her question. But when he looked down again, he merely shook his head. "Mighty tough to get a ship, if you're aimin' to go that route."

She sighed and tugged at the tough, pliant grass between her knees. "Would you want to come with us?" Only after the words were out did she realize what she had just said.

Kan-Kon's face went pale. His eyes seemed to focus very far away, his lips trembled, and he began coughing.

"That's okay. I didn't think you would," Jael said hastily. She waited until his coughing subsided. "Anyway, I'm hoping my partner, Ar, can help me come up with a way when he gets back." She shrugged. "If there's anything you remember that might help . . . I mean, you never know what might be useful."

Kan-Kon's eyes were still focused elsewhere. He seemed to be in shock over the very idea of going back to that place. He sat still for what seemed a very long time; then, without warning, he stood up and brushed off his pants. "I must be going," he said softly. He began to stride away.

"Wait!"

Kan-Kon looked back.

"I'm staying at the rigger dorm!" she yelled. "Jael LeBrae. Call if you think of anything, all right?"

Kan-Kon might have nodded, or it might just have been her imagination. Then he walked off along the waters that lapped at the grassy shore.

Jarvorus saw his opportunity and took it. One of the ifflings was venturing closer to the human presence, a little apart from the others. It was whispering, trying to send words of encouragement.

Jarvorus flashed across the gap and caught the iffling in his burning flame. It took only a moment to focus his energies on the startled being; it took only a moment to send the thing on to oblivion. Its fellows, reacting at once, dove toward him—but by then, he was already flying back to the company of his remaining fellow warrior. The ifflings retreated, wailing.

Just two of them left, Jarvorus said to his companion.

Shall we strike now?

Wait. The time will come.

The other warrior was eager, restless, sorry to have been so slow as to have missed out on the kill. But Jarvorus, while rejoicing, was thoughtful. He had caught a glimpse of the iffling-creature's thought as he had destroyed it. And what he had seen puzzled him.

It was not the iffling's intelligence or knowledge or purpose that disturbed him; it was something else. He had sensed in it . . . a willingness to sacrifice its life. Not a lack of love for its life, but a willingness to give it up if required to. He thought he sensed echoes of that same willingness in the human, as well—and he didn't understand it.

Who *were* these enemies, these strange beings, the ifflings? The question troubled him. He thought he might like to know more about them before he killed them all.

The days passed with excruciating slowness. The voices never quite seemed to go away, but neither did their owners become visible again. Jael's dreams were like turbulent waters—troubled and restless, but never taking a clear course. The next time she saw Kan-Kon, he was drunk; but he looked at her with frightened eyes that said he hadn't forgotten. Mostly, she spent the time alone, hoping for word from Ar.

When he finally did arrive, she almost missed him. She'd checked with the registry early in the morning; and unable to stand the thought of waiting around, had bought a ticket for a day trip out of town. Her train was late, and tiring of the wait, she went to a com booth in the depot and called the dispatch office one more time.

There was no word on the arrival of *Corona*, the ship Ar was supposed to be flying for Mariella Flaire. But there was a node message from Ar: "*Arriving 1130 today on train from New Tilly. Meet me?*"

Jael's breath went out in a rush. Arriving on the train from New Tilly? That was a port halfway across the continent. Had he been diverted? Eleven-thirty: that was fifteen minutes ago! She bolted out to see if the hi-speeder from New Tilly had come in. It had—just—and was beginning to pull out again. She watched the silver cars glide past on their magnetic cushion, accelerating, as she looked frantically up and down the platform. "Ar!" she shouted. Most of the passengers were already on their way out of the depot. She rushed back to the lobby.

"Jael!"

Ar was standing out front, waving. His tall Clendornan form was impossible to miss: the nearly wedge-shaped head, flat on top with grey hair, the triangular face with silver-blue skin, the zigzag smile. As she ran toward him, his crystal-orb eyes glowed, and he strode forward to meet her. She threw her arms around him and hugged him ferociously. Ar laughed with a hiccuping sound. They broke their embrace and held each other at arm's length. Ar's face was cracked by his zigzag smile. "It is good to see you, my partner," he said as he studied her.

Jael, ready to explode with words, could only grin. She broke away from him and spun around in joyous relief.

"You received my message?" Ar asked.

Jael shook her head helplessly. "What happened? Why did you come in on a *train?*"

"Well, I had to take a different ship back, with another crew." And the way Ar said it, she knew that he had a story to tell.

She interrupted him. "Did Mariella change your assignment? Did you see her? Oh, Ar, we have to talk! We might have to ask Mariella to do us a huge favor. Do you think she'd be willing?"

His eyes flickered with puzzlement, then dimmed. His expression brought her words to a halt. This time, Ar's tone was subdued. "I doubt she'll be able to. That's why I had to come back on another ship, Jael. Mariella's company has gone bankrupt."

Chapter 12
RIGGERS WITHOUT A SHIP

IT TOOK Jael several heartbeats to regain her breath. Mariella's company, out of business? "Ar—that can't be!" she gasped.

Ar cocked his head sympathetically. "I'm sorry to drop it just like that. I'd wanted to celebrate our reunion first."

Celebrate? Jael could hardly find her voice. "What are we going to do?" she whispered.

The Clendornan made a purring sound. "Don't worry, we'll find other people to fly for. We have a good record, so it shouldn't be too hard." He gave a rippling shrug and hefted his duffel. They began walking toward the glideway that would take them to the rigger quarters. "I feel worse for Mariella than I do for us. She hit some tough economic conditions, and I think her partners made some bad decisions while she was traveling and out of contact." Ar sighed. "I guess we knew it couldn't last forever."

Jael's heart pounded in misery as they walked. Everything she'd been bursting to tell Ar was now sunk in a swamp of hopelessness. What Ar was saying was true, of course. Two years ago, Flaire had endured some hard times with her company. But she had recovered, and continued employing them on a regular basis ever since. But Jael, who as an adolescent had watched her father's business fail, should have known that no business was immune to bad luck—or bad judgment.

"That's my only news," Ar said, trying to sound a cheerful note. "It is very good to see you again, Jael."

She nodded, not looking at him. All of the joy of their reunion had been robbed from her. She didn't know what to say. They rode the glideway to the rigger dorm, and walked to Ar's quarters. She perched on the end of his rigid, almost unpadded bunk while he unpacked some of his things. "Do you want a little time alone?" she murmured.

Ar's mouth crinkled in a smile. "Perhaps ten minutes for a mist and a change? Then would you like to go for a walk? I haven't been outside much in a long time."

Jael's heart was heavy as she rose. "Meet you downstairs."

By the time Ar rejoined her, she'd managed to get her thoughts in order. As they walked toward the lake, she told him her news—first, about Kan-Kon and her decision to break their long silence about the dragons. Ar listened thoughtfully. "I hope this fellow isn't adding our story to his public exhibition," he remarked. They sat down near the lake's rippling surface. Ar began humming a dissonant tune, and Jael trembled at the sound. Ar's predilection for off-key tunes had once nearly driven her to distraction; now it was comforting.

"I don't think so. Ar—"

"You have more to tell me?"

"Yes—" And she related, in stumbling words, what had happened one midnight, such a seemingly long time ago. She told him what the ifflings—or voices, at any rate—had said to her. *Windrush needs you. Go to him.* The words resonated out of her memory of that dark night, and when she actually spoke them aloud, she felt as though she were giving freedom to something that was alive. Giving freedom so that the pain of keeping it in could stop.

Only the pain didn't stop. Windrush was in trouble, and there seemed nothing she could do. By the time she finished she was crying, rocking backward and forward, her eyes squeezed shut against the noonday sun. She could not stop shaking.

Ar laid a hand on her shoulder and made muttering sounds that she knew were supposed to soothe. But really, nothing could soothe her except finding a way to go, a way to answer the ifflings' plea. And she knew that Ar had no way to give her what she needed.

Back in her room, Jael flicked on the holo projector. "Ed!" Ar boomed. "How are you, my feathery friend?"

"*Scrawwwww!*" The bird flashed his colors and took to wing from the stondai tree. He batted about the room in jubilation before circling to land on Ar's shoulder. "Back! Rawk! Back—you're back! Scrawww!"

"I am indeed back, and I missed you. I trust you've been keeping Jael good company," Ar said, making a tickling gesture under the parrot's holographic chin.

"Yep, yep. Good company." Ed sat back and cocked his head about the room. He gazed at Jael and then at Ar. "She tell you? Awk! She tell you? Graggon-things here! Haww!"

Ar gave him a crinkly smile, his eyes glowing purple at the parrot. "You mean the ifflings?"

"Ifftings, ifftings—haww! That what they were?"

"Apparently so. I guess she told you about them?"

"Rawwk! Ed saw. Ed *saw!* Strange things, awk—*talking.* Woke Ed up! Scary—hraww! Scared Jayl, scared Ed!" The bird fluttered his wings.

Ar cocked his head to peer at the bird. "You saw it, too, Ed? Are you sure?"

"Hawwwwk! Ed sure, all right! Scared Ed!" The parrot launched himself from Ar's shoulder and whirred about the room before landing on Ar's knee.

Jael looked at Ar with a wry smile. She remembered a time, a couple of years ago, when Ar had doubted her story of dragons in the Flux. "Did you think maybe this was another figment of my imagination? Like Highwing?"

His silver-blue face darkened slightly. "I did not doubt you, Jael. But it is helpful to have confirmation. It could make our needs more . . . credible . . . if we seek . . ." He paused to grope for words. "Well. It will not be easy for us to get back there, will it? But it seems we must try."

Jael drew a sharp breath. Until now, Ar hadn't come right out and said that he wanted to return with her. Her pulse raced, and she gazed at him with gratitude. They were no closer to having a ship, perhaps, but it felt to her as if the gulf between her and the dragon realm had just closed a little. Maybe, just maybe she would sleep tonight without her dreams of anxiety, and with hope in her heart.

This fight Jarvorus did not start. He was content to watch and wait as the two ifflings bobbed in the distance, whispering their irritating encouragements to the human. It was his fellow warrior who took the initiative—stupidly, blindly hoping to destroy the ifflings in a display of boldness and strength.

Erupting with anger, the ifflings pounced back upon Jarvorus' companion. Jarvorus watched in dismay, holding back for the sake of the mission, as the warrior was annihilated. He regretted losing his companion. But the important thing, more important than aiding his fellow, was to remain vigilant for a chance to lead the human astray. It did not matter if the ifflings lived or died, only that their purpose be thwarted.

His fellow had destroyed one of the ifflings before being consumed in the fire himself. Jarvorus briefly considered striking now, while the last iffling was weakened. But what he saw emerging from the fire was not a weakened foe, but a blazing and indignant foe.

Jarvorus silently thanked his late fellow for his foolishness and bravery; but he, Jarvorus, would wait. Only he, now, could see to it that his mission was fulfilled.

By the next afternoon, they had been over every avenue they could think of to acquire a ship—from applying for grants from the rigger-space research institutes on various worlds, to buying a ship or stealing one. The first seemed unlikely, and would certainly take far too long, and the last was hardly a serious consideration. That left trying to buy one.

Ironically, *Seneca*, the ship they had flown for Mariella Flaire, was right here on Cargeeling, where it had been in the tanks for a refit for most of the last ten weeks. That, in fact, was one reason Jael had stayed here while Ar had made his interim flight. They had expected to return to service with *Seneca* when the ship itself returned to service. But with Flaire's company going out of business, she wondered what would happen to the ship.

Could they, perhaps, afford to buy a ship at auction? Between them, they had more assets than Jael had guessed. But the cost of a rigger-ship remained far beyond them. Could they get financing? It seemed unlikely, without a persuasive business plan.

Ar was determined to devise a way. Perhaps he could secure a loan on his home planet. Perhaps Mariella could still help somehow. Ar would check on the status of *Seneca*. Jael's task was to compose a description of their intended use of the ship—aside from visiting dragons, of course. She was to be truthful, but to make it sound as if they still had a grip on reality.

None of this afforded much hope. But it was all the hope they had.

The passage of the days took on a surreal quality, as they worked and planned and saw no progress. Jael found herself thinking of her late father. Willie LeBrae had done a lot wrong in his life, and she had spent a good part of her own life hating him for it. She had eventually managed to forgive him, but only after coming to a painful understanding that he really had cared for her, even if in a hopelessly flawed way. It was he, after all, who had enabled her to attend rigger school and to learn the very profession that he had ultimately come to despise.

Willie LeBrae had been a shipper and shipowner—initially a legitimate one. Later, when the tides had turned on his business fortunes, so too had his legitimacy. In the end, he had abused many an innocent rigger, though hardly more than he had abused his own family. Still . . . Willie LeBrae would have known how to acquire a ship, even under the most difficult of circumstances. Perhaps not a ship that one would personally want to fly; but that sort of concern had never stopped him. Jael wished now that she had learned more of the business from her father. It was perhaps the first time since she'd been a little girl that she had wished she could emulate anything of Willie LeBrae's life.

She wondered if it was too late to learn.

Five days after Ar's return, she was in the spaceport administration building, waiting for Ar, who was inquiring into the status of *Seneca*. It seemed that *Seneca* had been impounded by the shipyard that had overhauled its flux-pile and rigger-net systems. Until the overhaul bill was paid, the ship could not be moved. Ar was hoping to acquire the use of the ship from Flaire, if they could raise the money for its release. Flaire, he thought, might be open to the idea; but she was on Vela Oasis, sifting through the ruins of her business, and fluxwave communications with Vela Oasis were erratic, and very expensive. So far, he'd been unable to reach her.

Jael was standing in the hallway, studying the ships-for-sale bulletins on a wall-screen, when she heard footsteps. She glanced—then stared in amazement at the last person she expected to see here. The ex-rigger was smooth-faced and neatly dressed, with his long hair molded into a tidy appearance. "Kan-Kon?" she whispered.

"Whaaat?" Startled, he came to a halt. "Miss . . . Jael," he said, flashing a sudden sheepish grin. "Mighty surprised to see you here." He shifted from one foot to the other.

You're surprised to see *me?* Jael couldn't quit staring at him. She had never imagined him well groomed. And she'd thought he had long since given up everything having to do with space. "I—" Before she could think of what to say, she was rescued from her embarrassment by the sudden appearance of Ar at her side. The tall Clendornan's lips were pressed into a thin line as he nodded to Kan-Kon. "Ar . . . this is . . ." Jael gestured, trying to force out the name.

"Kan-Kon," said the ex-rigger in a husky voice.

Ar's eyebrows jumped. "Rarberticandornan," he said, shaking hands. "Please call me Ar."

"Ar . . . yes. You are Miss Jael's rigging partner, then," Kan-Kon murmured, bowing slightly. "Most pleased to meet you."

Ar bowed back. "And you are . . . the one who . . ."

"Yes," Kan-Kon said quickly, glancing away self-consciously. "I'm afraid I gave her a bit of a start just now. I don't always—that is, I don't think . . . well." He smoothed down the front of his tunic. "I think she was surprised to see me here. But yes, I am the one who—" and he shrugged with a forced smile. "Are you still trying to—find a ship to—"

"Go back," Jael whispered. "Yes." She looked questioningly at Ar. He shook his head. Her breath went out in a sigh.

Kan-Kon's eyes darted from Jael to Ar and back again. "Forgive me. Am I—?"

Jael shook her head. "No, it's all right. It's just that . . . well, we've been trying to get the use of one particular ship, you see. A long shot. But so far . . ." Her gaze went back to Ar.

"No word from Mariella," Ar said. He stroked the ridge over his temple, his eyes glimmering moodily. "And the repair yard has already filed for the right to go to auction. If they succeed, I don't think we can do much about it." He glanced at Kan-Kon, who was studying his fingernails. "Jael, I fear we are being rude. May we invite your friend to join us for tea?"

Kan-Kon looked uncomfortable. "Tea?" he murmured, his voice cracking a little. "I don't really—that is, I've finished my business here for the day. How about . . . something a little stronger?" Ar raised his eyebrows, and Jael shrugged, and they all walked down the corridor together.

Settled in a nearby lounge, Kan-Kon drew deeply on a draft of ale. He sighed with noisy satisfaction, thumping his mug down onto the table. Jael watched uneasily, wondering if he would be transformed before her eyes into the man she had met before. As if reading her mind, Kan-Kon murmured, "I expect you're wondering . . ." He paused.

"Do you still, uh, do business, here at the spaceport?" Jael stammered, trying to fill the awkward silence.

Kan-Kon tipped his head noncommittally. The question

seemed to make him uncomfortable. He grinned, drumming his fingers on the tabletop. "A little, here and there. I keep my hand in." He hoisted his mug again, hesitated, then laughed abruptly and took another great swallow. He seemed to want to say more. But he turned to stare out the window instead.

Jael glanced at Ar, whose expression was unreadable. "Well," she said, "I guess Ar might like to hear about your experiences with—you know."

Kan-Kon tensed, still looking outside, tapping one fingernail on the table. He finally nodded, and turned back to face them. "I reckon you know what she means, Ar. It was nearly seven years 'go, standard." He cleared his throat noisily, and quit drumming on the table. "I was flying a duel rigger with my friend Hoddy—up from the south toward Lexis. Don't even remember which one of us it was got the idea. But we thought, let's take a detour and see if those rumors're true—about the dragons. I mean, here we were, just like everyone else, avoiding the mountains. And it seemed sort of foolish to us. I was a pretty good rigger, back in those days. Cocky, though. We didn't really think it *was* true, about dragons. So we went into the mountains."

"And?" Ar asked.

Kan-Kon guffawed bitterly. "Oh, it was true! And it wasn't a very long detour, either, not once the dragons showed up. . . ."

Jael stroked her throat nervously as Kan-Kon told his story. Ar displayed the same noncommittal politeness with which he had first heard her tell of meeting Highwing. Kan-Kon, so far, had stuck mainly to the duel, which had ended with their capture. He had not yet mentioned the one thing that had convinced her of the truth of his story. She cleared her throat. "Tell Ar how it was you heard the . . . prophecy."

There was a sudden glimmer in Ar's eyes. He took perhaps his third sip of ale since they had sat down.

Kan-Kon grunted. "Right. Well, they had us trapped— caught on a kind of rock plateau, surrounded by four of 'em. Couldn't flee, couldn't fight. They had us stuck in some kind of a *spell*, you'd almost say, as though our feet was glued to the rock. But then—" He shook his head as if in puzzlement. "They got to arguin' amongst themselves about whether we were some kind of demons or something. About whether to just barbecue us, or turn us into lizards, or I don't know what. There was some noise about a prophecy, but they didn't say anything I could make sense out of. Not till the iff—the iffling—appeared."

"What did the iffling say?" Jael asked, glancing at Ar.

Kan-Kon sighed. "Said they was making a mistake. It sort of . . . *sang* . . . this prophecy to them. But I swear, it seemed to be lookin' right at me and Hoddy the whole time. Mebbe that's why I remember what it said so well." Kan-Kon shuddered, taking another swallow of ale. He swayed a little, as though the power of the memory were too great to contain.

"And—"

"Ah . . ." Kan-Kon slowly drew himself straighter. He seemed a different man from the one who had stood before a crowded bar and shouted the words. Now he spoke them softly. "It went somethin' like this. 'From beyond life and hope will come one. Friendless will come one. And the realm shall tremble.' " He peered at Jael. " '*Giving her name* will come one. Challenging darkness will come one. And the realm shall tremble.' Something like that, anyway." He drew a breath and continued, " 'From that one comes a beginning. From that one comes an ending. And you bet your—' er, that is, 'and *surely* the realm shall tremble.' " He cleared his throat and frowned down at the table. He glanced up and took another drink, a long one. His sobriety was fading visibly.

Jael felt her temples pulsing. "And what did they do then?"

"Well, that's when Hoddy took it in his head to try to make a break. The spell somehow loosened, and he jumped. And they grabbed him in an instant and—" Kan-Kon's voice caught, then turned angry. "What they did was—" his voice cracked—"they *tore him right out of his body*. Killed him there on the spot. I don't know how—or even why. They jus' did it. Somethin' happened in the Flux, like a big quaking, and then I saw his . . . *spirit*, y'might say . . . lift right out of the net. And then somehow they just crushed the life out of him." Kan-Kon stared at Jael, then jerked his gaze away. "It was like watchin' a flame snuff out. He was just *gone*. But o'course, his body was still right there in the rigger-station. And I had to—to take him out and put him in the . . . freezer. And bring him back."

He squeezed his eyes shut for a moment, then blinked them open and continued in a husky voice, "They cremated him here on Cargeeling. Put it down as unexplained accident. Flux abscess or some doodoo cowpuckeyshit like that. He's still . . . I mean, I go out every once in a while to the place where they . . . where the marker is." He drained his mug in a single long gulp and savagely punched the table pad for another, then stared in silence at the table.

Jael asked quietly, "Why didn't they do the same to you?"

Kan-Kon pressed his lips together to keep them from quivering. "I . . . I guess the iffling . . . finally got through to 'em. All along, it was sayin', 'He's not the one. He's not the one! And even if he were, don't you think doing that to him would just make him stronger?' " Kan-Kon paused. "That's what it said. And I still, to this day, don't know what the damn thing meant by it. But the dragons seemed to know. At least—in the end, two of them made the others set me free."

He cocked his head at Jael. "And I guess mebbe that's one reason I believe you—that not all dragons are bad, I mean. But lemme tell you, I never—*never*—was so glad to leave a place in my life. Still, you know, to this day . . . there's something about that place that just won't let me go. I don't know why." He shook his head, then bowed it, pressing his hands together prayerfully in front of his nose. A thin line of tears was running down his cheek.

Ar stirred. "Your words trouble me, Kan-Kon." The ex-rigger snorted, as a robot delivered a fresh mug of ale to the table. "But not, perhaps, for the reasons you think."

The backs of Ar's eyes glowed like coals. Twilight was deepening outside the window of the lounge. A starship, locked to a tow, rose from the field beyond the administration buildings. The tow's space inductors glowed orange, rising and dwindling into the sky as the tow and ship accelerated away.

Kan-Kon grunted. "So why, then?"

Ar stroked his temple ridges. "It's more because . . : well, I guess you heard our story from Jael already." When Kan-Kon nodded, Ar said, "It's because, well, I believe that Jael . . ." Ar hesitated.

"She's the One, if that's what you're havin' trouble sayin'. Hell, I know that already," Kan-Kon said.

Ar looked disconcerted. He sat back, glancing at Jael. "Did you—?"

"Naw," Kan-Kon said. "I know what you're thinkin'. That maybe she went around braggin'. But she didn't, she jus' told me what happened. And the rest—hell, it was obvious. And I guess tha's why you need to go back. Because there's somethin' there that you're destined for. I can't tell you what, and I don't know if it's good or bad. But I'm *damn* sure it'll be dangerous, and it might even—"

He swallowed, and his voice softened suddenly. "Well . . . I thought I heard these words, too—when the dragons were babbling about the prophecy, not the iffling." He cleared his throat, several times. "*From that one's death will . . . something something . . . ending be wrought.*" He stared at her. "I don't know what it means—or if it means anything. But . . . well, if you're destined, then I guess you have to go. But be careful!" His eyes suddenly came afire, his hands in the air, waving. "*Get yourself a ship, Jael!* Don't let this thing stand in the way of your destiny!"

Jael felt a chill. "What do you think we're trying to do?"

"Don't take no for an answer! If it's money you need— *aahhhhh*—" Kan-Kon groaned and abruptly looked away, glaring into space.

Jael watched him, waiting to see if he would finish his sentence. Finally she whispered, "Do you know where we could get—?"

"Nahhh," Kan-Kon said, breaking the spell. He shook his head, belched, and took another long pull from his mug. "Well!" he said, straightening up suddenly. He was still avoiding Jael's eyes, and he looked acutely uncomfortable. Clearly he had said something he wished he hadn't. "Anyways," he blurted, "you shouldn't be listenin' to a washed-up old fart like me. I guess I should be gettin' along on my way here. I wish you two . . . luck . . . findin' a ship to go, and all. I know how it is, when you got a call and you jus' have to do somethin', someway, somehow."

Jael could only stare at him in bewilderment.

"I guess I'll maybe see you two good riggers again before you leave. Anyways, thanks for the . . . tea." Kan-Kon heaved himself up and walked, swaying, from the room.

Chapter 13
A PARTNERSHIP FORGED

THE POSTING of the auction came with shocking speed. The name *Seneca* appeared on the bulletins two days after the default on the bill at the repair yard. There still was no word from Mariella Flaire, but apparently the management of the yard was either pessimistic about the chances of being paid or, more likely, eager to turn a profit on Flaire's misfortune.

"What are we going to do?" Jael asked, feeling what remained of her hope slipping away.

Ar was silent for a time as they stared at the bulletin. "Either we triple our money in the next two days or we give up on *Seneca*—"

"And find a cheaper ship." Jael nodded dully. She had been steeling herself for the inevitable. But what kind of a wreck could they afford to buy? Probably one that couldn't qualify for a spaceworthiness certificate. Ar was clearly thinking the same thing. Just remember, she thought, Willie LeBrae made ships fly that had no business flying. If he could do it, so can I.

But as they walked away from the boards, even Ar was slumping.

The auction was scheduled for two days later. The next day, Jael received a message on her room com: "*Miss Le-Brae—we urgently request you call our office at Krakow Spaceport concerning a matter of great import to both of us. Please call today. Herbert Connolly, AAA Refitting and Resupply, Unlimited, Krakow.*" Jael was puzzled, to say the least. She'd never heard of the company, or of Herbert Connolly. Finally she called the number. The secretary who answered could tell her only that Mr. Connolly wished her to visit the office as soon as possible.

Ar was off on a round of visits to finance companies and probably wouldn't be back for several hours. After some thought, Jael decided to go alone. The address turned out to be in a line of small offices at the edge of the spaceport. The area was dreary, the buildings a dirty grey. Only a faded number on the front distinguished the building at the address she'd been given. Inside, she found dim hallways and doors with grimy windows. At the end of a long hall, she found AAA Refitting and Resupply. It was only a little less depressing on the inside. Behind the front desk were ancient holos of three obsolete spaceships, all impossibly bright and shiny. The pictures had a slight distortion-shimmer to them. She was sure they were at least two decades old. The side wall boasted last year's calendar.

A matronly seeming woman walked out of a back room. Jael drew a breath. "Is Mr. Connolly here? I'm Jael—"

"LeBrae? Yes." The woman touched the com. "Ms. Le-Brae here to see you."

"Thank you, Mrs. Murdock."

A wiry black man emerged from the back room and gestured her in. He took a seat behind a plain, but immaculate, oak-topped desk. He stared at her for a moment, without speaking. Jael perched on the edge of an old wooden chair and returned his stare. His eyes had no whites; they were entirely charcoal grey, except for the black pupils. Against his ebony skin, his eyes seemed to recede into the distance. Jael blinked, and started to say, *You sent me a message*, when she realized that he had just introduced himself. "*Meez* Le-Brae," he continued, in carefully clipped syllables, his hands folded before him—and he hesitated, as though reluctant to continue, before giving a long, wistful sigh, "*eet ees* my understanding that you are in need of a sh*eep*. Eef I may ask . . ." He hesitated again, then shook his head and continued, in an accent which she did not recognize, "Is thees so?"

Jael hesitated, then nodded. How did this man know? Did rumor travel that fast here in Krakow?

"Well-l-l, then," he said, with a scowl, "it may *bee* that I can be of asseestance to you. Or—I should say—one whom I represent wishes to hel-l-lp you." He twitched his nose. As she was about to ask, with considerable suspicion, what exactly he was talking about, he added emphatically, "This ees not my idea. But . . . we have heard of your eenterest in a sheep named *Seneca*—which is schedul-l-l-ed to be auctioned. *Eef* I may ask—is that correct? You have flown this sheep before?"

Jael felt her brow furrow up as she forced her head to nod. She felt paralyzed by bewilderment. Who the hell was this man, and who was his friend? Why should she speak to him? She wanted to run, screaming, from the room. She wanted to fall to her knees and beg him to say more. What did it matter who he was?

"Ah-ha." Connolly steepled his fingers on his desk, seemingly unaware of her reaction to his question. "*Meez* LeBrae, I may have a proposition of mutual inter-r-rest." He coughed delicately, as her breath caught in her throat. "That is . . . your friend, and my partner, Meester Gonzol-l-l-es, has asked eef we might join with you in the purchase of the aforementioned sheep. He has expressed his desire to share with you and your partner in the ownersheep of that sheep." Connolly paused, puckering his mouth. "If you would be inter-r-r-ested . . ." He sat back and stared at her, as though expecting her to take over the conversation. When she didn't, he asked with some impatience, "Would that eenterest you, Meez LeBrae?"

Jael stared at him stupidly.

Connolly looked pained. "Meez LeBrae, I am given to understand that time is somewhat of the essence in thees matter."

Jael struggled to reply. Who the hell was Mr. Gonzoles? Someone Ar had talked to? Had he already made it all the way down to this . . . dump of an office, looking for help? Tears began to well in her eyes, and she tried to make them stop.

"Meez LeBrae?"

Had this man just offered to help her buy *Seneca?* Or was she hallucinating . . . ?

"Meez LeBrae, you know who I'm talking about, yes? If I may say, you l-l-look sl-l-lightly confused—"

She shook her head, blinking. "I don't *know* any Mr. Gonzoles!" she blurted finally.

The charcoal eyes stared. "Meester *Kan-Kon* Gonzol-l-les? You don't know *Kan-Kon* Gonzol-l-les?"

Kan-Kon? she thought, certain she must have misheard. *Kan-Kon* Gonzoles? "Excuse me," she whispered. She shook her head. "That's ridiculous. Kan-Kon couldn't possibly be—I mean he's, he's—" A drunkard. A failure. A misfit.

"Yes," Connolly agreed, as though reading her thoughts. "That ees true. Nevertheless—"

"Are you telling me," she demanded, "that Kan-Kon is in a position to help me buy a *ship?*"

Connolly looked disconsolate. "Yesss, Meez LeBrae. I'm afraid so. I assure you, thees idea is as unsettling to me as it is to you." He hesitated. "But shall we continue?"

Jael swallowed and stared at him in disbelief. Connolly seemed to take that as assent, and went on to present the particulars of the proposed arrangement: a pooling of resources, a joint effort. It all seemed more than a little hazy to Jael; she began to feel as if she were flying in the rigger-net in some sort of syrupy landscape, unable to make her thoughts keep up with the events streaming by. Connolly talked, and she answered, but with only scant comprehension of what she was saying. Kan-Kon Gonzoles was going to help them buy the ship. *Kan-Kon.*

Only after she had shaken hands with Mr. Connolly and left the office, promising to return with Ar, did the feeling begin to dissipate. Even then, her head seemed to be ringing so loudly she could scarcely hear a sound around her. But by the time she returned to her quarters, she was beginning to believe it, and to become excited, filled with the strange conviction that things were at last starting to turn her way.

* * *

By the time Ar came back, it was well after the close of business hours. Nevertheless, after she'd explained the situation to an incredulous Ar, she called Connolly, and he urged them to come right down.

It was now dark in the industrial park. There was a nightglow billboard on the side of one of the buildings, spelling out a graphic enticement for an erotic-aid product, with glowing, billowing green images and words that seemed to rise out of the flat side of the building. Jael was glad, as she walked past it with Ar, that it was too dark for him to see her flushing with indignation.

The hallway leading to Connolly's office was even gloomier than it had been in daylight, but the office itself was blazingly lit with ceiling panels. Mrs. Murdock was still there, along with Connolly and one other person. Kan-Kon was half leaning, half sitting on the windowsill beside Connolly's desk, his head bowed, fingers stroking his chin in thought. He looked sober, intensely so. He didn't stir for a few seconds after Jael and Ar came in. Then his eyes rose to meet Jael's, and at once darted away again, in embarrassment. She thought she glimpsed a faint upturn of one corner of his mouth.

"Now, then, do wee all-I-I know why wee're her-r-re?" Connolly asked, in a tone of obvious sarcasm. He looked from one to another with a gaze that seemed disapproving. Jael suddenly had a feeling that Kan-Kon and Connolly had been arguing.

Ar waited for Jael to answer, but when she didn't, he murmured, "Well, as I understand it, we're here to discuss terms for the purchase of a ship." He set his glowing eyes upon the silent ex-rigger. "Kan-Kon. Mr. Gonzoles. I am . . . surprised. I believe I speak for Jael, also."

There was an awkward pause. Kan-Kon suddenly looked up and grinned broadly. "Guess I never told you, when I quit riggin' I went into the shippin' business."

Ar shook his head, his lips crinkling ever so slightly. "I believe you omitted that fact. But then—" and he glanced at Jael—"I suppose we never asked, either."

Kan-Kon continued to grin. "But I *tol'* you I kep' my hand in."

Jael flushed. You did, she thought. And we never asked because we thought you were a hopeless drunk. We thought you slept in the street at night. Go ahead and say it, Ar, it's true.

"I reckon it's understand'ble," Kan-Kon admitted. "After all, I don't 'xactly—well—that is, I do have my problems. I'll be th' first to admit it. And I don't exactly run what you would call a *high-class* shippin' firm—do I, Herb?"

Jael found herself quaking with silent, astonished laughter. "You mean, this is—" Her voice failed, and she gestured around.

"My outfit, more 'r less, yep." Kan-Kon cackled suddenly. "Not that Herb here would let me brag much about my contribution to the day-t'-day operation—would you, Herb?"

Connolly steepled his fingers on the desk, looking long-suffering but near the end of his patience. "*Eef* I may say—*weeth* all respect—we do a profitabl-l-le enough business here. That is—" and his gaze darkened even further—"when we refr-r-rain from . . . unwise purchases."

Kan-Kon suddenly became serious. "Yep, we make a pretty good profit—thanks almost entirely to Herb Connolly, who don't drink near as much as I do. An' if he owned any more of the company, he'd prob'ly kick me out on my rear, an' I couldn't much blame him. And o'course, the whole place would fall apart without Mrs. Murdock—isn't that right, Mrs. M?" He glanced at the older woman, who merely sighed, shaking her head in disapproval.

"But you two don't give a dinglydamn about that. You need a ship. And mebbe I can help you." He paused, while Jael and Ar looked at each other and back at Kan-Kon, who grinned again. "Wouldn't you know, it happens that we've been known to buy a ship or two at auction. Thing is, right just now, we don't have the capital to buy your ship, *Seneca*, right out. But I thought just mebbe, if we put our heads together, we could become *shared* owners—Herb's

quite proper reservations notwithstanding, you understand. Then you could take that flight you been dreamin'
about to certain regions of the civilized realm." With a
sidelong glance at Connolly, he winked at Jael. She could
not help trembling with hope.

"*Eef* I may say—" Connolly interjected.

"No, Herb, you may not," Kan-Kon barked, with sudden vehemence.

Connolly stiffened. "I am onl-l-ly trying to prevent a
terribl-l-e mistake. Do you know what it could cost you
to—"

Kan-Kon shook his head. "Sorry, Herb. Yes, I do know.
But this time I'm pullin' rank on you."

"Then perhaps-s-s you should theenk about finding another operations manager-r-r."

Kan-Kon sighed. "Herb, Herb—don't take this so personal, will you? You can go right back to runnin' the whole
show and makin' us lots of money, just as soon as these
folks is on their way."

Ar spoke before Connolly could reply. "May I ask
. . . *why* . . . you're offering to do this? It's not that I'm
unappreciative, but . . ."

Kan-Kon glanced at Connolly, who looked away—then
suddenly leaned forward. For a moment, he seemed to be
gathering some inner strength. He closed his eyes and said,
"Yeah, I guess I can tell you. Or try, anyways." When he
opened his eyes again, they were burning with intensity.
"There was a time, once, when I didn't do somethin' I
should've done." His voice caught. "When I ran . . . instead
of standin' and doin' what a rigger might've done."

"You mean—" Jael began.

"I mean—I don't know what I coulda' done to save him,
exactly, but I do know my partner's dead because I was too
scared to try." Kan-Kon drew his lips together, touching
his chin with one hand, looking as if he were thinking of
something that he was afraid to speak of, even now. He
shook his head slowly. "At least, I'm pretty sure he's dead.
And if he's not . . . oh holies, I bet he wishes he were."
Kan-Kon's breath whistled out in a nervous sigh, and his

next words were whispered. "Because I know from what the iffs—ifflings—said, that there's somethin' dangerous out there. Somethin' mighty big, and dangerous, and growin', and—well, I guess you know it as well as I do, you told me about it yourself. You called it—what—?"

"Tar-skel," Jael whispered with a shudder.

"Right. And that's really, I figure, what got Hoddy. It scares me to think about it, even after seven years. But . . . mebbe I coulda done something about it then—for Hoddy, anyways—but I didn't. And mebbe now I got another chance."

Connolly looked disgusted. "Dangerous *fantasies*," he hissed. "You run from fantasies, and now you dr*eenk* and you won't take the treatment for it because—"

"*Not* fantasies!" Kan-Kon shouted. "*Real*." His voice softened as he turned back to Jael and Ar. "Real. And maybe you two can do somethin' about it, in my place. Just maybe."

Ar stared at him for a few moments. "What exactly are you proposing?" he asked quietly. "*Seneca* goes up for auction day after tomorrow."

"Don't y'know." Kan-Kon drew himself up, and nodded as though dismissing his disagreement with Connolly. "But what 'f we paid off her refit bill? What if we stopped that old auction and bought her at a favored price from your old employer? You think he might go for that? Hell, at auction, he'd be lucky to cover his legal fees, anyway."

"She," Jael croaked.

"Beg your pardon. She. But she might jus' do better, and *we* might do better, if we cut a deal on that ship and get her off that auction block before she gets on. What do you say? Can you reach her?"

"She's on Vela Oasis," Ar said.

Kan-Kon frowned. "Long ways away. If we can't reach her, I don't know if we could do it. We could pay to spring the ship, but how do we know she'd honor the deal?"

"I'd trust her," Ar said slowly. "But it would be better to have confirmation, certainly."

Kan-Kon pointed to the com, finger tapping. "Fluxwave

is as close as your phone," he said cheerily. "Class One 'gram, and you pay for it?"

Jael winced at the thought of the cost. But Class One was the surest way to get through. She swallowed and nodded to Ar. He stirred, but before reaching for the com, he asked one more question. "Exactly how much were you looking for us to invest?"

Kan-Kon whooped and grinned at his unhappy partner. "How much you got?"

Even after the answer came back from Flaire on Vela Oasis, approving the sale price, it was no easy matter to work out all of the details. Jael gratefully left most of that in Ar's hands while she completed her research on the fastest course from Cargeeling to the distant mountain realm.

When the dust had settled, Jael and Ar were listed as first and second in command, respectively. Kan-Kon, or rather, AAA Refitting and Resupply, Unlimited, was listed as minority shareholder. Kan-Kon could have demanded more, and they would have given it to him, but as he said, "Hell, you think I want it on my shippin' record that I *ordered* one of my ships to fly the mountain route? It's outta my hands—outta my hands. Just pay me my share o' the profits." There was some discussion about a cargo manifest for the trip—which might, after all, recover the costs of their voyage once they reached Lexis or another port. Jael was reluctant to take on the responsibility for a cargo, but they finally settled on a small manifest of surplus optronics parts that AAA had purchased at auction some time ago and had been unable to get rid of.

There was one more thing that seemed to be on Kan-Kon's mind, but he seemed to be having trouble getting around to saying it. Jael thought perhaps she knew what it was. "Would you . . . Kan-Kon, are you changing your mind? Would you like to come with us?" She glanced at Ar, who merely looked puzzled.

Kan-Kon turned white. "By the holies, no!" he whispered. "But—" and he hesitated and swallowed hard, and Jael realized that she had, perhaps inadvertently, touched upon what was bothering him. "There is somethin' I want to say before you go," he murmured. "And that's . . ." He swallowed again.

"What is it, Kan-Kon?" Jael asked softly.

"Well . . . it's about when I was there. With Hoddy. When I . . . when I let him . . . die." Kan-Kon's hands were moving in small circles around one another, wringing and clasping; Jael had never seen him look so nervous before.

"You didn't *let* him die," Jael whispered. "You couldn't have stopped it."

"Couldn't I?" Kan-Kon said plaintively. "Couldn't I? You don't know that—".

"But the dragons! What could you have done against the dragons?"

Kan-Kon nodded and wrung his hands some more. "I don't . . . exactly know. *But Jael—remember this! You can change things in the Flux! You can change things!*" He groaned, almost whimpering. "I forgot, Jael. I forgot that. Don't let the same thing happen to you, okay? Okay?"

Jael nodded. "Okay."

He seemed to brighten, and looked from Jael to Ar and back again. "Good, then. Good!" He picked up a hardprint from his desk and waved it in the air. "Shall we go give our new ship a look-over?"

Jael jumped up without answering. She didn't have to. It was all she could do to keep from running across the spaceport field.

By the beginning of the second week following, *Seneca* was reregistered, fueled, provisioned, and waiting on a liftoff pad. They would depart in the morning.

Jael could scarcely wait. Tonight they would sleep aboard ship. Tonight, she knew, she would sleep the restless sleep of a soldier before battle.

Chapter 14
INTO THE STREAMS
OF THE FLUX

SPACE!

Liftoff came precisely on time, at 0842 local. The tow carried them swiftly into space and left them on an outbound course, rising out of the plane of the ecliptic of Cargeeling's sun. After a check of the rigging systems, Jael took up her station in the starboard rigger-alcove. Reclining in the couch, she took a deep breath. Her vision of the console overhead darkened, and her senses sprang outward into the net, into the mists of the Flux. She was floating in space, the ship invisible behind her. There appeared to be a white layer of fog below her, a morning mist clinging to the surface of an infinitely deep sea. It was a mist that no morning sun would ever burn away.

Ar joined her in the net like a swimmer slipping silently into the water. They exchanged glances, and together they took the ship down, a gleaming silver submarine dropping beneath the waves into a world that knew no limits in time or space. The Flux seemed at once quieter and vaster, and yet more alive, than the realm of normal-space. Once they began moving, Jael became aware of the distant whisper of worlds moving through the currents of the water, far, far away.

Time passed, as they reacclimated themselves to the net and to the Flux. For Jael, it was her first time rigging in fourteen weeks, and she felt like a swimmer whose muscles had tightened from disuse. Even Ar had to reorient himself to the ship. Not only had he just come from flying another ship; but *Seneca*'s flux-pile systems had been completely overhauled, resulting in a different feel to this once-familiar net. Together, they flew carefully, testing the ship's movements, until they were sure they were ready for the faster layers of the Flux.

Ed was another matter. Ar favored waiting until they were well under way before bringing the parrot into the net, on the theory that the more smoothly they were flying, the easier it would be to merge his rigging personality with theirs. Jael thought it better to sort out any problems now, while they were still in the easy waters. Soon enough, they would be flying for all they were worth. Ar conceded, and soon afterward Ed was flying around in the net, happily scrawwwwing and screeeeing as he exuberantly tested the limits of the bubble surrounding them, and pausing occasionally to pluck at the fruit of a tropical cybertree that Jael had introduced into the net for him.

They kept the submarine-bubble image for a while, extending large ghostly fins into the currents to carry them along. The image was of their making, but the actual currents were objectively real, sensed by the rigger-net and transformed through their personal intuition into images that they could craft and control. That was one characteristic which distinguished the mountain realm of the dragons from other regions of the Flux. The landscape there was far less mutable, their control over it limited mostly to the altering of their own physical form. Why this was true, she could only guess: perhaps it was because of the living beings there—the dragons, ifflings, and who knew what else. She in truth knew little about life in the dragon realm, or the rules by which life was lived there.

In her rigger-school training, when the subject of the dragons-in-space legend was first raised, the instructors had spoken at length of the dangers of taking legend too seriously, of mistaking one's own prejudices and expectations for realities inherent to the Flux. That was good wisdom; but those instructors, she guessed, would never have believed the truth of her experiences along the legendary "mountain route."

Just the thought was enough to remind her of the urgency of their mission. Without a word, she began pushing herself harder. The faster, deeper currents beckoned, and time was fleeing. . . .

The surviving iffling-child nearly missed its opportunity to follow the human rigger. While keeping its distance from the dangerous false-iffling, it had been trying to save its strength, drawing energy from the distant light of this world's sun, while keeping a silent watch on the human rigger's spirit-presence. It felt fairly confident that its message to her had been heard. But it was shocked when it realized that the rigger-spirit was suddenly rising away from the surface of its world. The iffling shot upward in pursuit. Outside the atmosphere, the sunlight was stronger, giving it just enough strength to pursue and intercept the speeding vessel in which the rigger Jael had clothed herself. Should it continue to follow at a distance? the iffling wondered. Or should it try to penetrate the conducting enclosure of the vessel? Something odd was happening around it, some sort of disturbance in the flow of space and time. What was the human doing?

As the iffling-child wondered, it saw the enemy-spirit appear, momentarily, from *within* the vessel. The thing darted back into the ship, no doubt having spotted its adversary. That left no question: the iffling streaked forward to catch the gleaming ship. Wary of the enemy, it slipped in through an opening where energy pulsed, gaining a breath of strength as it did so. It darted through the shadow-structure of the ship, seeking a place of safety from which to watch the human.

It found a spot near the focal point of the disturbance. Hardly had the iffling settled into place when the disturbance deepened without warning. Dizzily the iffling clung to the structure, aware of the enemy also watching from the far side of the vessel. The web of space-time opened in the center of the disturbance, the threads separating from one another, the vessel sliding into the underrealm of this strange human reality. The threads closed behind it as the vessel plunged deep into the underrealm.

The iffling was both terrified and relieved. An instant

later and it might have been left behind, alone in human space, the rigger out of its reach forever. The iffling clung to its position ever more guardedly, watching the enemy, watching the human in its ship, waiting to see where it would go.

Home, perhaps. Home.

Jael, do you want to rest awhile?

She glanced from the bow position, where the bubble was spearing through the fast-flowing waters, back toward Ar, who was sitting at the stern wielding a long-handled tiller. The image was absurd: a submarine with a sailboat's tiller. But it was working. Their course was taking them over a rising and dipping bottom surface, following the contours of a strange abyssal plain as the light-years flowed around them. Jael shook her head. *This is no place for one person to try to handle the ship,* she answered, focusing her control on the steering planes at the prow of the ship.

We could ease off and drift higher for a while, Ar said. *We need to rest sometime, you know.*

He was right, of course. Nevertheless, she shook her head. The current was moving in the precise direction she wanted, and she didn't want to lose any time because of something like a need for rest. She knew she was being stubborn—but sometimes, she thought, stubborn is the right way to be.

Ar didn't ask again, though they had been flying for most of a shipday. They both knew it was a question not only of how long it would take to get there, but how tired they wanted to be when they arrived. Would they be flying into a fight? Would they find Windrush on trial for his life, the way they had found Highwing—or would they find something they couldn't even imagine? Whatever the answer, Jael knew this: she didn't want to mourn over fallen friends because she had answered the summons too late. She could forgive herself for many failings, but not that.

They fell endlessly downward through an atmosphere of pastel clouds. It was their third day of flight, and the deep-sea imagery was long behind them. *Seneca* was dropping like a floating seed through an atmosphere reminiscent of a gas-giant planet. In reality, they were crossing downward through the galactic plane, seeking new currents that would angle back upward from the south, toward Lexis and the other Aeregian worlds. She had no interest in reaching those star systems; but somewhere below, coursing upward toward them, were currents that swept past a landscape filled with images of mountains. Even farther to the south, and outward on the galactic radial, lay a small backwater planet named Gaston's Landing, where Jael had been born and raised. She had not been back there since her fateful trip with Mogurn.

Heads up, Ed!

The parrot responded to Ar's call by banking left, then right, as a billowing cloud fled by them. Ed was driving, leading the way now and doing a superb job of steering them through the patchwork of clouds. But he had a tendency to be hypnotized by his own flying. *Arrk,* he muttered, bringing them back on course. *Air so deep! Rawk! Hit bottom soon?*

Jael had been wondering the same thing. They had been dropping for a long time now, and it was hard to be sure of their progress. The nav libraries were helpful, but only up to a point. The currents and forms of the Flux changed constantly—as did the galaxy itself, of course—but on a much faster time scale than the normal-space galaxy. One took note of other riggers' flight reports, but one also expected to be surprised.

Jael was plagued by a recurring fear that her intuition about the Flux, and about their course, was not entirely clear, that she was being subtly influenced by . . . she didn't know what . . . momentary waking dreams, perhaps, or by her imagination of what might be happening in the realm in her absence. There was a voice that seemed to speak to her in the silence of the net, telling her there was no reason to hurry, or to be going at all. And yet at other times another voice seemed to whisper that the need had never been greater.

She wondered, sometimes, if she was descending into madness. But she knew which way her heart spoke, and it made her want to fly faster than ever.

The bottom of the atmosphere came up like a fist, flat and massive and dark. Ed saw it first and squawked, and Jael called at once for a new image. *Ar! Aerobat!* she cried, extending her arms.

The ship sprouted the stubby lifting surfaces of an aerobatic aircraft, and she began hauling up hard on the nose, taking care not to overstress the wings. The net shuddered but held, as Ar and Ed joined her in the effort.

It was going to be close. The ground rose to meet them. Their dive slowly flattened out. *Hawwwk! Hawwwk!* Ed cried, beating his wings fiercely in an effort to pull them into a climb.

Ar, hold it steady! Jael cried, pitching the nose up still harder.

They were in level flight now, but a series of hills loomed up before them. The wind screamed in her ears. They began to climb, turning their speed back into altitude. But the hills seemed to grow as they loomed closer. She had only moments to decide: go around, or over? In her instant of hesitation, she felt Ed give a powerful kick upward. Grimacing, she held the wings level. The hills rose . . . and the ship rose just a little faster . . . and the hilltops flashed beneath them with a *whump!* of turbulence.

Then the hills were gone behind them, and a flat plain opened up below. A powerful downdraft swept them down to the plain, and they sped along just above its surface, all three of them gasping, their momentum carrying them with astonishing speed toward a region of murkiness ahead.

Jarvorus knew they were drawing closer to the home-web, to the realm that had spawned him. He could not say how he knew, but there was a feeling deep in his being, a feeling that bore the name "home." He knew, as well, that the time for completing his mission was growing short. The human was returning to the realm, as foretold. But to whose influence would she return? His task was to take her to Rent, and ultimately to the Nail, to the one who had created him, who had taken a mere cavern sprite and transformed it into Jarvorus the warrior. He did not intend to fail in his task.

He kept his watch on the remaining iffling, and knew that it was watching him just as carefully for any sign of weakness or inattention. But Jarvorus had the advantage. He had only to draw the human just a little astray, to keep her clear of the dragons and lead her instead to his Master. There she would serve the prophecies, but not in the way the enemy expected. She would die, yes, and the realm would tremble, yes—but with the victory of the True One, the True Power, the Nail of Strength.

Jarvorus had only a dim knowledge of the prophecies and the lines of battle ahead. But he trusted and believed his Masters; he could feel the coming victory already. There was a change coming up in the underreality, and Jarvorus thought he sensed the power of the True One in that change. He was glad of that; he would not be fighting alone much longer.

The murk turned into darkness, and soon they were underwater again, but this time moving like catfish, feeling their way through an almost impenetrable gloom. It was apparently a boundary layer of some sort, and if they could just get through it, Jael hoped that they would emerge into a faster-moving layer, one that would transport them quickly toward the mountain realm.

She had her hands outstretched, moving over the bottom. It was stony and slick, the current slow but steady. It was almost too steady, and that made her nervous. There ought to be at least a little turbulence. It was almost as if some outside force were bracing the current, like a muddy river in a channel. It was only a feeling, but she had learned long ago to trust her intuition in the Flux. Should she trouble the others with her feeling? she wondered.

She was just on the verge of voicing her unease when the murkiness vanished, like a curtain being torn away. They were floating in clear, midnight-blue space, but the space was half filled by something that took her breath away. It was an enormous, transparent . . . creature? . . . or structure? It filled much of their view with a tracery of luminous webbing, like an enormous spiderweb. Beads of light moved in and out along its radial strands, like liquid drops, and waves of light and shadow flickered along the arcs of the webbing. It appeared hundreds of times the size of their ship, and they were moving directly toward it.

Ar?

I don't know what it is, either, Jael.

Ed fluttered up and down, and from one side of the net to the other. *Rawk! Too big! Too big! Make it small! Hurry! Make it small!*

We can't, Ed, Jael said urgently. *Please settle down and help us try to understand it.* She stared at the thing, and shivered suddenly. *I feel a . . . presence . . . here, Ar. As if it's alive, and it knows we're here. I feel a . . .* She hesitated. *I feel danger. I don't know why, or what kind.* She glanced back and could see Ar's eyes glowing in the darkness, and the faintest outline of his face. *Do you feel it?*

Ar looked disturbed, but didn't answer.

The ship seemed to be moving inexorably toward the thing. Whether her premonition of danger was correct or not, there was little they could do about it. The current was growing stronger, and it flowed directly toward the web. It occurred to Jael that if indeed it was alive, this might be how it fed itself, by seining whatever came along, like a whale filtering plankton with its baleen. The idea was alarming.

Ed perched between the two humans and tried to make himself small. He trembled with fear, and made clucking sounds under his breath.

Can we steer through the gaps? Ar murmured. *I don't see any other way.*

Jael nodded silently. She saw no alternative, either. But there remained that internal voice, warning of danger.

The thing grew visibly larger as they approached. It stretched far to their right, and to their left, and above and below them, creating the illusion that it was wrapping itself slowly around them. Or was it an illusion? The threads of the web were close enough to see more clearly now; they looked like soft glass tubes, with liquid light streaking along their lengths. The threads flexed slowly, and several strands were bending inward toward them, as though to entrap the ship in its mesh.

Ar, look out! she cried. *Aim for the center—if we can maneuver at all!*

Ar joined her in steering away from the strands. The shape of the webbing became foreshortened like a halo around them as they sped toward its center. The current was irresistible, and she felt a mounting sense of danger, a feeling that something malevolent was peering at them through this web. Oddly, her fear of being trapped dwindled; instead, she began to feel that they were about to be flung onward—but in what direction? They would have only an instant in which to determine their course. The tiniest error could mean light-years of difference.

She was sure that this thing was alive. *We're not your enemy!* she cried out in desperation, in the instant before they flew into the plane of the web.

What happened next occurred in an eyeblink, yet seemed to take forever.

The ship flashed into the darkness of the gap.

It was like a circuit closing. The rigger-net came alive with electricity. Jael glimpsed Ed and Ar alight with fire, becoming transparent like the web; she glimpsed their thoughts and memories streaming out into the webbing like wildfire. She knew she was as transparent as they; she felt her own thoughts pouring out, her hopes, dreams, fears—most of all, her fears about failing her dragon friends—and glimpsed them being drawn into the web.

What if you fail to reach the realm? What if you're destroyed here and now? The fears seemed to rise up from the Flux itself. She heard Ar calling out to her, but he sounded light-years away.

In this frozen instant, she *knew* that the web was alive, toying with them. And now something was erupting from it—a face in their path, an enormous face outlined with the same light that rippled through the webbing. It was a bearded, rheumy-eyed face, a face she knew and hated with all of her being. *Mogurn! You can't be alive!* she whispered. Was it possible? Could this webbing have caught her old captain's life energy from the Flux and preserved it, preserved him in all his evil?

No, no, no, no . . . !

Another voice was crying frantically that it was not real, she was being deceived. But Mogurn's presence was overwhelming: the malevolence that poured from him toward the one who had denied him, who had killed him.

Mogurn, damn you forever! Get out of my way! she cried. She kicked the ship hard and slewed past him, and the face exploded into streams of light that ran back up into the web.

In the same instant the net blazed white around her, and all sound and thought were obliterated by the roar. It was too much for the net to handle. She was suddenly certain they were going to die; they *were* dying, she felt death moving through the net as synapses burned and evaporated. She felt no panic, only regret. She had no awareness at all now of her fellow riggers, and the thought flashed that she hoped she would know them beyond death. *Windrush, I'm sorry!* she whispered.

She felt a searing pain as the brightness became unbearable. Then it was gone and everything was lost to blackness.

PART THREE

THE REALM

PROLOGUE

IN THE luminous spaces of the Dream Mountain, the choir of voices was soft but unceasing, even as individual draconae joined and left the choir, where the retelling of the words kept the memories alive in the heart of the Mountain. Among them was a memory passed down through uncounted generations, from a time just after the dark one's earlier defeat in a terrible battle with dragonkind. This memory was treasured above all. This memory was of the time when the prophetic visions had appeared. . . .

In those days, reverberations of the first war with Tar-skel had not yet died down; but so weary were the draconae, and so preoccupied with tending the hatchlings and fledglings, that the watch on the dreamfires had, for a time, diminished. Just one aging dracona named Sunfire was tending the Forge of Dreams at the heart of the Mountain, when the fire blinked—dimmed—and to her astonishment, produced a dark opening in its blazing light, where figures appeared to move and cry out. Sunfire, half lost in her own dreams, came to alertness in fear and bewilderment. At first she thought it an astounding glimpse of the Final Dream Mountain, where departed souls dwelled in the warmth and light of the fires. But some inner sense told her that this was something different, something extraordinary; it was a glimpse into another world . . . or another time. She heard a voice whispering to her . . .

Before she could make sense of any of it, Sunfire fell into a trance, visions pouring into her mind like tongues of fire from the dream forge. How long she lay that way, she didn't know; but she knew she was not wholly alone, she felt another there with her, a being of shadow and stealth, a being neither of the Mountain nor of the fire. When she awoke, it was to the rustling of glassy wings, the cries of other draconae coming to her aid. Were they the ones she had felt? No—she recalled a sharp movement and a glimpse of the shadow darting away, down into the underrealm from which it had come. Her cry of warning was too late; the servant of the Enemy was already gone, or hidden. But perhaps it made no difference: the Enemy had already been defeated. What harm could its servants do now?

As she opened her mouth to explain to the others, utterly different words rose unbidden in her throat. Unable to stop or control them, she heard herself crying:

> The dark one returns
> Its spells to weave
> That those who forget
> Lose all they believe.
>
> The realm will quake
> But little know
> The power that yet
> Remains to grow.
>
> To tear from its midst
> The fires of being,
> That dragons may die,
> Unknowing, unseeing.

Sunfire gasped for breath, nearly overcome by astonishment at her own words. She knew that they came not from her, but from the vision in the fire. The draconae murmured and rustled, repeating her words as she spoke them. Her voice deepened as she sang:

> From beyond life
> will come one
>
> From beyond hope
> will come one

> *Without friend*
> *will come one*
>
> *And the realm shall tremble.*
>
> *Innocent of our ways*
> *will come one*
>
> *Challenging darkness*
> *will come one*
>
> *Speaking her name*
> *will come one*
>
> *And the realm shall tremble.*

The words poured from her throat in great waves, filling her with dread and wonder. The old dracona nearly fainted as she sang, and finally groaned:

> *The one will fall*
> *as the battle is fought*
>
> *Upon her death*
> *is the ending wrought.*
>
> *From that one*
> *comes a beginning*
>
> *From that one*
> *comes an ending*
>
> *From that one*
> *all paths diverge*
>
> *And surely the realm shall tremble.*

As she gasped for weary breath, she glimpsed the shadow-thing again, fleeing through the underrealm, out of the Mountain—and she knew that it had heard it all, heard all that the other draconae were chorusing and repeating, committing to memory. The others seemed to understand already what Sunfire was only hazily beginning to see, that these words were for the heart and soul of dragonkind. They were not for the present but for the future, for the ages to come.

Chapter 15
TREASON AND TREACHERY

WINDRUSH BLINKED his eyes open. He glimpsed several sweepers scurrying out of sight, carrying his night scales and puffs of dust toward their dens. Was that what had awakened him? He forced his thoughts up into the glare of true wakefulness. He sensed that it was very early, scarcely dawn on the outside. He had hardly found sleep at all, and what he had found had been restless and unsatisfying. It was not the sweepers but his own thoughts that had awakened him.

He thought of yesterday: the iffling, the demon, the vision. And FullSky. There was so much to think about, so much to be understood. He vented a breath of steam. He could not remember when he had felt so tired. But he sensed that sleep was beyond him now; what he should do is fly to the camp and share his knowledge with those he could trust. And Farsight and WingTouch needed to know that their brother FullSky still lived.

Crouching, he let his thoughts drift down into the underweb of his cavern's protective spells. He leaped, tugging at the exit spell as he spread his wings and beat downward. The cavern vanished from around him, and he was airborne over the mountains under a rose-and-violet dawn. He flew south toward the main encampment.

When he arrived, he found considerable commotion in the camp. The guard dragons greeted him somberly as he circled overhead, and when he landed, the dour figure of Rockclaw limped out toward him. Rockclaw was too old and frail for battle, but he had the sharpest memory of all the draconi, and it was his duty to gather information and report it to the leaders. Usually when he came to report to Windrush these days, it was with bad news.

"Rockclaw. You are about early, today."

Rockclaw regarded him with dusty-seeming eyes. "Yes, Windrush. But not gladly. Have you heard the news of your brother?"

Windrush exhaled a plume of steam. FullSky? Had the others learned, somehow, of FullSky? That was impossible . . .

"WingTouch did not return from last night's patrol," Rockclaw said, with a shake of his head. "Nor did Loudcry." The old grey dragon gazed moodily toward the south. "His patrol was attacked by drahls. Most of the drahls were destroyed—but those two have gone missing. FireEye said he felt *someone* die." Rockclaw sighed. "A search has begun, but—" He shook his head and left the sentence unfinished.

Windrush's breath left him. WingTouch, killed by drahls? He could not have regained one brother in the night, only to lose another! "No!" he whispered.

"It is hard news," Rockclaw agreed.

"NO!" Windrush thundered, ignoring the looks he drew from the camp. Turning from Rockclaw, he leaped into the air and beat his wings, climbing in anguish toward the target cliff at the south end of camp. "WINGTOUCH!" Gaining altitude above the cliff, he banked and dove toward the target wall. "WINGTOUCH! LOUDCRY!" He loosed a great flame onto the wall and veered away, climbing again with pounding wingstrokes, circling for another pass. *"Die, drahls!"* he cried, as he hurled himself toward the wall for another pass. His flame scorched the rock.

By the time he had started his third pass, at least half a dozen others had taken to the air to join him, and more were bestirring themselves. WingTouch and Loudcry had both had friends, and even those who did not know them as friends mourned them as brothers fallen in the war. Soon there was a small army of dragons flying out their grief and anger against the target wall—and even after Windrush had spent his own immediate rage, the others continued their grief flight, targeting the wall with fire that they were helpless to turn upon the Enemy.

Windrush let out a long, flaming breath and spiraled down to land. He felt spent, and utterly at a loss. "Is Farsight about?" he asked the nearest leader, Stronghold. The tan dragon shook his head darkly, staring back at Windrush. "What is it?" Windrush asked, sensing that the other dragon had something to say.

Stronghold clenched his talons, and grumbled throatily. "How much longer will you wait, Windrush? How much longer?"

Windrush blinked and regarded the leathery, powerfully muscled dragon. "What do you mean?"

"Strike at the Enemy!" Stronghold said. "Before we do it ourselves! Do you not hear your brothers calling for action? Will you wait until they challenge you for a new leader? *Act, Windrush! Act!*"

Windrush stared at the dragon in shock. "Do you doubt my leadership? My garkkondoh? My honesty?"

Stronghold hissed furiously. "No one doubts your honesty, Windrush! Certainly not I. But you are losing the will of your brothers. You are so absorbed in your . . . *underrealm*—" and he puffed great clouds of steam, which almost hid from Windrush's sight the other dragon's amber-glowing eyes, and the faces of others who were gathering close to listen—"and your *demons* and your *visions*. You test our patience, as we watch our brothers fall, and our lumenis vanish!"

Windrush was nearly speechless. "How can you say— don't you understand—?"

He was drowned out by a rising grumble from the dragons gathered around. "Take us to battle!" a dragon behind him cried. "Or someone else will!"

Windrush drew a long, deep breath and turned to see who was present. Many were simple warriors, some were leaders. Their voices told him that Stronghold was telling the truth. If he wanted to keep the dragons united behind him, he could delay no longer. This was not the time to tell anyone about FullSky, or to speak of the ifflings, or of Jael.

He saw it in the eyes of the dragons gathered, and in those emerging from the sleeping warrens to learn what was happening, and in those just now landing from their grief flight. These dragons were angry. They wanted battle, not patience, and if they did not find the leadership in Windrush, they would find it in SearSky, or in another. "I see," Windrush said at last.

"Do you—?" began another dragon.

"*Silence!*" Windrush roared.

The grumbling stopped.

Windrush hardened his gaze to a glare. "Leaders! To the Vale of Decision! Now!"

Cries of triumph went up. Windrush expelled a long plume of smoke, and ignoring the shouts, leaped into the air. A dozen or more dragons followed, while others trumpeted their approval from the ground. Windrush flew southeast, over the target wall and over a low ridge of mountains, flanked by the flight of angry dragons. He crested the north wall of the Vale of Decision and dropped toward the dry stream bed at the bottom of the rocky vale. He landed on the flat command stone at the head of the valley and watched as the dragon leaders came in, soaring and blasting the air with fire. Farsight was not among them; the meeting would have to go on without him.

"My *brothers!*" he called, his voice thundering out over the vale. He, too, was being carried along by rage. "It is said that the time has come to let our anger burn against the Enemy! What is your voice?"

A rumble of approval went up, with smoke and fire.

"One at a time! Give me your counsel! Give me your thoughts!"

Another roar went up, as the dragons vented their rage. He waited a few moments, then bellowed for silence. When he had their attention, he called to the dragon sitting closest on his left, "Winterfall! Your counsel!"

"Strike at the Black Peak!" trumpeted the sandy-white dragon.

A fresh cry went up. Windrush expelled a doubtful plume of smoke. The Black Peak was a battle already fought. It was true, they had not stretched their limited fighting power to hold the peak where Jael had won her victory. And in the absence of spell-wielding guardian dragons, the peak was, for all practical purposes, under the Enemy's control again. But its value at this point was unclear.

Windrush kept his doubts to himself. "Hailfar! Your counsel!"

"Strike at the Dark Vale!" thundered Hailfar, next in the row.

A less animated roar went up. Strike at the Enemy's heartland? The seat of Tar-skel's sorcery and terror, and perhaps his own dwelling place? If they could conceivably destroy the Enemy at the Dark Vale, the war would be won. But the Dark Vale was heavily protected by drahls, by Tar-skel dragons, and most of all by sorcery. Windrush knew perfectly well that his dragons could not win such a battle—not without far greater strength in the underrealm. Not without the knowledge and power of the Dream Mountain. Not without Jael. To strike there would be brave and futile, and would probably mean the end of dragonkind.

Windrush nodded without replying. "SearSky! Your counsel!"

To his surprise, the great black dragon hesitated. "Strike at the east camp of the Enemy!" SearSky finally called.

Windrush flared flame from his nostrils. That, at least, was more sensible. The Enemy's east camp was a large gathering place of drahls and Tar-skel dragons—no easy target, by any means. But it was within a day's flight, and it was a target where they might have *some* hope of hurting the Enemy more than they would be hurt themselves. At least, they might, *if* they flew with this kind of rage in their hearts, but kept clear thinking in their heads.

"Longtouch!" Windrush called. "Your counsel?"

"East camp of the Enemy!"

"Deepclaw! Your counsel!"

"Black Peak!"

"Stronghold! Your counsel!"

"East camp!" thundered Stronghold.

"Stonebinder . . ."

The roll call continued. The greatest number, in the end, favored the east camp. Certainly, it was the only place that Windrush could in conscience lead his dragons with even the slightest hope of meaningful victory. When the roll call was finished, Windrush sat silent for a few moments as the other dragons fumed among themselves. Finally he looked across the gathering and thundered, "Listen, then! Gather in three flights, two watches before the next dawn, to strike the east camp of the Enemy! Prepare, brothers—but do not speak of the target beyond this vale! Gathering dismissed!"

A triumphant cry went up. Even those dragons who had wanted the greater targets voiced their approval. In truth, most of them did not care much about the target, only that they struck *somewhere.*

Windrush watched as the dragons flew from the vale. His anger at WingTouch's death had not left his thoughts. But he could only hope that the dragons' anger, and the recent feeding, would be enough to fuel their bold action tomorrow.

Upon his return to the main encampment, Windrush was told that Farsight was urgently looking for him. He found his brother on a high outcropping, searching the camp with his silvery-clear eyes. The younger dragon looked deeply disturbed, and Windrush assumed that he knew why.

"Farsight!" he called, shouting up to his brother.

Farsight leaped down with half-furled wings. "Windrush, we must speak! Can you fly with me now?"

Windrush agreed, and the two took to the air at once. Farsight urged them to fly northward, where they would be less likely to encounter others. "I missed you at the leaders' meeting!" Windrush said when they were alone in the sky.

"I heard about WingTouch," Farsight muttered, his voice heavy with grief. "I'm afraid I have other distressing news, for your ears alone."

"More bad news! First I must tell you—we fly against the east camp of the Enemy tonight. I trust that WingTouch's spirit will go with us. But I too have news that I have not yet spoken aloud. It concerns FullSky and the ifflings, and it gives me hope."

"FullSky!" Farsight's eyes flashed. "You are full of surprises! If you can offer hope, then I will be grateful indeed. Because I must tell you what I overheard last night, in the darkness of the mountains. Windrush, we have a traitor among us. . . ."

By the time the two dragons had shared all of their news with each other, they had flown well north of the main encampment. Somber and silent, they circled back the way they had come. Farsight was cheered to learn that FullSky lived and fought with them, and that the ifflings were reaching out to the static realm to find Jael. But for Windrush, the news of a traitor was as troubling as the death of a brother.

If only they knew the traitor's name! He did not criticize Farsight for avoiding a confrontation in the night—it had been the right thing to do, he was sure—but he desperately wished that he had been there himself. Perhaps he could have sensed the dragon's identity through the underrealm. Now they could only be watchful, and live in fear of betrayal.

"Do you think, Windrush, that we should call off tomorrow's attack?" Farsight asked finally, voicing the question that both were pondering.

Windrush beat the air with his wings. "I'm afraid," he murmured, "that that might cause even more harm. Our brothers are angry and impatient. I may have erred in calling for an attack—and yet, if I had not, I doubt that my leadership would have survived this day, or the next. The others have no understanding of the unseen battles; they only want to wage war with flame and wing."

Farsight's eyes reflected the morning sun, as he answered cautiously, "Many of our brothers are foolish. But I think you may be right, Windrush."

Windrush accepted Farsight's appraisal with a hiss of steam. "We will go on with the attack—but not speak of strategy until we are on wing. That much we can do to thwart our spy, at least. Farsight, we must keep this to ourselves. It will do no good to have rumor flying, and false accusations. But you and I must be alert."

"Shrewd as drahls and more silent," muttered Farsight. Windrush glanced at him sharply. "Perhaps that, yes. What a way to put it, though. Farsight, I think I would like to know more of what happened to WingTouch. Shall we go speak with the survivors of his patrol?"

Farsight didn't answer. But he began beating his wings harder, flying grimly back to the camp.

Chapter 16
DRAGONS IN FLIGHT

THE NIGHT was cool but not cold, as the dragons took to the air. They flew with a fierce determination, and they flew as quietly as a flight of more than seventy dragons could fly. They moved like a gust of wind over the valleys and ridges. On Windrush's orders, they strove to disturb nothing, to be heard by neither wakeful nor sleeping creatures, to give no warning of their approach. If a stirring animal, or a drahl, should have glanced upward toward the faint night-time glow of the sky, it might have sensed the pattern of shadow against the clouds, or heard the muted fluttering of wings. But if good fortune flew with the dragons, they would strike the enemy without warning.

If good fortune flew with them. Windrush's thoughts were heavy with the report of WingTouch's patrol from last night, and the near certainty of WingTouch's death. He was nagged by an undefinable sense that this attack was somehow a mistake. But he kept his doubts to himself, so as not to infect anyone else with them. He tried to think like Rocktooth and FireEye, who had eagerly joined this mission hoping to avenge WingTouch's death.

It would be a demanding flight for the dragons—not so much for the distance to the enemy camp as for the terrain they had to cross to reach it—especially the treacherous ridge of the Borderland Mountains, a jagged range which lay just beyond the Valley Between and which clearly demarcated the beginning of the Enemy's territory. If they could cross the Borderland Mountains without incident, and without being detected, that in itself would be a great success.

It was not Windrush's plan to pass over the mountains

in a single formation; rather, they would divide into three groups. One, led by Stronghold, would veer far to the left to the Hermitage Pass and approach the enemy camp from the south, on the Enemy's side of the ridge. Another, led by Farsight, would fly northward to the Pass of the Black Mountains, not far short of the Black Peak itself, where a glowering fire from the static realm still shone over the broken mountains. Farsight's group would come upon the enemy from the north. The main group, led by Windrush, would go straight west, over the summit of the Borderland Mountains.

That crossing lay ahead of them yet. They had just completed their flight over the ragged slopes of the Scarred Mount Ridge, site of many small conflicts between dragons and their foes, including the one that had claimed Wing-Touch. As that ridge receded behind them, they soared high over the dark plain of the Valley Between, flying west toward the Borderland Mountains. The Valley Between was not a place where dragons dwelled now, but it was far from deserted. Dragons of both sides patrolled here, and drahls were often spotted moving up and down the ridges in their missions of spying. Numerous shadow-cats made their homes here, too, as well as small flyers and sprites and lesser animals. Most of them had no role in the conflict, though a few did serve as sentinels for the dragons—and others, Windrush suspected, served as spies for the Enemy. If any of those spies witnessed the dragons passing, he hoped that their reports to the Enemy would not arrive before the dragons themselves.

In a happier time, lumenis groves and draconic gardens had speckled this broad valley. All were destroyed now, ravaged by the servants of Tar-skel, or by his sorcery. Passing over these dark lands that had once borne such fruit, Windrush felt an ancient anger rising from deep within, raging against the one who had done this to the land. He nurtured the anger; it would make him fight all the more fiercely. He sensed that the others, flanking him, felt the same rage as they flew over the Enemy's desolation.

The night was wearing long as their flight brought them

over the foothills of the Borderland Mountains. Windrush spoke softly to the others, sending word back through the company that the north and south flanks were to split away now. "Quietly," he urged them. "Quietly!"

Glancing back, he saw the flanks separating, the glowing coals of myriad dragon eyes vanishing to the north and to the south. Behind him, the center group continued strong. Windrush faced into the west wind and picked up the pace of his wingbeats. It was time to start gaining altitude, to climb for the crossing over the most difficult mountain range in the realm.

The air felt strange this high. It had a different character, a different quality of presence, a different undersmell. Perhaps it was the mountains more than the altitude; perhaps it was the nearness of Tar-skel magic. Windrush knew that it was possible to fly higher—he had done so himself during the lumenis vision—but few dragons ever did, and even at this height, he had a sense of flying near the very edge of the realm. Exactly what might happen if he flew beyond the limits of the realm, he didn't know; but he thought it would not be good to try. Even now he felt a sense of separation between mind and body that reminded him of movement through the underrealm.

Ahead and below, the summits of the Borderland Mountains were dim, icy pyramids, rising up from the predawn mists as though to provide otherworldly perches for the dragons as they passed. Even to dragon eyes they were dark shapes, though the faint skyglow from a cloud-covered moon cast enough light to make their outlines visible. The dragons intended to stay as high above the peaks as their strength and skills could take them, not only to avoid the perilous downdrafts that could dash them onto the rocks, but also to remain inconspicuous to sentries.

Windrush felt excitement coursing through his body as he pumped the air, flanked by his fellows. It was not yet the energy of battle-fever; that would come soon. This was the rush of night-air-over-mountain, and it was one of the most powerful sensations that Windrush knew. Battle-fever was shallow compared to this. He trusted that the power would stay with him throughout the morning to come, giving him strength for the battle.

The sharp summits passed slowly beneath them. The sky was already growing lighter with a cold, eerie predawn light. It was a deceptive light, and it made the massive summits seem so perilously close that Windrush almost felt that he could reach down with a talon and touch the ice on their caps as they passed below. But he knew from the stillness of the air that they were much higher above the peaks than appearances suggested. He tried to use his undersense to seek out any enemy sentries, but he was flying too hard; it was impossible to focus deeply in the underweb while exerting himself so strenuously, and he dared not pause. He would just have to use his eyes, ears, and nose to detect the enemy. Soon they would be upon the foe and secrecy would no longer matter.

The mountains fell away into the darkness. They were over the ridge, well into the Enemy's territory. Attack or counterattack could come from any direction. Windrush whispered a command to his flanking leaders: begin descending under the cover of darkness.

The final leg of the flight passed with dizzying swiftness. Mist curled up from the ground as they dropped toward the valley of the enemy warriors. It grew difficult to distinguish mountain from vapor. Shadows among wisps of vapor looked like drahls, and more than once, the dragons quickened their wingbeats to catch an enemy who was not there. Excitement burned through the dragons like the fire of lumenis; Windrush could sense talons twitching and fires rising in the backs of dragons' throats. To his left, he could see SearSky's eyes glowing red with eagerness. To his right, the dusty-white Winterfall nodded in readiness. The minutes fled, like the mist beneath them.

Real dawn was breaking as they swept down into the hollow where the enemy encampment lay. A rosily glowing, cottony vapor half concealed the land. There was an eerie beauty in the dawn; how ironic that in moments this place would be a cauldron of battle. How many of them would not live to return? Windrush shook aside the thought. His scales rippled as he prepared to attack. He imagined that he was not alone, that the spirit of Highwing flew invisibly with him—and he thought, If you can see this, Highwing, we will fight to make you proud.

Emerging from the mist was the form of an amphitheater and the dark shadows of entrances to warrens. "Spread out to attack," Windrush rumbled. Any instant now, drahls and Tar-skel dragons would come boiling up to meet them. Windrush glanced each way. "NOW!" he thundered.

"NOW!" echoed the others.

Flanked by forty dragons, he dove with a roar into the encampment. Flame billowed from his throat, chasing away the mist. He scanned left, right, ahead, looking for the enemy warriors who would be rising to meet them. Flame danced hot in the back of his throat. "COME FACE US!" he bellowed, his voice one in a chorus of dragon challenges.

The answer came in a great uproar and billowing up of shadows from the ground—below and behind the dragons. "Drahls!" came the cry, repeated many times at once. The dragons wheeled and turned upon the enemy shadows, fire flashing from dragon after dragon. "Die, drahls!" SearSky boomed, stretching out his black claws to rake any drahls that evaded the flames.

Moments later, the shouting died away, replaced by silence—then rumbles of puzzlement. The shadow-drahls were evaporating like the mist, even before the dragon fire touched them. The dragons who dove after them were closing their claws upon thin air. A deafening peal of laughter reverberated in the valley like the sound of a thunderstorm. It was not a dragon laugh, but something unearthly, demonic.

The dragons rose again, peering about in confusion as they tried to pinpoint the source of the laughter. It seemed to come from everywhere at once. "Press the attack!" Windrush cried, lifting his voice above the din. "It is sorcery! Do not be deceived by the Enemy's sorcery!"

Roaring in agreement, the dragons wheeled around to

renew their assault. They raked the ground with fire, challenging the enemy warriors to appear.

Their own cries echoed back to them as they overflew the central amphitheater, belching fire. There was no answering cry, and the empty shadows of the warrens remained empty. No one emerged to meet the challenge, no one rose into the air to flee. The amphitheater, clearly visible now in the scattering mist, was deserted.

"SearSky and center dragons, make another pass!" Windrush shouted, trying desperately to keep his vanishing hope from infecting his voice. *"Winterfall and flanks, search the heights! Longtouch and scouts, climb and search the skies! Call out what you find! All others silent!"* As his words echoed back through the air, a haunting quiet came over the valley. The beating of wings, and the occasional crackle of fire, were all that broke the stillness. As the dragons split up according to his directions, Windrush climbed for a better view. Had the camp been deserted all along? No—here and there, firepits used by the enemy warriors were still smoking.

As SearSky's wing of dragons flew slower and lower over the encampment, sending flames into the warrens, they were met again by shadows boiling up from the ground. The dragons attacked, and again found their targets vanishing before them into the air. New cries of demonic laughter pealed through the valley. The sound seemed to Windrush to echo from the hills and the warrens, to reverberate out of the underrealm itself. It was Tar-skel, laughing through his sorcery at the bewilderment of the dragons.

From the greater height, Windrush could see more clearly that these shadows were as empty as those which had fooled him back in Hodakai's cavern. His fellow dragons were being deceived by the same trickery of the Enemy. Furious, he scanned the slopes on either side of the valley, looking for further signs of a trap. It was clear that the Enemy had known they were coming. Were drahls waiting to fall upon them as soon as their company disintegrated into chaos? He dared not risk that. *"Keep your formations tight!"* he called down. *"Beware of treachery!"*

He had a feeling, though—a twisting of humiliation and rage deep in his gut—that the Enemy had already won this battle, had made fools of them by inviting them to attack an empty valley. Where were the Enemy's servants now? No doubt far out of reach, waiting for the dragons to abandon their effort. Windrush leveled off high above the ground, trying to use his undersenses. But there was too much commotion; he could not focus.

Reports were starting to echo back on the wind. "No enemy here!" "None on the north slopes!" "None on the south slopes!" "None in the warrens!"

Windrush cursed silently—cursed the air, and the Enemy and his tricks, and the spy who must have warned him that they were coming. What should he do now? Attempt to occupy the camp, to establish a foothold in the Enemy's territory? Some of the dragons might call for that; but it would be impossible to hold this place for long, so far from home. How many dragons would it cost them to try?

Windrush felt a stinging uncertainty. They had come to punish the enemy warriors, and had met only frustration and treachery. He had been a fool for pressing the attack after learning of the traitor in their midst.

"Who betrayed us?" someone shouted from below, his words echoing Windrush's thoughts. "What spy told them we were coming?"

The words were met with angry mutterings. For a moment, Windrush felt tempted to shout down that one of their number was a spy—and the sooner they found him the better. But he knew that an angry brawl among the dragons here would serve the Enemy's cause far better than their own. It would take careful and determined effort to locate the traitor, the real traitor.

"*Silence in the valley!*" he shouted at last. His command reverberated across the empty camp, stilling the grumbling. He called out for small parties to search the warrens, and for the rest to form a defensive circle about the camp. "If the Enemy returns, let him be met with our fury! Scouts, keep a watch on the sky. Search for any sign and search for our arriving flanks.''

They had not long to wait for the latter. Before the scouts had even climbed back above the bordering slopes, Windrush felt the approach of new dragons. An instant later a cry from a scout signaled the arrival of Farsight's flank, from the north. Soon Stronghold's flank flew in from the south. The leaders gathered around Windrush, circling in midair.

Brusquely, the dragon asked for reports. Farsight's flank had noticed nothing unusual in their northern passage through the mountains. Stronghold's, however, had been interrupted at one point by a call from ToweringTree, at the rear, that he had seen something moving in the Valley Between—just a glimpse of one or more shadows in the air, shortly before they had reached the southern pass. But after a brief search had turned up nothing, Stronghold had ordered them to hurry on, so that they would arrive in time for the battle.

At Windrush's call, ToweringTree rose from the circling company and joined the leaders. "The shadows you saw, back in the Valley Between—which way were they moving?"

ToweringTree's eyes flickered worriedly. "To the east. That was why I asked Stronghold to wait. Windrush, if the drahls aren't here—"

"Then they might be attacking *our* land," Windrush said, voicing aloud the fear that they must all have been harboring. The enemy could have moved as stealthily as the dragons—perhaps more stealthily. The dragons had not left their land unprotected; but even so, a large part of their fighting strength was right here, circling uselessly in the air.

A cacophony of laughter rang across the valley, jarring him from his thoughts. Was the Enemy listening to their words and thoughts even now? He felt a bone-chilling cold rising out of the underrealm. As the eyes of the dragon leaders flashed around him, he knew that they were all realizing the magnitude of their mistake. "We must return!" "Quickly!" "The defense cannot hold—" The murmurs rose around him.

"*Wait!*" Windrush commanded. "We must return, yes! But not thoughtlessly. Gather your flanks and prepare to fly, but give me a few moments of silence, to see what I can learn." Without waiting for any argument, he veered toward the south slope and landed on the nearest outcropping. He raised his head to smell the air—and let his thoughts sink into the underrealm.

What he found, once he had passed beneath the surface layers of the underweb, was a tangle of deception, overlaid with vapors of confusion and the smells of enemy sorceries. It made him dizzy to try to follow the threads of the Enemy's treacheries, and he knew that he had neither the time nor the skill to sort it all out. But the one thing he could search for was some hint of where the enemy warriors had gone, what their goal was. They might have left some imprint of their paths in the underrealm. But there was such a confusing welter of signs . . .

And yet, there in the middle of it all, almost as though it had been left for him to find, was a thread leading away from this place, leading in a direction that was not exactly east or west, or north or south. But it bore a clear direction of intent; it was almost as though the groves gleamed at the end of the thread, shining all the way back to where Windrush peered in horror.

If only he could send a blast of flame through the underrealm to destroy the enemy before they did their terrible work!

Emerging from the underrealm, Windrush leaped from the outcropping, wings thumping the air. "*Away!*" he thundered. "*Abandon this place! Return to the north and south groves! The lumenis is in danger!*"

Chapter 17
THE VALE OF TAR-SKEL

FOR THE captured WingTouch, the flight westward into the territory of the Enemy was a nightmare of pain and exhaustion. The drahl said little, but kept its claws in the base of the dragon's neck as they flew. The pain was no longer constant, but it returned instantly if he flagged in his speed or strayed from his course. In the company of the drahls that had joined them in the Scarred Ridge, they had flown westward until long after night had given way to the morning. WingTouch had seen the last familiar territory disappear behind him in the cold light of the early morning, and then they had begun the long climb over the Borderland Mountains. From that point on, they were flying ever deeper into the Enemy's territory.

WingTouch's hopes that he might at least observe the Enemy's activities were cut short when, after the crossing of the mountains, the drahls wove a tight net of darkness about his head, blinding him to his surroundings. He navigated by the whispered instructions of his captor, and by sharp jabs of pain when he got an instruction wrong.

He had plenty of time to think, at least. He was sure that by now his dragon brothers must have concluded that he was dead. He wished he could let them know that he was not. Windrush, in his place, might have been able to call out, to communicate somehow through the underrealm. But lacking such skills, WingTouch was wholly isolated. Despair teased at the edges of his mind, but he was not one to give in easily to despair. He didn't think much about why; he just knew that there was nothing to be gained by it, and one discipline he did have was the ability to shut out unhelpful thoughts. Still, there was little enough in his situation to support hope.

He could not guess how long he had been pumping his wings, without even a gliding break. He knew that he was deep in the land of Tar-skel. The drahls laughed from time to time, apparently joking among themselves. Their voices turned into rasping croaks as they veered close to taunt him. Was that the natural timbre of their voices, when they dropped the sorcerous intonations of beauty?

On and on they flew, until WingTouch thought his wings would fail.

After an eternity, he heard a hoarse whisper: *"Land now, dragon—if you have the skill!"*

WingTouch felt a flush of anger. He was supposed to land blind, then? So be it. He let himself lose altitude, straining to judge by the feel of the air when he was approaching the ground. He ignored the laughter of the drahls and focused on new sounds, a murmur that sounded as though it might be rising from the ground. There was a curious moment when he felt a sudden change in the texture of the air, a strange kind of *thickness*, and the sounds of the voices suddenly became more distant. He was passing through a layer of sorcery, he was sure.

He felt a backwash from his wings. As he flared to settle to the ground, the drahl tightened its claws in the back of his neck. A lance of pain shot through his wingblades—just enough to cause him to spill air from one wing, then the other. He hit the ground with a sideways skid, and tumbled over. As the drahl tumbled with him, it clenched its claws in his neck, and a blinding pain obliterated all other sensation.

There was a sound of raucous laughter. He struggled to rise. The drahl let go and dismounted, but he could feel the throbbing wound it had left between his wingblades. The drahls' laughter subsided, and one of them hissed: "Prepare, dragon, to meet the true source of power in the realm. Prepare to beg for your life. The Nail of Strength does not look kindly upon those who oppose his will."

Nail of Strength. WingTouch subdued a rumble of defiance in the back of his throat, as he fought to push himself upright. He could guess how warmly he would be received by the one to whom he had once foolishly given his allegiance. He shivered, turning his head blindly.

He felt a chill on the back of his neck—the breath of a drahl. The next breath could easily kill. "If you are fortunate," murmured the drahl in a sonorously beautiful voice, "you will see the insignificance of your power, compared to the least of the Nail's servants. Then perhaps you will understand . . ."

The drahl left its words unfinished. The darkness fell away from around WingTouch's head. He blinked hard, and gasped out a long hiss of bewilderment as he turned his head one way and then another.

He was in daylight again—but it was a daylight unlike anything he had ever seen. There was a swirling, shimmering, unnatural quality to it, as though a darkness existed *within* the light, as though the light were somehow subordinate to the darkness. For a moment, he could not focus upon anything physical at all. The air and light took all of his attention. He could only think of them, together, as a *strangeness*—something not of this realm. Was this a naked sorcery of Tar-skel? If so, the Enemy had grown far bolder in his displays in the time since WingTouch had so blindly and stupidly served in his shadow.

* **Are you surprised, dragon-called-WingTouch?** * whispered a powerful, but silken, voice that seemed to come from within the strangeness itself.

WingTouch shivered at the familiar sound of that voice. He'd never thought of it as being the voice of Tar-skel, not during the time when it had so beguiled and commanded him. Then it had seemed the voice of a near-equal, perhaps just a touch wiser and more worldly—offering him choice and power. In the end, of course, it had given him neither, only blindness and fear.

"I have not offered you my name," WingTouch protested, trying not to let his voice tremble.

* **Oh, but you have—long ago,** * sighed the voice. * **As did your brother Farsight.** * The voice suddenly hardened, as WingTouch narrowed his gaze. * But your other brother, Windrush, never learned. And you—you forgot my teachings. You abandoned me. Do you not remember? *

WingTouch did not answer. Of course he remembered. Yes, he had given his name to that one. But it had never given its name in return. WingTouch had made his escape when Jael had shown him the way out. At least he'd tried to, or wanted to. He wondered now: was it ever really possible to escape?

The Enemy seemed to understand his thoughts. It laughed softly. * You thought you could run away. * Its laughter ended on a hard note. * Do you think, once you've given your name, you can ever take it away? *

WingTouch trembled, remaining silent. The light and air suddenly changed, and he became aware of shape and form around him. It was no less strange than the formless light of sorcery. The drahls flanking him looked like pure shadow—not at all like creatures that once had been dragon, before Tar-skel had altered them. They were jagged, threatening shadows, and though he could not quite *see* it, he felt that there was a pale light flickering within each of them, the light of their living spirit, perhaps even the spirit of the dragonlings that they had once been. The sight made him shudder and turn his gaze away.

In front of him, something altogether different, and incomprehensible, had appeared. It was a floating geometric pattern: a series of hollow, nested, angular shapes, each closed inward like a ring, but with four or five straight sides of unequal length. At first he thought that they were floating one inside another; then he realized that one floated *behind* another. He was staring down a sort of tunnel, down a profound emptiness that ran through the center of the figures as they diminished into the distance. The strangeness of light and air seemed to originate here, within this thing, a power of sorcery that flowed like a river from a source hidden in that tunnel.

The sight was so disturbing, so *alien*, that WingTouch was almost hypnotized by it. At last he shifted his gaze. The drahls were still present, floating threateningly around him. Behind them was a landscape—not of ground, but of streaming, coiling clouds. It was as though they were all still in the sky; and yet he knew, the muscles and sinews of his wings and feet had told him, that he had landed on the ground. A watery sort of light shone down upon the clouds, which glimmered darkly from within, with flashes of red and purple fire, like eerily tortured storm clouds.

Rising out of those mists, he saw several narrow, spindly peaks—more like needles than mountains. Spots of shadow circled around the tips of the peaks, orbiting in regular rhythm, with none of the dipping and swaying that any flying creature would display. What were those spots, and those peaks?

WingTouch glanced higher, and was startled to see that the sky itself shimmered, though not with the light of a sun. There was a fine tracery of webbing that seemed to enclose the sky, and *it* shimmered, and something about it was familiar. It took WingTouch a moment to remember his brother's vision. Windrush had described a great, treacherous web encircling the realm.

Binding the realm.

Crushing the realm.

* You see. But do you understand? *

The voice jarred him back to the present. He had been allowed to look at all of these sights, to absorb the mystery, to wonder at the power. But for what purpose? To plunge him into despair? WingTouch turned his gaze back to that strange geometric structure and trembled, remembering how he had once done the bidding of the one behind it. He opened his mouth to speak, then blew a wisp of steam instead. He wasn't ready to give in to despair.

The voice chastised him. * You would be wise, young WingTouch, to understand the nature of the power you challenge. Perhaps you should search again for that wisdom which seems to have deserted you. *

WingTouch blinked. This time he found words. "I recall only one time when wisdom wholly deserted me. That was when I abandoned my father and gave my allegiance to a power that wanted to destroy the realm where I dwell." He subdued the flame that rose in his throat, and vented smoke from his nostrils instead. "But that was before you let your true nature be known. Before you began attacking our groves. Before you took away the Mountain."

He was answered by soft laughter, rising against the stillness, and echoed by the croaking laughter of drahls. The strangeness seemed to deepen, the geometric shapes to distort in a way that confounded his eyes. "What have you done with the Dream Mountain?" he demanded, angered by the laughter. "Are you afraid to tell me?"

The drahl-shadows began to converge upon him, then stopped, hissing.

WingTouch blinked slowly. "What could it harm you to tell me?"

* I tell, * whispered the voice, so deadly and soft that he had to strain to hear, * those whom I wish to tell. *

"Are you afraid to tell?"

* Do not test wits with me, impudent fool! * There was a pause. * You will lose—now, and every time. *

WingTouch glanced at the drahls which he knew were awaiting the command to kill him, or torture him. But he had already decided: he would not allow despair. "Highwing was right. You deal in fear, and yet you yourself are afraid."

Soft laughter once more. * Afraid? *

Drawing a breath, WingTouch said, "Yes. Afraid of the prophecy—"

His words were cut off by a clap of thunder. It seemed to rock from one side of him to the other. The swirling clouds flickered with lightning. A bolt snapped up out of the clouds and across, striking him in the chest. He gasped, could not gasp, as the shock paralyzed him, blinding him with pain. He could not speak, but he could hear. The next words seemed to reverberate from the clouds, like the thunder. * Do not speak to me of prophecy, or you will suffer . . . suffer . . . *suffer* . . . no matter how long you might plead, or how pitifully you might beg. Is this understood? * WingTouch gasped, could not speak. * IS THIS

UNDERSTOOD? * Another bolt hit him, and he blacked out.

It was only an instant, it seemed. But when his eyes blinked open, and his vision returned, he focused on something new, something that had appeared over the clouds, over the slender peaks that spiked upward out of the flashing mists. There was an enormous shape floating there—a mountain peak, broad and sloping and translucent. A dazzling light seemed to glimmer in it and through it, as though barely contained by it. The sight made him tremble in awe. It was true, then. The Enemy controlled the Dream Mountain, held it captive—by what sorcery he could not imagine. There was no visible point of connection between it and the other peaks, or even the clouds. It seemed to rise out of a nearly invisible mist high in the sky. How could it be? he wondered helplessly. The thought of a power that could do such a thing sent shudders of fear through him.

The Enemy controlled the Dream Mountain, as the dragons controlled their tiny patch of territory and their tiny lumenis groves.

As he watched, the mountain faded from the sky. But the image persisted in his mind like the lightning that flashed in the clouds.

Without warning, a third bolt flashed out of the clouds and struck him and in the blast of pain the dragon lost consciousness altogether.

WingTouch awoke to darkness, and to the sound of murmuring voices. Tar-skel's voice? No—these were voices of torment and despair. He couldn't even tell if they were dragon voices. "Who is there?" WingTouch murmured, but he heard no answer.

A short time later, he heard the sound of footsteps. They were not the footsteps of a dragon. He squinted into the darkness, where he was now able to discern some shapes. He seemed to be imprisoned in a large open area, some sort of crater, surrounded by dark, jagged shapes of stone, just at the edge of visibility. He tried to move, but his legs were frozen in place. The effort to move sent shudders of pain through his body. The wound at the back of his neck throbbed. He peered down at his feet and saw that they were embedded in solid stone. Enraged and humiliated, he could only vent steam.

A figure came into sight before him, nearly obscured by his breath. WingTouch grunted in surprise. It was not a dragon, nor any other creature of the realm. But it was a *kind* of creature he knew. It was a *human*—a human like the rigger Jael. Only not like Jael—taller, more muscular, darker in demeanor. But, surely, a rigger. His mind was clouded with confusion. A *rigger*. What was a rigger doing here, in the Enemy's camp? Was this . . . could it be . . . a rigger of the prophecy?

The human walked around an angular boulder and stood before him. It stared at him for a time, then said, "You have gazed upon the Dream Mountain." Its voice rippled like dragon scales, smooth and yet threatening.

WingTouch stared back at him, trying to decide what to make of this being.

"Do you begin to understand how useless your struggle is?" the human asked.

WingTouch drew a slow, difficult breath. After knowing Jael, if only for a short time, he had come to think of humans as allies, as forces for good from a realm beyond the realm. But he suddenly recalled Windrush's report of the human-spirit he had met in the abandoned warren to the south. WingTouch didn't remember that one's name, but it had seemed clear enough that it had counted itself no friend of dragons. WingTouch decided, staring at this one, that perhaps it was of the same order as the being his brother had met.

"Are you a spirit?" he asked the human.

The rigger drew itself up, in surprise. It did not appear pleased by the question. "Do I look like a spirit?" it barked. "You are exceedingly impudent for one who has no hope, dragon-named-WingTouch!"

WingTouch closed his eyes for a moment. That was certainly true. He had no hope left for himself, and he didn't know why he persisted in taunting the Enemy and his servants with his own . . . yes, *impudence*. Except that . . . he refused to admit despair into his thinking. Even now.

He blinked his eyes open. "You have me at a disadvantage, human—or human-spirit, as the case may be. You know my name, but I do not know yours." *But I have not given* you *my name, remember that*, he thought.

The human laughed. It was an ugly sound. "I have you at a disadvantage in *many* ways, dragon. But for the sake of convenience, since I harbor some expectation that you and I will become colleagues, you may call me *Rent*." His tone of voice made it clear that he was giving a form of address only, and not his true, full name. Not his garkkon-rakh, not the key to his inner being.

"Rent," the dragon murmured. It was, he thought, not nearly so attractive a name as Jael. It was, however, a suitable form of address for a servant of the Enemy.

Rent nodded, and strode around the dragon with his hands on his hips, studying the captive. "Now, if these questions are out of the way—"

"Not yet!" WingTouch said, wheezing with pain. "You haven't told me—" and he paused, breathing slowly— "whether you are a spirit or a true human."

Rent returned, scowling, to face the dragon. "You are most persistent, WingTouch. Headstrong, I should say. That *could* be to the good—if coupled with common sense and wisdom."

"You evade—" WingTouch began—and cried out as a sharp new pain clamped onto the back of his neck. Rent waved his hand, and the pain vanished, but left him shuddering.

"Let that be a lesson. Do not *ever* speak disrespectfully to me."

WingTouch vented silent steam.

Rent smiled. "But I will answer your question—because in doing so, I may help you to understand something important." He waited for a reaction from WingTouch, and nodded when the dragon remained silent. "Good. You're learning. Now, then. I am a spirit, yes—a spirit from another realm. You know the meaning of that, I believe?" He paused. "But perhaps you don't know *this*. It is with the power of the Nail of Strength that I walk in the form that you see. I was once bereft of my form, through the viciousness of your own kind. But now I have my form once again, and it is far greater and stronger than ever before." He studied the dragon. "Do you understand what I am telling you?"

WingTouch considered before answering. "I understand. Your form, as I see it, is not yours at all. It is a sorcery-thing, a trick of the underweb, a—"

The pain this time was blinding, and it lasted for a longer time than he could measure; it lasted nearly forever.

When it did finally stop, he was reeling. He needed desperately to shift his stance, to lie down—but with his feet embedded in the stone, he could not move at all, he could only wobble in pain. Shuddering, he knew that the torment was only beginning. The suffering of being trapped immobile like this could alone drive him mad, if it lasted long enough.

Rent was watching the dragon from atop a nearby boulder, where he was sitting with one leg drawn up and his hands clasped around his knee. "Had enough?" he asked.

WingTouch contained his anger. His legs ached fiercely, and were shaking. He tried to flex his claws, but they were locked solidly inside the stone.

"My point, dragon-WingTouch, since you seem unwilling to perceive it for yourself, is that your allegiance to *this* side—to the side of Strength, to the side of the *Nail*—will serve you far better than your meaningless persistence in your present frame of mind." The human leaned forward, gazing at him. "It is not, after all, as if we would ask you to fight in any way that is wrongful or unnatural. Is that what you fear?"

WingTouch felt his weight shifting dangerously. His leg muscles trembled on the verge of spasm. He did not answer the demon-spirit.

"You're suffering. Allow me to help you." Rent stretched out a hand toward the struggling dragon. The stone softened and melted away from WingTouch's feet, freeing him. He sank down in shuddering relief, letting the weight off his legs. "You see, we are not without understanding," Rent said.

WingTouch breathed quickly, gulping air. He struggled not to act on his greatest desire right now, which was to incinerate the demon with his breath.

"Now, then. What we are asking for is really just some information," Rent said, rising to his feet. "Your brother Windrush is the leader of all the dragons—we know that. He has sent for the demon Jael to help him—we know that. The battle has not much longer to run before we are the victors—we know that. But . . ." He paused, stroking his chin. "We wish not to prolong the suffering. And so we would like merely to know certain aspects of your brother's plans—"

WingTouch could not hold back a snort.

Rent raised one human eyebrow, and continued with apparent patience. "So that we might quicken the end—end the suffering, and quicken the release of the Dream Mountain for the benefit of all." His gaze sharpened. "We would like to know, for example, if the demon Jael has reappeared in the realm."

This time WingTouch kept control. He made no sound, no response to the human's ridiculous claim. No response to the question. He had no knowledge of it, in any case—but he was not going to tell the human that.

"If you are wise, you may share in the pleasure and the rewards of the victory," Rent pointed out. "Just as, for example, your brother FullSky has chosen to cooperate with us—"

WingTouch lurched to his feet. *FullSky!*

"Oh—you didn't know?" Rent asked mildly. "Why, yes—your brother has long been a part of our effort."

"FullSky . . . is . . . alive?" WingTouch whispered, not wanting the human to hear the anguish in his voice, but unable to keep his silence.

"Why, yes. Yes, indeed. And being a wise and strong member of your race, he is doing all that he can to help us—"

"You are lying, demon!"

"Watch your tongue, *dragon!*"

WingTouch swayed on his feet, drawing himself into a crouch. He felt fire tingling at the back of his throat. What if the human wasn't lying? He and Farsight had once been that foolish. Suppose FullSky was alive—and still a traitor? WingTouch did not think he could stand to know that, even if it were true. He would rather die now.

"FullSky is a noble dragon of the Nail," Rent said. As he spoke, he suddenly began growing in size before the dragon. "*He* will see the Dream Mountain freed, even if your other foolish brothers do not. They with their stupid attacks! Even now we are turning more of their precious lumenis groves to ashes."

WingTouch could stand it no longer. He loosed a breath of fire upon the loathsome human, drenching him with flame. *"Die, demon-liar!"* he cried.

The flame crackled harmlessly through the human, who did not move a muscle until it had passed. WingTouch drew breath for another blast of flame, but his breath froze in his chest as Rent raised a hand and waggled a finger at him.

Molten stone rose to swallow his feet in agonizing heat—and hardened in an instant, locking him into a trembling crouch.

"You are a great fool," Rent said, and turned and walked away.

WingTouch bellowed and bellowed in helpless rage.

Chapter 18
SECRETS IN THE DARK

THE WATCHER floated silently past the dragon FullSky's kuutekka—a ghostly jailer in the underrealm passing over the ghostly spirit of its prisoner. Suddenly the Watcher struck downward, flashing with fire and shadow at a movement in the adjoining, lower cavern, where a great chasm seemed to drop out of the bottom of the underrealm. FullSky froze in mid-movement. He had been slipping carefully along the walls of the prison, probing tirelessly at the spell-weave that had held him for what seemed a lifetime. But the last thing he wanted to do was provoke the Watcher, or attract attention of any sort. After a moment, when the Watcher had not reappeared, he stretched his kuutekka forward to the lip of the opening between the coalfire-walled cavern where he was imprisoned, to peer down into the larger, darker cavern where the murmuring voices and flickering lights of imprisoned, bodiless spirits never stopped floating up from depths of the underrealm.

FullSky caught a glimpse of fire erupting from the chasm. The angry shape of the Watcher flew back up toward him. He retreated hastily; but even so, the Watcher shot a flare of punishment in his direction, a blue flame that crackled around him in quick, hot circles, darting and biting at his kuutekka before finally expending itself. FullSky gasped, and tried not to shudder in the underrealm as he recovered from the casually administered punishment.

One corner of his mind felt his body shake and tremble in the outer world, where it was chained to the rocks of Tar-skel's dungeon. He strove to disassociate himself from the pain that burned through his body. Though he could not wholly ignore the pain, his effort to do so gave him just enough relief to retain some semblance of endurance, of purpose in his underrealm consciousness.

Eventually he found the strength to peer back into the glowing labyrinth of the Enemy's underrealm. The Watcher, the fire-serpent, the creature of the Enemy— whatever the terrible thing was—was gone for the moment. Gone elsewhere, tormenting other imprisoned spirits, no doubt. This was probably a good opportunity to creep out again into the glowering light, to seek other pathways, other windows in the underweb that might conceivably be of benefit. Escape, of course, was out of the question. His physical body remained chained here, and the Watcher would certainly notice if he tried to reach out of this place with his thought for more than a few minutes at a time. But it was those breathless minutes, snatched when the Watcher wasn't looking, that were as precious to him as life itself.

Cautiously now, he began to stretch his kuutekka out again from his body, probing the hazy underrealm walls of the dungeon. Something didn't feel right. He paused, concealing his presence against a wall. An instant later, he felt a quivering in the underweb, and the Watcher flashed back across the cavern, answering some new movement, punishing some feeble challenge to its authority as jailer.

FullSky slipped back into his body, so quietly as to make no disturbance in the underrealm at all. He had worked very hard at learning to move stealthily in the underrealm; but there were times when it was best to wait, and clearly this was one of them.

There would be opportunities later to try to reach Windrush. There would always be opportunities. He had to believe that, or he would lose hope altogether.

Time, to FullSky, had become something that shifted and moved in his mind with little connection to the world beyond. Pain had come to seem eternal in his body, imprisoned and broken by the Enemy's spells of cold and darkness. His imprisonment and his pain were something he was determined, not just to endure, but to turn to good purpose. He knew now he could not do that without help—though, for what had seemed an eternity, he had tried. But that had been before he had learned to open silent, secret passages in the underrealm—before he had learned to reach out, even in imprisonment, to his brothers on the other side of the realm.

It had not happened quickly. For many seasons on the outside, he had raged uselessly against himself for falling prey to the Enemy—for his own foolishness in toying with the Enemy's sorceries, so long ago. In those days, the Enemy had not yet revealed his true identity, but surely there had been enough warnings—from his father, from the ifflings, from his own inner heart. Still, he had succumbed to his own pride in his underrealm skills. Naive in his innocence, he had challenged the master of deceits—and the Enemy had trapped him neatly in his web. His ensnarement in the underrealm had quickly led to his physical imprisonment as well. It had taken him a long time even to begin to forgive himself.

It had taken him longer still to realize that he was not altogether crippled, or blind. From his spell-prison, he had been permitted to watch the imprisonment of his father Highwing in the Black Peak, and the sentence of exile. But he had also glimpsed Jael's triumph and the humiliating defeat of Tar-skel at the Black Peak, and the subsequent release from bondage of many hapless dragons who served unwittingly under the dark one's shadow. Jael had bought freedom for many, including two of FullSky's brothers— but not, unfortunately, for FullSky or any of the other *physical* prisoners of the Enemy.

Nevertheless, FullSky had rejoiced in the outcome of that battle. His rejoicing earned him a lifetime of the drahls' brutality—but the Enemy, having more urgent treacheries to weave, displayed no further personal interest in him. FullSky was tortured by servant-jailers, yes—but his mind remained free, and he retained some ability to peer out of this dungeon of power, through the underrealm. As the realm was torn by open warfare, and the number of prisoners grew, the watcher-spirits who guarded the dungeon's underrealm seemed almost to encourage his awareness of the suffering of others—indeed, it fed his despair.

Over time, though, the watch over him grew lax, and he discovered that he could peer out through numerous small openings in the spell-weave of the prison, and even observe the comings and goings of the Enemy's servants, and on occasion overhear fragments of their conversation. With care and stealth, he was able to explore nearby areas of the underrealm, beyond the limits of the prison, without drawing his jailers' notice.

Eventually he decided that perhaps his role in this world was not yet ended, though he could not clearly foresee what he might do. He was learning much about the Enemy's plans. He caught glimpses of the sorcery that blocked the way to the Dream Mountain—not a clear view, but far more so than was likely possible from the outside world, or for any of the free dragons. Though he did not fully understand the sorcery, or know how to defeat it, a tiny flame of hope grew in his heart that he might learn useful secrets and somehow pass them out to the faithful dragons of the realm.

He grew more bold in his explorations of the underrealm. It seemed that as long as he made no effort to create spells of escape or power, he could move relatively undisturbed. He discovered that it was possible, with care, to stretch his thought outward for a considerable distance. He found himself in a game of testing and trying, feinting and retreating—risking discovery to gain more knowledge of the Enemy's actions and plans, or to whisper to ifflings that he thought he sensed passing just beyond reach. At times, he imagined that he felt the touch of his father Highwing's spirit, reaching out to encourage him from the heartfires of the Final Dream Mountain. In the dungeon where he lay broken and crippled, his drahl-jailers subjected him to continuing abuse; but in the underrealm, his skills seemed to grow in proportion to the cruelty inflicted upon his body.

It was only a matter of time before he sensed the distant movements in the underrealm of his brother Windrush—and sensed, as well, Windrush's terrible need and the need of all the realm. It was out of that desperate need that FullSky finally risked crafting the terrifying vision that he cast across the underrealm into his brother's lumenis-heightened awareness. It was out of that need that he risked exposure in the underrealm, opening passages that could help Windrush find him, speak to him, and hear *his* need.

His final reach outward, touching Windrush's thoughts in that place of wilderness and desolation, had unfortunately drawn the attention of the Watcher—and ended in a blinding pain that made the warning clear. He was fairly sure that neither the Watcher nor its Master knew precisely what he had done, but now the Watcher seemed to appear much faster when he stretched out beyond his body. If only it would leave him untended, just a little longer!

As if in mocking answer to his thoughts, the Watcher swept back into the cavern and floated one way and then another, scanning prisoners. Finally it hovered directly over the point where FullSky's kuutekka huddled within his broken body. The Watcher was silent as always, watching him with whatever terrible undersenses it commanded. FullSky did not move, or make any acknowledgment of the Watcher's threatening presence. But he felt it pulsing hatred like waves of heat, and he could not help feeling that the Watcher meant to taunt him, perhaps daring him to challenge it to a duel of power that he could not hope to win.

Once, he might have been tempted to take up such a duel. But he knew that his hope lay not in foolish challenges. For all of his hard-learned skills, he had little real strength left, and it was well within the Watcher's powers to destroy him, if it chose to do so.

The standoff lasted for what seemed a very long time, but was probably only a few heartbeats in the outer world. The Watcher spat a contemptuous gob of fire in his direction and moved off to the other side of the cavern, where it hovered, flickering with light and shadow.

FullSky was not even certain exactly what the Watcher

was. It was like, and yet unlike, a drahl. It had the power to punish and to terrify, and it spent its power lavishly upon both the bodied and disembodied spirits trapped in this place. It was probably itself a trapped spirit, transformed and made terrible by the Enemy. What its original form had been, FullSky could not even guess. He had watched it take various forms, using whatever power was most frightening to those it opposed. It used fire, it used darkness, most of all it used fear. It *became* these things— even the power of fear itself, and he had seen no one resist it, especially not these defeated spirits, kept alive here for the dark purposes of the Enemy's sorceries.

Even from where he huddled now, FullSky could sense distantly the crepuscular web of sorcery that Tar-skel was drawing about the realm. He did not know how, but he knew that all of these trapped spirits—including, he feared, his own—were lending power to that sorcery through their pain, through their fear and their despair. The web was growing stronger, growing with the despair of the dragons and the ifflings and all those who lived in the realm—and perhaps even those beyond the realm, where the Nail of Strength sought to cast his influence. The completion of Tar-skel's web of power would be the final undoing of all who stood against him.

So long as it remained uncompleted, the sorcery could still be broken. But it would take more than the strength of dragons to break it. This, he was certain, was the time which the prophecies of the draconae had foretold. The rigger Jael was the One spoken of, the One for whom the realm would tremble. It would take Jael's help to break the sorcery, and the help of the ifflings, and of all those who knew the Enemy and were willing to risk everything to defeat him.

And if he, FullSky, were to have any hope of playing his part, he would have to act soon. It meant risking his silent life in the underrealm, in a brazen try for freedom. He could not do it alone. The Watcher was too powerful. But if he could just reach out once more to his brother Windrush. . . .

* * *

As if in answer to his prayer, the Watcher flickered suddenly and floated out of sight on some other errand. FullSky waited a little longer, to be sure. Then he slipped his kuutekka through an almost invisible opening near the end of the underrealm cavern, where the floor fell away and where, not far beyond, the abyss of spirits yawned. He moved quickly, but with desperate care, hoping that he could pick up a trace of his brother's presence near one of the concealed windows that he had left in the underweb of Windrush's cavern.

FullSky's hope was that the Watcher's own powers could be turned to its disadvantage, and bring him his freedom. His *fear* was that the failure of his plan could make his brother a captive here alongside him—or worse, in the chasm of spirits.

Without hope, FullSky could not live. This was a terrible risk, but it was one he had to take. He hoped Windrush would be willing to take it, as well. Not for his sake alone, but for the sake of the realm.

Chapter 19
TRAITOR SEARCH

THE COMPANY of dragons entered their final, exhausted glide from the crest of the Scarred Mount Ridge, swooping down into the small lumenis grove that lay between the ridge and the main dragon camp. Windrush had not allowed any respite in the flight back over the mountains from the Enemy's land. Even so, he saw at once that they had arrived too late.

The lumenis groves were a smoking ruin, and a brief probe of the protective spells showed them shattered by a far greater sorcery. The dragons who had remained to guard the groves were nowhere to be seen. They had either fled or died. Windrush raged helplessly at the Enemy, and at himself for spending so much of their strength on a mission driven by anger and frustration, rather than by wisdom.

The dragons would miss these groves sorely. Windrush wondered if other groves had been attacked, as well. It seemed likely. But how many others?

"Scouts!" he called, banking back toward the other dragons wheeling in the air. "Fly ahead to the Valley of Fallen Light! Return at once if they need help there!" Four scout dragons, already bone-weary, soared away at once to the east, toward the most precious lumenis grove in the held land.

Windrush's thoughts were interrupted by a call from the guard warrens, below.

"Survivors!"

Windrush landed immediately. Emerging from the stone shelters, moving with great difficulty, were two badly injured dragons. One was dragging a broken wing; the other bore terrible open wounds from the talons of enemy warriors. They squinted into the sun, croaking helplessly to their too-late rescuers. Windrush approached, venting black smoke at such atrocities perpetrated upon his land.

One of the injured was groaning, "We tried . . . tried to defend . . ."

"Of course," Windrush rumbled reassuringly, moved by the anguish in the dragons' eyes. "The others—were they all killed?"

The guard dragon nodded. "All that we saw. Except us. Help came . . . from the camp . . . too late. We sent them . . . where they might still do some good . . . hid ourselves to report . . ." The dragon wheezed for breath.

Windrush sighed. "Rightly done. What happened?"

The story was exactly as he had feared. Hordes of drahls had appeared just before dawn, hurling themselves into a frenzied attack up on the grove. At the same moment that the dragons were attacking an empty valley, the drahls were inflicting terrible damage here. The defenders held as long as they could, struggling to keep the guarding spells knit against the invasion. But the drahls, working the Enemy's sorceries, overwhelmed them. Once the guarding spells were broken, the defenders, vastly outnumbered, had no chance at all.

Windrush listened, trembling with anger. At last, he turned away, leaving others to get the final details. He feared for the Valley of Fallen Light. If the scouts he'd sent out had found the enemy still there, they would need help, and quickly. Calling together the leaders, he gave new instructions. Half of Stronghold's dragons would remain here. All the rest would fly on with him to see if drahls were still abroad in the realm.

With growing despair, he left the ruins of the grove behind.

The flight took them over the main camp, where a few dragons on sentry duty rose to give their report. Moments later, the scouts he had sent ahead earlier returned to meet them in the air. And on this day filled with such crushing humiliation, Windrush at last heard good news. The Valley of Fallen Light was safe—the approach spells intact, the guard dragons unharmed, the valley undisturbed. The enemy warriors had attacked two other smaller groves along the flanks of the Scarred Mount Ridge, but had not struck this far to the east.

Apparently the Enemy's purpose was to harass the dragons, to wear away at their reserves, to weaken them without confronting their greatest strength directly. Though the Enemy's attack today had been less than the final death-blow Windrush had feared, Tar-skel must surely have reveled in his chance to turn the dragons' angry offensive into a costly humiliation.

Now, Windrush knew, *he* had to find a way to turn despair back into hope. If he could not, who would? This morning, the dragons' unity of purpose had been overwhelming. Now it was shattered. Already he had overheard some grumbling about Windrush's decisions, Windrush's mistakes, Windrush's failure to find the murderous traitor. And perhaps the complaints were not wholly without justification. But recriminations could only turn this defeat into an even greater catastrophe. Bad enough that they'd lost lumenis. If he lost the dragons' support, the struggle was as good as over.

That meant he must regain the confidence of his followers—and he knew what had to be done. *The traitor must be found, and there must be no mistake.* He summoned Farsight to speak privately at the edge of the main camp. "We must eliminate the treachery from within—and I see only one way."

Farsight stared at him dazedly. "How, Windrush? I've already heard more rumors than you could imagine—dragons accused of dropping out of formation to consort with drahls, dragons accused of speaking to the Enemy through the underrealm, dragons accused of *being* drahls. I think there are more suspects than dragons."

"That," Windrush said, "is what worries me—more, even, than the actual treachery. It is the effect of this rage and suspicion on all of us. No good can come of the innocent being accused with the guilty!"

Farsight's clear eyes focused upon his. "What do you propose?"

Windrush drew a long breath. "To demand a private union of garkkon-rakh with every leader. Every leader in turn—and then with every follower. I must see for myself who is truly garkkondoh, and who is a betrayer of dragons. It is the only way."

Farsight's eyes glowed with astonishment. "Every dragon? Windrush, you cannot demand such a thing!"

"What choice do I have?"

Farsight blew a cloud of steam. "They will never agree! Their trust is already shaken. To propose such a thing—it has never been done! Not union with *every* dragon!"

"It has been done in ages past," Windrush snapped. "It can be done again." He said it with greater assurance than he felt. All he really knew of past ages was fragments of draconae stories remembered from his days as a fledgling. But he knew this: there had been a time once when dragons had far more readily shared their innermost thoughts with each other, especially in time of need.

Farsight spoke in a low sigh, turning his head from side to side, as though afraid that someone might be overhearing. "Ages past? This is another time, Windrush! I do not know even close companions among us who bind in union except under the most extreme circumstances."

"What could be more extreme than this?" Windrush asked. "If our brothers cannot agree, then I doubt we will find the traitor—and if we cannot eliminate this poison from our midst, then I doubt that the realm can be saved." Windrush drew a deep breath of mountain air. His resolve had become clear in his mind, even as he'd spoken of it with Farsight.

Farsight's eyes glowed and he breathed sparks. "Very well. But for you to examine each and every dragon? Not even you could endure that much, my brother. Why not call upon a group of us to do this? What of Winterfall, and Longtouch, and Stronghold? They are well trusted." Farsight hesitated, blinking soberly. "To be honest, Windrush, I think there are many who would choose—if they must submit to this—to be judged by one of them, rather than by you. This is a most awkward time in your leadership. There is no point in denying the truth."

Windrush glared, but realized that Farsight was right. "If the four of you are willing—very well. But I will join with each of you before you begin. There must be no suspicion. There will be no dragon who is not tested by another—including me."

Farsight blew a flame of approval. "Perhaps, then, you should begin with me—and move on to the others."

Windrush peered around at the scattered and demoralized company of dragons. "Yes. We should do it in the presence of the others." He drew a deep breath and bellowed into the air: "ALL LEADERS, GATHER IN THE VALE OF DECISION! GATHER NOW!"

His cry echoed throughout the camp. Other members of the dragon company began to stir again—some looking eager, some sullen, some puzzled and angry. Windrush nodded to Farsight, and together they took once more to the air, leading the way to the Vale of Decision.

After murmuring privately with the dragons that Farsight had named, Windrush addressed the company from the command stone. "Dragons, you all know that the Enemy learned of our plans before we took to the air last night. You all *suspect* that we have been betrayed by one of our own. Well, it is true. A traitor was overheard, in the night, conspiring with a drahl!" A loud murmur rose; he called for silence. "BUT—we do not know the identity of the traitor. I propose to undertake *now* to find the one, who could be among us right here in this vale."

Another mutter went up, and several names were rasped out by bitter voices. *"Enough!"* Windrush cried angrily. "There will be judgment! But by the realm, it will be a fair judgment. I will not have brother turn against brother. If any of you has *evidence* against another, he may speak now. If you have no evidence, be silent!"

He paused for a minute to see if any dragon would come forward. Few of the assembled would even meet his gaze. It was impossible to guess whether there might be a dragon out there attempting to conceal his guilt. "Very well, then—this is my command! There must be a test of *each one of us*, by someone else known to be true. We must each submit to a union of *garkkon-rakh to garkkon-rakh!*" There was an immediate rumble of protest, and he raised his voice to the volume of a battle command. "THERE WILL BE NO ONE EXCEPTED! I will be tested first of all! Each of you will be tested! And each in your companies, and every dragon still out on patrol will be tested! *Garkkon-rakh to garkkon-rakh!*"

The rumbling grew louder. He shot a crackling flame skyward until he had their attention. "We will begin at once—with me! I will link with Farsight—in your presence—and after Farsight, Stronghold—and then Winterfall—and Longtouch. They will each test me—and I will test them. If we are found loyal, those four will examine all of you gathered here. None will be excused! I know you are weary—but we must, *and we will find the traitor!*"

An uncertain mutter of approval answered him. He expected no better than that. Many of them, he imagined, were too shocked by his command to know how to answer. But he knew—they all knew—that they would be here, gathered in this vale, for a long and grueling time to come. He hoped he could keep them from rebelling until they were done.

Windrush's gaze locked with his brother's. Farsight's clear, silvery-faceted eyes glimmered with a concealed inner fire. It was in that fire that he held his most closely guarded thoughts and memories; it was that fire which held, and would soon reveal, the dragon's soul. Windrush's gaze passed inward through the deepest facets of his brother's eyes; he felt his brother's gaze passing into *his* eyes. Even as brothers, he and Farsight had only joined this way once previously as grown dragons, and that was long ago, before their father's death. He felt a moment of profound hesitation, and then a shudder of release, as Farsight dropped the barriers surrounding his privacy and secret selfhood, like a veil falling away.

Flame blossomed around Windrush's vision, and his spirit, as Farsight's thoughts and memories bubbled up to join his . . .

His brother was even angrier about today's treachery than he was—and beneath the anger burned the memory, the infuriating memory of the voice of a dragon plotting treachery with a drahl. (If only I could recognize it . . . if only I could recognize it . . . !) Farsight's inner mind murmured over and over. Windrush shared the churning memory and the frustration. He strained to identify that voice in his brother's memory, to recognize what Farsight could not. It was so tantalizing . . . and yet finally impossible. There were a dozen dragons whose voice it might have been.

Farsight felt *his* frustration, as well, and together they let go of the memory, as so many other images rushed up to displace it. There were memories of their father, Highwing, teaching them to fly and to duel; bright memories. And long-ago memories of their mother, Skytouch, of her chiming voice and her lenslike beauty, wings and body of glass, flying against the sun like a thousand jewels. It was she, in the beginning, who had taught them of the Words, and the histories that were the domain of the draconae and the puzzlement of the draconi. Once grown out of fledgling-hood, they saw her rarely, living as she did in the Dream Mountain; but when she flew to them, she was like a living sunset. And then one horrifying day, Highwing came and told them of her brutal death: a singing jewel, knocked from the sky by young dragons who were already under the influence of the unseen, unrevealed Tar-skel. Highwing had destroyed those fledglings, then helplessly watched her die.

Skytouch's death changed their father. Though the brothers had seen it in different ways, they both knew of her words to him at the end, Words of the prophecy. Highwing believed that, like it or not, he had become a part of the enactment of those Words when the rigger Jael came into the realm, changing the course of dragon history.

Darker images welled up in the link then—images of Farsight's and WingTouch's time of blackness, of their seduction by the Enemy's claims and promises of power, and their desertion of their father when the dragons of the realm attacked him for befriending an outsider. It was a shameful and humiliating memory, but Farsight made no effort to conceal it. They both knew that it was down there, among the very darkest of the memories, that Windrush must especially search, to see if any loyalty to the Enemy lingered, to see if there was any chance that Farsight himself was culpable as a traitor.

And search Windrush did, without apologies. At the same time, Farsight was searching *his* memories—of his contact with FullSky, and of *his* times of weakness, when he had doubted his own leadership, and of a time earlier, when he too had been afraid to defend Highwing, until shamed into it by an outsider named Jael. There were failures enough to go around.

But in Farsight, though he found a deep shame for the past, Windrush found no trace of disloyalty since.

(You musn't doubt it, either of you.)

Windrush started. He thought he had heard a voice whisper those words, a voice that was neither of theirs, and yet was so familiar that it caught his attention at once—and Farsight's, as well.

(You mustn't give up.)

(Farsight?) Windrush whispered.

(Windrush?) whispered Farsight.

Their locked souls burned like lumenis. *(Highwing?)* Windrush did not mean to voice the question into the bonding, but of course there was no way not to. And he realized that Farsight had thought, and spoken, the same question at the same time.

There was no clear answer, but he thought he heard the voice again, growing fainter. *(Seek out the one who cries, "Friend of Highwing!" Without her, you are lost. . . .)* The final words were so faint that Windrush was scarcely certain he had not imagined them. So often before, he had thought that he had felt the silent, invisible presence of his father's spirit, perhaps reaching out from the heartfires of the Final Dream Mountain—but never had he heard his father's voice in words.

He gazed into the soul of Farsight, and knew that his brother, too, had recognized the presence of Highwing. And Farsight, too, was unsure what to think or say.

(I do not doubt you, Farsight,) Windrush said at last.

(I do not doubt you, Windrush,) answered his brother.

And they dissolved the link, and Windrush let a long, slow sigh escape from his throat. The fire between them flickered and went out, and he blinked and widened his gaze. Surrounded by the waiting dragons, his brother was staring back at him, with a tiny ray of new hope gleaming in his eyes.

When he entered into union with Stronghold, his thoughts were already ringing with deep memories, with hopes and regrets. Amber flame blossomed within Stronghold's eyes, and he felt the memory of his link with Farsight bubbling up at once. It could not be helped. Stronghold shared those memories with surprise and interest, and gave as well as he received.

There was so much to be seen, so much to learn. With astonishment, Stronghold discovered the depth of Windrush's memories of Jael—and of his recent contact with FullSky. From Stronghold, there were the memories of the practice of battle as a young dragon, and the lure of the duels, and the promises of dragons gathering to destroy any from the outside who would come to change their world. Stronghold, too, had been fooled by the unseen spirit of Tar-skel, ensnared by a promise of glory, trapped by a subtle sorcery from which he was freed by the victory at the Black Peak.

Windrush searched Stronghold's heart carefully—and he found there much discouragement and frustration, and indeed, more than a little dissatisfaction with Windrush's abilities as a leader. He examined that dissatisfaction closely, and with considerable discomfort. But Stronghold's trust in Windrush's character and garkkondoh remained steadfast, and whatever his concerns about means and strategies, he showed not a hint of disloyalty. Above all, he bore a burning desire for the defeat of the Enemy who had once enslaved him.

(I do not doubt you, Stronghold.)

(Nor I you, Windrush.)

Spilling over with memories and reflections that he wished he could spend a season studying and understanding, Windrush opened his gaze to Winterfall's. Their memories fell together like a swirling snowstorm.

Winterfall had never trusted the Enemy, never been swayed or seduced, never wanted anything but to rid the realm of anything that echoed of the Nail of Strength. Winterfall was a cautious dragon, who loved to fly more than he loved to fight. Like Windrush, he had gone into hiding during the times of subtle treachery when Tar-skel's hidden influence had darkened the realm, twisting the behavior of dragons who did not even suspect that the Enemy of legend lived.

After the Black Peak, Winterfall had emerged to assert his strength—and had called vocally for Windrush's leadership in the struggle. Now, in his deepest soul, he harbored terrible doubts about whether the dragons could prevail. But he would rather die than betray those doubts—or his own people—to the Enemy.

Heady with exhaustion, Windrush joined with Longtouch—a dragon whose clarity of inner sight and whose focus of thought were so keen that Windrush felt his own inner maelstrom settling and calming in the other's presence. Windrush had never joined with Longtouch before, and he was amazed at the silent wisdom that he found. Longtouch had no idea who the traitor was, but his mind blazed in search of clues. Here, Windrush realized, was one in whom he should place far greater trust. When he ended the union, he felt as though he were leaving the presence of a dazzling fire.

* * *

Four unions in a row was enough. Windrush's mind was ringing, but he was satisfied. "Leaders!" he called out. "I leave these four to continue the search for the traitor. I trust them completely."

"As we trust Windrush," called Stronghold, echoed by the other three.

The gathered dragons rumbled restlessly, but Windrush continued without pause. "I must now search elsewhere for knowledge that may be vital to us." Weary though he was, he felt an urgent need to continue his search of the underrealm.

Farsight's gaze touched Windrush's just enough to murmur silently, *(If you find FullSky again, tell him of our need.)*

(I think he knows already, better than we do,) Windrush said.

With a throaty rumble, he left the gathering and took to the air at once for the mountains north of the camp, and his cavern.

Chapter 20
WORDS IN THE UNDERREALM

FLOATING IN the dark, the troubled rigger-spirit was going crazy with the taunting of the cavern sprites. They seemed to be everywhere around him, plaguing him for no apparent reason.

"Can't make up his mind, he can't."

"Poor Hodakai." Giggle.

"Poor, poor Hodakai."

"*Shut up!*" he screeched, which only made them laugh and giggle all the harder.

They knew just how to get to him. Hodakai had been obsessed, lately, with trying to decide what to do about Rent, and the dragon. Rent was becoming increasingly hard-edged about trying to get him to join up with Tar-skel. The last time they had talked, Rent had warned him that if he did not agree to help soon, he might be cast from his present isolation into a spirit-dungeon that would be far worse.

That had made him angry. Angry and frightened and confused.

He didn't know what he was going to do.

In particular, Rent had been trying to convince him to entrap the dragon the next time the serpent made contact. Hodakai wasn't at all sure that this was something he wanted to do. It wasn't that he was feeling any particular affection for the dragon, but he didn't like the risk. He wasn't much of a risk taker, really—never had been—notwithstanding the one, eternally regretted time when he and his partner had stupidly gone looking for dragons.

Furthermore, there was something the dragon had reminded him of last time that had stuck in his mind: that it was the *Tar-skel* dragons who had imprisoned him here, then abandoned him. And the Tar-skel dragons were on the same side as Rent. Tar-skel controlled the power that could allow Hodakai to walk as a man again, as Rent was so fond of reminding him. But it was Tar-skel, really, who had stripped him of his body in the first place.

It was Tar-skel who had the power to enslave.

The power to free from slavery.

The power to embrace the entire realm in a web of sorcery that might never be broken, if the ambitions that Hodakai had heard trumpeted were true.

These were powers that Hodakai had once found fascinating, in a morbid sort of way. But upon deeper reflection, he now found them terrifying. They certainly didn't make him want to *trust* Tar-skel.

Hodakai scarcely knew what he wanted anymore. His feelings were increasingly at odds with everything he thought he had decided in the past. He found himself almost wishing that the dragon would visit him again, just so that he would be forced to make a decision one way or another.

"Hodakai, Hodakai!"

"Rent will be so . . . so . . . angry . . . !"

"*You* sprites, *SHUT UP! SHUT UP! SHUT UP!*" he bellowed, dancing furiously in his prison. He could not wait for the dragon to visit again.

It would be good to know at last what his decision was going to be.

Windrush's cavern seemed a place of cold silence, removed from the dangers of treachery and war. He knew, of course, that this could be a deadly illusion. His safeguards had already been breached, after a fashion, by the ifflings and by FullSky. A sufficiently sorcerous enemy, if it knew or cared about where to find Windrush, could probably defeat his guarding spells. Windrush watched two of the sweepers scurrying across the floor with his fallen scales, and he felt a momentary suspicion. Could these small creatures be spies of the Enemy? He smelled carefully in their direction, and found nothing but the smell of innocence. What did the sweepers care about the matters of the larger world? Their highest cares were about the shapes of the tiny scale-sculptures that they left about the cavern. Windrush noted a new one, a slender, bent-tipped pyramid of gleaming silver, in the corner.

Settling down, the dragon turned his attention inward. His mind was afire with images and worries, hopes and cares. Sleep was impossible. He let his thoughts sink deeper.

The underrealm was like a quiet, hissing ocean, after the distress of the outer world. The windows, all but one, remained exactly as he had last seen them, surrounding his cavern with opportunities to mystery and danger. The one exception was the passage that had led him into the wilderness with FullSky. That one was now missing, as if it had never existed.

He thought of the ifflings, and wondered if they had succeeded in reaching Jael. Whether they had or not, he knew he had to continue his search as best he could. Today Tar-skel had defeated them, badly. He had done so by knowing in advance what the dragons were doing, while the dragons struggled in ignorance. There had to be a way for Windrush to learn sooner of his adversary's intended actions. There just had to be.

Windrush turned, somewhat doubtfully, to the window that led to Hodakai.

The imprisoned spirit seemed even more agitated than usual when Windrush made contact. The dragon allowed his kuutekka to take form within sight of the rigger-spirit—which seemed only to alarm it.

One called Hodakai, why are you so nervous? Windrush asked, attempting to sound solicitous.

Ah, dragon—it is you, Hodakai said, twitching uneasily.

It is I. Windrush waited, hoping the spirit would settle down. *Have you given any more thought to our last discussion?*

The figure of light danced, becoming even more agitated. *What are you talking about?*

Windrush shook his head at the creature's excitability. *About the wisdom of choosing the right friends. Don't you remember? I believe I pointed out to you that your present friends were unlikely to be trustworthy in the long run.*

The spirit-flame became almost still. *I do recall something of the sort, I suppose.*

Windrush waited for the invective that would surely follow. When none did, he said, *I perceive that you have a certain sense of honor, Hodakai. It's a worthy quality.*

If you think to flatter—

Not at all. Why would you need it?

Then what—?

I was simply wondering if you'd become disillusioned yet with the other side. You see, they have no sense of honor.

Hodakai hmmphed for a moment. His spirit-presence seemed to bend in thought. *Tell me something, dragon.*

Yes?

What is it you want from me? I'll tell you right now that I can't help you find your precious Dream Mountain.

Windrush considered that assertion. It might be truth, or might not. But there was no good in trying to argue the point. *That is not the only thing we need,* he said finally.

What else, then?

The dragon took his time in answering. *It would certainly help us . . . to know more about the Enemy and his plans for battle.*

Hodakai laughed. *You don't want much, do you?*

Well . . . perhaps it is a lot. Windrush let a small plume of steam spiral up from the nostrils of his underrealm image. *But anything we can learn increases our chances of ridding the realm of him and his terror.*

The spirit-flame shivered. *I see. And, of course, you have in mind some benefit that I will see from helping you?*

Windrush rumbled with impatience. *You will benefit the same as the rest of us. I cannot promise you any reward, Hodakai. I cannot even promise you freedom from your spirit jar—except, possibly, for your flight to the Final Dream Mountain.*

The other says that he can let me walk again as a man, Hodakai sniffed.

So you have told me. And as you have pointed out, I cannot do that. Windrush paused. *But—*

What?

Think of the price you might pay for choosing the other side.

The spirit snorted, but did not seem altogether certain of itself. *What price, pray tell?*

Your garkkon-rakh, Hodakai. Your soul.

Hah. So you say!

Windrush hissed at the spirit, silencing him. *I note,* he said, *that you have not chosen the other's side, in all this time. I think you know that I am right. As I said, you do have a sense of honor. I will be truthful: on our side, it is possible you will lose your life. But at least if you fly to the Final Dream Mountain, you will do so with honor.*

Hodakai twitched, bending and straightening. He did not speak for a long time. Windrush, sensing that the spirit was deep in thought, did not interfere. Suddenly Hodakai made a stabbing movement toward him. *I can tell you this,* he hissed. *The danger is greater than you think. Far greater.*

Windrush exhaled silently. *What do you mean?*

Hodakai's voice grew stronger and harsher. *You are concerned about your petty realm here. But to Tar-skel, your realm is just one little stepping-stone to a much greater sorcery. Each victory here takes him a step closer to ruling space itself. You think of weavings in the underweb; I speak of great edifices of power being shaped—all so that he can reach out of this realm, out of the Flux, even into what you call the static realm. His ambitions are terrifying, dragon! You and your people are only pebbles to be ground underfoot. I don't think you can stop him. But if you're going to try, you'd better do it soon. Once his web is complete, you will never break it.*

The rigger-spirit fell silent, but his words seemed to ring on in the emptiness of the underrealm. Windrush's thoughts reverberated with memories of the lumenis vision, and warnings made by FullSky and by the ifflings. He did not doubt Hodakai's words.

And you are right about one other thing, Hodakai continued, in a softer voice. *Without the Dream Mountain, you have no hope. That is why he has hidden it from you. You must find it—before he becomes its master.*

Before? Windrush asked in surprise. *Does he not control it now?*

Hodakai hesitated, then shook his fiery head. *I don't think so, no. He holds it. But he is not its master. Not yet. At least, that is my impression. He seems to want something from it that he can't have.*

Windrush studied the rigger-spirit with no small astonishment. *Will you not help us find it?* he asked softly.

I told you. I do not know the way. I do not have the answers you want. Hodakai was starting to sound wary again, as though for a few moments he had mustered his courage, and now was losing it again.

Perhaps not. But you could watch. You could listen. You could tell us what you hear of the Enemy's plans. In that way, you could help us defeat him.

The spirit flickered. *I . . . perhaps, yes. But how would I . . . that is, you have not even told me your—*

My name is Windrush, son of Highwing, the dragon said abruptly—and in afterthought, added, *That you may call me, and to that I will answer.* He wondered if the spirit understood by his qualifying statement that he was not granting him full exchange of trust, but just the first step toward trusting one another. *I give you the sound of my name, Hodakai, though not yet the fullness of my being. We are now equal, in that respect.*

Windrush, the spirit repeated suspiciously. *Windrush. And how might I reach you?*

It is not safe for you to try. I will reach you. The dragon was suddenly aware of something shifting in the underweb around him—and of Hodakai becoming nervous.

Begone, dragon, the spirit hissed. *At once!* As Windrush cautiously began to withdraw his kuutekka, Hodakai screamed, *BEGONE, DRAGON! I WILL HAVE NOTHING TO DO WITH YOU! BEGONE, YOU DEVIL, YOU FOUL WORM!*

Windrush retreated hastily, breaking the contact. The underrealm seemed to swirl around him even as he pulled back from the connection. Something was approaching Hodakai from another direction, but he could no longer sense it. Was it the Enemy, or one of his servants?

Windrush drew himself back into his own lair, pausing at the underrealm window. Nothing seemed to be pursuing. Had he escaped without revealing his presence? Could he trust Hodakai to keep the visit to himself?

There were no guarantees, none at all.

Windrush secured the opening to the best of his ability. He sighed, trying to make sense of what he had learned. The Enemy did not yet control Dream Mountain. He knew he should rejoice—but his mind was too full of cares, and too tired. Perhaps he ought to get some sleep.

Unless an iffling showed up in the next few moments to distract him, that was what he was going to do. The moments passed, and no one, iffling or otherwise, came visiting. Very well, then. He closed his eyes—and he listened, as time stretched around him, to his own heartbeat. It seemed only to grow louder with each passing moment, and the cares dancing in his thoughts more urgent.

Chapter 21
AWAKENING

HER AWARENESS wavered about her like a holo going out of focus, its dimensional integrity flickering and holding for a fraction of a second, then disintegrating again. Jael was struggling to return to consciousness. But her efforts seemed disconnected from reality, somehow, divorced from her own mind. She felt herself gently rocked by aftershocks, distant gongs and pings, echoing through whatever . . . awareness . . . or reality . . . surrounded her. They were, she knew in some dim recess of her mind, aftershocks of the force that had hurled them to . . . wherever she was now. She felt the shock waves, but was separated from them . . . and from her companions. There was a boundary layer . . .

She felt that she was clawing her way upward through an endless sea, holding her breath, praying that she could reach the surface before her lungs burst. The surface shimmered out of reach, but she kept swimming toward it, trying to cry out, but unable to make a sound. She wanted to weep, not knowing where in this ocean she was, or if she was alone, or if she was even really alive. She was aware of pain, but it too was separated from her.

She heard someone calling her name, calling . . .

And then it all began to slip away. The voice faded. She felt herself sinking back into unawareness, into the quiet tidepool of the unconscious from which she had risen.

Jarvorus' recovery from the shock of passage came slowly. The stunned feeling of bewilderment was gradually fading. Whatever that enormous thing was that had hurled the human vessel across several layers of space and time, it had done so with an astounding force. Despite Jarvorus' abilities to skate across space-time boundaries, he was nonetheless amazed to find himself unharmed, and still securely ensconced near the vessel's power source.

As he regained his faculties, the warrior looked around for the others. The iffling was still there. It looked as though it too had been stunned, but was now awakening. He thought briefly of attacking, but he himself was hardly prepared for a fight just now. In any case, he felt a curious reluctance. He recalled his earlier feeling that there was something about this creature that he liked . . . that he wanted to understand. As long as the iffling did not interfere with his mission to lead the One where she was supposed to go, its continued life would not be a problem.

The human and her shipmate were glowing with life, as well, but not moving. They appeared not to be conscious. There was also that strange, cold light that flickered and rasped, the thing that seemed in a way almost alive, but not quite like any of the others. It was making odd hacking concussions now, which conveyed no meaning to Jarvorus.

Jarvorus turned his attention to the real question, which was, where were they?

He peered past the shimmering layers of energy that protected the vessel from the surrounding medium, and was startled to see a landscape full of sharp craggy rises and deep dips, and a multicolored sky. The ship was lodged against the side of one of those crags. Strong winds outside were making the ship shudder. There was something about the sight . . . something in the air that made him ache strangely, that made *him* shudder as well, that had nothing to do with the force of the wind. There was a sharp, challenging smell in the air that seemed to urge him to leave this vessel, to fly free. He felt, for a moment, almost as if he remembered this place. An image rose unbidden in his thoughts of an enclosed place of rock, a cavern—life winking in the crevices, most *un*warriorlike beings chattering and singing. The image puzzled him.

Was this home? He scarcely remembered his life prior to his time as a warrior. Had they arrived back in the realm of his origin, the realm he had been remade and reborn to protect? Jarvorus studied the landscape with wonderment, pausing only for an instant to glance in the direction of the iffling. It was glimmering with energy, apparently taking stock of its own situation. Was it reacting in the same way he was? Did it have memories of a past life here? He couldn't tell.

He knew that his mission was the opposite of the iffling's, and that troubled him. They had been together for so long, even as adversaries, that he could not help thinking of the iffling—and even Jael herself—almost as comrades of a sort. They had all just been through a great trauma together. He knew he should not be thinking such thoughts, but it was difficult not to.

In any case, his concern now was not with the iffling. He had other needs, and he was bursting with desire to explore this strangely wondrous and familiar world. And yet . . . he must consider his mission. If the riggers awakened, he had to be ready. Except that he was a little unclear about what he was *supposed* to do next. Even if they were in the home realm, he had no idea *where* in the realm he was, or for that matter, where exactly he was supposed to lead the riggers. Had he somehow forgotten—or was it a missing part of his instructions? He needed to discover his next course of action.

He was suddenly aware of an almost overwhelming urge to explore beneath the surface of the observable world. Perhaps this was no coincidence; perhaps that was where he would find his answers. If he could keep just a corner of his attention upon the iffling and the human, he could let the rest of his senses sink down into the body of this land, to search out the land beneath the land.

Even as he thought it, he felt it happening, as though it were something he was born to do. A whole new world opened up to him. It was not a world of open space like the wind and the rocks, but rather a vast, gloomy network of threads and passageways that seemed to lead in all directions. As he peered down one, then another, he glimpsed distant lights of life, winking in caverns. He trembled with a sudden desire to reach out, to discover who those lights belonged to. One of them was different from the others, more distant but far stronger, and now it seemed to pulse and beckon almost irresistibly.

Perhaps, without losing his present position, he could just reach out to it . . . make contact . . .

Jarvorus was startled to find himself suddenly, wholly, in the presence of that light. He had not meant to *jump*, only to reach—but it was as if the light had opened the pathway completely, and swept him in an instant into its presence. He felt a stab of panic. Would he be able to find his way back?

Welcome, my helper-warrior! cried the light, driving away his alarm. *I thought I felt your return to the realm!*

Jarvorus quivered with amazement and uncertainty. He felt that he ought to know this being, but he could not quite grasp the memory.

The light coalesced into an almost solid shape that, strangely, reminded Jarvorus somehow of the human rigger. In no way would he have mistaken it for Jael, but he could not help wondering if there was some sort of similarity between them. The light spoke again. *Do you remember who I am?*

Jarvorus struggled. *I think I . . . Are you the one who . . . ?*

Made you? Yes. Indeed, I am pleased that you remember, said the being. *I am the one who created you, made you over. With,* it added quickly, *the wisdom and power of the Nail of Strength.*

You sent me on my mission, Jarvorus ventured.

I oversaw your creation from the simple being that I found floating uselessly in a cavern, and I gave you your mission, and prepared you for your journey. You called me Master Rent, before you were born into that other world.

Fragments of memory drifted up into Jarvorus' awed mind. He recalled awakening in the other realm. And before that . . . he found vague memories of life in a cavern, with others of his kind, a gentler and less perilous life. Sometime in between, he'd experienced a time of terrifying transformation, when he'd been changed somehow, and imbued with specific knowledge and instruction and abilities, which had awakened in him upon his rebirth as a warrior. And that must have been when he'd learned of the Nail, and the treachery of the dragons. And now he was again in the presence of his creator and master!

What report do you have for me, brave warrior? asked Master Rent, studying him closely. *How have you and the other warriors fared? Do the others guard the human rigger now, while you report?*

Jarvorus was suddenly overwhelmed by shame and fear. *Master Rent*, he confessed, *I am the only survivor of the warriors. The others . . . fell to the ifflings.*

To the ifflings!

Only one iffling now remains, Jarvorus whispered. *The human rigger is . . . in the realm, but not conscious.*

The figure of light and shadow approached him, its voice deepening and becoming hypnotic. *Show me what has happened, Jarvorus.*

The warrior felt an electric touch between them. His memories from the other realm stirred in him, rising and flowing out to the one who made him. He did not speak, nor did he need to.

I see, Rent said, after a few moments.

The warrior-elemental could not tell if his master was pleased or displeased. *Should I have done something differently?* he asked timidly.

Rent seemed to consider. *I might wish that you had not let the iffling live. But even that could have its uses. I perceive that you struggled bravely, and you kept the mission paramount in your thoughts. No, it seems you did well, warrior. But—your work is not yet over.* The voice became harder. *Much remains for you to do.*

I am ready to serve, Jarvorus murmured, though a part of him wanted to cry out that he was tired, and surely he'd done enough already.

He sensed a great pulsing activity within the figure of Master Rent. He sensed that the master was thinking, and perhaps speaking to others, even as he was present here with Jarvorus. Was he planning the next assignment? Jarvorus felt a nervous anticipation—and a growing urgency to return to the vessel carrying the rigger Jael. The iffling was still there, and she should not be left unwatched for long.

You are going to lead the rigger Jael to a place where she may not wish to go, Rent said suddenly. *I will give you everything you need to do that. But I have something else for you to do first.*

Dare I leave the rigger alone any longer? Jarvorus asked weakly.

Do not question my orders! Rent snapped. *I will send others to guard the rigger—and when you return to her, you may command them. But first I require you to perform an errand elsewhere. I wish you to take the form of an iffling when you do so. Can you manage? You seem to have had ample opportunity to observe the ifflings.*

Take the form of an iffling? That would be easy enough, as long as only the outward form mattered. Jarvorus bowed in acknowledgment. As he did so, his master flared momentarily, and he felt the sudden, electric touch of Rent delivering words into his mind—a message to be delivered, along with a tiny spell of persuasion. He felt implicitly the instruction that the content of that message was none of his business. *Shall I bring the rigger Jael to you afterward?* he asked, meaning to acknowledge the instruction.

Rent darkened with anger. *You will not! You will do precisely as I say! Is that understood?*

Jarvorus bowed again.

Now then, snapped Rent, *I will explain what you are to do with the rigger. Pay attention! You will take her to a place I have selected, safe from the dragons. There she will be bound, so that her sorcery cannot . . . interfere . . . with our work. Until the time comes*—Rent paused. There was a certain breathless urgency in his instruction, which surprised Jarvorus.

Forgive me, Jarvorus said. *But surely you're not afraid that the rigger could hurt us.*

Rent's image flared, darkened, flared again. *What are you implying, warrior?*

Nothing, Master—nothing! Forgive me!

A bolt of lightning flashed through Jarvorus, stunning him more than hurting him. *Forgive you? growled Rent. In time, I may. But now, curb your insolence, or I shall return you to the life of a powerless sprite from which you came.*

Jarvorus waited fearfully.

The rigger Jael is a powerful sorceress. Until the proper times comes, she must be kept far from the powers and workings of the Nail. Is that understood? Furthermore, she must not be permitted to see or to speak with a dragon, or her powers may become magnified. Rent focused a stern gaze upon the warrior. *And you will keep her FAR FROM THIS PLACE, at all times!*

Then where—?

SILENCE! You are a clever and ambitious warrior, and that is to your credit—and mine. But you will listen in silence!

Jarvorus listened in silence.

There is a place prepared for her, a place known as the Pool of Visions. It is an ancient place of power, a place long forgotten by the dragons. It is a place where we will begin to take control of the rigger's ambitions and powers, and turn them at last to the final destruction of the dragon threat.

Jarvorus listened in growing awe.

Open yourself now and I will give you all of your instructions. I will teach you to change shape, to become as one more pleasing to her eye, to gain her trust. And I will grant you a power reserved for the most special of my servants. I will bestow upon you the "power of eyes"—a power never before granted to one of your kind. Open yourself, my warrior, and receive.

Jarvorus obeyed. Fearfully, excitedly, he bowed to receive the direct thoughts of his master.

It was a very long contact. When it ended, Rent seemed to become large before Jarvorus, and yet to draw back. *You are released to go. Those warriors who will serve under you have been dispatched. You may go to deliver your message. You know the way.*

For an instant Jarvorus thought to speak, then thought better of it. He felt light and dizzy with new thoughts. He bowed his flame in acquiescence and backed away from his master and creator.

Rent disappeared behind a veil of fog. Behind Jarvorus, the darkness of a passage opened, and he felt himself turning and jumping outward through the realm beneath the realm.

Hodakai was as nervous as a sprite keeping a secret. Ever since he'd talked to that dragon Windrush, he'd been out of his mind with anxiety. He had tried to escape into fantasies of rigging, but found it impossible. Here, he'd as good as promised Windrush that he would serve as a spy, but now he was anything but certain that he wanted to go through with it.

It hadn't helped to have the dragon's visit interrupted by Rent. It was positively demonic, the way Rent seemed able to sense when Hodakai was feeling anxious. He didn't think Rent had actually seen the dragon; but Hodakai was a poor liar, and knew it. Rent hadn't stayed long, had said he merely wanted to see how Hodakai was doing, and to offer him a little more time to make his decision. Hodakai was virtually certain that Rent had some other purpose in mind, but if so, he had gone away without revealing it.

Now, just a little later, Hodakai felt the underweb trembling with another visitor arriving. For an instant, he thought it was the dragon returning. But to his astonishment, what appeared was neither the dragon nor Rent; it was an iffling. An iffling?

The being floated in his presence like a sprite—but more than a sprite. It was more somber, and clearly more intelligent, than a sprite. It spoke his name softly, even in the quiet of the cavern, though there was no one else around to hear. *Hodakai*, it said.

Hodakai could not imagine why an iffling would visit him. He hardly knew what to say. Finally he just said: *Iffling?*

The thing floated closer. Something about it seemed a little odd, but he could not say what. The truth was that he had seen very few ifflings in his life, and for all he knew, they came in as many shapes and styles as humans in his own universe. This one glimmered with a particular intensity. *Hodakai, we must speak.* Though its voice was soft, it commanded attention.

About what? Hodakai murmured.

About your relationships with certain dragons, whispered the iffling.

D-dragons? Hodakai, though he had no body, nevertheless felt a breath-holding reflex take over. He pulsed with self-consciousness. *Wh-what dragons?*

Come, Hodakai. We both know about it. Why deny it?

Hodakai was stunned. How many people in this wretched land knew about it when he talked with Windrush? *I guess I have had some conversations,* he said finally. *But what of it? It was dragons who captured me. Why shouldn't I have conversations with them?*

The iffling glimmered. *I do not say that you shouldn't, Hodakai. Far from it. But the question is, do you understand how they are planning to deceive you? That's what I came to warn you about.*

What do you mean?

For a moment or two, the iffling remained silent. It floated before him, making him very nervous. He had no great love for ifflings, but when it came down to it, the one thing he'd always heard about them was that they were truthful. Irksome, yes. Capricious, yes. A nuisance, yes. But truthful.

Hodakai, are you aware that the dragons have summoned another human to this realm?

What?

And that they have done so for the sole purpose of cementing their private stranglehold on this world?

You mean the Tar-skel dragons?

Listen to me, Hodakai! I'm talking about the dragons who oppose the Nail!

Hodakai fell silent before the flamelike iffling. He was stunned, and bewildered. If this creature was speaking the truth, then he had just been made a fool of by Windrush.

Don't you see that they're planning to betray you?

Who?

The dragons who have been visiting you! They're trying to enlist your help against the other side, aren't they?

But I thought— He hesitated. *Well—*

The iffling pulsed.

Hodakai felt as though a cottony web were closing around him. *I suppose, yes, they are,* he said dully. *Not that I've listened to them.*

Of course not, because you are perceptive. You sensed that their purpose in seeking your trust, in appealing to your better nature as a human, *is to further enslave you.*

I . . . Hodakai struggled to find words. It was Rent who was trying to enslave him, not the dragons—wasn't it? Or was it the other way around? Why couldn't he think?

Hodakai, we ifflings are a peaceful folk. But one thing that makes us angry is untruthfulness! These dragons claim to fight for freedom. And yet, they seek to enslave an innocent person like you!

Hodakai bobbed in confusion. It was true that the dragons had always made him suspicious. They always seemed to want something, but never could he remember them offering anything in return. They controlled his life and his death. Except for a few pitiful spells they had left in the cavern, he was helpless here.

Unless, of course, he joined up with the other side.

Hodakai—you must not be without hope.

What do you mean? Can you free me?

Not I. You. You can free yourself, replied the iffling. *Free yourself from bondage. Defeat them at their own game. Join with those who would never betray you!*

Hodakai felt his soul churning. Who was he to believe? *I always thought you ifflings and dragons were friends! Why are you coming and telling me this, if you're friends? I don't get it.*

The iffling floated backward for a moment. Hodakai felt an odd rustling in the underweb, and for just an instant felt a breath of clarity. A moment later, the iffling floated toward him again, and that cottony feeling returned. *You must understand. To us, right and truth are more important than passing friendships.* The iffling's voice sounded aggrieved. *It is true that we have had friendships with dragons. But when those same dragons abandoned truth, in favor of their own selfish wants . . .*

Almost against his will, Hodakai found his own anger returning—a very old anger. Anger against those who had trapped him in this universe and killed his only shipmate. He remembered all the times that dragons had lied to him, promising to set him free, and humiliated him, before leaving him here alone to rot with the cavern sprites. And to think that he'd almost decided to trust one of them! That worm Windrush—if that was even his real name!

If you're wondering what you could do—

Yes! he cried.

The iffling drew close. *If you have their trust already, there are many ways to deal with betrayal. May I suggest that you treat them as they treated you.*

They're liars, Hodakai whispered.

Indeed. And I suggest that you reflect their own lies back upon them. My guess, Hodakai, is that they have asked you to serve as their spy.

Hodakai acknowledged with an embarrassed flicker that that was true.

Then you hold a potent weapon in your hands, rigger-spirit. When they come to you for information, give them misdirection instead. What better way to help us end this struggle!

I don't care a damn about the struggle, Hodakai said. *I'll tell you that right now.*

Nor do we. Except to end it.

Hodakai was startled. *Well, if that Windrush tries anything . . .*

The iffling brightened at the sound of the dragon's name. *You are wise, rigger. Most wise. If I may be so bold as to make an offer . . .*

Of course.

We would be pleased to provide you with misdirection to thwart the dragons' efforts. Would you like us to do this?

Yes. Thank you, he whispered.

You are welcome. I trust you would not mind if, on occasion, we passed this information to you through an intermediary? Such as your friend Rent?

Rent? he thought in amazement. *Rent? But I—I don't—*

Be assured that you may trust Rent implicitly.

I— His words choked off, leaving him speechless. Rent? He was going to have to trust Rent? Perhaps he had misjudged the man. Was it possible that the iffling knew more about Rent than he did?

Is that agreeable? the iffling asked.

Hodakai, feeling slightly . . . stunned . . . finally flickered his assent.

Thank you. And now, Hodakai, I must go. You will hear from us again soon.

So long, Hodakai whispered, as the iffling slowly faded into the underrealm. He stared after it for a long time, before turning his thoughts inward. As he remembered Windrush, his thoughts burned with humiliation. He had come so close to agreeing to help the dragon. Well, he would show it. Yes, he would. Truth and justice, not dragons, would prevail if he had anything to do with it.

Jarvorus slipped through the underrealm like a breath of wind, returning by an instinct he didn't even know he had, directly to the place where he had left the riggers unconscious in their cocoons of energy. He was mystified, but pleased, by his successful mission on behalf of Master Rent. In his guise as an iffling, the words had come to him as needed, welling up out of his unconscious like waters from an underground stream. Rent, exactly as he had promised, had provided him with everything he had needed to deliver the message to that terribly strange rigger-being, Hodakai—along with the ludicrously simple spell of persuasion.

If he didn't precisely understand the reasons for that mission, he put the question out of his thoughts now. He had his primary mission to think of, and that was to lead Jael to the Pool of Visions.

Emerging from the underrealm near the spaceship, he found all as he had left it—except for the presence, glimmering in the hills on all sides of the ship, of the new warrior-sprites sent here by Rent. They were watching, doing nothing. Excellent.

Jarvorus moved past them to take charge once more.

Chapter 22
A BATTLE IN THE DARK

It SEEMED as though half the night had passed, by the time Windrush gave up on sleep and blinked his eyes open to the dark form of the draxis in the cold hearth. He sighed. It was useless. There was too much to do, too much to learn. Too many duties weighing on his mind, including the many dragon guardian holds he knew he ought to inspect as leader. He thought of the minor lumenis groves throughout the held land, each with loyal dragons standing watch; and the Grotto Garden of the Forest Mountains, to the south, perhaps the only surviving dragon garden in the realm; and the Deep Caverns, far to the east, where powerful, ancient spell-weavings were now only a memory, but a potent memory . . .

And yet with all these places to visit, he knew that the place he had to start was right here in his own cavern. There were two more underrealm windows that he had not yet explored.

He stretched, unkinking his neck. He let a breath of steam rise toward the ceiling, then blew a flame into it, warming the cavern. Finally he sank back into the underrealm and smelled about for spies or intruders. Satisfied that he was alone, he considered his next action.

Of the two windows, he was tempted by the one that smelled of woodland and salt sea. But something seemed to tell him that it was not yet time to look that way; there was something he needed to see first. He felt himself drawn toward the window of glowering underground fire. He didn't know why. But he sensed that someone, or something, was calling him from that dark place.

He smelled the sulfur, even before his kuutekka was fully

formed in the window. Stretching his thought out through the weave of the underweb, he found himself entering what seemed a labyrinth of underground pathways, a maze that seemed to increase in complexity as his thought ranged out, trying to find an underlying pattern. It was a place of darkness, and somewhere in the distance, a place of fire. He smelled danger. It made him think of the Enemy, but he did not think that this place was a creation of the Enemy. Perhaps, he thought, it was a natural feature of the underrealm that now bore the mark of the Enemy's passage and use.

Windrush felt more than a little anxious as he probed down one pathway, then another. Would there be drahls? Would he find Tar-skel, waiting to draw him in to his death? He fought to clear his thoughts of such questions, to keep from radiating his apprehension like a beacon through the underrealm. He wished he knew what he was looking for, or which direction to look.

After a time, he returned in discouragement to a point near where he had entered, and he rested in silence awhile, listening. Eventually he heard sounds he had not noticed before, sounds such as might be heard deep in the earth, traveling from great distances. He heard groans, as of stone rubbing ponderously against stone. He heard trickles of running water. He heard voices, so soft that he could not even distinguish whether they were dragon voices or something else. He heard footsteps, tiny running footsteps and slower walking footsteps. They might have been the steps of innocent sweepers underground, or of the Enemy's heaviest servants; the distance so confounded his hearing that it was impossible to tell. None of them seemed to be drawing near. He sensed distant threads being drawn through the underrealm, and knew that somewhere magic spells were being crafted. By friend? By foe? It could be either. It could be both.

After a time he began to grow restless, but something in the back of his mind told him to remain still and be patient. And so he remained, listening to the sounds as they came and went. All were almost impossibly faint, and it was only through his utter silence that he was able to hear them at all.

In time he heard a new sound, a voice that he recognized as distinctly dragon. *Windrush.* He remained still, listening. A trap? Or a friend? *Windrush.* He tensed, but again held his silence.

He felt a sudden stirring of air around him, and detected a sharp new breath of sulfur. The voice, the third time, was louder—*Windrush!*—and he recognized it with a gasp of relief.

Here, he whispered at last. *Where are you, FullSky?* He strained to distinguish from which of the various passages the voice was coming.

Follow that one, FullSky whispered, when his gaze brushed a twisting pathway from which the faintest red fire seemed to glimmer. *Move carefully, and keep a guard about you.*

Mindful of the enemy presence that had intruded upon his previous encounter with FullSky, Windrush moved silently down the passageway, his kuutekka stalking like a cat along the cold wall of the passage. The passage turned and twisted, and descended. It descended a very long way, it seemed, and Windrush paused twice to peer back uneasily in the direction he had come, listening carefully. The only thing he heard was, twice, FullSky's whispering voice urging him on.

He lost track of time, moving like a spirit-being through the meandering passageway, lost track of the turns, and of the distance he had descended. He was startled to realize that the faint reddish illumination had grown brighter, to become a dull, ever-present glow suffusing the air before him. It seemed angry, threatening. Beneath the smell of sulfur and smoke, there was an undersmell that made him hesitate, made him want to turn and flee. It was the smell of the Enemy. He hesitated.

Just a little farther. Please. I cannot help you if you don't come the rest of the way. It was FullSky's voice, quiet, urgent.

Windrush took a slow breath. He floated forward and rounded one last bend in the path. His breath escaped in a gasp. He had expected to be surprised, and even frightened—but he had never dreamed of the sight that faced him now. The passageway opened into a great cavern. The floor of the cavern was split by a tremendous, gaping fissure that glowed and flickered as though from a deep subterranean fire. The air seemed to rise in shimmering waves.

Windrush, I need your help.

Startled, the dragon lifted his gaze to peer through the shimmer of the air, to the far side of the crevasse. There he saw FullSky's kuutekka, wavering almost as dizzyingly as the air. He looked only half solid, and yet his presence was terrifyingly real. It was his familiar, almost-glass face, with dark hollows where his eyes should have been. It was a haunted-looking face, a face that seemed almost beyond pain. It seemed that FullSky's kuutekka emerged from an opening in the cavern wall. Windrush could only glimpse his brother's hindquarters and tail, but it appeared that he was being crushed under a heavy slab of stone. Did his kuutekka reflect his condition in the outer world? The dark emptiness of his eyes seemed to be focused directly upon Windrush's, but the waves of heat made them appear to dance and veer.

FullSky, Windrush whispered, *what is this place? What are you doing here?*

His brother's great, glassy head swung back and forth, as if he were struggling to get a clear line of sight—or as if he were ducking from something. Windrush caught sight of a tendril of fire whipping around FullSky, lashing him as he moved. Windrush crouched instinctively, making his kuutekka ready to spring. But which direction? He couldn't tell if the whipping fire was holding FullSky where he was, or punishing him. After a moment, it seemed to burn itself out, leaving the younger dragon gasping in pain. *Please help me!* FullSky whispered. *I am trapped here!*

Windrush hissed into the dancing air. Though that thing of fire was gone, he felt danger jangling all around him. There was powerful sorcery at work here, without question. A sorcery of Tar-skel? How could he hope to fight that? *How can I help you?* he hissed, voicing the doubts that swirled in his thoughts. *Where are we? What am I seeing?*

The air steadied for an instant, and he saw clearly the pain etched into FullSky's face. *Dark Vale!* FullSky gasped. *The Enemy's dungeons. A Watcher holds me. If you could— defeat it—I might yet—!*

Before he could finish, an arm of fire erupted from an opening in the cavern wall and whipped around his head and neck, blazing bright and choking off his words. This time the fire did not fade, but instead grew, until Windrush realized that he was looking at an entire living being—a creature of fire—one moment a single, flowing serpentine shape coiling about the dragon's head, and the next a lacing of fiery strands, each one sprouting a head, and biting and lashing at FullSky's kuutekka.

Instinctively, Windrush shrank into a defensive posture. What was this thing? The Watcher? The name *fire-drahl* sprang into Windrush's mind; he had a sudden vision of a natural being of the underrealm, altered and twisted by the Enemy. If it wasn't aware of Windrush yet, it would be soon. It was clearly punishing FullSky; it was enraged, driving him back toward the cavern wall, back from the crevasse, and back from Windrush.

Help me! came FullSky's almost silent cry.

Windrush drew a difficult breath. What could he possibly do? FullSky's skills were far greater here than his own. He felt fire building at the back of his throat, but he had never felt so helpless. What powers could he control in the underweb to defeat a thing of fire? He could project an image of fiery breath—but could a being of fire be hurt by fire?

He groaned with uncertainty as he crouched, separated from his brother and the Enemy's servant by the gulf of subterranean fire. FullSky was struggling, no longer crying out. Was he trying to keep the Watcher from noticing Windrush, so that Windrush could strike? But how? If he made the wrong move, if he misjudged the Watcher's powers . . . Windrush imagined himself like his brother, his kuutekka imprisoned here while his body struggled in vain to bring back its spirit. And if he were imprisoned or destroyed here, how would he be helping dragonkind, or the realm?

Windrush, please! his brother gasped suddenly, breaking free only for an instant before a new whippet of fire lashed him.

If it was his brother, and not a trap. Windrush felt a sudden, shuddering doubt. He had been deceived by the Enemy's sorcery before . . .

Help me! the dragon-kuutekka pleaded. *Free me—to act—!*

Windrush rumbled. For his brother, he should risk anything . . .

He strained to catch FullSky's gaze through the wavering air, but there was too much heat in the air—or perhaps a sorcery of obscurity. Bringing himself to the brink of the chasm, he drew a weaving in the underrealm with his thoughts, trying to create a transparency in the air. It worked: he felt a change in the underweb as the air turned clear. The other dragon seemed to harden into solidity, and its gaze, glowing out of the dark hollows of its eyes, glowing fiercely across the chasm, linked directly with Windrush's. Windrush felt the sudden rush of the other's thoughts into his, felt his mind spiraling madly into the maze of pain, searching for the heart of the mind, the garkkon-rakh. He found it, found his brother FullSky crying desperately, *(Windrush, hurry!)*

Windrush's mind was filled with images caught from FullSky, but there was no time to look at them. The Watcher was rising, turning, expanding toward him, its fire brightening. It had felt the change in the underweb, too, and if it hadn't seen Windrush before, it did now. Its rage crackled in the air, violet-red fire lashing toward its new enemy. Windrush leaped low and hard over the chasm toward FullSky, his kuutekka floating weightless. Fire flashed over his back, and into his vision, blinding him—and more than blinding him.

Everything seemed to change in that instant. It was as though he had passed into a new level of the underrealm—where he was blinded, and yet he saw, by a kind of ghostly spirit-illumination. The fiery chasm below had come alive with luminous, writhing figures—living spirits crying out from where they were held captive. Windrush was aware, too, of another living spirit—the Watcher, encircling him with great arcing tentacles of blazing power, around and above and another coming up from below. In another heartbeat, it would have him tightly in its grip.

Instinctively, Windrush dove—downward into the chasm, darting past the arm sweeping upward. He made it past, but as he dodged away, peering in horror at the writhing spirits imprisoned far below, he felt the lash of flames on his back. He fled sideways, and up—and as he sought escape, he heard a wordless, crackling anger that made him shudder. He turned and saw the face of the Watcher, a hole of darkness surrounded by fire; he knew that it was a devouring spirit, and he was the one it meant to devour.

A snake of fire flashed above him, and he dodged downward again. He was being forced back down into the abyss, toward the other prisoners. He was growing dizzy, and was having trouble controlling his movements. Where was FullSky now? He felt as if his kuutekka were being pulled from its anchor. He must resist! *FullSky!* he cried. *What is it doing? How can I fight it?*

Above him finally he glimpsed the presence of his brother, imprisoned in arms of cold lightning, unable to move—but able to see, to call out. *Windrush, change your form! Change!*

What? Change his form? His kuutekka?

Keep that which is you, Windrush! Guard your garkkon-rakh! Don't let it distract you!

But how—?

*You must outwit it, you must out-*believe *it!*

Even as FullSky spoke, Windrush could see the Watcher begin to change *its* form. It was becoming a great meshwork of fury and fire, coalescing into the shape of a many-headed serpent, lashing its head one way and then another, cutting off Windrush's avenues of escape. Its feet were rising from below, fiery talons glittering. Windrush felt his fear tightening. Keep that which is you . . . what did FullSky mean?

No time to think. Windrush imagined himself smaller, imagined the shrinking spell that the demon Hodakai had once used on him. He dove away from the Watcher's fire-spitting head, and an image came to him, and without even thinking about it he transformed his kuutekka into a small, fast flyer called a bat. He shot past the whipping head of the Watcher, easily evading it, then swooped back up, high above the fires of the abyss, and circled, warily eyeing the specter that had attempted to trap him. He suddenly realized where the image had come from: it was from his memory of the rigger Jael's thoughts.

He had just done an astonishing thing, turning his kuutekka into the shape of another being! He had done as a rigger did, changing his form in the underrealm! He did not even know what this animal was, except that he had once seen Jael imagining and taking on the form of one. The Watcher raged and hissed at him as he dodged its flame. Windrush veered left and right, up and down, streaking to the top of the cavern and diving back toward the abyss, evading the Watcher with a great zigzagging swoop. He felt a rush of joy in his success.

The joy evaporated a moment later. Overhead, the Watcher had turned itself into a huge, fine-meshed net, a living web of flowing silver, with no openings large enough even for a bat to fly through. He fled to one side and along the edge of the flaming chasm, desperately searching for an opening, and finding none. He dropped lower, toward the imprisoned spirits. The net fell after him, dropping closer and closer. Furious with himself, he sped back up to meet the net of the enemy. If he couldn't escape it, he might at least hurt it. Another Jael-image surfaced in his mind: a sleek, silver, water creature with a long, sharpened beak. He became the image, and as he met the net, climbing, he lashed his beak ferociously back and forth, slashing at the mesh.

Fire exploded around him, and he felt an intense flash of pain. The cavern and the abyss flashed dark and bright, and his vision went black for a terrifying moment, then returned to that strange, ghostly light of battle with the

Watcher. He tried to ignore the pain as he fought against the net—until he realized that he was already through it—he had sliced an opening and was careening back toward the ceiling. The pain was gone.

The danger was not. A great blanket of blackness was swarming upward to meet him. It was not just something black that was stopping light; it was a being that was devouring light, and he could almost feel the coal-red glow of the abyss being swallowed by it.

He circled warily, watching the creature rise. How could he fight something that destroyed light itself?

He flitted from side to side, despair rising in his heart. How great was this thing's power? If he changed his form again, the Watcher would do likewise. Didn't it ever tire? He glanced across the cavern and saw his brother FullSky, forgotten by the Watcher, etched in a cold, hollow light, struggling to rise from the place where the Watcher's fire had chained him. Another image sprang into Windrush's mind.

As the black emptiness rose to meet him, Windrush became a fire-elemental. He felt himself burning into flame, like an iffling, sacrificing all bodily form. He struggled not to panic, not to think: The Watcher is already winning. Then the panic vanished as he felt strength rising in the heat of his flame, like the strength of a dragon who has just eaten of lumenis. This was the strength of pure fire, the strength of hope . . .

For an instant, he even believed that this was not just his strength alone, but someone else's combined with his. A power reaching to him through the underrealm . . . FullSky's? His father's?

The thought fled as the blackness rose and engulfed him. The cavern vanished, and his brother with it. His hope vanished, too, and as darkness swarmed around him, he felt the bone-biting cold of despair. The heat of his fire was gone. From the numbing silence of the blackness, he heard a harsh laughter, ringing in his consciousness. Then his consciousness began to fade.

Keep that which is you!

The memory of FullSky's words brought him back from the abyss of utter, eternal darkness. *Keep that which is you.* He remembered how, moments ago, he had been burning with blazing fire, the light and heat of his strength, his hope. The blackness had swallowed the fire, made him forget it . . . distracted him . . . but had not quite extinguished it. He reached within, found a flickering spark within the darkness of his soul, and determinedly blew it back to life: a flicker of light, a tiny flame against the devouring darkness.

Laughter screeched again through his mind, deafening him and filling him with dread. The flame flickered and guttered.

Do not let it distract you.

NO. I burn with flame.

His spark shot up hot and bright against the darkness. He felt it lock in mortal combat with the darkness, the living darkness of the Watcher's malice. If there was to be a victory, it must be a victory of light against dark. Flame against darkness.

His flame blossomed.

The cold of the darkness fought back; it was a living breathing hating darkness, a knowing and raging darkness, and it was determined to strangle the flame, to kill it. The darkness had the power to imprison countless souls; it was the darkness of death. How could he possibly overcome death?

With a sudden intensity—as if someone had just passed the memory to him—he remembered Jael's fierce determination when she'd flown into the static realm to rescue Highwing. It was an impossible mission with no hope of success, with only death awaiting her and her friends. But she'd won nevertheless, she'd saved his father, allowed him to die bravely, allowed his spirit to pass to the Final Dream Mountain. *You must outbelieve it.* As Jael had outbelieved the odds.

No, hissed the darkness.

Yes.

Windrush drew his strength from somewhere, and not from himself alone; he knew, unshakably, that his flame could burn brighter and hotter than the strength of any darkness. The flame of his kuutekka, of his garkkon-rakh, of the soul of his very being, welled up and burned with a fierce white heat. He felt the darkness recoil from it, felt it recognize a power that it suddenly realized it could not withstand. An image flashed in his mind, and he knew now that this was how more than one iffling had stood against the darkness. He burned hotter, brighter; he *believed* that his light would prevail. He knew he was no longer alone.

The blackness screamed in anguish and shrank away. The Watcher's soul was in the blackness; it had never imagined that its power of terror could fail. Windrush pursued it, growing even brighter. He knew that he alone could not be burning so brightly; and if the help was coming from his brother, or from his father in the soulfires of the Dream Mountain, or from the ifflings, he didn't know or care. The light was blinding now, filling every corner of the cavern.

The underweb burned with the strength of his light. The Watcher, locked into its blackness, coiled inward upon itself. It flickered madly. With a last convulsion, it shrank and vanished before the light.

Windrush's power faded in intensity. With considerable effort, he drew himself painfully back into the ordinary form of his kuutekka. The ghostly light that the Watcher had cast over the scene of the battle was gone.

The darkness was gone. The lines of fire that had encircled his brother were gone. But FullSky was still etched in light, glowing against the far side of the cavern. *My brother, thank you,* whispered the dragon of light. He no longer seemed paralyzed or crippled, not here in the underrealm at least.

FullSky rose from the stone floor and floated toward Windrush. The far wall was visible through him. *I can join you now in the battle.*

Can you escape? Windrush asked, barely able to speak.

Not in the outer world. My body will never leave Tar-skel's dungeon. But here in the underrealm, I will fight as I can. You may not see me again, but we will be struggling together, and we will be together again in the Final Dream Mountain. The glowing being that was his brother seemed to breathe upon him then, to touch him with its light.

Windrush shivered as a thousand images cascaded into his thoughts from FullSky's mind, then disappeared into his unconscious like a basket of stones dropped into a pool. He shivered, unable to make any sense of the images; but he knew he would need them before this struggle was over. He felt FullSky draw away.

You must flee now.

Windrush struggled for breath. *FullSky, wait!*

There is no time. You must flee, before you are found. The dragon of light that was his brother drew back across the abyss and gazed at him just once more, before fading away through the cavern wall. The cavern suddenly seemed very empty, except for the glowering abyss of spirits. And from that chasm, Windrush heard a rising murmur, like a rushing of wings, the sounds of spirits freed, flying away through the underrealm to whatever Final Dream Mountain awaited them. He suddenly realized that he had prevailed not just for his brother, but for all of those others, whoever they were. He had a feeling that they were about to erupt before him like flames from a forest fire.

You must flee now.

A deep thrumming sound was growing to fill the cavern, a rumbling from some distant place. A hot wind seemed to be rising, blowing in his face. Something or someone was coming to investigate the source of the disturbance in the underrealm.

Windrush departed with the speed of thought, his kuutekka shrinking to a tiny spark of light, bright but fleeting in the gloom of the passageway as he fled from that place forever.

Chapter 23
VOICES IN THE WILDERNESS

AGAIN SHE heard someone calling her name . . .

Jayyyl . . . Jayyylllll . . . Jayyyllll . . .

There was something very familiar about that voice, but she couldn't quite awaken enough to make the connection. She was in an ocean, swimming, struggling toward the surface . . .

Jayyll, awwwk—are you there? Wake up, Jayl!

The dancing-mirror surface drew near, at last. She strained, kicked, lungs burning bursting struggling not to expire, reaching up, arms and fingers stretching . . .

She touched the surface and it shattered in liquid silence. The boundary opened then, and a cacophony of sound exploded. A parrot was screaming, hurling itself back and forth in a damaged rigger-net, trying to bite and claw its way out. Ed . . . Ed . . . its name was Ed.

She suddenly remembered . . .

The web . . . ship out of control . . . had to regain . . . impossible . . . ! She remembered now the slamming force of the thing that had launched them, ejected them across space and time, and she'd thought she was dying.

Even now she wasn't certain that she had not died.

She could not seem to move or talk.

Is this what death feels like?

Ar—was Ar alive? Or was he with her . . . in death?

Nothing seemed quite right here. Ed was flying around violently, trying to reach her. She could almost touch him. They were so close now . . . and yet she could not. The rigger-net seemed to be torn somehow, keeping them apart. She could not see Ar, or hear him, or tell if he was alive.

JAYL . . . ?

Jayl . . . ?

Jayl . . . ?

The parrot's cries echoed down through several layers of separation in the net. As she probed, she finally heard the parrot's voice directly. *Jayyyl!*

Ed! she croaked.

The parrot screamed and flew straight toward her, growing larger and larger and finally imploding into her vision. *(Jayl!)* he cried, within her mind. *(Ed!)* she whispered joyfully. She felt his thoughts swarming around hers, felt him looking out through her eyes.

She blinked, suddenly aware that there was an outside reality. Where were they?

She focused her eyes on a mountain landscape. The ship had come to rest on a steep slope, nestled against a crag of some sort. They were motionless, except for vibrations from the wind. She could not be sure, but it certainly looked like the mountains of the dragon realm. As she craned her neck to look around, she half expected dragons to appear out of the clouds. But she saw nothing moving except snow, swirling in the wind.

She remembered Ar's reaction the first time they had arrived in the realm together and been dumped on a snowy slope not too unlike this one. He wasn't going to be much happier now. But where *was* he? Had he left the net?

She couldn't tell with any certainty, but there was a *weightiness* to the net that made her think he was still here with them. The net felt fragmented, in a way she had never experienced before. It occurred to her that perhaps she should withdraw and regroup with her shipmates outside the net. But first she wanted to learn all she could.

She took a deep breath and called: *AR?*

There was no answer.

She felt Ed, still trapped inside her mind, frantic with joy that she was alive—and in terror over what was happening. Having gotten into her head, he seemed unable to get back out. Perhaps if she withdrew from the net, he would be freed—and she could begin to make sense of things.

Her first effort to withdraw told her at once that something was wrong. The net quivered, but did not yield. The way out was blocked somehow. She tried again, and the net trembled but did not yield. She couldn't see what the problem was, but it frightened her. This shouldn't be happening. *Ar?* she whispered. *AR? Rarberticandornan?*

The only sound was a low rumble in the background, a neural interference that suggested something wrong in the physical projection of the net itself. She couldn't identify its source, but she sensed that she might not be able to exit the net until it was corrected. She fought back a fresh surge of fear. What if they were all trapped here? Stop it! she thought sternly. There were many possibilities—and one was that Ar was already on the outside, trying to help her.

(Ed, can you hear me?) she whispered.

She felt the parrot fluttering in her thoughts. *(Awwk,)* he croaked, in a voice taut with fright. She glimpsed images of his fear—memories rushing up of a time when he had been trapped in the wild, imprisoned in a cage, drained into a data nodule. His fear resounded like the tapping of a snare drum. *(Awwwk-k-k. What hap-p-pened? Jayl?)*

(I don't know,) she murmured. She found the situation nearly incomprehensible. But she remembered that Ed had bridged some sort of barrier in coming to her. Maybe he could do that again. *(Ed? I need your help.)*

(Aw-w-w-wk. Y-yes-s-s.)

(Look for Ar for me. I can't see him—but he may be in the net somewhere, trying to reach us. Can you move around at all? Can you reach outside of where I can see—and tell me if you hear him, or see him?)

(C-c-can't, Jayl.)

She shuddered at his feeling of helplessness. *(Try, Ed— please? We're hurt. I don't know how badly, yet. But I can't see Ar, and maybe you can reach into areas where I can't. Please!)*

(Urk-k.)

She sensed the parrot cocking his gaze about uneasily, trying to spot openings that his human riggermate could not. It all looked rather foreboding. But now there was a shadow, way off to one side. Could that be Ar, in another part of the net? She felt Ed moving his thoughts that way;

then she felt a sudden, fluttering release. Ed had found a way to stretch beyond the limits of her thoughts. Good! She decided to let him do what she'd asked, while she looked elsewhere.

Her gaze went back to the mountain wilderness outside the net. There was something in the air that she could almost smell, that told her that this was dragon country. But whether it was *friendly* dragon country was another question altogether.

There was one way to find out, of course. "Cry, 'Friend of Highwing!' and I will hear you, though all the mountains lie between us," Highwing had once told her. Highwing was gone now, but his son Windrush had renewed the vow.

Did she dare? She was helpless, if hostile dragons came along. But she was helpless anyway.

She took a shallow breath, and barely whispered the words: *Friend of Highwing . . . friend of Windrush . . .* Her voice caught. She swallowed hard and forced her voice to rise to a croaking cry. *I am . . . Jael . . . friend of Highwing . . . and Windrush!*

The landscape sighed with emptiness. If there was anyone out there to hear her, she couldn't tell. Even if there had been, she could hardly expect her pathetic cry to carry far. She drew a ragged breath, determined to shout this time.

Before she could make a sound, a voice hissed: *Do not cry out again! It is not safe!*

She choked in astonishment. It was not Ar's voice, but it was familiar. She thought it was the voice of . . .

The creature materialized in front of her before she could complete the thought. It was a creature made of fire, gathered into a vaguely dragonlike shape. It floated in the air just above the boulder against which the ship rested. It had an ethereal and magical appearance, and yet it pulsed with an urgency that seemed personal and immediate. When it spoke again, its voice seemed to float like a whisper of wind in the night. *You must not reveal yourself yet. We will show you the way.*

Jael hesitated. *Who are you?* she asked, though she

thought she knew already. She thought it was an iffling, though it did not look quite like any she had seen before. Did ifflings take on dragonlike form?

You know who I am, said the being.

Jael frowned. *Are you the . . . iffling . . . who told me to come here? Are you the one who visited me in the other . . . in the static realm?*

Of course. And I have been with you ever since. But now we must see that you continue your journey, without being led astray.

Am I in time? she wanted to cry. If it was not safe to call out openly, did that mean that her friends were in hiding against danger? Her voice trembled as she asked, *Can you tell me, iffling, what is happening here? How are the dragons faring against . . . Tar-skel? How are Windrush and his brothers?*

The iffling seemed to flicker for an instant. *Your questions will be answered soon. But right now you must follow me! We are in great danger!*

Jael didn't know if it was even possible for her to move. She couldn't tell much about the state of the rigger-net, except that it was damaged. And she wasn't even sure that she herself was in any condition to fly. *I don't know if I can move.*

You must! hissed the iffling. *Without delay!*

Jael shivered. She supposed she hadn't come this far just to give up because they'd gotten banged around a little. *Ed,* she called softly, *if you can hear me, keep trying to get through to Ar. I'm going to see if I can get us moving again.* She felt a flutter of acknowledgment.

Drawing upon some inner strength she barely knew she had, she reached out through the net to touch the rocks beneath her. They felt solid and icy cold. The ship, behind her, was a massive extension of her own body. She nudged it hesitantly, to see how difficult it would be to move. To her surprise, it *did* move—it felt like a great, empty balloonlike container behind her, nearly weightless, but with great bulk and inertia. She thought a moment, then began to change the image of the ship, shrinking it down behind her. At least she still had that much control.

Hurry! urged the iffling.

Jael frowned and gave another experimental push. The ship felt heavier—probably an illusion caused by its greater compactness. She refined the image: the ship became a backpack, strapped to her shoulders and waist. She would try to walk . . . and carry it. Taking a deep breath, mindful of the iffling's impatience, she took a tottering step forward. She felt traction on the rocks under her feet, felt the movement of the ship's mass behind her. She stepped carefully, descending to a more level stretch of rock—not quite a path, perhaps, but passable.

Ahead of her the iffling floated, bobbing and glimmering, beckoning.

The iffling-child struggled to revive itself. Whatever had hurled the ship into this place had nearly destroyed the iffling in the process. But now all seemed quiet. This *was* the realm of the dragons, the iffling felt, though it could not have said how it knew. It had, after all, been born into life in the realm of the humans. And yet . . . there was something here that touched its mind and said: *Home is nearby.*

But where, exactly? The iffling was having trouble perceiving space clearly, as though there were splintered layers of underrealm obscuring its vision. It sensed the human rigger, still alive, but the iffling was separated from her by one of the layers of brokenness. The other, nonhuman rigger was present and alive, too, and somewhat closer to the iffling; but that one had not yet returned to full consciousness. The ship, nevertheless, was moving—under Jael's shaky control. And Jael appeared to be following someone . . . someone whom she took to be an iffling.

She was following the enemy, the false-iffling.

You must not, you are being misled! the iffling cried out, but it knew that its words had not carried far enough to be heard. It was certain that the false-iffling was leading Jael astray, taking her in a direction that was intended to thwart her true purpose. What exactly the enemy was up to, the iffling couldn't tell. But it was not taking her to Windrush, that was clear.

The iffling called out again, but there was no indication that it was heard, much less understood.

If it couldn't reach Jael, could it do something about the enemy, the falsifier of truth? Probably not. The iffling was too weak to fight—and now it glimpsed more distant pulses of light outside the ship. More false-ifflings, joining the other? If so, the true-iffling would have to be even more careful. But the false-one seemed unconcerned about fighting, or about the true-iffling at all. It seemed concerned only that Jael follow it.

Follow it in its lies.

There seemed little the iffling could do. It wondered if there were others of its own kind here, others who could help. Perhaps so—but it dared not leave Jael to look for them. That left the other rigger, the one called Ar. Perhaps it could make contact with that one. *Rigger, awaken!* it called softly, reaching out. *Rigger Ar, you are needed!*

There was a stirring in the rigger's mind. The iffling felt a spark of hope. *Rigger Ar, you must awaken! You must speak with Jael!*

There was a fluttering of wakening thoughts. *What? Who's there? Jael?*

The iffling's hope brightened a little. *Jael cannot hear you. You must listen, rigger! Listen carefully . . . !*

Ar had awakened to a nightmare. He was alone—where? He felt no physical sensations. His mind was awash with images of serpents and fire-beings and moving mountains—and the distant, frantic squawking of a bird—and now a voice calling in a whisper out of the darkness of the void. He was enclosed by darkness, and by a web . . .

You must listen, rigger!

He was abruptly conscious, the image of the web and the darkness gone. A voice was calling to him. Where was he? He was encased in a kind of layered translucency, the remnants of the rigger-net, separated by prismatic fracture zones, which seemed to enclose him like a cocoon. He could not see very far, or move at all. Off to his right, through the translucent barrier, he saw a shadow moving.

He thought it might be Jael—but it looked like a figure walking. That made no sense. He called out to Jael, but there was no answer.

There was that squawking again. Ed? Ar looked in all directions, but couldn't see the parrot.

Rigger, there is danger! You must help me speak with Jael!

The voice again. *I cannot speak to her,* Ar whispered back, his words full of a deep sadness that he had not even been conscious of until now. *I cannot reach her. I do not know why.*

The voice answered, *It seems there has been a . . . splintering . . . around you.*

Splintering? Like cracking ice? Once, years ago, they had intentionally caused such an effect *outside* the net, breaking through an icelike boundary layer in the Flux. But now the net itself seemed to be splintered. This was an alarming realization. Their once-gleaming, newly tuned rigger-net was in ruins.

Worse, he discovered, he could not leave the net to analyze and correct the problem. His presence and Jael's, and perhaps even Ed's, were blocking the way out from each other, like shards of broken glass choking a drain. And yet . . . the ship was in motion. He could see a snowy landscape outside, moving past with painful slowness. He could tell that someone, no doubt Jael, was guiding the movement. But where was she going? Were they in the dragon realm?

She is being led astray, whispered the voice.

Ar blinked. He was still in something of a state of shock, and it had only just hit him that he seemed to be speaking to a ghost. *Who are you?* he demanded.

Iffling, he heard, and in the same instant he caught sight of a tiny flame through one of the spidery fracture patterns that enclosed him. The bit of fire flickered, as though in weariness. He wondered if it was trapped, too.

Jael? he asked.

Alive . . . but I cannot reach her.

Ar nodded. *Are you trying . . . to get us to Windrush?* He remembered that Jael had spoken of other voices, confusing and conflicting voices.

Windrush, yes.

Then who is leading her now?

A false-one. False-iffling. The creature flared for a moment. *You must reach her! Warn her!*

False-iffling? Ar let out a weary breath and set about to see if there was some way he could reach Jael. The damage to the net was profound, and it would take a great deal of work, and probably luck, to repair. He hoped it was possible; he hoped he could do it before it was too late.

Past another fracture-layer in the shattered prism, he glimpsed a shadow of a bird fluttering its wings. He heard again a distant crying and screeing. Perhaps he could make a connection that way, and work onward to Jael. *Ed!* he called. *Ed, if you can hear me—fly this way!*

He couldn't tell whether the parrot heard him or not. But the damage in that direction seemed less intractable. He began tugging at nearby folds of the net, attempting the impossible task of fusing the shreds back together again.

The wind swept a haze of snow across the landscape, like blinding sand. Jael had been picking her way along a winding, descending trail. She paused on a level patch to heft the ship on her shoulders. It felt extremely odd to be carrying the ship like this. She still had no idea where in the realm they were, or where they were going. She tried to scan the landscape; but the obscuration of the snow shifted, moment to moment, giving her only fleeting glimpses of the wider land. She really had no choice but to follow her guide and hope that, sooner or later, the view would clear.

She felt Ed moving about, trying to contact Ar. She felt sure that the Clendornan was here, that it was just a technical problem keeping them apart. What was *that?* An echo of Ar's voice? Perhaps . . . but now it was gone again.

The iffling reappeared through the snow, glowing and pulsing urgently. *Follow,* it whispered. *Follow quickly. We must hurry.*

She sighed and followed. The snow parted to reveal the ground at her feet, then closed again, leaving her to walk in blindness.

* * *

Stay back! Jarvorus commanded. *Do not interfere with the ship!*

The sprite-warrior flickered and moved away from the shimmering form of the human ship's manifestation. The rigger herself was visible at its prow as a complex interplay of light and shadow. Deeper within the ship, half concealed by veils of light, were the large nonhuman rigger and the small one, and the iffling. Something had happened to the weave of space, causing it to entrap them in its tangled shreds. A fold of space seemed to have emerged from the underrealm, intruding itself into the curious structure of their net, keeping them apart. Jarvorus had not planned such a thing—it was an unexpected result of their violent entry into this realm—but he found it useful.

Jarvorus had decidedly strange feelings as he led this procession. Several times now, he had had to warn his helpers away from the ship. He did not want the human, or any of the others, injured. The sprite-warriors were hastily altered cave sprites who had little of Jarvorus' knowledge and wits. It was good that they followed his command; he could imagine the havoc that they might wreak otherwise. But he was determined to conduct his charges safely.

He ducked close to the ship. *Follow!* he urged the human. He sensed her hesitation as she tried to renew contact with her fellows. *Hurry!*

The image of the rigger flickered and shifted and stretched into motion, the ship floating over her. He began leading the way again. It was not that much farther, he thought. Not much farther at all to the Pool of Visions, and to the trap that awaited.

Chapter 24
FREE IN THE UNDERREALM

As FULLSKY had hoped, it was the Watcher's strength that became its undoing—transforming itself into a living darkness, a thing that swallowed hope and turned it to despair. But its darkness could not stand against a dragon transformed into light. In the moment of the Watcher's death, FullSky felt a tremendous release. His body might remain crippled and chained by the Enemy, but his spirit, his kuutekka, was freed from the oppression of the Watcher's power.

The weaving he had prepared in secret came together now, threads of the underweb whirling and tightening. His heart leaped for joy, as the physical pain of his body was bound out of the weaving of his kuutekka. He couldn't abandon his body altogether, but he could stretch out from it. He rose from the floor of the cavern, his senses yearning to reach out into the pathways of the underrealm beyond.

He crossed over the chasm of spirits to where Windrush, stunned, was struggling to understand what he had done. FullSky touched his brother's kuutekka, and Windrush's thoughts reached out to him in bewilderment and joy. Could FullSky escape and join the others? he wanted to know.

FullSky wished he could answer yes—but that was impossible. His role in the struggle lay elsewhere. There was much he might yet do, but only if he moved quickly, before the Enemy knew that he was free. He was skilled at crafting spells in the underrealm, but his power was no match for the Enemy's, if that one came after him directly. And if his body were destroyed? He had no idea how long he could survive then. Perhaps not at all.

Windrush, I do not know if you will see me again. But I will be fighting alongside you. We will be together again in the Final Dream Mountain.

FullSky—!

Realizing how hopelessly slow words would be, and how fleeting their safety here, FullSky probed directly into his brother's thoughts. He saw there the hope for Jael's appearance; and he saw also the bitter disappointment of the dragons' failed attack, and the frightening destruction of the lumenis. And he saw Windrush's futile efforts to find the Dream Mountain.

He would give Windrush such hope as he could—in images that he knew might not reach Windrush's awareness at once, but would surface in their own time. He showed his brother the blow he had just struck against Tar-skel's web of power—freeing many spirits along with FullSky, and thereby breaking one small strand in the Enemy's web. It would perhaps set the Enemy back only a little, but every hope was precious. Even small setbacks could delay the completion of the web. *Windrush, you are not alone,* he sang softly. *I'm sorry to have put you at risk—but believe me, you are not alone. And now you must flee!*

He pulled back from his brother's kuutekka. *Flee now! Flee before you are found here!*

Windrush gazed at him in amazement. FullSky blinked once, and departed back across the chasm of spirits. He peered back as Windrush turned away, up the pathway though which he had come. FullSky tugged at the weave that had kept that pathway open. There was a shifting of the underweb, and the path vanished as though it had never existed. Another similar opening appeared in its place, leading to another part of the realm altogether. If the Enemy came searching, FullSky hoped that that detour might, for a little while, lead him astray.

In the chasm, the spirits of the captured dead were swarming out of their imprisonment, perhaps in flight to the Final Dream Mountain, perhaps elsewhere. They were making a considerable disturbance in the underrealm. This was good, FullSky thought. The distraction might give him the cover he needed.

Passing out of that place, he hurried back to his anchor point and the beginning of his own journey.

FullSky did not leave the Enemy's lair at once. He wanted to learn what he could of the Enemy's activities nearby, and this might be his only chance.

He was floating in the dungeons of the Dark Vale. In the outer world, he knew it was a blasted landscape, filled with craters and honeycombed with spaces into which captives were crowded, half embedded in stone. Here in the under-realm it was a place of brooding powers, throbbing with glowering light. There were few shadows in which to hide. He would have to move about like a luminous ghost in a place that reeked of poisonous fires. Fortunately, the Enemy and his servants were preoccupied with their own sorceries, and they probably never imagined that a spirit of the opposition might be moving freely through the under-web of their dungeon. If they sensed his movement, he hoped they would dismiss him as one of the harmless dead, freed from the chasm.

In this level of the underrealm, the dungeons were a vast, open network of caverns and cells, separated by slender pillars and archways and glowing, fragmentary walls of melted-looking stone. The captives floated like trapped, luminous fire-beings, anchored in their bodies. Most had no evident awareness in the underrealm, though a few seemed to peer dully at FullSky as he floated past. Some of the captives were dragons caught in battle; others were dragons who had voluntarily joined with Tar-skel, only to learn too late that their standing in his realm was not what they had hoped. Many were not dragons at all, but shadow-cats and sprites and slope-climbers, and other beings that he did not recognize.

Guardian spirits moved among them like drifting lanterns—brighter, but often no steadier, than those they guarded. These guardians were witless and slow, compared to the slain Watcher, but still quite capable of sounding an alarm. FullSky moved with care, keeping his radiant presence close to the glowing walls. Since he could hardly float into the underrealm presence of the Nail himself and ask what was happening, he wanted to see if he could decipher anything of the Enemy's plans from the spells that were woven here.

It was risky. The Enemy would soon realize that a part of his web had come unraveled, that some of the strength stolen from captive spirits was gone. And in time, FullSky's kuutekka would be noticed. But he didn't intend to remain long.

Drifting along the walls, he memorized the shapes of the threads and lines and seams of the sorceries that held this place together. He had no specific idea what he might do with the information, but any knowledge was potentially useful. Indeed, if he learned enough, he might eventually find a way to free some of his fellow captives. But he dared not try that now. It was the Enemy's larger spells that he wanted to decipher. Most of all, he wanted to pursue threads he had glimpsed before—threads that might, however indirectly, connect to the Dream Mountain.

Still, he could not resist an urge to skim close to the nearest captives, wondering if he might recognize anyone. He did not—at first, anyway. But wherever he could do so without attracting attention, he brushed the thoughts of the captives and offered a silent whisper of defiance and hope against the pain.

He had nearly reached the end of the caverns when he caught the first undersense of something, or someone, familiar. It took him a few moments to locate it, on the extreme far end of this last cell: a flickering spirit that somehow seemed to shine with greater stubbornness than most. It must, he thought, be a dragon recently captured—someone still hoping against all odds for escape.

FullSky drifted across the bottom of the cell toward it. Several outerrealm guardians, likely drahls, were clustered around the captive; but they displayed little or no awareness in the underweb. Perhaps he could move just close enough to probe the captive with a tendril of thought. It was indeed a dragon, he realized. He gently touched it—and almost cried out with surprise. *WingTouch!*

He fought to maintain his equilibrium. WingTouch back in the Enemy's grip? Both WingTouch and Farsight had been freed by the breaking of the Black Peak sorcery. How had WingTouch been recaptured? Hovering perilously close to the guardians, FullSky struggled to think. Had his brother been seduced back? There were no threads of entanglement or deceit around him. WingTouch was throbbing with pain and anger. He had been captured, then—captured fighting. FullSky touched his brother's throbbing mind and felt it shudder with confusion. WingTouch felt his presence, but didn't yet know who he was. WingTouch had indeed been taken in battle, but the Enemy was trying now to persuade him to become a traitor. That was the source of the dragon's anger, and of much of his pain. He burned, even now, with defiance.

That, at least, was good. Very good.

But did he dare identify himself to WingTouch? It might bring him hope. But it could also be dangerous, if WingTouch were closely questioned by the Enemy. FullSky moved cautiously about his brother's presence. WingTouch had little skill in undersensing. How strong a contact would it take? He dared not make too large a disturbance. He approached closely enough to feel a growing turbulence in WingTouch's thoughts.

The anger was intense.

The pain was terrifying.

He could not leave his brother without speaking, no matter the risk. He called, softly, *WingTouch.*

The dragon's mind jerked, startled.

FullSky watched for any reaction on the part of guardians, and remained ready to flee.

Who is it? WingTouch peered around helplessly in the outerrealm, but kept his cry of pain to himself.

FullSky drew closer still and whispered, *Do not speak aloud. It is FullSky. I am here with you.*

A tide of rage and anguish exploded from WingTouch's mind. *FullSky! I do not believe that you are a traitor!* he hissed, barely containing his words. *But if I learn that you are, I will kill you myself!*

FullSky was stunned. Why would WingTouch think him a traitor? He drew back to watch for ripples in the underweb. When there was no sign of awareness by the guardians, he slipped back in, probing WingTouch's memories. In a few moments, he found the Enemy's false accusations. He answered: *The Enemy is lying. Never doubt that.*

He gave WingTouch an image: a dragon bound in stone, its head held high, fire flaring from its throat. He meant it as a symbol of his own adamance against the foe, but also as an encouragement to WingTouch, fellow prisoner of Tar-skel. His brother stirred uneasily at the image.

I cannot help you now—but I will try later, if I can find a way, FullSky whispered.

WingTouch struggled in his bonds, with a startling ferocity. FullSky, like most of the others, had been broken and crippled physically soon after his capture. But as he probed in WingTouch's thoughts, he guessed that the Enemy was saving him, apparently hoping to seduce him back, or to intimidate him into betraying the rest of dragonkind. But why was the Enemy bothering? Could it be that Tar-skel was more insecure about his victory than he would have had others believe? Was Tar-skel afraid of the ancient prophecy, even now?

In WingTouch's heart, FullSky saw a strong defiance— but also something else, something that had not existed in his brother's heart before, but was just beginning to take root: a tiny grain of despair.

It was hardly surprising. FullSky remembered how long it had taken him to grow out of his own despair in captivity. But time now was short. His brother might not have the luxury of growing out of his despair. WingTouch knew the state of the dragon companies, and much of the thought of their leader. The Enemy would not permit him to remain defiantly silent for long.

Still, the Enemy's insecurity was cause for hope. And FullSky had to convey that hope to WingTouch—to extinguish that grain of despair before it could grow larger.

The enemy is lying, he whispered. *His victory is not yet assured. There is still hope—always hope!*

His words drifted into WingTouch's mind, but if they were having any effect, he could not tell. The guardians suddenly moved closer, flickering with a more intensive attention. He was forced to pull away at last, leaving his brother behind.

He would return later, if he could. Perhaps he could find a way to help his brother; but in the meantime, he could only trust that the seeds of hope he had planted would grow—that WingTouch would survive, somehow, intact.

The underweb trembled with the approach of more drahls. Perhaps they were coming to torment WingTouch, or to question him. FullSky longed to stay with his brother. But there was nothing he could do with so many of the Enemy's servants about. And the most important thing now was to survive, himself, and to learn all that he could.

To learn, if possible, of the Dream Mountain.

It was time to move on.

He floated regretfully away. But it was not long before he glimpsed, through an opening in the glowering cavern, the very thing he had been looking for. It was a meandering thread, apparently vanishing into the mists of the under-realm. But just above it, a presence shone through the mist, like a diffuse beam of light. It was not an actual image, but he was sure that he recognized it. He had glimpsed it before, from the dungeon—but now he saw, for the first time, the faint pathway that might lead there. That thread, he was sure, led to the sorcery that kept the secret of the Dream Mountain.

He hesitated only an instant; he had been lingering here long enough already. Gathering himself, FullSky caught that path and fled from the cavern like a spark into the night.

Chapter 25
READINESS FOR BATTLE

WINDRUSH AWOKE to the sight of several sweepers scurrying away from the latest of their creations—a tiny sculpture at the edge of his hearth. He squinted as the little creatures vanished into the hidden crevices of the cavern. Muttering to himself, he studied their handiwork. Made entirely from his own fallen scales, it featured a small, conical, mountain-like shape raised above a flat, horizontal surface by a slender arm fashioned from pinched dragon scales. The flat surface was dull and rough, the color of dead, faded scales; but the object shaped like a peak had been polished to a bright silver.

Windrush puzzled over the structure for a few moments, trying to draw some meaning from it. Were his diminutive houseguests making these structures with some intent directed at *him*. Did they somehow sense his search for the Dream Mountain? Was this supposed to be a representation of the Mountain? If so, he could not decipher what he was to learn from it.

He felt a rush of weary annoyance, and drew a breath to blow the thing away, so as not to be plagued by such questions. Before he could do so, he heard a sudden rustling, and a squeak. One of the sweepers, a tiny creature with oversized eyes and ears, and a long tail, crept out of the shadows and pushed the sculpture along the ledge, toward Windrush—almost as though offering a gift. Windrush held his breath, then finally let it out softly. Very well. The sculpture could remain.

"Creature, do you wish to speak to me?" he murmured softly. The thing squeaked just once, then darted quickly out of sight. He could have sworn that the squeak had been a sound of approval.

Because he had saved its handiwork? There seemed no way to know.

Windrush stretched, as other questions crowded the matter out of his mind: the memories of last night, when he had enlisted Hodakai as an ally, when he had fought in the underrealm to free his brother FullSky. It was rushing back to him like a dream. But it had been no dream: one of the four windows in the underrealm was now gone. He was greatly cheered to think that, whatever else had happened, he and FullSky had struck a blow against the Enemy—and FullSky, in some way he did not understand, was now free.

FullSky had touched him, in the dizzying aftermath of the underrealm fight—but to impart what? Windrush's memories of those moments were confused; he thought FullSky had been more intent upon communicating *hope* than information. And yet, beyond the hope had been an uneasiness. Was Tar-skel preparing another attack?

Windrush could not recall anything specific, except an awareness that the Enemy was gathering his power and momentum. And this: that the dragons must be prepared for dark days to come, and must guard against fear.

He could not do that alone. It was time to rejoin the others. He had been fighting in silence and privacy long enough this day.

The sky was striated blue and pale green, and crisp with morning chill. Windrush swallowed airborne particles of lumenis that glittered on the wind, as he soared southward toward the dragon camp. It was, he thought, a good day for replenishing, for building hope.

At one point, as he snatched at the glowing bits of lumenis, he thought he heard a voice whisper in his mind, calling to him. Another lumenis magic? When he listened again, it was gone. He could not say whose voice it was, but it made him think of Jael. Was she returning at last? He longed to hear the answer *yes*, but there was no answer in the air.

He flew hard to the camp, and arrived to find the grounds

quiet in the morning stillness. But Rockclaw was up and out, and he hailed Windrush with grim urgency. Windrush strode across the grounds to speak with the gnarled dragon. "Did they find the traitor?"

"Stonebinder," Rockclaw barked, as though he'd been waiting all night to pass on the information.

Windrush vented his breath in a hiss. "Stonebinder?" That was disturbing news indeed. Stonebinder was one of the leaders of the guardian-spell dragons—a friend of SearSky, but one who had served well enough, though to be sure he had been heard to complain from time to time of the Enemy's superiority. "Who found him?"

Rockclaw spat sparks onto the ground. "He betrayed himself. Fled when it was getting close to his turn." The recorder dragon looked furious. Windrush had never seen him so angry.

"And was he stopped?"

"No!"

Windrush drew half a breath.

"He waited until there was a commotion over the testing of SearSky—*the fool*—"

"SearSky?"

"He objected to the testing, said that—forgive me, Windrush—that you and your leaders were full of yourselves, and you had no right to test dissenters—"

"We tested everyone," Windrush rumbled.

"Of course. We all knew that. But SearSky made a disturbance about it, and that was when Stonebinder escaped." Rockclaw gouged the earth with his front nails, as if he might somehow draw Stonebinder back through sheer force of will. His eyes glowed with anger. "Many gave chase, of course. But he was quick with a spell, and eluded them." Rockclaw drew a raspy breath. "Windrush, I am sorry to present you with bad news again."

Windrush scowled about him at the sight of the camp: the harsh cliffs with dark warrens in which warrior-dragons slept, the charred face of the target wall, the shreds of cloud drifting overhead. This was hardly a fit place for dragons to live; it looked more like something the Enemy would create. But for many who had joined in the war from the east and the south, or who had fled from the land taken by the Enemy, or whose caverns had been destroyed, this was home. And now even this place was threatened—by a traitor who could share the secrets of the defenses with an enemy who already held the advantage in the war. "He carries the spells that protect the lumenis," Windrush murmured, so low in his throat that Rockclaw could hardly have heard him.

Nevertheless, the old grey dragon nodded.

"Is that all?"

"So far. Farsight can tell you more, perhaps, when he returns."

"Returns?"

"He led a search party to the Scarred Ridge, in case Stonebinder hid instead of flying all the way to the Enemy. I have little hope of that, myself." Rockclaw stamped the ground and glared about the camp.

"And what of SearSky?" Windrush asked sharply.

Rockclaw peered at him with dusty eyes.

"Are we certain that SearSky did not create a distraction so that Stonebinder could flee? Was SearSky actually tested?"

Rockclaw's gaze sharpened. "I do not know, Windrush. But SearSky was among those who joined in the search."

Windrush grunted. It did not prove SearSky's innocence that he had flown with the searchers. He could as well have been trying to protect his friend, the traitor. But Windrush had no proof of that, either. He did not much like SearSky, but that didn't make the arrogant fool a traitor.

"Farsight called for another meeting tonight at dusk," Rockclaw added.

Windrush nodded and turned away.

"Where will you be?" Rockclaw called.

Windrush paused in thought. "I intend to visit some of the guardian holds. I'll be back for the gathering tonight." He was tempted to inform Rockclaw of the battle he had fought for the freedom of FullSky; he saw the hunger in the old dragon's eyes for any good news. But, he thought,

Farsight ought to be present for the first telling of that. "I believe a new attack may be coming," he said finally. "But all is not dark. You must keep hope, Rockclaw. Be my ears and my eyes here. If there is news or rumor, bring it to me. Can I count on you?"

Rockclaw's eyes flared. "When have you doubted me?"

Windrush nodded. "Then good-bye for now." He spread his wings and flew into the air as one driven by silent need.

Windrush traveled far that day, dropping down to speak with dragons on the ground, even in the smallest encampments and groves. Twice he flew for a time with patrols that he met in the air. He flew southward along the Scarred Mount Ridge, to a patrol camp near the south border of the held land, and asked for news of Jael, or of drahls, or of any stirrings of the Enemy. There was no news, only dread; but he did what he could to provide encouragement to the dragons there.

If only he could linger a while longer in these places! He was aware of a profound sadness for what could be lost in this war; and at the same time, an unreasoning hope was growing within him, and an admiration for all of the dragons who remained ready to fight and perhaps die for the realm.

Flying on to the east, he wished that he could visit the whole of the realm today. It was impossible, of course. Some strongholds were too far away for one day's efforts. From a promontory at the edge of the Forest Mountains, he gazed south toward the Sawtoothed Ridge, just a jagged shadow on the horizon. It was deep in that desolation that he had found Hodakai alone in his prison. Windrush could not help thinking wistfully of the places of abandoned magic that lay that way—places once frequented by dragons, but now too remote to be guarded. In the Streams of Song, fast-moving brooks made music in the ground; and there, in times past, draconae had gathered to share song and history. And at the Pool of Visions, dragons in a previous age had joined garkkon-rakh to garkkon-rakh, drawing upon the soul-shaping power of the pool as they sought wisdom from one another. In the Moon Sea, to the south and west, the moons could at times be viewed passing *beneath* the realm. It troubled him to leave such places undefended, but what choice did they have?

There was one place of lost magic that the dragons *did* hold yet—the Deep Caverns, far to the northeast, at the extreme edge of the realm. There the currents of the underrealm had once run deep and strong, the strongest outside of the Dream Mountain itself. There, wielders of magic once created innumerable works of beauty. But the Deep Caverns' significance, too, lay in the past. Most thought that the power had gone out of the place; others believed that the dragons simply had lost the skill to use the power that was there.

But in Windrush's heart, the Deep Caverns held a place like that of his father's magical garden: a wistful memory of something that had been beautiful and precious. He'd insisted upon their defense; yet he could not defend them heavily, not with vital lumenis groves to guard, and so few dragons to guard them. He doubted that the Enemy would trouble himself with an attack there, unless maybe after all else was won. Nevertheless, he thought, the dragons guarding the caverns deserved encouragement as much as any. Perhaps tomorrow, he would visit there.

But this day was wearing on, and he had one more important stop before returning to the main encampment. He flew northeastward over the Forest Mountains, toward the Grotto Garden and the last known dragon egg.

The Grotto Garden was a deep, wedge-shaped vale, well hidden in the northern flanks of the Forest range. Banking inward, he was challenged by two guard dragons. Recognizing him at once, they escorted him to a landing near the upper ridge of the vale. "Windrush! I was beginning to doubt that I would ever set eyes upon you again!" cried Greystone, the leader of the guards, a dragon whose seagreen eyes always reminded Windrush of his brother WingTouch's. "Have you come with news, or with need?"

"I have come to see how you are holding out," Windrush answered. "And to look in upon Treegrower, if she will see me."

"Hah!" Greystone snorted. "Do you think she is so feeble she would turn away the leader of the draconi?"

Windrush blew a breath of steam. "I hope not. How is she? And how are *you*, my friend?"

Greystone arched his wings, then shrugged them downward. "How am I? Not as well as I used to be, when we flew for the joy of it and thought the lumenis would never end! But I guess I'm better off than most of you battling the Enemy head-on."

"You guess?" asked Windrush, with a fleeting wistfulness for the carefree days when he and Greystone had flown together with other fledglings to hear the teachings of the draconae. If they had known then what they knew now, how much more they would have valued those times! But Greystone, more than most, had taken the teachings to heart. He had never been much interested in fighting, though he believed passionately in guarding such beauty in the realm as he could.

"Well, it is awfully quiet here, Windrush. Not that I'm complaining!" Greystone led the way down into the garden, pointing his head one way and another, as though to ensure that Windrush would see how well the place was being preserved.

It was, indeed, a reassuring sight. Windrush stopped to peer at a cluster of bushes with purplish, upturned cups for leaves. The cups held a clear liquid which drew floating insects and several small, colorful flyers that hovered, sipping the nectar. The flyers reminded Windrush of Jael's rigger-friend Ed. He watched them thoughtfully, aching to know what had become of Ed, and Ar, and most of all, Jael. After a moment, he blinked and turned to follow Greystone.

Passing a swirling pool in a rock basin, and a row of lantern-trees, Greystone continued downward into the vale. He nudged a shadow-cat out of the way with a good-natured swing of his snout and continued down the path toward the carved-rock grotto at its bottom. Windrush paused a moment, as the shadow-cat peered out at him from beneath the low-hanging threads of a curtain-tree. The cat was practically invisible, but its eyes blinked alternately like stars winking on and off. Windrush returned the creature's gaze, and for an instant, felt a linkage. The cat, too, felt the encroachment of darkness over the land, and Windrush sensed a plain and poignant desire in its simple heart for the dragons to make the darkness go away. *We will try,* he answered silently. *We will try.* The eyes brightened for an instant, then vanished under the tree.

Greystone swung his great head around to peer questioningly, and Windrush strode after him.

The grotto at the bottom of the vale was a graceful series of openings in water-carved stone. It held within its breadth a cluster of arching, cavelike spaces. The dracona Treegrower was resting inside the third of those spaces. Her glassy head was raised, gazing at the two draconi as they approached. "It seems to me you are *always* complaining," she said to Greystone in a softly chiming voice.

"Hah!" rumbled the dragon. "Are you eavesdropping on my conversations again?"

The dracona's golden eyes turned to Windrush. "Certainly not. I've no wish to die of boredom." She sighed deeply. "Windrush."

"Treegrower," he answered, bowing his head.

"You never come anymore."

Windrush felt a flash of regret, though he knew her remark was half teasing. "I'm sorry. I try, but—"

"Nonsense. Too busy fighting to worry about draconae and eggs. Do you come with news?"

Windrush studied the dracona, her eyes luminous gold, but dimmed with age, and cloudy. A few rays of the afternoon sun penetrated the cave to refract through her gemlike scales, but there was a dusty look to her. She looked older and weaker every time he saw her. If she were not the only living dracona outside the Dream Mountain, and therefore fiercely determined to survive, he was sure she would have given up and fled to the Final Dream Mountain ages ago.

But Treegrower was the caretaker of the last egg, laid not by her, but by the dying dracona Moonglass, shortly after the disappearance of the Dream Mountain. Moonglass had not lived, but Treegrower had—and she'd vowed that this egg would survive, despite the fact that it could only grow and hatch in the Dream Mountain. Were there other eggs in the Mountain? Perhaps—but no one outside the Mountain knew for sure.

"Not news, perhaps, but encouragement," Windrush said. His gaze dropped at last from Treegrower's eyes to the polished silver sphere she held protected between her front legs, a sphere about the size of her nose. So small—and so vital to all of the hopes of the realm! How long had she protected that egg, and how much longer could she do so? He tried to dispel doubt from his voice as he spoke. "I come with hope," he said at last. "I have felt my father's presence, more than once, from the Final Dream Mountain. And I have found hope in the underrealm. And . . . Jael . . . may be coming."

Treegrower studied him. "*May* be coming?" Her eyes blinked and shifted to peer longingly out of the cave. She was so weak now, Windrush realized with a pang, that she would find it hard even to leave the cave. "I labor within, to keep hope alive," she whispered, as though to herself. Under her breath, he heard her murmuring words, probably of prophecy. Her gaze shifted back to Windrush. "Hope in the underrealm, you say?" she asked, her voice cracking. "Can you tell me—?"

—*before I die, hopeless?* he seemed to hear, under her voice.

At that moment, he forgot his resolution to tell Farsight before anyone else. Cautioning both Greystone and Treegrower to silence, he told them of his battle in the underrealm, and of FullSky's freedom. "I don't know what it means, really," he said—and stopped trying to explain. His words suddenly seemed unimportant, because Treegrower's eyes had indeed come alight with hope, genuine hope. He glanced at Greystone, who seemed more guardedly encouraged.

"Thank you, Windrush," the dracona sighed, her voice chiming more clearly than it had since his arrival. She blinked her eyes and nodded slightly, and he sensed that it was time to let her rest.

"Be well, Treegrower," he said, taking his leave. Speaking to Greystone on his way out, he warned the guardleader about the danger of Stonebinder's defection, then said, "Keep her well, my friend. Whatever else you do, keep Treegrower well to see the return of the Dream Mountain."

Greystone's sea-green eyes flickered, and he exhaled a flame in reply.

Windrush returned to the encampment late in the day and found that the search parties had come in without any news of Stonebinder. Apparently the traitor-dragon had fled to join his Master. Farsight was organizing the night's patrols, and it was a while before Windrush could speak privately with his brother. When he did, he questioned Farsight about the events of last night. His brother's silver-bright eyes darkened as he recounted the confusion of Stonebinder's escape. "Winterfall had linked only briefly with SearSky, but he believes that SearSky is loyal. I would like him to be more fully examined," Farsight said.

"How many others have not been tested?"

"Enough to keep us busy for tonight, at least." As Farsight slumped, head low, Windrush realized just how tired his brother was.

"I have some news that will brighten your eyes," Windrush said, and told Farsight of FullSky's release. "I think," Windrush added, "we should not speak openly of this. There may yet be traitorous ears among us, and it would not be well for the Enemy to know of FullSky's activity."

Farsight angled his head and nodded. "Bad enough that Stonebinder is undoubtedly betraying our spell-secrets. We must be more vigilant than ever." He glanced up, where numerous dragons were circling in the sky. "It is time, Windrush."

The dragons were gathering toward the Vale of Decision.

This meeting was the most rancorous yet. The air itself seemed aboil with anger at Stonebinder for fleeing—and at those known to be his friends, or even suspected of being his friends. Windrush called for the testing to continue, to learn if there was more than one traitor; and Farsight, risking open hostility, proposed that the renewed testing begin with those whose examinations were interrupted by Stonebinder's flight—namely, SearSky, Sharpclaw, and Thunderwall.

SearSky objected violently, claiming that he had been subjected to enough examination already. Not so, asserted Farsight. The testing had been interrupted, and it was crucial to confirm the loyalty of all dragons. SearSky refused, until Windrush rumbled, "No one flies with us who has not shown himself trustworthy, garkkon-rakh to garkkon-rakh. SearSky, I have never doubted your loyalty—but you make me wonder. What do you have to fear? Will you be tested?"

SearSky shot him an angry glance, red-flame eyes blazing out of a craggy black head. For an instant, Windrush feared that SearSky, too, would fly away—to be pursued and brought down by his fellows. Finally SearSky belched a flame into the air. "I will not have my loyalty doubted!" His voice crackled. "Do your worst to me—for what pleasure it will bring you!" He glared at Windrush. "Bring on your deputies—if you are afraid to test me yourself!"

"I have no such fear," Windrush answered coldly. "But I do have other tasks that call me. If you show yourself loyal to any of these—" and he nodded at Farsight, Winterfall, Stronghold, and Longtouch—"I will gladly fight at your side."

SearSky snorted, but protested no further.

Windrush drew Farsight away to speak privately. "Again I must leave you in charge. Warn the others to be alert for

new attacks, and organize the patrols well. I will rejoin you
tonight, if I can."

"Be swift, and be careful," Farsight said.

"You as well," Windrush replied.

The underrealm passage to Hodakai's prison seemed eerily
quiet. It was not that Windrush expected the presence of
any other being in the passage; but there was a stillness that
was disturbing—as though a certain background murmur
of life were missing. The dragon paused as he approached
the rigger-spirit's presence.

The spirit was dancing about nervously. Windrush
waited for Hodakai to settle down. *Rigger-spirit*, he said in
greeting.

Dragon, answered Hodakai. *Windrush, I presume?* There
was a sarcastic taunt to his voice.

Indeed. How are you, Hodakai?

The spirit pulsed, not answering his question. *Have you
come . . . for the reasons that we discussed earlier?*

The dragon gazed at him, puzzled by the spirit's demeanor, but unable to discern the creature's thoughts or
feelings. *You have not had cause to change your mind, have
you?*

No—of course not.

That is good. Because I hope you can help us.

Of course, of course.

You seem nervous, Hodakai.

Well . . . I suppose I am. I'm taking a big risk, you know.

We all are, Windrush said. *But I do appreciate the risk to
you, as well. Do you have anything to pass on to me?*

Hodakai was silent for a moment. *What . . . exactly
. . . did you want to know?*

Windrush drew a slow breath. *What are the Enemy's
plans? I have reason to expect a new attack. Have you heard
rumor? Have you heard where he plans to strike?*

For an instant, Windrush wondered if he ought to have
asked so directly. But the words were out—and they didn't
seem to have taken the rigger-spirit by surprise.

Hodakai swayed in his jar for a moment, but when he

spoke, his words seemed confident. *Yes, Windrush—I have heard.* He paused, as the dragon waited. *There have been rumors, indeed. Rumors that one of your number has fled, and taken with him secrets to the safety of your—what do you call them?—lumenis groves. Places that you value highly, in any case.* Hodakai paused again. *If I were you, Windrush, I'd put everything I had into defending those groves.*

The dragon gazed at the spirit's kuutekka. *Do you know exactly where they're planning to attack? Or when?*

Hodakai seemed to stare him right in the eye. *I do not, dragon. Not exactly. But I would guard your most precious— what do you call it—the Valley of Light? The Nail, I think, would have great pleasure in taking that place from you.*

A direct assault upon the dragons' main strength? The Enemy might well be feeling that confident, after his recent victory. Windrush growled inwardly. *Tell me something else, Hodakai. What do you know of the Enemy's web of power?*

The spirit pulsed. *What would you like me to know of it?*

How close is it to completion? Windrush asked sharply. *This is important! Not just to us, but to the realms beyond, as well!*

Hodakai seemed reluctant to answer. He danced silently, until Windrush grew impatient. At last he said, *I don't know, dragon. But I don't . . . think you have much time.*

Windrush stared at him.

Anything else? the spirit asked.

Windrush drew up his kuutekka to depart. *No. But if you learn more, tell me. Hodakai—you've been very helpful. We won't forget it.*

I'll bet you won't, Hodakai thought as the dragon vanished into the underrealm. I'll bet you won't. Not when you pick yourself up from the ruins. You'll remember for a long time what happens when you try to double-cross me. You'll remember, all right.

He danced with excitement; the danger made his spirit quiver and soar. The question about the web of power had almost thrown him—especially the business about its endangering his own realm. But he remembered the iffling's words, warning him of the dragons' treachery, and his mind was made up. It all seemed so clear now. There was only one person he would serve, and that was Hodakai the rigger.

And now it was time to call Rent and tell him what had happened. Just as soon as he had spent a little time recovering his equilibrium. Just as soon as he had flown a bit in the rigger-net of his mind, diving and soaring and reveling in the ultimate freedom of the Flux. . . .

Chapter 26
FIST OF TAR-SKEL

FULLSKY FOLLOWED the underrealm thread as it wound away from the Dark Vale and climbed toward a glowering, truculent sky. It was an extremely fine, silvery thread, only intermittently visible. To most eyes it would not have been visible at all, but FullSky's long experience in the underrealm had taught him to perceive trails that others missed. Just for an instant, before starting along this path, he had glimpsed at its other end the presence of something he was willing to risk his life to reach—the Dream Mountain.

What he was doing now was extraordinarily dangerous. Having slipped away from the fire and shadow of Tar-skel's dungeons and the camouflaging commotion of the Enemy's lesser servants, he was venturing into an open sky where watchful eyes might notice him more easily. He was still tied by a thin wisp of his kuutekka to his physical body in the dungeon, but he could think of no way to protect that lifeline, except by trying not to be seen. He assumed that there would be guardians somewhere along this thread, and he did not wish to lose his newfound freedom through carelessness.

The path had not been easy to follow, but once he'd felt his way past the upturn in the spidery thread, and risen out of the murky confusion of the dungeon's underrealm, the rest of the Mountain-concealing sorcery had come into focus quickly enough. It was as if he had climbed up and out of a foggy soup which kept the rest of dragonkind from seeing what he saw now: the layers and encircling arcs of power that cradled and shrouded the Mountain. The appearance here in the underrealm was of a mountain somehow *floating* high above the land that the dragons inhabited.

It was not that Tar-skel had in reality *moved* the Dream Mountain; rather, he had encircled it with spell-weavings that kept the draconi from reaching it or even seeing it. So cleverly had he coiled layers of the underrealm *around* the Dream Mountain that it was as effectively removed from the realm as if he had physically uprooted it. No dragon could penetrate that shroud, except through the underrealm—and even in the underrealm, it probably could only be reached by starting where FullSky had—in the heart of the Dark Vale.

He rode close to the silvery thread now as it spun upward through a clear-sky underweb. The clarity lasted only for a few moments. Then the thread took him into smoky layers of sorcery that made him think of storm clouds over volcanic fire. It seemed to him that the sorceries flashing around him did more than just isolate the Dream Mountain from the rest of the realm; they were a part of the underpinnings of the great web of Tar-skel, the weaving that seemed to reach outward from the underrealm toward the boundary layers that kept this world apart from all others. FullSky noted this, but tried not to be distracted by the larger implications. He tried to focus solely upon threading his way along the path to the Mountain. The storm layers flowed downward past him like layers of smoke, as he rose. A low, bass thrumming filled his mind.

Abruptly, the clouds fell away and the thread streaked upward into a new layer of clear sky. FullSky paused, with a sudden fearful feeling that this was too risky; he was too likely to be seen. He caught sight of a branching path, winding off sideways along the top of the cloud layer from which he had just emerged. Hesitating for only an instant, he took the detour. It looked as though it might later twist back up toward the same destination as the main thread; but it was the difference between a fine, clear mountain passage and a thin, perilous, twisty one bound in fog. He hoped he could find his way through the fog.

He had scarcely made the detour when he heard voices behind him, harsh crackling voices. A blanket of cloud caught him, then flashed away again, leaving him exposed.

The larger silvery thread was still visible behind him, climbing into the sky. Two figures of jagged, pulsating fire—watchers, perhaps—were streaking up the thread that he had just abandoned. He continued his own movement without changing rhythm, hoping to be less conspicuous in steady motion than he might be if he stopped and tried to hide.

The two watchers vanished, flickering, up the thread. How many more of those would there be? he wondered, his relief mixed with worry. Would he find the Dream Mountain guarded by them? If so, how could he hope to get through?

No matter; he was committed. He flew through the patchwork of fog, following the side trail, peering through every opening in the shroud for a glimpse of the ultimate direction of this path. He prayed that he had not been misled in following it, that the mist would not part to reveal guardians in his path.

The clouds began to darken and grow turbulent. Looking up through breaks in the cover, he saw layers of storm cloud overhead, in fast motion against the sky. Something in the movement was dizzying, and it took him a moment to realize that it was a circular motion. Before he could think more about it, the thread bent abruptly upward—and he flew from the concealing layers straight up into a great, storming whirlwind.

As he clung to the thread, he found to his relief that it passed into the relatively calm center of the maelstrom. But he was astounded by the power and momentum carried by those clouds, now racing in a vast circle around him and above him. Lightning flashed within the cloud walls, and the layers churned as they spun around, as though each wisp of cloud were vying for the inside position. The sheer power was terrifying enough; but more than that, he had the impression that there was a purposefulness in the movements within the cloud wall, as though there were a strength and intelligence there, not just in the crafting behind the storm, but dwelling in the storm's power itself.

Almost as though . . . it were alive . . .

As though . . . it were not just a *creation* of Tar-skel, but an actual coiling of the Enemy's own personality through the underweb. And if that was true . . .

FullSky had a sudden, terrible feeling that the Enemy himself might be breathing within those clouds, and looking out through them. FullSky had never actually met the Enemy face-to-face; but this dark, endlessly spinning mass was making him quake with fear.

He slowed, but did not stop. He tried to draw his kuutekka close about him, making his presence as small as it could be. Around him, the great walls of cloud were turning, racing in the sky. The pale thread continued upward through the eye, but edged frighteningly close to the cloud wall.

Something new began to happen now. A great fist of cloud erupted from the far side of the storm, pushing out into the stillness in the center, then turning upward, moving with agonizing slowness—and yet, for a cloud, with shocking speed. FullSky felt faint at the power he sensed in that fist . . . or was it a *Nail?* . . . pushing into the sky. He shivered, and fought to keep his fear from shining out through his kuutekka. There was an overwhelming presence inside that cloud; it was a presence he had contested once, and lost to, and did not want to battle again. FullSky felt a tremendously oppressive dread in his heart; he was sure now that it was Tar-skel he was seeing, the Enemy's kuutekka manifest in the underrealm, the Enemy looking out upon the face of the realm that he was claiming for his own.

A current of air was rising beneath FullSky, carrying him upward, closer and closer to that great, swelling fist. He could not turn back now if he wanted to, not without battling the current, not without drawing attention to himself. How small could he make himself? he wondered desperately. As surely as if he were physically here, he felt himself holding his breath, riding the updraft as a fleck of dust or a droplet of water, riding it wherever the winds would take him, spiraling and spinning about the path-thread, but drawn inexorably toward the eruption of the Nail's presence.

The fist seemed to be closing around the thread-path, as though to clutch it. FullSky was flying headlong into its grip. He felt a rushing despair as he rose, helplessly, ever closer to the impossibly dense cloud. He became aware of tiny, churning microstorms on its surface, and imagined that those tiny disturbances were eyes, peering out into the sky. *Peering . . .*

He was certain that that was Tar-skel's gaze shifting to and fro, taking in the sight of his underrealm. How could that gaze miss the kuutekka of a dragon rising alongside it? As he struggled to reduce himself to an invisible speck, he thought of his physical body, captive in the dungeons of the Dark Vale; and he knew that if Tar-skel recognized him, no matter what evasions he might try here in the underrealm, his body could be destroyed within a moment of the Nail's command. The only mountain he would reach then would be the Final Dream Mountain, the soulfire of death.

Lightning seared the air around him; and as the thunder rumbled, he saw not just the lightning glowing against the clouds, but the Nail's web of power, as well—a fine woven outline visible through the clouds. The lightning flashed, illuminating the fist of Tar-skel with great jumping sheets of light and shadow; and the web seemed to burn brighter. It was not finished—there were strands incomplete and missing—but it was strong, and growing stronger.

FullSky, spun by the winds, streaked ever faster upward toward a grey ceiling of sky that loomed overhead. He was level with the fist of cloud, practically surrounded by its massive bulk, still mushrooming outward. It was impossible that he would not be seen! Each flash of lightning illuminated more to the Enemy's gaze, and surely that gaze was circling around toward *him*. FullSky's fear and hope were knotted tightly in his heart. His fear must be blazing out like a beacon in the night!

And yet, perhaps not. As he watched, the stormy eyes seemed to slide past him. With each flash brighter than the one before, he felt the power in the Enemy's gaze drawn outward toward the vastness of the web. The Nail was admiring his own handiwork, and missing altogether the puny presence of a dragon's *kuutekka* rising through its center. FullSky heard a rumbling voice, a voice of anger and satisfaction, of arrogant pride; and he knew that the voice was reveling in the lightning and thunder, in the dreadful structure beyond. And though FullSky could practically have reached out and touched the surface of Tar-skel's fist, he remained absolutely still and shot upward and away from it in terror, a scrap of leaf on the wind.

A heartbeat later, he was above the storm, untouched. He felt as small as a grain of sand; he could hardly remember what it was like to fly as a dragon. He caught his breath, and tearing his gaze from the Enemy's terrible presence, gazed upward again. Directly overhead was a thinning in the cloud ceiling, and a frail thread-path twisting up through that opening. Far off to the side, almost lost in the wall of the great storm below, FullSky glimpsed the larger main thread that he had left earlier, and saw that it turned away from where he wanted to go. He had chosen correctly, in leaving that path.

From above, Tar-skel's fist looked a little less dark now, a little less ominous. He was not by any means out of range of the Enemy's sight, but he began to feel hope again. The roiling of the Enemy's presence seemed turned away from him, and he was rising faster and faster away from it. The grey ceiling overhead was dropping upon him like a blanket. It was wispy thin, right here in this one place above the Enemy's gaze, but before he could even think about it, the fog whipped closed around him and cut off the sight of Tar-skel's storm.

A few seconds later, the fog layer fell away below. Looking up, FullSky trembled in wonder. There were twists and turns in the path yet, but above him as he rose was the astonishing sight of a vast, magnificent, translucent mountain.

Dream Mountain: a sharp-featured peak of glass, glowing from within. FullSky, after the first heart-stopping moment, recovered his concentration and reached out his presence toward it.

There were no further barriers of the Enemy. Apparently Tar-skel was so confident of his grand sorcery that he did not trouble to station any of his lesser servants here. FullSky followed the thread-path without difficulty to the base of the Mountain, and there he felt familiar draconic spells of entry; and with a shudder of pleasure, he tugged at those threads and found himself inside the Mountain.

The transformation was instantaneous. He was in a place bathed with sunshine, so bright he could see nothing else, and he heard the voices before he saw their source. They were like chimes ringing in a shifting breeze, like glass singing in a fire, like a stream chortling in a carved channel. They were surely the voices of the draconae, and FullSky for a moment could not move or breathe or utter a sound to make his presence known. Nor did he have to.

You who have entered, said a voice floating toward him. *You are different from those who have tried before.*

Indeed, FullSky whispered. *I am a friend. I cannot see you. But if you are the draconae, the dreaming, the singing ones—*

We are—

Then—and he paused, barely glimpsing the presence of the others, fluttering in the Dream Mountain's under-realm—*then know that I am FullSky, son of Highwing and Skytouch, and I am reaching out to you in desperate hope, from the dungeons of the Dark Vale.*

There was a sound of rushing wind, and another change, not quite instantaneous, more like an eyeblink. He was wafted into a darkness, but a warm darkness—and he felt something stirring near him, the flutter of fragile wings. He felt a breath close, and he glimpsed the movement of pale luminous figures, almost too dim to be seen. *Wait,* he heard.

Chapter 27
THE POOL OF VISIONS

THE SWIRLING snow was finally abating, the air clearing to reveal a landscape that took Jael's breath away, even through the distortion of the fractured rigger-net. The mountain trail was winding down out of the barren heights toward a glen of some sort; she glimpsed trees rising from the shadows. In the distance an oblate red sun shone over a majestic range of mountains, peaks gleaming with ice and snow, the lower flanks jutting angles of maroon and brown rock. As she descended, ship on her back, she saw clusters of trees below, with burnished purple and gold leaves. She glimpsed a stream tumbling down from a cliff face. Ahead of her, floating down into the glen, was the hazy and ethereal iffling, in the shape of a dragon.

Jael felt her spirits lifting. This looked like the sort of place where dragons might gather, and perhaps share word with her of the struggle. But as more of the glen drew into sight, she searched in vain for any sign of dragons, or any animate life other than the iffling. Her spirits sank again.

She felt terribly lonely. Ed had not returned from his search for Ar. Once, she thought she had actually heard Ar's voice, calling out—not to her, but to Ed—but only once, and then the voice was lost again in the cottony interstices of the damaged net. Jael knew she had to forget Ar and Ed and put the most urgent tasks before her, and not give in to fear. But her heart ached for the company of her friends. She was terrified that she had damaged the net irreparably, and that this was where they would all die, uselessly. Words had come back to her from a conversation with Kan-Kon, words she'd not paid much attention to at the time, distracted as she'd been by other thoughts.

"*From that one's death . . . will the ending be wrought . . .*"—words that he seemed not to have understood particularly, but which now made her sick with fear. She longed for Windrush. He could make sense of all this. She desperately wanted to believe that he had heard her call, or somehow sensed her presence.

The trail twisted to the left, dropped steeply for a few steps, then bent back the other way and sloped more gently down into the glen. The iffling, ahead of her, was pulsing. It seemed to want her to hurry.

She wondered again if she really ought to trust it. But what choice did she have? There had been a time, long ago it seemed now, when she had decided to trust a dragon. She hadn't known him well, either. But she had decided to trust him; and in the end, that decision had led her not only to a friendship with Highwing and his sons, but also to a deeper healing in her own heart. Did wisdom call, then, for her to trust this being, as she had once trusted Highwing?

The iffling floated back toward her, a glimmering dragon of light. *We will stop here, for now. You have many questions. In this place, we may find some answers.*

Jael blinked, wondering if the iffling had read her thoughts. *What is this place?* she asked. *Is it a place of dragon magic?* She remembered Highwing's garden of powers, which he had shown her during her first visit to the realm, and she wondered if this would be something similar. *Will we meet dragons here? Can we call to Windrush?*

The iffling dimmed, flickering as though with uncertainty. Then it brightened again. *It is indeed a place of powers—though not, precisely, of dragon magic. The Pool of Visions, this place is called. It is possible to see . . . much . . . and learn much, here. And perhaps . . . to call out to Windrush. Much will depend upon how much you trust . . . me. For here we must seal . . . our trust.*

Jael wondered at its words. It was not that she did not trust the ifflings; indeed, she had trusted them in returning to the realm in the first place. And yet . . . she remembered that at least one among them was false. How could she know which was which? Windrush! Where are you? Or

Highwing! Lord, how she missed Highwing! He would have guided her faithfully through such questions.

You remain uncertain, the iffling observed, its wings of light trembling.

Yes, she acknowledged.

The iffling's wings fluttered. *Come, then, and you will see.* It turned and floated down into the glen, without waiting for a response.

Jael trudged after it, until she suddenly realized that they were surrounded by trees. She paused to look around. The glen was not quite as it had seemed from a distance. The trees, which she had imagined as beautifully delicate creations arching up from the ground, were in fact arid-looking bushes that might have been standing here for centuries. Their leaves, so luminous from above, were a dull rust-color on the undersides. They rustled stiffly in the wind.

Over here! the iffling called. It was hovering at the edge of a pool where a water-carved basin caught the mountain spring she had glimpsed earlier, streaming over a cliff face. A few strides from where the water splashed into the pool, it overflowed into a twisting ravine that carried it out of the glen and down the mountain.

Jael stood by the iffling, gazing into the pool. The water was clear and dark, and curiously unrippled by the splashing inflow. Flashing down from above, the water seemed to be made of light, rather than substance. But in the pool, it became hard and almost mercurial. It appeared as though everything in this spot had to be tough rather than delicate, as though fragility had no place here. There was a beauty in this starkness, but it was nothing like the exquisite fairyland beauty of Highwing's garden of powers. But that place was gone, destroyed by the Enemy. Perhaps, in these times, this stark sort of beauty was the only kind that survived.

The Pool of Visions, murmured the iffling. As Jael looked up again it said, *Here, rigger, I invite you to share a draft of water with an iffling. Here, where knowledge is revealed through the underrealm, I invite you to join your thoughts with mine, and to share in the visions.*

Jael blinked in puzzlement.

The iffling pulsed, continuing. *What visions? Visions of the realm, of the dragons, of the powers and principalities. Can you not see glimmerings of them in the water, even now?*

Jael bent and peered into the water again. She saw her own reflection, and the reflections of the sky and the cliff. She shook her head.

The iffling dimmed slightly. *None? Then, it is all the more imperative that you join with me. It is the only way.*

Jael frowned.

I perceive your uncertainty, your apprehension, murmured the iffling. *Perhaps I can help.* It suddenly began to change shape. It settled to the ground, and quickly became more solid and less luminous—and shrank out of its dragonlike shape. Seconds later, it had transformed itself into an animal—a cross between a mountain cat and a lemur, with plush, tan fur and bright green eyes.

Jael stared, astonished—and remembered the iffling that had visited her in Windrush's cavern, two years ago. That one had taken on an animal form, too, though a more delicate one.

This is my other form, said the creature. *I thought perhaps you would find it less frightening.* It turned to gaze at the water, smelling it delicately. Looking up again, it cocked its head, as though a thought had just occurred to it. *The sharing of water. Is this not an ancient ritual among your people?*

Jael blinked. What would an iffling know about human rituals? *I . . . suppose it is,* she murmured.

Yes, said the cat/lemur. *It is a most sacred exchange of life.* Its eyes shone, gazing at her. *But here, at the Pool of Visions, it is more than sacred. When we share water here, it has the power to bind us together in heart and thought. Then, together, we may study the visions of the pool, and learn the fate of your friends. But it does require that you . . . trust me.* The iffling sat back on its haunches, gazing straight into her eyes.

Jael was unable to answer. She didn't know if what the creature proposed was even possible. How could she consume something that existed outside the net? Nothing in the Flux was supposed to be *substance* at all—though the reality of the dragon world disproved that. Nevertheless, it must be a very different kind of substance. How could she draw it from the Flux into the net, much less dare to drink it? The idea seemed crazy.

And yet . . . the iffling's green-eyed gaze was a powerful magnet, drawing her toward the pool, making her want to believe its words. She felt almost hypnotized by those eyes.

Something felt wrong to her, but she couldn't identify what. In the back of her mind, she knew there was a profound urgency. Windrush and the others were in need. Whom could she trust but this being, to help her find her friends?

Would it make a difference, the iffling murmured, slowly blinking its cat/lemur eyes, *if, first, I shared with you my name?*

Jael drew a breath. Exchange names—as she had with her dragon friends? When she had first met Highwing, she had blurted her name to him, without thought—and he had taken it as a profound token of trust and innocence. His sons, likewise, had accepted her name with great solemnity, as something by which they would be bound for life. She didn't fully understand the power of names here, but she knew it was a power to respect. *If,* she said uncertainly, *it is a way for us to know each other's hearts . . .*

That, said the creature, *and more.*

Jael let out her breath, and nodded.

The creature's eyes widened and darkened to pools. *My name . . . is Jarvorus.*

Jael felt a sudden lightheadedness. *Jarvorus,* she whispered back. As she gazed at the large-eyed creature, she felt a compulsion to give her name in exchange. *I am . . . Jael.* As she spoke her name, she felt a power going out of her—not a great power, but noticeable, a flush in her heart. She imagined it reverberating in the pool of water beside her. She blinked, and shook her head. She thought she had seen circles of light rippling through the water, in its depths. She realized that her vision through the rigger-net had suddenly grown clearer.

Does this mean—? She stopped. Had she just heard something?

Jarvorus watched her in puzzlement.

Jael's head was ringing, and she was no longer sure what was touching her from the inside or the outside. She felt a sudden thump, then parrot wings fluttering inside her head. Ed was back in her thoughts! She couldn't see him, but she felt him peering out through her eyes. *(Ed!)* she cried, dizzy with relief.

What is it? the iffling whispered urgently, its gaze sharpening.

(Jayyyyl!) she heard. *(Found Ar! Found Ar!)*

(What?) Jael was almost overcome by the dizziness. And Ed was so overjoyed at having found his way back to her that it took him a few moments to calm down. Finally Jael found her voice to ask, *(Is he all right? Can you lead me to him—?)*

The iffling interrupted, urgently. *Jael, we must not delay! What is the matter?*

It couldn't see Ed, apparently. No matter; she could explain later. She felt the parrot scowling in concentration. *(Caw! Found, yes! Okay—awwk! But lost him again! Couldn't get to him! Almost—awk—couldn't get back!)*

Jael struggled to think clearly. *(Did you talk with him? Does he know we're alive?)* The iffling's intense, puzzled stare was making it even harder to focus.

(Rawwk—yes. Danger, Jael! DANGER! Must find graggons!) Jael felt Ed spreading his wings abruptly, between her temples. He looked about, with abrupt movements. *(Scrawww! What's that? What's that?)*

Jael's breath caught. She tried to calm herself. *(That's . . . Jarvorus. His name's Jarvorus, and he's an iffling. He's trying to help me . . . find Windrush.)*

The parrot shifted his head nervously back and forth inside Jael's eyes, staring out at the waiting iffling-animal. *(Danger,)* whispered Ed. *(Find graggons. Quickly!)*

(Yes. That's what we're hoping to do.) Jael blinked, realizing that Jarvorus was growing quite impatient.

What are you doing? it whispered. *To whom are you speaking?*

My shipmate, Jael murmured. *We have been separated. Our ship is damaged.*

Yes, yes. That is why you do not see clearly. But have you not noticed, your vision is clearer now?

The iffling's words were true; especially since their exchange of names, her ability to see out of the net had improved. It was as though the boundary layer between her and the Flux had stretched thinner, and grown more transparent. She wished that the same could be said of her thinking; she could barely focus at all now.

Jarvorus spoke again. *Jael, the urgency grows. We must let the pool show us your friends, if it will! Surely the . . . dragons . . . are waiting!*

Jael nodded foggily. In her head, she sensed Ed rumbling with unease, but felt his urgency, as well. He was desperately eager to find Windrush, to put an end to all this uncertainty. *Yes,* she whispered.

The cat/lemur sighed in satisfaction. *Yes,* it said, and stepped to the edge of the pool. Bowing, it delicately touched its tongue to the water. Raising its head, it commanded, *You, now. You need only touch it to your lips.*

Jael drew a breath, not moving. Her head was swimming, but she could not make herself step to the pool's edge.

You must—if you would find your friends! Jarvorus hissed.

Jael let her breath out in a rush. She could almost feel a force propelling her forward, toward the water. She couldn't tell if it was her own volition or something else, but neither could she resist it, or even want to. She would not actually drink the water; how could it harm her? She *wanted* to overcome her fear, to join with the iffling and share in its visions of the realm! She stepped forward and knelt at the water's edge, taking care not to overbalance the spaceship on her back.

Yes, yes! hissed the iffling, close beside her.

Jael drew a final, nervous breath, and dipped her hand down. The water quivered oddly, and her cupped hand filled with clear, glittering silver. She raised it to her mouth, and hesitated one last time. Then she touched it to her lips . . .

(Jayl, no—stop—hawwwwwk!—he's not—!)

She felt a flash of ice as the water touched her, and the ground seemed to shift beneath her. For an instant, she thought she would topple into the water; then she felt a great rushing sensation, as though she would float away. Ed was flapping wildly in her mind, screaming in anguish. But she didn't quite understand why—until her eyes focused on the pool's surface, where the burning water was spilling from her hand. She saw Jarvorus' reflection grinning at her. Iffling? No! she realized at once. He was no iffling—he was the false-one, and his razorlike teeth were showing in his grin, and his eyes were ablaze with triumph.

In that instant her gaze and Jarvorus', reflected in the water, came together. Something changed deep in the net, or in the realm around her, and she felt Jarvorus' thoughts plunge into hers like a burning knife into butter. She saw his spirit now, revealed in all of its falsehood. But it was too late to stop the process; the sorcery was unfolding exactly as Jarvorus had intended . . .

Windrush! Help me please—! she struggled to shout.

Deep in her mind, Ed was screaming in her defense, lashing and biting at the invading presence of the false-iffling's thoughts. But his efforts were futile. She felt Jarvorus' thoughts turning to strike in anger at Ed. She panicked as she saw it poised to kill, to stab and strangle. *(No!)* she cried, and enveloped Ed's presence in her own thoughts, shielding him from the attack. Ed was saved for the moment, but it was all the opening Jarvorus needed to whirl his threads of sorcery around Jael's innermost being. She fought to repel him, but uselessly; she could feel the spell tightening around her like a noose. *(You're no iffling!)* she hissed in futile rage.

(No. Not an iffling.)

(Then what are you?) she gasped.

She felt a rumble of triumph. *(I am a warrior in service to Rent, and to the Nail of Strength—the one against whom the dragons war in vain.)*

Tar-skel.

Jael felt ice water flowing in her veins as she realized the magnitude of her blunder. She wanted to scream in rage, to physically hurl this being from her thoughts. She could not even muster a whimper of protest.

(*Your power is our power now,*) whispered the being.

Jael's gaze fell helplessly on the Pool of Visions, and she no longer saw only her reflection and the false-iffling's; something new was shimmering into focus, deep in the waters. It was an image of dragons on wing . . . dragons tumbling through the air . . . dragons dying in battle, in great numbers. She glimpsed a coiling darkness, and felt a terrifying surge of malice toward her, and an incontestable power; and surrounding everything, enveloping all the mountains of the realm, she saw a fine, glowing spiderweb of sorcery . . . and she saw herself, dying in battle, and the web of sorcery blossoming in power.

(*The prophecy fulfilled,*) crooned the false-iffling, in a voice that sounded almost drunk with triumph.

Jael felt a crushing despair. She didn't wholly understand the vision, but she didn't have to. The vision revealed death and defeat, not just for her, but for all the realm. She became aware that her hand was immersed in the icy waters of the pool, and she drew it out. Her arm moved as though trapped in molasses. As her hand slowly came up and out of the water, the vision disappeared. She held her hand before her face, watching the silvery drops fall away, in slow motion. (*What have you done to me?*) she cried silently.

Javorus' thoughts rose within her own. For a disbelieving moment, she imagined that she glimpsed *sympathy* in the warrior's thoughts, and a heartbeat of hesitation. Then a new resolve swept all that away, and the Enemy's creature said, (*I wish you no harm. But I have sealed you into our power, and now I must bear you away to a place where you will be safe.*)

(*Jayllll!*) Ed wailed, his voice distant and ineffectual.

(*Safe?*) Jael repeated dully, her hope utterly broken.

(*Yes—safe—so that at the proper time, the prophecies will be fulfilled,*) answered the creature named Jarvorus.

Jael felt herself rising to her feet. Jarvorus had turned back into a being of fire, but no longer did he assume a dragonlike shape. (*Come,*) he said, his voice frighteningly melodious in her thoughts. *(It is not too much farther.)* She might have tried to resist, but she was unable. She could not turn away or refuse to move. Jarvorus controlled her will now.

They left the Pool of Visions, and the glen, and set their feet upon a new path back into the mountains.

In a distant corner of her mind, she felt the net crinkling, and she heard a voice calling, as if across a vast distance. It was Ar's voice, reaching her at last. He was calling out a desperate warning: *Do not trust . . . the false-one . . . false-iffling . . . beware of treachery . . . !*

But the warning was far too late.

Chapter 28
THE DRACONAE

THE DRACONAE entered FullSky's mind so swiftly he had no warning at all. He instinctively reacted to close his thoughts—then realized what he was doing and ceased resisting. This was what he had come here for. But his mind was bubbling with questions, and he couldn't get them out.

It was a strange and astonishing contact. The draconae revealed nothing of themselves, even as they laid open with remarkable clarity his memories and thoughts. His battles in the underrealm and his contacts with Windrush rose like great gleaming bubbles in water, expanding and turning for the draconae's inspection.

(Is he true—?)

(Is he alive and true—?)

(The Words speak of hope from beyond death—)

(But he has not died—)

(He has come from a place more inescapable—)

(Does he bring news of the One—?)

(Only the hope—the promise—)

(But his brother—)

(Windrush tries to reach us, but the barriers of the Enemy are too strong—)

The questions and observations swirled around him in a tempest. But the draconae knew and understood far more than he did. He had to get his questions out, while there was still time!

(Patience—)

(Our son, we know of your needs and your questions—)

(We all share these needs—)

He was beginning to feel disoriented, as in a lumenis feeding, full of fevered passions and sensations bubbling up out of the deep places of the mind. Was it because of the draconae's probing, or was this the way of the Dream Mountain, to be a place of confusion, of beautiful sounds and dizzy wonderment? Or was it, he thought fearfully, the beginning of his kuutekka's losing contact with his physical body, the beginning of death? He couldn't tell.

(Enough—)
(He is true—garkkondoh—)
(Let us show ourselves—)

There was another change, another eyeblink. He was bathed again with sunlight, and surrounded by movement. His kuutekka blossomed back around him as he had not felt it in a long time. He felt like a dragon again, instead of a dying spirit; his thoughts were once more his own. He heard the sounds of water tumbling and splashing in a pool. He turned his head one way and another; all around him was the fluttering of gossamer wings, and the flashing of glassy dragon faces—but confusingly, as though everything were broken into a myriad of facets.

He had not seen the Dream Mountain since his departure from the outer slopes as a youngling, a time he remembered only in fleeting images. He had never seen the inside of the Mountain at all, much less from the underrealm. This was the province of the females—not just now, but throughout most of dragon history. The inside was for singing, and remembering, and dreaming; it was for the draconae. It was for the tending of the Forge of Dreams, the fire at the heart of the Mountain, which brought life to the realm. It was not for the male dragons to tend those fires; their hearts were in the skies, and in the deeps of the external mountains. FullSky realized that even he, whose heart was the closest to a dracona's heart of any male dragon, knew precious little of the real powers of the dreamfires.

But now he was inside the Mountain, peering out through the shimmering lens of the underrealm. He saw the sun drenching the outer slopes, pouring into the Mountain through refracting surfaces of clear and translucent stone.

He was in a hollow, rocky glade, surrounded by noisily splashing streams and by *trees* and by the musing ones, the females, the draconae.

The draconae! There were dozens of them surrounding him: creatures of glowing jewel and glass, with wings that seemed made of crystallized air, their eyes flashing like shards of erupting lumenis. Some of the draconae were shimmeringly reflective, others glowing and transparent, some round and smooth, and others all angles and probing facets. Each dracona presented him with a different face of mystery as he peered into one gaze, then another. Their kuutekkas were faces of spirit and song: they seemed to dance and waver, as though he were seeing them through rising thermals, or a pool of water.

Am I seeing your outer-world appearances? he whispered in wonderment.

You see us as we are, as nearly as your underrealm vision will allow, murmured a faceted emerald dracona, her voice like wind piping through hollowed stone. *We had to see you clearly, though perhaps too abruptly for your comfort. But our needs were great.*

I understand.

But now we wish to answer your questions. And to help, if we can.

Yes. He hesitated. All of his deeper questions had fled from his mind, driven out by astonishment. *But . . . who are you? What are your names?*

There was a sound of laughter, a chuckling stream. There was a sadness that reverberated in the sound like distant waves.

I am Deeplife, said the first, the emerald-glass dracona.

Gentlesong, said a creature of smoothly polished curves.

Lavafire, rang a resonant voice, from a dracona who glowed within like fiery embers.

Cooltouch, said another, with mirrored scales.

Starchime, sang one who made him see blazing, impossibly concentric circles of fire.

Seatouch, whispered a voice like water hissing on sand . . .

And the names continued, one after another, dizzyingly, until he could scarcely keep the names and the draconae straight. But he rejoiced to meet them all, knowing that these draconae held the prophecies in their hearts, and held the knowledge of how the realm might be saved. So many questions rose in his mind that he could not even begin to sort them out.

You want to know, chimed the emerald Deeplife, whose eyes were unfathomable gems, *whether the One has returned.*

Jael, he said, and heard a murmur of agreement. *And—?*

Several draconae fluttered their wings. *We had hoped you would know,* answered . . . Starchime, was it? *The ifflings sent their last children to her. But whether they can bring her safely here, we do not know. Nor do we know exactly what she is to do here—or whether sufficient time remains. The Enemy's power grows steadily stronger.*

But, murmured Cooltouch, *the Words seem to promise that no victory can be won without her—*

We cannot be certain, said another, and there was a quick, rippling discussion before Deeplife called for silence.

FullSky reached for words. *How can you know . . . so much of what is happening in the realm? Are you not trapped here by the Enemy?*

Indeed, but the Enemy—

In his confidence—

His arrogance!

—permits us to see many things, finished Deeplife, hushing the others. *He wishes to persuade us of his invincibility. He wishes us to despair, to surrender our Mountain to him.*

But . . . he already controls the Mountain, FullSky thought.

His words, though not spoken, were heard. Deeplife replied firmly. *He has imprisoned the Mountain. But he does not control it—or us, though he may hold the power of life and death over us.*

He can destroy you. He can destroy all of us.

Deeplife nodded, glittering. *But he cannot command us. He needs us yet, to control the Forge of Dreams. He needs the despair of the dragons to strengthen his sorcery. But in time, if his web grows strong enough, he may find his own way to control the powers that emanate from this Mountain.*

FullSky listened carefully, gazing at the fragile beings who surrounded him. He remembered Highwing's story of how Skytouch, his own mother, had died at the hands of fledgling dragons whose hearts had been ruined by Tarskel. And he thought: How easily these draconae could be destroyed, in the same way!

You think truly, FullSky. If the Enemy no longer believes he needs us, he will destroy us.

And when—FullSky hesitated—*when might. he no longer need you? How strong must he become?*

The draconae stirred. There was a long pause before Deeplife said, *Who knows what Tar-skel, in his pride, will believe—or when? But the Words say that an ending will come, and a new beginning, when the One falls in battle.*

Hearing those words, FullSky brooded silently.

Another dracona—the glowing Lavafire—spoke up, in a resonant voice. *On that last matter, there is disagreement, even among us.*

You mean . . . as to whether it's true?

No, we are certain it is true. The Words came, after all, from the dream forge itself, through an opening in time, we believe. An opening into the future—a future that in our age has become the present. But whether the ending that is foretold will favor the Enemy, or the realm, no one truly—

Before she could finish her thought, she was interrupted by a sudden disturbance. Several of the draconae turned away, rustling and murmuring in agitation. Lavafire queried in rumbling tones, then announced, *We have seen something in the Dark Vale. Please wait.*

FullSky waited—terrified that the Enemy had discovered his connection with the draconae. He felt a movement, not in the outer reality of the Mountain, but in the underrealm. The light around him faded, and he realized that the draconae were flanking him in an underrealm window, a place of near-darkness.

A vision was coming into focus: a vision of dark, winged creatures taking flight against a deepening evening sky. The sight made him shiver; it was a legion of the Enemy, both drahls and Tar-skel dragons, gathering in the air. Gathering for battle.

The strength of Tar-skel rises, murmured a dracona who evidently had been among the first to see the vision. *I heard their leaders speaking. They are bound for the Deep Caverns.*

That set off a great commotion. *The Deep Caverns are scarcely protected*, one of them said. *Windrush strengthens the defense elsewhere*, said another.

FullSky listened with alarm. Why the Deep Caverns? Were they more important than the dragons had realized?

Has anyone felt the contact of an iffling? Deeplife asked the others urgently. *Can we send warning that way?*

The ifflings are failing, whispered the hushed voice of Seatouch. *Their strength is nearly gone. They cannot reach us now.*

Deeplife spoke to FullSky. *Have you any way to reach Windrush, quickly?*

Not now, FullSky whispered, with a breath of steam.

Then we can only watch.

That is why we are being allowed to see this, Deeplife said softly. *So that we might watch, and despair.*

FullSky hissed quietly to himself, but said nothing. He knew that despair was the Enemy's greatest weapon, and if the draconae succumbed, there would be little hope indeed.

The drahls and dragons gathered, rising over the harsh twilit peaks of the Enemy's territory. Instead of taking flight to the east, however, they flew in formation in a great, spinning circle. Gradually they closed their orbits inward until they were turning dizzyingly fast, like the storm clouds FullSky had braved in reaching the Dream Mountain. He sensed that threads of the underrealm were being stretched and altered, even as he watched. The empty air in the center of the formation shimmered and *opened* somehow, and the drahls banked and fell inward through the distorted air, and vanished.

FullSky blinked, feeling a disturbance in the underrealm. The Enemy, he knew, had just released a potent sorcery, sending his legions through some astonishing shortcut to their target. FullSky stared at the image of empty sky over the Dark Vale and felt more helpless than ever.

Leaving the darkened window, three of the draconae—Deeplife, Starchime, and Gentlesong—remained close to FullSky in the underrealm, but drew him to a place where they could speak quietly. They all knew that the dragons, back in the held land, must even now be fighting for their lives. But there was nothing any of them could do about it, and they had agreed that FullSky should learn all he could while he was among them, in hopes that he might take some useful knowledge back through the underrealm with him.

They seemed to be perched on a ledge overlooking a place of silent but intense draconae activity. They were granting him a glimpse of the Forge of Dreams, a place where draconae skilled in the powers of the Mountain labored to maintain the defense of the dreamfires, and through them the integrity of the entire realm and the underrealm, and everything that lived there. From where FullSky sat, the view seemed to shimmer between a darkened cavern with draconae gathered around a glowing hearth—and a breathtaking and impossible-to-grasp view of an all-enveloping darkness full of stars, and a blazing source of light and heat that seemed to be everywhere and nowhere in that darkness, all at once. The underrealm itself seemed to pulse and breathe around the power that flowed from that source.

There are not many to whom we would show this, Deeplife said. *But even now, we must keep from you any greater knowledge of the dreamfire. Though it saddens us, you may be vulnerable to the Enemy.*

FullSky nodded. He was grateful to be seeing this much.

You took a great risk, venturing past the Enemy to come here. Your presence encourages us, murmured Gentlesong. In the underrealm, she presented a kuutekka of graceful arcs of light, somehow coming together in the shape of a dragon.

My risk increases, the longer I remain. There is so much that I would like to know!

We will share with you—

But, said FullSky, *I hardly know where to begin! I wonder what can help us to prevail!*

Deeplife spread her wings. They flared with multiple colors, as though sunlight were passing through them. Her eyes seemed infinitely deep, one facet leading into another, and another . . .

She sang softly:

> *A word names the nameless*
> *And light dawns from dread*
> *To the heart of darkness*
> *Are the fearful ones led.*

And she was echoed by the other two, who sang, like repeating chimes:

> *And the realm shall tremble . . .*

Raising her voice slightly, Deeplife sang:

> *Challenging darkness*
> *will come one*
>
> *Speaking her name*
> *will come one*
>
> *From that one*
> *comes a beginning*
>
> *From that one*
> *comes an ending*
>
> *From that one*
> *all paths diverge.*

And the other two echoed:

> And surely the realm shall tremble.

FullSky was silent.

Those, said Deeplife, *are the Words that have been foremost in our hearts lately. They sustain us in both our hope and our fear.*

Words, FullSky thought. He feared them, and longed to know their secrets. But could words defeat the Enemy?

The Enemy knows those Words as well as we do, Deeplife said. *And make no mistake—he fears them.*

FullSky gazed at her in puzzlement.

Starchime coruscated with radiating circles of light. *He fears them because he does not understand them. He knows there will be an ending, and a new beginning. But he does not know what kind of ending, or beginning. Nor do we.*

FullSky admitted, *I hardly know, myself, whether to draw hope from them, or fear.*

The draconae made chiming sounds of assent. *That is their nature. But we choose to draw hope.*

Hope, FullSky thought. How difficult it was to feel hope when the Enemy was so powerful, and so . . . unknowable. For all of his encounters with the Nail of Strength, he still scarcely knew what or who Tar-skel was.

None of us knows for sure, whispered Gentlesong. *But much has been handed down in wisdom from of old.*

Legends, he whispered back.

More than legends. Told through legends sometimes, but real nonetheless. Open your thoughts to us, FullSky, and learn of our foe.

FullSky stared at the dracona, and at last met her gaze. He felt her thoughts slipping deep into his . . .

The images stirred melancholy memories. As a youngling he had been taught much that he had since lost to the dimness of time. Like most draconi, FullSky had not really *wanted* to remember such things, not when he was a youthful dragon, eager and invincible. These were dark memories, the memories of Tar-skel.

(Indeed,) whispered Gentlesong. (But the time has come to face them, and to learn.)

The Enemy entered the realm in a time before even the draconae's memory (Gentlesong murmured). His life before that was known only through his boastings, recalled and passed on by his servants and foes alike. He came from another realm altogether, where he had been an influential being in a race of immortals or near-immortals. There he had been an artist of some sort, a shaper-crafter of wondrous powers and great renown—but not, it seemed, renown enough. His pride grew with his work; and with that pride came a darkening of his spirit, as his fellows granted him too little praise, too little understanding, too little bowing to his wisdom and his power.

(Was he driven by jealousy?) FullSky asked wonderingly.

(By jealousy, pride . . . and in the end, madness,) answered Gentlesong.

The seeds of madness, perhaps, were present from the beginning. But the rise in fame of another shaper, whose work overshadowed his, brought about a final eruption of envy, and a lust for mastery and revenge. What truly happened then, no one except Tar-skel himself could say now. But somehow he found the power to destroy that realm and all who lived in it, and he fled with his own life. And as he did so, he called himself Nail of Strength, his anger and pride burning hot as a sun.

Over the eons, his anger cooled somewhat, but never went out. After unknown wanderings, he came in time to the dragon realm. He arrived quietly, and studied the realm carefully, before gathering his power here.

(Was he known to the dragons then?) FullSky wondered, trying to recall his own earliest times of learning.

(They knew of his presence, but not yet his nature,) murmured Gentlesong. (Our ancestors were not as wise as they might have been. Many followed him without knowing that they did so.)

(Then little has changed,) FullSky noted, and Gentlesong

could only agree, as she continued conveying the images to him.

Tar-skel's sorceries in the underrealm were unparalleled, but that explained only a part of his success. He drew a growing following of dragons under his sway, through appeals to greed, to power-lust, and to fear. He seduced many with promises of great magics, and he offered overproud dragons a chance to rule over others who were more fearful, weak, or timid. These were the early times of dragon civilization, and the dragons had little tradition of history and order. Even the draconae were only just learning the powers of memory and word, and the quiet taming of the dreamfires. But they knew enough, even then, to guard control of the Forge of Dreams from this one.

Across the ages, numerous wars erupted between those who served him and those who hated the turmoil he had brought to the realm. Dragons died in those wars, but Tar-skel did not.

(And yet he was defeated,) FullSky recalled.

(Yes, in the greatest of those wars, he lost most of his followers, and his sorceries were broken,) said Gentlesong. (Some thought that he was dead. But in fact, he only slept, leaving the realm untroubled for a time.)

As Tar-skel slept, stories and legend grew up around his name, keeping his true nature from burning too deeply into the dragon conscience, sparing dragonkind the pain of remembering its own failures. He was portrayed as a spirit that punished wicked dragonlings, or draconi whose courage failed. He became a tragic figure, a dragon whose ambitions outstretched his abilities—a character whose story revealed the price of becoming powerful, but not powerful enough. Many said that he never lived at all, that his was just a name given to an ill wind that blew in the hearts of some dragons—a name given to an impersonal evil, to render it less terrifying.

Thus the true history diminished in dragon memory. The reasons for past wars vanished in a murk of discarded guilt and shame. As the draconi forgot their own misdeeds, the fictions became so entangled with reality that even by the draconae, the truths were sometimes misremembered. And so the Enemy was reduced to a fable who had no true life, no true name, no true power.

But though silent for many generations of dragons, Tarskel indeed had life, had a name, had power.

FullSky, remembering his recent brush with the Enemy, knew well that one's power. Gentlesong paused, sensing his unease, but FullSky urged her to continue sharing . . .

Quietly, while the draconi were forgetting that he had ever lived, the Nail of Strength gathered his resources, his forces, his legions of twisted and altered beings. If from time to time a young fledgling vanished from the slopes of the Dream Mountain, the draconi preferred to believe that accidents were to blame, fledglings who tried to fly before they were ready, or caretaking draconae who were inattentive to their charges. But the singing ones knew, and perhaps even a few of the male dragons suspected: the invisible one was stealing fledglings, stealing them and twisting them into something terrible and deadly, and calling them drahls, servants of the Nail. But of the draconi who flew and dueled and maintained (or so they believed) the strength of the realm, most refused to recognize the truth.

Once again, Tar-skel grew strong, cloaked in silence and invisibility. His darkest works were performed in secrecy; his influences were whispers in the darkness to those who did not even know whose voice they were hearing. If he did speak audibly, it was in a voice of unworldly beauty. Some, like FullSky, were drawn in to challenge his magics, and were captured. His presence was concealed by senseless disputes among the draconi, by brooding distrust of outsiders, by a growing belief that anyone or anything not-dragon—such as a rigger, or even an iffling—must be demon. And this time, his silence lasted . . . until one such outsider was befriended by a dragon, mirroring the ancient prophecy . . . until his sorcery, to his fury, was defeated by that same rigger.

(Jael,) thought FullSky. (The One.)

(So we have believed,) Gentlesong sighed.

Tar-skel's malice, if anything, flourished following that humiliation. He had already quietly concealed the way to Dream Mountain from dragons who were too absorbed in their duels and disputes to notice. He was determined to complete his ultimate weaving of power, a web that would draw not just this world, but all those beyond, into his grasp. But he was angry, as well; and if he could avenge himself against the rigger in his moment of success, so much sweeter would be the victory that he had long craved—the mastery of *all* worlds.

(But what of the prophecies?) FullSky whispered, awed and terrified by the recounting of their foe's staggering power.

(The Words came to us in the days following the last great war,) said Gentlesong. *(And not just to us, but to a surviving servant of the Enemy.)*

An aging dracona, Sunfire, standing watch over the Forge of Dreams, had witnessed the vision and spoken the Words aloud. And the rest of the draconae had remembered them, through song and verse and vision, for the ages to come. And the Enemy's servant had fled, bearing the knowledge of the same Words to its master.

And over the generations, the draconae—and, it was believed, the Enemy as well—had been striving to understand those Words. Friend and foe alike now, all were waiting, waiting for the final story to unfold.

Even as Gentlesong poured the images into FullSky's thoughts, much of it echoed back from his deepest memories of early teachings. But even hearing it, and seeing it in his mind, he felt an unreasoning desire not to believe that they, today, could be facing this same, legendary Enemy. He seemed too powerful, too terrible, too . . . immortal.

(Can he really be so ancient?) FullSky hissed, barely able to speak even in the privacy of his own mind.

(More ancient than our memory,) said Gentlesong.

A wisp of steam curled up slowly from FullSky's kuu-tekka as he reflected upon his Enemy's, and his own people's, history. He was grieved by the tragedy of the dragons' failure to remember their past, and grateful for the draconae's preservation of the truth against the erosion of the ages.

He all but forgot his own precariousness in the underrealm as he whispered to the dracona, *(Tell me, please— what can I do?)*

Chapter 29
BATTLE FOR THE DEEP CAVERNS

WORD OF attack came in the night, not from the Valley of Fallen Light, or from the outposts to the south, but out of the darkness to the east. Windrush had been flying vigil with the guardians of Fallen Light, and left Farsight in charge of continuous patrols out along the western border and the Scarred Mount Ridge. The border seemed secure. Nevertheless, Windrush felt a vague but growing suspicion that something was wrong; and several times, had landed so that he could probe the underrealm for any signs. But it never did any good; he felt that something was stirring, somewhere, but until it broke out into the open, he could not tell what it was.

And so, despite all of their preparedness, it came as a shock when a flame-billowing messenger appeared out of the east, shrieking: "Attack! The Enemy has attacked! Send help to the Deep Caverns! Send dragons to the Deep Caverns!"

The dragon did not even slow down, but trumpeted his warning as he passed the Valley of Fallen Light on his way to the main encampment. Windrush rose to intercept him and flew alongside toward the camp. "Report!" Windrush called. "Your name! How many of the enemy? What have they done?"

The messenger's angry flame flashed in the night. "Sky-piercer, Windrush! More drahls than we could count—and enemy dragons, too! It was sorcery—they appeared out of nowhere! They are destroying our guard, and the caverns as well. If we don't have help, the caverns will be lost!"

Windrush was dumb with astonishment. Why the Deep Caverns? Did some power remain there, after all? He beat the air furiously. "Tell Farsight, in the camp!" he commanded Skypiercer. "Gather all that can be spared! I will take some from the valley and fly ahead!"

"Enter at the Amethyst Cliffs! The guard there is still holding. But hurry!" Skypiercer cried.

Windrush broke away and sped back toward the Valley of Fallen Light. As he approached the valley, he called out to those on guard. "I need six to fly with me against the Enemy! The rest of you stay, and be more vigilant than ever! Who will come?"

Within moments, he had his six: Longnail and Rocktooth, formerly of WingTouch's patrol, Hardscale and FlyForever, two lanky dragons from the south, plus WindSpear and—to his surprise—SearSky. Farsight had probed SearSky and pronounced him as cantankerous and illnatured as ever, but utterly loyal to the realm—and not just ready to do battle, but eager.

"We'll fly fast and hard, and be outnumbered when we arrive," Windrush warned, as the seven climbed away, eastward, from the lumenis grove.

"The better to show the Enemy who is stronger!" SearSky growled, from the left flank. "It's time we did some *fighting*!"

His cry was echoed by the others, and Windrush nodded. He was not one to feel easy readiness for battle, but he knew that a fighting spirit was exactly what they needed now.

As they flew eastward into the dark of night, Windrush tried, but could think of no specific target that would draw the Enemy to the Deep Caverns. Their past powers diminished, the caverns were now hauntingly empty, a place where even a dragon could feel an oppressive loneliness. Windrush had maintained their defense, but sparingly. He wondered now if he would regret that. If the caverns were so useless, why had the Enemy mustered the sorcery to attack them, all the way on the far side of the dragon-held land? Did Tar-skel know something about the Deep Caverns that the dragons should have known?

"Who would have thought?" he heard Rocktooth mutter aloud. "Why the Deep Caverns and not the groves?"

Windrush said nothing, but as he worked his wings tirelessly in the night, he thought of a certain demon named Hodakai to whom he intended to put some harsh questions. Defend the lumenis! said Hodakai, and Windrush had believed him. Not that defending the lumenis wasn't a prudent thing to do. But not a hint had Hodakai given him of the real target.

Windrush smelled the air ahead, filled with scattered storm clouds, and he smelled the underweb stretching out toward their distant goal. He smelled the Enemy. He smelled destruction.

The Amethyst Cliffs emerged from darkness with starlight glimmering through them, so that they seemed insubstantial, a great ghostly wall in the night sky. The dragons approached the cliffs at their westernmost, and narrowest, point. From there the wall stretched eastward for a short distance, before bending to the northeast. The farther along the wall they flew, the greater its height; but at its base, it dropped away into nothingness. A pair of dragons appeared out of the darkness and met the seven. It was the sentry patrol, and the two urged Windrush and his companions to hurry.

"I can fly faster, if the rest of you can," SearSky growled from behind Windrush's left wing.

Windrush replied, "We will all fly faster now. *Prepare to dive, brothers! Downward, to meet the Enemy!*"

The dragons behind him echoed his cry as one. In tight formation, they pitched over and dove, seeking the bottom of the Amethyst Cliffs.

To many dragons, the Amethyst Cliffs marked the edge of the realm as they knew it—a place where the bottom dropped out of the world. And that was very nearly the truth. Windrush and his fellows were diving off the edge, into another world—into inky darkness, an abyss of emptiness like the night sky turned upside down. It was a long dive, an endless dive. In the near-darkness, it was hard not to fear that they had lost their way, and were falling into an emptiness from which they would never return.

"Where are we?" murmured FlyForever, probably the youngest dragon among them. It was an understandable question: their only point of reference was the vertical cliff wall, which in the faint starlight seemed to recede from the eye, to vanish into the night.

"Where are we?" SearSky laughed, spilling air from his wings to fall faster. "On our way to the darkest hole in the realm. Do you want to challenge drahls in the utterest darkness? This is the place to do it." Laughing again, he blew a tongue of fire downward into the abyss. Like a torch in the night, his flame vanished into darkness, but not before it momentarily illumined a small section of the wall. The fire was refracted back out of the faceted-gem surface, like a gleam of light in a dragon's eye. For the briefest instant, one could see how, in the morning sun, the cliffs might blaze with blue fire.

When the flame went out, the dragons dropped in a darkness that seemed more enveloping than ever. "No more fire," Windrush warned, trying to steer a true course downward, parallel to the cliff wall. "Save it for the battle, SearSky. If any of the enemy were looking this way, you just announced our approach. Let's try to surprise them, and maybe we'll stay alive long enough to do some good."

SearSky snorted. But from then on, the wind was the only sound as they dropped into the endless bottom of the night.

The first hint of the Deep Caverns was a feeling that the cliff was steadily curving from them, no matter how hard they tried to stay even with it. For a moment, Windrush feared that he was losing his orientation, leading the others into the great void beyond. Then he saw the first sprinkling of stars through an opening in the wall to his left.

That was the opening to the Deep Caverns, and to the stars that shone through from their extreme opposite end. When they passed through that opening, they would pass *beneath* the realm, beneath the mountains, beneath the earth. And those were the stars of the sky beneath—similar in appearance to, but different from, the stars they knew above the realm.

His heart pounding with excitement and fear, Windrush pulled out of his dive and led the other six in a long, curving flight through the opening to the caverns. It was difficult to make out the forms in the dark, but the cliffs were above him now, a ceiling rather than a wall. He knew that stalactites and columns extended down from that ceiling, and they had to fly with caution to avoid a collision.

And where, in all of this darkness, was the enemy? And where were the dragons defending against them?

The caverns were vast, and stretched out in many directions. Were there no remaining sentries who could lead them to the battle? The enemy could be almost anywhere. But they must have come in search of the power that had once emanated from the underrealm here. Windrush recalled a place in one of the caverns called the Flowing Springs—a focal point, long ago, for a great potential in the underrealm. It seemed as likely a place as any.

He sniffed the underrealm as he flew, wishing that he could land to concentrate properly. But there was no place to land, and no time! The drahls might already have won their victory here. Windrush felt anger powering his wing-strokes, and flame building in the back of his throat.

Behind him, SearSky grumbled, "Where are they? Have they done their filthy work and left this useless place?"

"Don't be so sure the place is useless," Windrush answered. "The Enemy wouldn't waste his time here unless he thought he would find something of value."

"Drahls!" SearSky muttered. "That's what I want to find! Drahls to kill!"

Windrush spotted a faint nimbus of light, far off to his right. He banked that way. "You may get your chance." Now he saw a flicker of fire: dragon flames. "Battle ahead!" he called softly. "Be sharp! And stay quiet!"

Cavern-shadows flowed past them as they picked up speed. Windrush scanned ahead, trying to discern the shapes of dragons, of drahls, of anything that moved. He saw several more flashes of flame, and then they sped through a great dark archway. A pale moon came into view beneath the inverted horizon, shining up into the caverns from below. Its ghostly illumination was enough to let Windrush make out the outlines of the ceiling and walls. He strained to pick out, at last, the shapes of the dragons and the enemy.

It was a chamber called the Cavern of Clouds Below, roofed above with vaulting stone ceilings and floored with sky—and far below, a layer of cottony white, ever-present cloud. Windrush knew this place a little. The clouds below were a place where dragons never went, but up here in the cavern, dragons had once gathered in great numbers, perching on hollowed-out ledges and crooks of stone. Beyond this cavern, on the far side, was the place called the Flowing Springs. Whether the enemy was there or not, Windrush couldn't tell—because the Cavern of Clouds Below was swarming with drahls, and with a much smaller number of dragons who were trying to drive them away. It was clear that the dragons were in desperate need of help!

Guided by the flickering of fire—hot, yellow flames of dragons, and ice-blue flames of drahls—Windrush and the six arrowed straight for the center of the battle. Soon they could see the banking, climbing, diving shapes of the combatants, and they began to pick out dragons who most needed help. In the noise and turbulence, no one seemed to have noticed their arrival. Windrush thundered out a battle cry: "DRAGON BROTHERS, HELP HAS ARRIVED!" The six behind him echoed the cry, and for an instant the battle seemed to pause while everyone registered their presence.

The beleaguered dragons cried out, and hisses filled the chamber as the drahls realized that they faced fresh opponents. Windrush wasted no time: he dove upon the nearest drahl and blasted it until it tumbled, burning, toward the clouds. He turned instantly to climb again for a new target—and to avoid several drahls who were wheeling toward him. He heard the shrieks of several other drahls dying, and knew that his companions had joined him in taking advantage of their surprise.

The advantage did not last long. The dragons who had been defending this place were tired, and hurt, and reduced in numbers. They had lasted this long by darting in and out from sheltered places in the upper reaches of the cavern, but a look revealed that many of those shelters had been blasted away by the attacking drahls. These dragons would not have survived much longer. Windrush did not want to think how many the realm had lost already tonight. They were still outnumbered, but with the addition of his seven, they could certainly fight back. "TURN THE TIDE!" he called out. "TURN THE TIDE!"

He felt the chill of drahl fire on his right wing, and dropped and twisted sharply, glimpsing a drahl over his shoulder. He turned beneath the enemy. It could not follow quickly enough, and Windrush climbed steeply and twisted again to come back upon it. He saw a flame and heard a scream, and the drahl was falling, incinerated by SearSky. The other dragon's eyes gleamed as he passed close to Windrush.

There was no time for thanks or gloating. Three more drahls were upon them, and the two dragons blew flame and beat the air, and moments later were separated again. Windrush caught one of the drahls and raked it with his claws, and felt it shudder as it tumbled away from his grasp, out of the battle. He had no time to follow it for the kill. Another flew across his path, trying to evade the pursuit of FlyForever. Windrush blew flame and killed the drahl— but a flame from another direction caught FlyForever at the same moment, following his movement. Windrush came about hard, and cursed at the sight of FlyForever burning, spinning in agony—burned, not by a drahl, but by another dragon! The Tar-skel dragon, eyes afire, was diving away— toward Rocktooth, who was just shaking loose a pair of drahls.

"*Rocktooth! Enemy dragon!*" Windrush bellowed.

Rocktooth veered again and blew a breath of flame, but missed the Tar-skel dragon. Windrush shot a last, agonized glance at FlyForever, now falling out of reach, out of the cavern—and dove in pursuit of the enemy. He wouldn't have caught it, except that FlyForever's friend Hardscale thundered in from the right to join the pursuit and drove the enemy dragon upward and left, giving Windrush the chance to cut it off. *"You murder your brothers, traitor!"* he shouted, blasting a tongue of flame that caught the dragon on the left wing. The dragon spun around, eyes flashing with hatred, and belched fire at Windrush as it seemed to hang in the air, before falling tailfirst.

The blast hit Windrush in the face and neck, but he passed through it quickly. The enemy dragon had evaded him momentarily, but it was more badly hurt. Windrush banked over to come at the dragon again. But Hardscale was already upon the traitor, enveloping him in a withering flame, bellowing, *"FlyForever! This is for you!"*

Windrush felt sick rather than triumphant, as he watched the Tar-skel dragon fall to its death. An enemy gone, but one that never should have been an enemy. And a good warrior, FlyForever, gone before he'd fairly had a chance to fight.

"Windrush, dive!" he heard. He obeyed instantly, and saw a drahl shoot past. Rocktooth had shouted the warning, and it was a good message: Don't think! Just fly and fight! He turned back for another target.

The battle continued in the moonlit darkness for what seemed an eternity. The loyal dragons were still outnumbered, and were steadily being worn down. The fight was beginning to seem hopeless . . . until a new battle cry pierced the night. A dozen new dragons flew into the fray, sent by Farsight from the main encampment. Windrush greeted them with a grateful blast. The original dragon-defenders were exhausted, and several had fallen since Windrush's arrival.

"Burn the ones we saved for you!" SearSky trumpeted, cartwheeling across the vast cavern in pursuit of a frantically dodging drahl. He actually seemed to be enjoying himself. Windrush followed SearSky with his eyes, stunned by the dragon's fierce joy in the pursuit and the kill. He would not have wanted SearSky fighting against him; nevertheless, he shuddered at the bloodlust that burned in that dragon.

He had no time to think about SearSky, though. With the arrival of help, he realized that they might have a chance of clearing the drahls from this place. But even so, they were only fighting a rearguard action, in one cavern among many. What mischief was Tar-skel working, while the dragons and drahls battled endlessly here in the Cavern of Clouds Below?

"Two to fly with me!" he thundered, as soon as the new arrivals had joined the battle.

"With you, Windrush!" called Rocktooth, rising to join him.

"Where to, Windrush?" asked SearSky, cackling as he flew alongside. It wasn't clear if he was joining or taunting.

"If we're to learn what the Enemy is doing here, we must fly now, while the tide is with us," Windrush said. "Yes or no. I have no time for foolishness."

SearSky glanced around. "They need me here." The black dragon's teeth flashed, and his eyes glowed fiery red. "But you'll need me more, if you're thinking to fly deeper. Lead on."

Windrush flew high, passing above the battle. None of the drahls seemed to notice their departure. Windrush aimed toward the distant moon, then banked right. Ahead now, growing quickly, was another great archway. They sped through it.

Suddenly they had rock beneath them; they were flying through a half-enclosed tunnel, open on the right. A small shadow ahead grew, then turned away with a screech. It died in SearSky's flame before it could flee the way it had come. The dragons thundered past the drahl's body, falling to the floor of the tunnel.

The formation opened out into a new chamber, this one with a partial floor of stone. It was open on the right side; but to the left, a wall curved up and arched overhead. Perhaps a third of the cavern was open to the stars, directly ahead and to the right. Drahls were wheeling in the air, some distance away. They seemed preoccupied and did not immediately notice the dragons. The wall on the left looked damaged—as though a part of it had split away, perhaps falling out of the cavern and away into infinity. A stream of water was cascading down the broken section of the wall. The water glistened in the moonlight—and in the light of something else, as well.

"*Halt here!*" Windrush whispered urgently, braking to land. The other two complied, SearSky more slowly than Rocktooth. They muttered uneasily as they landed near him.

There was a strong undersmell of sorcery, but Windrush didn't need his undersense to reveal the Enemy's work here. He gazed in dismay at a glowing pattern of fine, ghostly light that stretched across the open sky ahead and to the right. It was a *web* of light, exactly like the Enemy's web of power that he had seen in the lumenis vision. It took him a moment to focus and realize that several strands of the web actually narrowed and entered the cavern. They ended near the waterfall, hanging in midair, glimmering.

Windrush's undersense was on fire. Power was flowing from that stream—he could not see it, but he could feel it—power such as had not flowed here in many generations of dragons.

"I must go into the underrealm," he whispered. "I must discover what is happening here."

"Those drahls will be upon us if we remain," SearSky said.

"Then you must protect me," Windrush answered, wondering if he could trust SearSky to guard him.

The black dragon shrugged his wings insolently. "Do what you must. But do it fast."

Windrush nodded, fearing what he was going to find in the underrealm more than he feared those drahls. With a last glance around, he closed his eyes and sank his thoughts into the underweb.

At first sight, the shape of the underrealm was little different from that of the outer world. But it was charged with different hues of light, as though the moonlight illuminating the cavern had turned to an eerie blue-green. The spring that tumbled down the wall was backlit by the sepulchral glow, and the sky off to the right was hazy with a faint blue airglow. But shining out of that sky was the luminous green web of the Enemy, which here in the underrealm seemed to breathe and throb with energy.

Windrush was flanked by two great, dark, still statues on his right and left—the two dragons guarding him. Their presence provided a silent reassurance. He knew they could do little to protect him against the greatest of the dangers here, but he hoped they could keep him safe from the other things casting their shadows in the underrealm, the shadows that were the drahls.

The real danger, of course, was the power revealed in that light. It was not a dragon light, nor a Dream Mountain light. It was a light of sorcery, a work of the Enemy. And yet, there was more to it than that. There was a natural power here: he could feel it flowing in the spring of water. It was a bitter realization; Tar-skel had found the power the dragons had thought long vanished. Was his knowledge of the underrealm so much greater—or had he learned secrets from the captive draconae? And what was his purpose?

Windrush gazed out at the web, remembering the vision of FullSky. He could imagine the Enemy's web reaching out, binding this place to similar places in other realms, in other skies. Did this web touch the static realm? he wondered. Did it touch realms that not even an outsider like Jael could imagine? Each strand seemed to pulse like a living fiber, breathing and growing, stretching from the Flowing Spring out into the infinity of the sky. In the outer world, the web seemed not to have touched the waterfall; but here he saw a pale ribbon of light connecting the two, and he could feel the power streaming out through that connection.

The dragon stared at the joining, wondering if he could interrupt it; but the sorcery-weavings appeared strong there. Moving up and down those nearer strands of the web were figures of light and shadow, so faint he had not no-

ticed them at first—figures that vaguely reminded him of
the guardian that had kept FullSky prisoner in the underrealm. Were they keepers of the spell? Whether they were
or not, Windrush saw no hope of interfering directly here.
If this was the object of the Enemy's invasion of the Deep
Caverns, then the battle was over. He could gather his
brothers to fight the drahls, but he had none who could
stand with him here in the underrealm.

He knew that he should leave before he was noticed. But
something made him delay a moment longer. If this battle
were not to have been in vain, he had to understand everything he could about the Enemy's work here. He peered at
the web shimmering against the sky. It appeared solid, and
yet ethereal; it was hard to see what it *was* exactly. And yet,
as he gazed at it, he began to see more of its larger structure.

One part of it coiled into the Deep Caverns, binding this
place into the web. Another part dwindled into the infinity
of the sky—binding this realm, perhaps, with others—
though he could not tell how complete that binding was.
Still another part seemed to coil around . . . something else
in the sky. It was coiled around a strange *emptiness*. A place
without stars, web, or airglow.

Windrush froze. *Emptiness?* A hole in the sky? Or in the
web?

With a sudden, unreasoning certainty, he knew that that
place around which the web coiled was something far more
than *nothing*. Was it the Dream Mountain, caught up in the
Enemy's web? He could not *see* that it was; and yet something told him *yes*. His heart nearly broke as he gazed at that
empty space. What chance was there of reaching the Dream
Mountain, if it was caught in the Enemy's web?

And yet . . .

Though there was power flowing from this spot into the
underrealm, and though it was under the Enemy's control
right now, it still did not *belong* to the Enemy, any more
than the power of the Dream Mountain belonged to him.
The web looked ominously strong, and yet he could see
that it was not altogether complete. Gaps remained, places
where not all the strands had been drawn together. It was

not yet finished. If only they could keep it that way! He wondered if that emptiness around which the web coiled wasn't in fact a *weakness* in the Enemy's plans.

Still, even as he sat here, power was flowing out of the Deep Caverns, bringing the sorcery closer and closer to completion. The time in which to act was growing short.

He sensed a movement nearby. It wasn't the guardians from along the web; it was something closer, a shadow. He tried to focus, then realized that he heard a dragon voice calling to him, urgently.

He wrenched himself out of the underrealm with dizzying abruptness. SearSky was growling furiously: "Come OUT of there, Windrush—come out NOW!"

Windrush grunted and blinked in the moonlit gloom, and glimpsed a flight of drahls flocking toward them where they were perched at the edge of the cavern. He struggled to react. "I'm here!" he gasped.

Rocktooth and SearSky sprang away instantly, toward the drahls. Windrush took a sharp breath and commanded his limbs to move. Swaying, he leaped and flew after his companions.

He wanted to call them back to fly with him out of this place of the Enemy—but the two were already on the attack. He could only leave them, or join them. Wearily, summoning his reserves of strength, he pounded the air until his wings screamed in protest; then he beat harder still, gaining more speed.

The drahls swept in a great arc to meet them. First SearSky, then Rocktooth bellowed out great tongues of fire. The drahls veered, scattering—but quickly circled back to surround the two dragons. They seemed not to have noticed Windrush following. Windrush let the fire rise hot in his throat as he sped upward. But before he could close the range, SearSky climbed in an abrupt spiral. His maneuver startled the drahls and caused them to turn awkwardly, trying to stay with him. SearSky pitched up sharply, then fell sideways into a spinning dive, his dark scales flashing in the moonlight. At least five drahls fluttered after him, breathing cold blue fire. Windrush crested his climb, above them now. He saw Rocktooth veering in front of a second wave of drahls, drawing them away.

Windrush pitched down and dove after the drahls chasing the spinning SearSky. His breath blazed out ahead of him, and he raked two drahls with searing flame before the others darted away. SearSky pulled out of his spin in a sweeping turn and glanced back in surprise at the tumbling, burning drahls. "Well done, Windrush," he remarked, eyes aglow.

Windrush began to reply, but was interrupted by a cry of distress. He looked around for Rocktooth.

The third dragon had succeeded too well in drawing the other drahls away. "Help, I—!" Rocktooth cried. His words were cut off by the freezing breaths of two drahls, crossing over him from either side.

"*Rocktooth!*" Windrush shouted, pounding the air to climb to his aid.

"*Windrush, watch out!*" rumbled SearSky, climbing past him on the right, belching flame.

Two more drahls broke off an attack that Windrush had not even seen coming. He caught his breath, looking for other attackers; then frantically tried to locate Rocktooth again. His heart stopped as he saw the young dragon with two drahls on his back, falling. Rocktooth's expression was locked in pain; the light was fading from his eyes. The drahls released him as he turned transparent as glass, and vanished in midair. "*You murdering hellspawn!*" Windrush cried, blowing fire, but too late to help Rocktooth.

"How could he be so stupid?" SearSky snarled, circling back. "Let's kill the rest of these—"

"*No!*" Windrush cut off SearSky's turn toward the drahls. "Rocktooth may have saved both our lives! Let's go! There are too many!"

"Too many for you, maybe!" SearSky snapped. But despite his words, he sent a single blast of fire to deflect the nearest drahls, then joined Windrush in speeding toward the cavern's exit.

They reached the tunnel and shot into it. They were outflying the drahls, but the air behind them was dark with fluttering pursuers. Windrush bellowed out a warning to the other dragons as they reemerged into the Cavern of Clouds Below. *"Drahls following!"*

"Windrush is back!" someone shouted over the sounds of battle, and the cry echoed across the cavern. "Windrush!" shouted another. "What did you find?"

He thundered back, "The Flowing Springs are taken by the Enemy! Withdraw, dragons! There is nothing more to fight for here!"

His cry reverberated through the cavern, and was answered by shouts of dismay. He repeated the command to retreat, determined not to lose more dragons in a futile battle. The Deep Caverns were lost. "We've learned what we need to know!" he bellowed. "Leave the caverns! This battle is lost, but the war can still be ours!"

"The war will be ours!" shouted a dragon, and that cry was echoed by others.

As Windrush swept through the cavern, helping dragons to break free of the enemy, he saw SearSky taking on several more drahls, raking them savagely from the air before continuing on with the rest of the dragons. As they sped out into the night beneath the vast, brooding Amethyst Cliffs, Windrush wondered silently whether he had spoken the truth.

Had he learned what he needed to know? Did they still have a chance of winning this war? Would Jael ever appear?

He had to believe that the answer was yes. Nevertheless, he kept his thoughts to himself as, with his flight of weary and wounded dragons, he began the long climb upward along the face of the Amethyst Cliffs, toward the top of the world and the realm that they knew as home.

PART FOUR

THE BATTLE

PROLOGUE

STANDING WATCH over the Forge of Dreams, the draconae crafted their guarding spells ceaselessly, wrapping threads of the underrealm around that one place that was everywhere and nowhere, a part of the realm and yet not a part of it. No fewer than seven draconae watched over the fires at all times, weaving their spells of protection, of creation, of preservation . . . and one *other* spell, held carefully in reserve.

The draconae were ever aware of the Enemy's desire to control the dreamfires, the powers from beyond the realm that nourished and sustained life and creation in all the realm. It was the one thing that might grant him final mastery, and it was the one thing that the draconae were utterly determined to deny him. The Enemy might imprison the Mountain, and he might bring an end to all dragon life and all iffling life in the realm; but he could not make the dreamfires do his bidding. Not yet, anyway. Not without the help of the draconae.

But what if, against all hope, he learned to use the fires himself? They could not forget the haunting Words:

> . . . *To tear from its midst*
> *The fires of being,*
> *That dragons may die,*
> *Unknowing, unseeing.*

If Tar-skel seized the dreamfires, did they have any remaining defense? Perhaps just one. They held in reserve a difficult and terrifying spell, woven in the sinews of the underrealm, to be used only in direst of need—a crafting that would release the bindings that held the dreamfires, a catastrophic release of *all* the bindings and *all* the power they contained. It would almost certainly destroy the realm—and with it the lives, not just of those in the realm now, but perhaps even those departed, those who lived beyond the realm in the soulfire of the Final Dream Mountain. That spell could sacrifice, not just the realm's future, but its living past, as well.

But if the alternative was Tar-skel's victory? Better to lose the realm.

And yet . . .

> *A word names the nameless*
> *And light dawns from dread*
> *To the heart of the darkness*
> *Are the fearful ones led . . .*

Even now, the draconae were not without hope. Those working at the Forge of Dreams wrapped their songs and words of protection not just around the fires, but around all the unborn dragons, the unhatched eggs that remained alive, but frozen in time, on the outer slopes of the Dream Mountain . . . just as the once-vibrant groves and streams where the draconae raised their young were now frozen, static, chrysalized in layer upon layer of binding energy. Those eggs, and those groves of life, were as much captive of Tar-skel's sorcery as the draconae on the inside of the mountain.

Light dawns from dread.

More than anything, they held hope for a release into life for those unhatched draconae and draconi of the future.

Chapter 30
THE VOICE STONE

RENT STRODE through the chasms of the Dark Vale with a pride that would have been beyond him just days ago. But everything that had happened in that time had been so *perfect*—just as his own body was perfect now, and his very existence. Around him the hardened shapes of a blasted land spoke eloquently of the power of his master, the Nail of Strength. Around him flickered the shadowy, and sometimes iridescent, shapes of the drahls as they moved about their master's business. Around him murmured the dragons who had entered the service of the Nail. Around him rose the groans of the captives, embedded in the stone prisons where the Nail's magic had sealed them—a magic that Rent himself had often wielded in the name of Tar-skel.

Rent felt a deep satisfaction in the knowledge that everything was now falling into place for the final victory, the victory of Tar-skel, and of a rigger-spirit named Rent, who had helped make the triumph possible. There was a confident power in his stride as he walked the sculpted paths of the Dark Vale, a power that he had never dreamed of as a mere human. If there was pleasure in walking in a human body, how much better it was to walk in a body shaped by Tar-skel, a body formed in a crucible of underrealm magic, a body that could be donned like a cloak or set aside at the pleasure of its owner! It was a body that could shape magic as no human being ever could. What man wouldn't give up his feeble, ordinary form, in exchange for such power?

Rent paused, resting one foot on a sharp volcanic outcropping, and surveyed the wondrous desolation of the Vale. He had had no small part in the forming of this place, with its maze of ravines and caverns, and the wondrous girding of underrealm spells that kept it intact. Life, he thought, was full of things to be proud of.

It had not always been so for Brenton Maskill, human rigger, human in another life. A past life—one from another time, another universe. It was a life of hatred and misery that he had left behind: hatred for a mother who had unwittingly exposed her child to an incurable and crippling alien disease—hatred for the other children, who had teased him, then pitied him, and finally shunned him—and hatred for his fellow adult riggers, whom he had utterly reviled, not giving them the chance to revile him first. He remembered being a rigger, and a skilled one. But what was the artistry of rigging, compared to this?

In that miserable life, rigging had provided the only outlet for a brilliant mind held captive in a ruined body. The time inevitably had come when stealing a ship seemed a more appealing prospect than working for shipowners who pitied and despised him. Killing his riggermates and his ship's master had been easier than he'd dreamed, and more satisfying. And once in possession of a ship, he had set out for the reputed dragon route, questing—with the insolence of blind and angry conceit—for a fight worthy of his skills.

Never had he imagined that the dragons would prove to be real, living inhabitants of the Flux. Never had he imagined how easily they would defeat him in battle, stripping him of his life and his form. And never had he dreamed that a silent, hidden power with a name like Tar-skel would witness the event and raise him up to a spirit-existence in the realm—and not only that, but would restore him to human form, a *perfect* human form, so that he could walk as he never had walked as an adult human. He not only walked, he strutted and worked his own mastery over the very dragons who had defeated him—a defeat that was to be his last.

Rent thought of Hodakai and laughed, shaking his head. Hodakai lusted for what Rent had. But they could not have been more unlike, either as human riggers or as spirits in the realm. Hodakai was simply unwilling to make the sacrifices that were required to become a favored one of Tar-skel. It was pitiable, but it was Hodakai's loss, not Rent's. Hodakai was one of those thoughtless riggers—not very bright, just bright enough to get himself into trouble. He was pathetically easy to manipulate; he'd not even questioned Rent's casual lie to him that his shipmate had been destroyed by the dragons. It was absurdly easy to maneuver Hodakai into doing what was needed; he was a perfect illustration of the price of weakness.

No such weakness for Rent. For him, and for the Nail of Strength, there was no longer any possibility of failure. There was only the long savoring, the anticipation of victory. With the conquest of the Deep Caverns, and the tapping of the power that had lain buried there, Tar-skel had brought almost to full strength the web of magic that was binding this realm to his will. It was true that the ultimate fulcrum of his power, the control of the singularity within the Dream Mountain, was not yet in his grasp; but that too was drawing closer with each passing day.

The dragons were enfeebled with despair, and yet the one thing they still did not comprehend was how perfectly their despair fitted into the Nail's sorcery. Tar-skel *wielded* despair, letting the dragons watch as their realm crumbled, piece by piece. Despair was his yeast, worked through his plan with infinite care, causing it to live and grow. Tar-skel *thrived* on the dragons' despair, and he was using it to create a work of such power, such sorcery, such magnificence and artistry, that Rent practically wept at the thought of it—and the thought of his own participation in it.

One day Rent would walk with his Master in bodily form on the world-surfaces of other realms, other universes. Perhaps he would even assist in the rule of the universe he had once called home.

* Rent. *

He blinked, his reverie interrupted. He thought he had heard a voice, deep in his mind. He wasn't certain; but it would not do to take chances. Turning from the view, he started up the long ascending path that zigzagged up one wall of the vale, toward the Voice Stone. He moved expeditiously, but without betraying haste. The land below him was broken and sectored like a great, shattered moon, where a blast of sorcery had fragmented the crust into the chasms that provided quarters for the servants of the Nail, and for the captives. He glimpsed a few of the latter stirring at his passage, and he smiled.

At the top of the path, he stepped onto a ledge that had been carved there, a platform edged by a low parapet overlooking the vale. A single guardian drahl waited there, cloaked in shadow. The drahl bobbed its head at Rent's arrival and withdrew into concealment.

Rent paused before the Voice Stone. It was a massive, finely polished slab of obsidian, embedded in the base of a towering wall. It was pierced by a star-shaped opening, as though a tremendous bolt of lightning had punched a hole into its heart. Far from looking burned, however, the inside of the hole was polished to a black-mirror sheen. It bored unfathomably deep into the stone, into the bedrock, into some place that was not *here*. From somewhere in the remote reaches of the underrealm, there flickered the glow of a distant and powerful fire.

Rent knelt before the stone. He dropped his gaze for a moment, drawing a slow and measured breath. Then he raised his eyes and peered down into the hole, staring deep, toward the distant fire. He could not focus upon the fire; it would not *allow* his eyes to focus. Slowly he released control of his sight, and with great deliberation, emptied his thoughts.

His mind filled quickly, but not from his own thoughts.

The underrealm shimmered around him as he sank toward what had been a fire, but was now the invisible center of a cyclone. He was drawn to a point of focus that he could not see, yet which he knew instinctively was the presence of Tar-skel. He never knew what form the Nail's presence would take. Darkness swirled around him, enclosing him in the eye of the storm. As he was about to speak, to acknowledge the call that had brought him here, there was a sudden flash of lightning in the clouds. The storm vanished and he was floating among stars, surrounded by the vast, rotating disk of a blazing spiral galaxy. And out of the galaxy, he heard the voice of the Nail.

* Servant, there is much to do. The time approaches when the realm will tremble! *Tremble!* *

Rent could not speak, even in his thoughts. His breath was caught, frozen.

* There is fear in the hearts of the winged serpents. *Fear!* But not yet *enough* fear. *

Rent struggled to swallow, to think. *But,* he whispered, *how could their fear be greater? Their groves are vanishing, they suffer dissension and betrayal, they have lost a spring of power that they were too dull even to realize they owned, they have lost many of their own number—*

* Are you reporting to me that which I already know? *

I—no—not at all!

* Have you forgotten the promise of the words of vision, which even the female serpents acknowledge? When the realm trembles, when the one falls in battle, then will come the ending. And the beginning. *

Exactly as we have hoped—as you have planned.

The majestic galaxy seemed to turn with greater speed, as though driven by an enormous urgency. * Yes. But we must be certain. Their despair grows, but not quickly enough! They must not even dream that they might prevail. We must cause their fear to mount until the very end, when the hope of even the female serpents will be crushed. Only when their hope is *gone* will we command them, and the power of their mountain. *

Rent was silent. It was true that although the pieces were now in place, the final victory had not yet been won. But he could not understand the concern over the prophecy. The "one" was in the hands of Rent's servants at this very moment. What could possibly interrupt the plan? The rigger Jael would be brought forth to die, in a final battle with the dragons—and there would die the dragons' last conceivable hope: the rigger whom they believed would set them free. Jael was powerless in his hands. And her death would seal Tar-skel's web of power forever.

The words of his master intruded.

* Servant, I perceive your thoughts. *

Yes, he whispered.

* Stop thinking—and do something for me. *

Of course. By your command. Though puzzled, Rent was not displeased. It had occurred to him, in moments of doubt, that in the instant of victory the Nail might be so satisfied with his own achievement that he would not fully recall the assistance that his servant, Rent, had provided. Rent would be happy to do whatever he could to reinforce his worth in his master's eyes.

* Create more terror for me. *

Rent smiled inwardly as he listened to his master's wishes. His kuutekka flickered and twisted, revealing his smile in the underrealm.

* Walk among the captives. Enrage them. They despair now. See that they despair more. *

Yes, Rent whispered.

Shadows flashed and surged in the coiling galaxy. * One thing more. *

Yes?

* Bring me ASSURANCE that the *one* . . . the *rigger* . . . has been secured. Then let the *serpents* know. Use that pathetic excuse for a spirit— *

Hodakai?

* Hodakai. Through that one, remind the serpents of how hopeless is their cause. *

Rent found himself hesitating. *I'm not sure . . . it might just make them fight . . . all the more desperately.*

* It matters not how desperately they fight. It matters not how many drahls they kill. Drahls are nothing; let them die. I wish only the serpents' hopelessness. I wish their rage, and their fear, and their despair. Can you do that for me, servant? IS THAT TOO MUCH TO ASK? *

The will of the Nail swept over him like a pounding surf. *No, of course not!* he whispered. *I will do so—at once!* It would not trouble him to deliver new instructions to Hodakai, the vacillating weakling, who would be terrified to receive them. All the better. Let Hodakai's terror be contagious; let him pass the news of defeat on to the next dragon who came snooping. *I will do so with delight*, he whispered again to his Master.

But this time he was talking to himself. The great glowing span of the galaxy had vanished, and he was staring alone into the flickering fire of the Voice Stone.

Chapter 31
A FINAL REGROUPING

Upon their return from the Deep Caverns, Windrush watched the others in the camp fly their grief flight for those just fallen, venting their sorrow against the target wall. Windrush was weary, and had no energy to spare for futile anger. As for those who had fought in the Deep Caverns, he sent them off with such encouragement as he could, to a well-earned rest.

SearSky, to his surprise, offered encouragement to *him*. "Don't fret over the Deep Caverns, Windrush. So the Enemy has another useless acquisition. It is the lumenis we should worry about."

Windrush accepted the spirit of the black dragon's words, but he was under no illusions about the Deep Caverns. Their loss was a serious blow. And he was worried about the lumenis, too. The fact that none had been lost tonight was scant reassurance; a new attack could come at any time.

"In fact," SearSky added, "it is the young warriors I worry about most. Will they have the heart for fighting, at the end? It's not going to get easier, you know."

"I have to agree," said Farsight. "Many of them are becoming discouraged. I don't know how much longer they can keep the will to fight." Farsight's half-silvered eyes seemed to rotate in distress. "Even now, I don't know if they truly recognize the Enemy for what he is. They stand by us out of loyalty—but they may waver and fall away, if we don't act decisively."

Windrush nodded, reluctantly. "I fear we must begin to prepare for the decisive battle. We may have to strike the

Enemy openly, at his heart, whatever the cost. There may be no other way."

"Now you're talking sense!" SearSky growled, his nostrils flaring with red fire. "Strike at the Enemy's heart! Enough of this nonsense about mystical answers! Leave that to the Enemy! What good will his sorcery do him if he's on his own walk to the Final Dream Mountain, eh?" SearSky shook his craggy head with barely contained battle lust, and turned to Stronghold, who was nodding nearby.

Windrush had no answer. He was continually amazed by SearSky's simplistic view of the world; and yet, at the moment, he wondered if SearSky might not be right. Perhaps they should just attack the Enemy, and when it was over, either the Enemy would be dead or the dragons would be.

"The young warriors fought bravely tonight," he muttered, thinking aloud. "Especially Rocktooth."

SearSky's eyes darkened as he turned back to Windrush. "They fought well enough for the Deep Caverns, maybe. But if we're to fly against the Dark Vale, they'll have to fight better. Smarter, faster, fiercer. And the sooner the better."

Windrush studied the warrior dragon for a moment. "In that case, perhaps *you* should train them, SearSky."

The black dragon's eyes flickered with suspicion. Behind him, Stronghold's amber eyes glowed with amusement.

Windrush cocked his head, nodding. "I watched you fight tonight—and no one in the realm fights better. You could teach the younger ones. Sharpen their skills, make them hunger for victory."

"There is no time for *training!*" SearSky spat. "The time has come to *fight!*"

"Indeed, you may be right. The time may be close—though there remain questions to which I need answers first. But—if you are right—then all the more important that you teach quickly, and well. Teach the young ones to fight as you fight."

"It is not their skill or their strength that I question," SearSky growled. "It is their *will*. Their *courage*."

"Then give them will. Give them courage. There is great need and little time. Best you start without delay." Windrush paused, raising his head. "Unless *you* need to rest first—"

Behind SearSky, Stronghold coughed. A wreath of smoke betrayed his amusement.

Windrush caught the black warrior-dragon's gaze again. He could see that SearSky *had* planned to rest, but was changing his mind. "Good. I'm counting on you." He turned to Farsight. "Assign your weakest patrols to train with SearSky when they are not flying. But be ready. We may set out with little warning."

"Where are you going?" SearSky protested as Windrush turned away.

"In search of answers," Windrush said without looking back.

Windrush knew, as he entered the underrealm in his cavern, that what he had said to SearSky was accurate, and yet incomplete. The dragons did need to fight with absolute ferocity when the time came. But unless he found some new hope, he knew that a face-to-face battle with the Enemy was almost certainly doomed to failure.

Where are you, Jael? he whispered to the darkness. *Why have you not come to us?*

And where were the ifflings? They had spent their strength trying to reach Jael. Were they gone now? Gone forever?

As he passed through the veil of the underrealm window, those questions were dispelled by the more immediate memory of what had happened in the Deep Caverns tonight. He felt his anger rising again as he broke into the demon-rigger's presence. *HODAKAI!* he shouted.

Ah—Windrush! the spirit answered, dancing nervously— too nervously, almost as if he had been expecting the dragon to appear.

Windrush glared at him. He had a feeling, suddenly, that he had interrupted another conversation—or at least, that Hodakai had very recently been talking to the enemy. He didn't sense the presence of anyone else here now; but there was, he thought, the lingering undersmell of a servant of the Enemy. *Hodakai, you lied to me.*

I did? the spirit squeaked.

You did, Windrush growled. *You told me to expect the next attack on the lumenis.*

The spirit writhed before his anger. *Wasn't it? Did I get it wrong?* There was a tittering quality to his voice that made Windrush certain that someone on the other side had succeeded in intimidating the rigger.

The attack was not on the lumenis. It was on the Deep Caverns—as I expect you know. Why did you lie, Hodakai? Is that what a rigger's word is worth? A lie? Windrush allowed his kuutekka to grow larger.

The rigger suddenly seemed to be gasping for breath. *You have no hope!* he rasped wildly. *No hope at all! Give it up, Windrush! Give it up!*

The dragon stared very hard at the spirit, until it twitched and grew still. It did not seem to be entirely in its right mind. *What do you mean?* Windrush asked, with a low threat in his voice.

Hodakai twitched again. *I . . . mean . . . you can only fool someone for so long. So you gave me your name! And you—you think you can trick me with it, but I won't be tricked.*

What are you talking about?

You lied to ME, Windrush! the rigger squawked. *You brought another rigger here to be your slave—and you thought you could enslave me, too! Well, it won't work, Windrush! It won't work!*

Windrush was so stunned, he hardly knew how to answer. *Enslave? You fool—if I wanted to enslave you, I would not have given you my name, you drahl-baiting cavern sprite, you—!* Windrush suddenly interrupted himself. *What did you say? Did you say another rigger has entered the realm?*

Hodakai laughed, his voice a desperate cackle. *Did you*

think I could not see past your lies? Yes, your rigger is here. But you'll never see her. Rent and the ifflings are making sure of that! You're so arrogant! You think you can—

SILENCE! Windrush bellowed. He glared at the spirit. *I'll say this once, Hodakai. I did not lie to you, and I have no intention of enslaving you, or anyone else.* He glared so deeply at the spirit that, for an instant, he caught the other's gaze and glimpsed a thread of his thoughts—and an astonishing network of lies that overlay his thoughts, held in place by a spell of persuasion. It appeared to be a simple spell, one that would probably only work on one as confused as Hodakai. Many of the lies appeared to come from another rigger—a Tar-skel rigger!—named Rent. Windrush grunted, understanding at last. This wretched creature truly had no idea what to believe.

Windrush tugged at a thread of the persuasion spell, trying to loosen it. He couldn't tell if he had succeeded or not. *You are misled by the lies of others,* Windrush growled into the creature's thoughts. *A rigger in league with Tar-skel! No wonder you're confused! And you believe that the ifflings are in league with the Enemy? Never!*

Hodakai pulled back indignantly, trying to gain release from Windrush's gaze.

What do you know of this new rigger? Windrush asked. *Where is she?*

That brought a snarl from the spirit. *Then as the iffling said, you do intend to—*

She is a FRIEND! Windrush roared. *A friend to the realm! Whoever told you differently was no iffling! It was the ifflings who brought her here! Do you understand? They risked everything to bring her to the realm!*

Eh? The spirit seemed completely bewildered now. Windrush tried once more to loosen the spell, then released the spirit from his gaze. Hodakai gasped and shuddered. *But it told me—*

Who told you?

It said it was an iffling!

Windrush nearly exploded with frustration. *It was not*

an iffling! Have you ever heard of ifflings siding with Tar-skel? Have you, rigger?

Well . . . no . . . The rigger flickered.

No—never! You have been listening to lies! Hodakai! Where is she? Where is the rigger?

Hodakai flared with uncertainty. Windrush couldn't tell if he was thinking for himself again or not. *How would I know?* he whispered plaintively.

You know she's here! What else do you know?

Well, I—yes, but—

Windrush rose enormous in the underrealm window. *Hodakai, do not test me further! If you intend to stand against me, say so!*

The rigger-spirit quailed. *I—NO! I don't know! That is—*

That sounded more like the old Hodakai. Windrush sighed wearily. *Tell me what you know,* he growled.

Hodakai was almost cowering. *Very little! Really!*

Tell me what you know.

Well, I—just that she's been captured.

Captured! Windrush tried to disguise his anguish. *Tell me where!*

How would I know? You tell me one thing, Rent tells me another! Rent said she was coming to enslave me.

Rent! Windrush cried. *Whoever he is, he's a liar! Think about it! Think! Why would a rigger come here just to enslave you?*

I—well—it's not that—I mean, Rent is a rigger too. Of course, he . . . I . . . Hodakai's voice choked off into inaudibility.

Windrush was so angry that he reflexively vented flame over the spirit jar—meaning it not so much for Hodakai as for this Rent, whoever he was. The flame-image passed harmlessly over Hodakai's kuutekka, but startled him nonetheless. Windrush asked tightly, *Where is the rigger now? Where has she been captured?*

Hodakai struggled to put words together. *She arrived— somewhere in the south mountains—that's all I know. That's really—all I know!*

Windrush stared at the spirit-flame. If that was true—if Jael had arrived in the southern mountains, if there was even the slightest chance that Hodakai was telling the truth—then he should send every dragon he could spare, to look for her. Except, how could he spare any? For an aimless search through the southern mountains?

Hodakai sniffed. *So—you got it out of me. What you do with it is your problem. But you should also know . . .*

Windrush waited.

You should know . . . Hodakai said slowly, but as though he were winding up to something. Suddenly he burst out, *Your cause is hopeless! Hopeless! The Nail has everything he needs to complete his plan. The Words will be fulfilled, and you will never see your Dream Mountain again. Unless . . .*

Unless what? Windrush growled.

Hodakai's flame quieted. *Unless you surrender now.*

Windrush stared at the spirit.

Hodakai spoke again, his voice like a chant: *No hope. Unless you surrender. Unless you give it up.*

The dragon hissed. *Who told you to say that? Rent?*

Hodakai became agitated, but didn't answer.

What else do you know that you're not saying?

I— The spirit-flame trembled violently in his jar. *I've said too much already! I CAN'T STAND THIS ANY LONGER! I've told you what I was supposed to! Now, get out of here, dragon—before they come!*

Windrush glared at the spirit, trying to understand what Hodakai was really saying. He didn't think anyone was coming; but someone, not Hodakai, had wanted him to hear the words he had just heard. Well—he'd heard them.

If they find you here, they'll kill me! Hodakai screeched, jittering madly in his jar. *Go! GO!*

Windrush nodded slowly. He would get nothing further from Hodakai now. He drew away; but before leaving the spirit's space, he rumbled, *Don't deceive me again, Hodakai. If you hear word of that rigger, I expect you to tell me!*

Without waiting for an answer, he departed. But his last impression was of a spirit who was sorely, sorely troubled.

* * *

Windrush stared at the last underrealm window, knowing that he must look there tonight. But suppose it led him to another battle in the underrealm! He was already so weary! Before he risked that, he desperately needed to rest.

Before he could even make his decision, he dropped off into a deep, dreamless sleep. But at some point, probably before dawn, he awoke with a start. An iffling was floating before him, little more than a flicker of luminosity in the air.

Windrush blinked groggily. "I wondered if I would ever see you again," he murmured.

We have not forgotten you, Windrush, whispered the iffling. *But our strength is failing. It is difficult.*

"Do you have news of Jael?" Windrush heard his own voice strain into near inaudibility.

We know only that something . . . has gone wrong.

Windrush remembered with a shudder his conversation with Hodakai. "Has the Enemy captured her?"

The flame flickered. *We are unsure. We have sensed treachery . . . a false-one.*

"A false-iffling?" Windrush nodded slightly. "I have heard of it."

Then you know, perhaps, as much as we. The iffling seemed to have to struggle to remain visible. *One child of ours . . . lives. We feel it. But we can do nothing to help it.*

"Do you know *where?*" Windrush asked quickly.

To the south . . . we think. We cannot be sure. We can only . . . trust in our last . . . child. And in Jael herself.

The dragon's breath escaped in a rush. "What have you come to tell me, then? Is there anything I can *do?*"

Search, if you can. The iffling almost went dark, then brightened a little. *And the last window. Do not forget it. Have not the sweepers been trying to tell you?*

Windrush blinked, startled. The sweepers? He glanced and saw a new scale-sculpture perched on the hearth. It looked like . . . a misshapen tree, he thought. He had no idea what it meant. "I have not forgotten the window," he said at last. "I was about to try it. Do you think it will offer guidance to finding Jael?"

We cannot say. Perhaps not. We only believe . . . that FullSky meant this for you . . . for a purpose. The iffling faded, and for a moment Windrush thought it was gone. But it flickered back into visibility just for a moment, in the cavern gloom. *Windrush, we must hope together.*

And as if that last whisper had exhausted the iffling's strength, it vanished for good.

Windrush stared uncertainly at the spot where the iffling had been. Then, with a last, puzzled glance at the sweeper's sculpture, he closed his eyes and sank again into the under-realm.

Perhaps because it was the last thing he'd looked at in the outer world, the sculpture's presence was the first thing he saw in the underweb. It was very small; he wondered if these things had been here all along. It looked only a little different here, more shadowy and asymmetrical. One branch of its "tree" made him think of a pointing claw. When he followed the direction in which it was pointing, he was startled to see it aimed directly at the fourth and last window.

Amazed, he turned and entered the window.

He encountered, at once, a smell that made him think of the sea—the tang of salt. Then sunlight filled his eyes, and his kuutekka materialized on wing, high over hills and woods and lowlands. Without understanding why, he found himself flying fast, toward the sun, over a metallic band of river that wound through the lowlands, and on through wetlands, toward a sunset glow at the horizon. The tang of the sea grew stronger. What was it that was drawing him on? He whispered FullSky's name, but heard no answer. It seemed that he was alone here.

Ahead of him now was a vast gleaming expanse of water, a pool that stretched out as far as he could see, to the sunset. It was the sea. But there was . . . something more than that, too.

He wasn't sure why he felt that, until the shoreline

passed beneath him. And then something materialized in midair, high above the sea . . . something massive and magnificent. He knew at once that it was the Dream Mountain, high in the air, floating on a wispy layer of cloud. It looked as though it were made of glass, and within it, a bright white fire burned. He ached to fly to it. But he already felt something deflecting him from it, even before he could draw closer. The spells of the Enemy, he thought.

Why had FullSky brought him here? To give him hope? It broke his heart to see the Dream Mountain, and to know that it was beyond reach. But something else was tugging at him, a feeling that there was something missing here. Not the Dream Mountain, but something else—a feeling that the window was not yet ready, for him to see all that it had to show him.

FullSky? he whispered, but still there was no answer.

He banked and circled, uncertain what to do.

As he tried to decide, he realized that the sea and sky and mountain were dissolving around him. He felt the window gently closing, the underrealm darkening around him. The time was not yet right, it seemed to be saying. He felt a stab of disappointment that it had not helped him to find Jael— but also a hint of reassurance, as though the underrealm itself were saying, there will be more to come.

But what? he wondered wearily. And when?

Back in his cavern, he was about to emerge from the underweb altogether, when he heard his name. The voice sounded very distant, and urgent. *Farsight?* he called back. Was his brother trying to reach him from the main encampment?

Windrush . . . at once if you . . . come at once . . . ! Farsight's undervoice sounded like the hissing of water on sand, and faded like a retreating wave.

Windrush called out an answer, but he sensed that Farsight was already gone from the underweb. His brother had no stamina for underspeaking; he must have just managed to shout out across the distance. Sighing, Windrush opened his eyes to the gloom of his cavern. His interrupted rest would have to wait a little longer.

He tugged at the exit spells and launched himself into the dawn sky.

"There was no warning—just an eruption of turbulence and dense storm clouds," Farsight said, swinging his head one way and then another, his diamond eyes flashing angrily, as though by force of will he would see to the ends of the realm. All around them in the camp, dragons were muttering in bewilderment and fury. Three lumenis groves had been attacked—but by sorcery, rather than by drahls. The groves had simply vanished into the Enemy's storms, and with them the dragons who had been inside them maintaining the guardian spells. Of those posted outside the groves, Farsight said, "When it was over, they just couldn't *find* the groves anymore. It was as if they had never existed."

Windrush fumed in frustration. "Was there *no* sign of them? Have you sent others to look?"

"Of course. But no—even the land that the groves grew on has vanished, and the realm has closed up around the empty spaces. And Windrush—the Grotto Garden, too! Treegrower, the egg, Greystone—all gone!"

Windrush drew a painful breath. Those groves were vital to the realm's survival. And the Grotto Garden! The last egg outside the Dream Mountain! His heart burned with the loss. What better way for the Enemy to strike at the dragon soul? He thought he knew what had happened. The Enemy had seized the groves just as he had seized Dream Mountain, probably using the power that Windrush had observed him tapping in the Deep Caverns. Windrush had imagined that they would pay for that loss eventually. But so soon?

As he peered around the encampment, he was beginning to realize that the time he had long feared was at last upon them. Too many lumenis groves were gone now. No longer could they continue to hold on, and hope. No longer could they search in vain for the Dream Mountain, or wait for

Jael to appear—Words or no Words. He would send a patrol to search the south mountains, but the dragons could wait for Jael no longer. Too few groves remained to sustain them. They faced starvation and certain death if they did *not* fly against the Enemy.

"The time has come, hasn't it?" he murmured, gazing westward, toward the mountains and plains that lay between the held land and the Dark Vale. "We must gather our strength—and fight, this time to the end."

He sensed Farsight nodding, but he also heard another rasping breath, and he turned to see SearSky, eyes and nostrils glowing. "You've not given me much time for training," the black dragon rumbled. "Did I not say that we should worry about the lumenis, rather than your places of magic?"

Windrush vented smoke. "It is no accident, SearSky, that we lost these groves *after* we lost the Deep Caverns. The Enemy's power has grown with his victory there."

SearSky snorted. "Then let us destroy him while we still have the strength to fly! Or would you rather we wasted away?"

"I agree," Windrush said, cutting him off. "We need your help now, more than ever. We will all feed, upon whatever lumenis remains. We will need all of our strength. Those who have gone the longest without lumenis will feed first."

SearSky seemed surprised to hear Windrush agree with him. "When do we fly?"

"Upon my command."

"Do you think they will still follow you?"

"Let us hope so." Windrush glanced at Farsight, and back at SearSky. "When this battle is done, they may follow whomever they wish."

"If any are still alive."

"If any are still alive," Windrush agreed. His voice hardened. "Until then, we fly on my command! We will take this battle to the Enemy! SearSky, are you with me?"

SearSky growled flame into the sky. "Can you doubt it? Take the battle to the Enemy!"

"To the Enemy!" Farsight agreed, matching gazes with his brother.

"Then call the leaders," Windrush said. And he added silently, to himself, Let us hope we find Jael before we all take flight to the Final Dream Mountain.

Chapter 32
IN THE CAVERN OF SPIRITS

JAEL'S MOVEMENTS, even the smallest gestures, felt ponderous as she floated with the false-iffling through the mountains, like a seed on the wind. She didn't know where they were going, and almost didn't care anymore. It wasn't just the exhaustion of being in the net so long; she was drugged by the spell in which Jarvorus had ensnared her. The false-iffling was always present now, stirring in her thoughts, and peering out through her eyes, much as Ed had done earlier. At times it was difficult to distinguish her own intentions from Jarvorus'.

Once or twice, she had tried to penetrate further into the false-iffling's thoughts, to learn what exactly it wanted, and why, and even what kind of a being it was. But its thoughts were slippery, like ice; she could find no purchase or place to penetrate and gain understanding. Sometimes she almost thought she detected a glint of *sympathy* in its thoughts; but every time she looked for it again, it was gone.

They were coming up on a small valley tucked in the midst of a seemingly endless parade of bleak, icy mountain peaks. Before she could gather her slow-moving thoughts to ask, she realized that they were drifting downward toward it. She wondered what was there.

Jarvorus' voice drifted through her mind. *(A place where you will be safe, until your time comes.)*

She accepted that statement dimly. With the presence of this creature in her mind, she felt more helpless and alone than ever. She knew that her shipmates were still here, in the splintered net, but the confining bands of Javorus' spell kept them isolated from her. At times, she could hear Ar's voice faintly, but she felt restrained from answering him.

Ed, too, had been barred from her presence. After several futile attempts to bite and claw through the binding, the parrot had given up in weary discouragement. Now he was huddled, despondently waiting for something to happen.

It seemed clear that her shipmates would be unable to help. But there was, at the outermost edge of her hearing, one other voice—like Jarvorus', and yet different. It was the true-iffling, she believed. Its words were hard to make out, but it seemed to be saying, *Remember* . . .

Remember what? she wondered.

As persistently, and quietly, Jarvorus seemed to be telling her to forget. But she did remember, foggily. She remembered who she was, and her mission. She remembered Windrush and his need.

(*The need is for the struggle to end,*) murmured her captor. (*That is the destiny for which you have come. Windrush is nothing. What matters is the new beginning. It is the only thing. . . .*)

Did she detect the faintest trembling of doubt in his voice? Jael felt adrift in her confusion. She knew there was some truth to the words of the false-iffling. The Words spoke of a new beginning. She had no idea how she was supposed to achieve that. *Upon that one's death is the ending wrought.* A layer of fear settled around her, like molasses. Was it possible, as Jarvorus said, that her friends here did not matter so much as the ultimate need to bring the realm's struggle to an end?

She would do anything for her friends.

Including die for them?

For her friends . . . perhaps . . . as she had been willing to die for Highwing, when he'd been cast out of the realm. But just to bring the struggle to an end? Even if it meant the other side winning? No, she whispered to herself. That made no sense.

Somewhere in the net she felt that Ar was listening, and she clung to a hope that somehow, *somehow,* he would find a way to help her come to the right understanding.

Remember . . . whispered a distant, lonely, voice. *Remember. . . .*

(Forget,) commanded Jarvorus.

Jael and the spaceship settled into the valley.

What now? Jael breathed. She was on foot again, with the ship on her back. She stood before a dark opening in the side of a mountain, and Jarvorus apparently intended for her to walk in.

Her feet moved, in wordless answer to her question. Soon they were inside a narrow, twisty passage that seemed to lead deep into the mountain. Just a few rays of light filtered in from above. She felt an oppressive and dizzying weight towering over her. As she walked farther into the gloom, the passage suddenly opened up into a great, vaulting space. It was an enormous cave, something like Windrush's cavern, but larger and starker, and more coldly unfriendly. There was a yellowish light glowing from off to her right, near the wall, and she walked toward it, across the stone floor. As she drew close, she saw, perched on a recessed ledge, a strangely shaped vessel that appeared to be filled with a glowing liquid.

(This,) Jarvorus murmured, *(is the Cavern of Spirits. You will be safe here, with one of your fellow riggers. Like you, he has been deceived and exploited by the dragons.)*

(What?) Jael peered around in the gloom for some sign of a "fellow rigger." The place appeared utterly deserted. *(What do you mean? Have you captured someone else with your lying tricks?)*

(I did not capture him,) Jarvorus answered. *(The dragons did. He is right there in front of you. His name is Hodakai. Ask him how trustworthy the dragons are!)*

Jael suddenly realized what Jarvorus meant: the glowing vessel. Stepping closer, she saw that it looked like a large, multifaceted crystal, glowing from the inside. It looked alive; it was slowly changing shape, with a writhing kind of movement that made its facets shift like living mirrors. Peering carefully within, she saw a small figure of shadow moving somewhat more energetically, inside the glowing light. There was something striking about that shadow; it had a flickering, firelike presence—as if it were not shadow, but a flame of darkness. *(What in the world?)* she murmured.

WHO'S THERE? A harsh-sounding voice echoed all around her. Startled, she glanced around. The shadow-flame danced and pointed a dark limb in her direction. *What's going on?* shouted the voice.

Before Jael could answer, Jarvorus spoke aloud. *I've brought you company, Hodakai! A rigger! Someone to talk to.*

The shadow-flame contorted and squirmed. Its voice sounded a little less harsh, a little more . . . human. *A rigger? What rigger?*

A rigger and her ship! said Jarvorus. *Look, Hodakai! Look!*

It took a moment for the twitching shadow to settle into a stable shape. Jael realized suddenly that it looked like an abstract figure of a man. It seemed to be staring at her, and past her. She was aware of her ship glimmering faintly behind her. *My name is Jael,* she found herself saying aloud, and her words seemed lost in a cottony haze even as she spoke. *Are you human? Are you really a rigger?*

The figure jutted forward and seemed to grow in size. *Oh, my—! It* jabbed at her with a shape that was vaguely like a hand. *I'll be damned! You're the one, aren't you? The one they've all been talking about—*

Jael, she repeated.

Yes—Jael. I'm surprised you told me. Everyone thinks names are very important around here. How'd you get caught? You're Windrush's . . . friend . . . aren't you? I knew it. Don't tell me this iffling is your—

It's not an iffling, it's a fake! Jael tried to cry, but couldn't quite.

The creature didn't seem to be listening, anyway. *I'm stuck here thanks to the dragons, myself, so I'm not exactly what you would call a "friend" of any of them. They didn't even give me a fighting chance—and they killed my buddy, too. But you—you got caught by an iffling!*

It's NOT an iffling . . . ! Jael managed to say, through the molasses of the spell.

(Jael, don't—!) Jarvorus whispered urgently, in a preoccupied voice from somewhat farther away. Whatever he

was doing, he wasn't controlling her actions quite as closely as before.

What? Hodakai suddenly became still. *What do you mean?*

Jael forced the words out. *It's a false-iffling! It did something to the real iffling, and tricked me.*

The shadow-flame peered at her, and she heard astonishment in his voice. *That's . . . very strange. That's exactly what Windrush said! But I wasn't sure if I should believe him. I wonder—*

WINDRUSH! Jael cried, suddenly realizing that he had mentioned the dragon's name twice now. *You know Windrush?* Her heart leaped, even in the binding of the spell. *Have you talked to him? Where is he?* She fought to get the words out. *WHERE IS HE? PLEASE!*

Hodakai pulled back, startled. *Well, hey—yeah. I mean—I know him after a fashion. He talks to me from a distance once in a while.* Hodakai seemed to angle a nervous glance one way, then another, as though afraid someone might be listening. *I expect he's pretty busy right now—with the war and all. Lot of fighting going on. But he's sure been heated up about looking for you, I'll tell you.*

Looking for me?

Hodakai seemed to shiver. *Well, he knew you were coming, apparently. But they haven't been doing too well—not that I feel much sympathy for them, mind you. He's been after me to help, but I . . . I didn't want to get into it, really—and anyway, this—whatever this iffling-thing is—*

It's not an iffling! Jael repeated.

Right—I got that, you don't have to keep saying it. Anyway, I thought it was an iffling, and it said that Windrush was going to make a slave of you, and me.

That's crazy! Jael cried.

Okay, but I believed it at first, Hodakai said defensively. *How was I to know? Of course, it also said I should listen to Rent. Now, Windrush says Rent is a goddamn liar, which I admit is certainly possible. So I don't know anymore what to—*

Wait, you're not making any—what are you talking about?

Hodakai fell silent. He twitched, and seemed to be looking past Jael. She glanced backward. For an instant, she thought she saw the glimmering form of a sharp-fanged animal, the shape that Jarvorus had taken at the Pool of Visions. Its eyes flickered briefly; then it flowed back into a blur of light, then vanished. But she had a strange feeling of a force shifting around her; it had done something to the binding spell. But Jarvorus was no longer occupying her thoughts; this might be her only chance. Jael turned back to Hodakai. *Tell me how I can reach Windrush!* she hissed urgently.

Even as she spoke, she felt a sudden, creeping chill, like a physical illness violating her from within. She shivered, and realized that the invisible molasses in which she was trapped was hardening around her. An image came to her mind, irresistibly, as though drawn by the power of Jarvorus' binding spell: an image of glacial ice forming to encase her in a clear, hard, impenetrable cell. As the image formed in her mind, a great mass of ice appeared physically, in the time it took to complete the thought—crystallizing out of nowhere to surround her in the cavern, encapsulating her in the Flux.

Scrawwwww—Jayl! wailed the thin, distant voice of Ed, barely reaching her through the barrier. His cry was echoed by Ar's, even more remote.

Hodakai's shadow-flame shook in astonishment. *Ice! That's incredible! What were those voices? Do you have shipmates? What happened to your net? Why can't I see it?*

. *Damaged,* Jael whispered, too shocked to say more. *Jarvorus, what have you—? Ar? Ed? Can you hear me?* Their voices were gone now. She was completely encased in the ice: Jarvorus' binding spell made solid and tangible. To Hodakai, she cried desperately, *Please! Help me reach Windrush!*

The crystal-shape that held Hodakai altered shape in slow surges, and he flickered within it. *Reach Windrush? You can't reach him! Look at yourself! You're a prisoner here—just like me!*

Jael stared at him through the thick layer of ice. She could not so much as gesture with a hand. It was as if the very currents of the Flux had frozen around her. *Prisoner*

. . . she murmured. Of course. Had she supposed that Jarvorus would let her go? He seemed to be gone now, but she had no hope of escaping. Only her thoughts were free.

I'm not saying that Windrush couldn't come here, of course, Hodakai continued. *Probably not in body, though.*

What do you mean?

Well, he does seem to get around pretty well through the underrealm.

Jael struggled to comprehend.

Hodakai flexed in his vessel. *The underrealm. You know it? It's—hard to explain. You might think of it as the next level down in the Flux, below the ordinary reach of your net. That's the best I can explain it. It's where the dragons and . . . others . . . do their magic. Where they draw the power for spells. They can travel in it, too—in spirit, I mean.*

You mean—in thought? Can you do that?

Well—mostly just to talk to Rent, Hodakai admitted. *I'm imprisoned here in this jar. I might be a spirit, but . . . I'm pretty well stuck here for eternity, as far as I can see.*

Jael stared at Hodakai, and his vessel. *Do you mean,* she whispered, *that you are only spirit now? You have no physical . . .* Her words trailed off.

Hodakai trembled in his jar.

Jael was shocked into silence. She thought of his words, and finally asked, *Who's . . . Rent?*

Hodakai guffawed unhappily. *Rent? He's a rigger, too. Do you believe it?*

Rigger? Jael asked dumbly.

Or was. He's a mean son-of-a-bitch, though. He's not . . . like this, either. He has a body, courtesy of Tar-skel. I expect you'll be meeting him soon enough.

Jael shuddered.

Don't ask me what they're planning, though, Hodakai added. *I have no idea.*

They—?

Rent. Tar-skel. The drahls. The . . . false-ifflings, I guess. They're all in this together.

Jael closed her eyes, overwhelmed by the sheer weight of everything that had gone wrong. She was not just overwhelmed, she was angry, she was *furious* . . . about Jarvorus and her captivity, about bringing Ar and Ed into this, about letting Windrush down . . . and the rest of the dragons, even if she had no idea what it was they needed of her . . .

And I guess you could say I've been stuck in the middle of it, too, ever since Kan-Kon and I hit the Flux thinking, Hey!—let's try something a little different this time—

If only she could talk to Ar, or Ed! She ached for their presence. She could just barely sense Ed, outside the ice, staring in at her . . .

—and damn-diddly, was that a mistake—

And now she thought she sensed Ar, farther away, whispering frantically. To her? She remembered the Pool of Visions, when he'd gotten a cry through to her, too late. She strained to listen, and thought she heard the words, *Pay attention . . . !* But now Hodakai was drowning him out again.

—had us completely helpless, lambs to the slaughter, and then some ifflings came and prattled on about prophecy, but a lot of good that did us—they grabbed me and I didn't even see them kill Kan-Kon. But Rent said they did.

Something clicked in her mind. *WHAT* did you just say? she cried.

The shadow-flame twitched. *What do you mean? When?*

Just now! Who did you say you were with?

The dragons? My partner?

Your partner!

Kan-Kon was his name. You wouldn't know him. That was a long time ago, and he got killed by the dragons—not even saved here like me—which, mind you, is probably just as w—

KAN-KON? Your partner was KAN-KON?

Yes, you wouldn't— Hodakai broke off suddenly, and his flickering form leaned toward her, causing the shape of his prison to distort. *Wait a minute! What are you saying?*

Jael heard a rushing like a waterfall in her head. *Is your name—* She groped helplessly in her memory, before retrieving Kan-Kon's partner's name. *Hoddy? Is that your name? Hoddy?*

The spirit flinched as though stung. *How do you—how do you know—?*

Of course! she thought. Hodakai. Besides, how many captured riggers could there be in the dragon realm? If only Kan-Kon had known that his friend was not dead!

You KNOW him? You know Kan-Kon? You mean, he made it out ALIVE? Hodakai made a series of little squeaking sounds. *But Rent said he was dead! Rent said the dragons killed him! How can this—oh my God—!*

The dragons let Kan-Kon go! Jael cried. *But HE thought they killed you!*

But then—why did Rent say—? Hodakai seemed utterly beside himself, bewildered and overjoyed. *How do YOU know him? Is he coming to get me—?*

He thinks you're dead! Don't you understand? He told us the whole story! He had no idea you'd survived! Jael hesitated, unsure what to make of Hodakai's weeping sounds. *I'm sorry. I'm sure he would have come, if he'd known. He . . . he doesn't rig anymore. But he got us a ship to come here.*

But where—? Hodakai gasped. How—?

Jael caught her breath. *He . . . runs a shipping company. On Cargeeling.*

Cargeeling! Hodakai wept. *That's my home! That's where I came from! Oh gods—that's where I wanted to be buried!*

Jael reeled, remembering what Kan-Kon had said, that Hoddy's ashes were, in fact, buried on Cargeeling. But she couldn't bring herself to say that.

Hodakai seemed lost in his own thoughts now, overcome by bitter tears. His words were muffled, but he was crying, *Rent! You lied to me! You lied, you miserable son-of-a-bitch . . . !*

As she listened to Hodakai weeping, she found herself wondering if any of this really mattered now, anyway. And where had Jarvorus gone?

Hodakai suddenly began laughing to himself. *And I believed him! Oh, you fool, Hoddy—you damn fool!*

Jael broke in. She needed this man's help. She had no one else to turn to. *Hodakai! Hoddy—please!*

The spirit slowly quieted to a mournful silence.

Hodakai—I came to help a friend, she said urgently. A

friend who needs me—who helped me—whose father helped me!

The dragon? You mean Windrush?

Yes, Windrush.

I've never heard of a dragon helping anyone . . .

They let Kan-Kon go, when the iffling asked them to. I'm sorry they didn't let you go, too. Please—will you help me? As a friend of Kan-Kon's?

Kan-Kon, Hodakai whispered.

Jael pressed desperately. *As a fellow . . . human? You remember, don't you, what it was like to be—?*

I remember, damn you! Ask the DRAGONS about it! Hodakai hissed.

Jael was stunned by Hodakai's outburst. But of course, he had good reason. *Look, I don't know exactly what—some dragons have done to you, or why,* she stammered. *But I'll bet they were under the . . . Enemy. Tar-skel.*

Hodakai shook. *That's what Windrush said . . .*

Believe him! Believe ME! she begged. *There are dragons here you can trust, and Windrush is one of them!*

Hodakai snorted, but with a certain hesitancy.

Jael realized that there was probably no way to convince him, except by telling him her whole story, as she had told it to Kan-Kon. It would take precious time. But what else could she do? What could she accomplish as a prisoner here? If she had any hope at all, it was to persuade Hodakai to be on her side. *Shall I tell you why?* she whispered. *Will you give me a chance to make you believe?*

Yes! she heard, a distant whisper. Was that Ar?

The shadow-flame gave a quivering shrug.

Jael stared at him. *I'll take that as a yes. I'll tell, and you decide.*

Tell, sighed Hodakai.

All right. Here it is, then. Jael drew a breath. *I don't know about you, but when I wandered into the mountain realm, I didn't actually expect to find dragons.*

Neither did I! Hodakai whimpered.

Jael nodded. *Well, I was lucky. The dragon I met was one named Highwing.* She closed her eyes, feeling a rush of sorrow, and adrenaline, as she remembered. *And that,* she murmured, *was when I learned, not just that dragons are real, but that there are dragons who are to be trusted . . . who are friends . . . whom it's worth risking your life for. . . .*

It took a long time to tell the whole story: Highwing's offer of friendship, over her own objections, and his help in casting out her own inner demons; her horror in returning to the realm and finding him condemned to death for be-friending her; and Windrush's and the ifflings' cooperation in helping her to save him. By the time she reached the end of her story—her terrifying rescue of Highwing from a fiery death in normal-space, and his subsequent death here in this realm, she was completely drained by the storm of longing and joy and grief that the memories brought back to her.

She was barely aware of her listener, his shadowy head cocked toward her. When he spoke, his voice was slow and troubled. *Is all this true?* he asked plaintively, but somehow with a clearer voice than she had heard before.

She nodded. Her own voice was scarcely audible, even to her. *Will you help me?*

I don't really know if I can, he said slowly. He hesitated, as though drawing a breath. *But if I can . . . I guess I will.*

For Kan-Kon? she whispered.

He sounded as if he were going to cry. *For . . . Kan-Kon, yes. And for . . . you . . . and your friends.*

Chapter 33
PRISONER OF MAGIC

AR COULD find no way to break through the barrier to Jael. Even before that demonic imposter of an iffling had enveloped her in a cocoon of energy, he'd been able to manage only glimpses of her presence in the net. And then he'd been dragged along, helpless to intervene, as she and the false-iffling had carried them to this cavern, apparently a prison for captured rigger-spirits. No one had paid much attention to him, or to Ed—and probably for good reason. They seemed unable to take any action whatever to help Jael. He had no idea what had become of the true-iffling.

Now he could only gaze in horror at his shipmate, encased in a block of ice. Ironically, he could see her more clearly now, though the barrier between them was stronger than ever. If only he could at least take some action to move the *ship*. But in the fragmented net, it seemed that Jael effectively had ship-control; and she was now completely immobilized, apparently unable even to see him. Could she *hear* him, though? Ar had tried to get a shout through—to alert her to what this being, Hodakai, was saying—that he was the former shipmate of Kan-Kon. What a terrible irony: that they had found a potential friend here, and he was a prisoner too!

Never in his life had Ar felt so frustrated. He kept pushing and tugging at his end of the net, trying to jostle the ship loose, trying to alter the image. But the Flux resisted his every effort; the trap was too strong.

The only hope he could find—and he was determined to find hope, no matter what—was in the chance that this Hodakai could help them, perhaps by calling Windrush or other dragons. It would require winning Hodakai to their

side, and Hodakai clearly disliked the dragons a great deal.
Ar could well empathize—he remembered the terror of the
Tar-skel dragons—but Hodakai needed to be shown that
not all dragons were like that.

Shall I tell you? Jael was asking.

Yes! Ar cried frantically. Whether Jael heard or not, he
couldn't tell, but in any event, she began to tell her story.

As he listened, it seemed to Ar that Hodakai was coming
around. But that still left the question: What could be done
from here? Was there anything that he hadn't yet thought
of, Ar wondered, anything that he and Ed could do? It
seemed hopeless; and yet he remembered a time, years ago,
en route to Vela Oasis, when he and Jael had been off
course, kept from their proper heading by a barrier of ice;
and it was Ed who had found the solution, Ed who had
broken through. *Ed!* he whispered, trying to reach the parrot without interrupting the rapport that was growing between Jael and Hodakai. *Ed!*

Urrrrrawk! muttered the parrot, from another fragment
of the net. He looked crumpled and discouraged.

Ed—do you have any ideas? Any at all?

The parrot rustled listlessly, with a flutter of scarlet and
green. Ar imagined he could hear the bird's thoughts grind-
ing like a spinning wheel, trying to generate hope. But in
this case, Ed seemed to have no answer, and no hope.

Jarvorus listened, entranced by Jael's story.

*. . . I didn't think we could hold Highwing in the air, he was
so weak from almost falling into that sun—but Windrush took
the weight and slowed him—and gave him a chance to fly one
last time, and speak to us before he died. And when he died, he
seemed to be rejoicing, Hodakai! He was back in his own realm,
among his own people! He turned to blazing glass in the sun, and
vanished, and his voice was like a chime, laughter on the
air. . . .*

Jarvorus wept at the end, moved by the unexpected
beauty of her tale, and stunned by the emotion it stirred in
him. He'd not intended to listen; in fact, he'd been on the
verge of leaving to report to his master. But he'd been

drawn back by her words, by the power of her memory. He'd found himself touching her thoughts again, not to control them but to marvel at her daring, risking her life to save her friend. Jarvorus *felt* her joy in the rescue, and the grief that followed as her friend passed from the realm.

Jarvorus was astonished and overwhelmed by this notion of friendship, by the willingness to raise friendship over self. He knew, even as he reacted to it, that he should not be moved by this, that it had nothing to do with his mission; and yet, he found its power irresistible. He felt drawn to her story and her feelings as a cavern sprite to an upwelling of warm, nourishing heat from the underrealm. It was irrational; it was foolish; it contradicted the training of his master. And Jael, he reminded himself, was his prisoner. But what, in his training by Rent, had prepared him for emotions of such power?

He had told himself that by listening to her story, he could more clearly identify and excise that troubling knot of *sympathy* that had grown in him for her. But instead, he found himself saddened and moved, and *liking* Jael, and even her friends. There were qualities about them that he was discovering he admired: compassion; mercy. Had he known those qualities before, in another time? He saw a few sprites floating about this Cavern of Spirits, and he felt a trembling knowledge that he had once been one of them . . .

A hazy memory was surfacing from the dimly recollected past . . . of a fellow cavern sprite dying, when it put itself in the path of an underrealm snare, one of Master Rent's weavings, which was about to engulf several young sprites. At the time, Jarvorus hadn't thought much about it; if anything, he'd thought it a foolish thing to do. Now, though, he wondered.

He started back from the memory, shaken a little. He thought perhaps he liked those sprites more than he liked the creatures made from them, the aggressive warrior-spirits hovering around under his own command. He even felt a grudging respect for the iffling, which in spite of everything, still remained hunkered in the shards of the rigger-net, trying to encourage Jael. It was a pity that they had to be adversaries. Rightly or wrongly, he felt a little ashamed for having caught Jael in this trap . . . even if his cause had been the right one.

It didn't matter, of course. Nothing could change what he had done—or had yet to do. He'd bound and sealed the One, using the powers that Rent had bestowed upon him. His presence and attention were no longer needed to hold her; in fact, he couldn't free her now even if he wanted to. In a while, her purpose would be fulfilled. That was a destiny that couldn't be changed.

But perhaps her understanding of it could be. Perhaps he could give her that much—as a gift—an understanding of what was to come. An understanding of the necessity, and the beauty.

He moved closer, to speak with her again. He noted the two riggers that shared her net, and satisfied himself that they were well secured by the spell-weaving and could cause no difficulties. Then he slipped back into the rigger's thoughts.

(Jael,) he whispered, *(I perceive that you are troubled. But do you not understand your part in the struggle? If you could escape and join with the dragons, you could do no good! You could only endanger the greatest work of power in all the universe!)*

(What . . . ?) She sounded fatigued, and confused.

Jarvorus spoke softly, aware of the Hodakai spirit watching Jael, and not wanting him to hear. He perceived that the grip of his persuasion spell on Hodakai had loosened, and he didn't want to involve Hodakai in this. He whispered to Jael, *(Don't you know what is being made here? You are a part of it!)*

She seemed to be returning to alertness. *(What . . . thing . . . being made?)*

The warrior-spirit hesitated. He wanted to share with her the vision he had been given by his master, but he wasn't sure how to do it. *(Look,)* he said, at last. *(I will try to show you.)* And he did something he had never tried before: he touched the net that surrounded her and wove an image there for her to see.

Jael gasped in surprise.

He slowly drew it into focus: a great web stretching across the sky, enveloping mountain and sky and space. *(You saw this at the Pool of Visions, but there was no time then to explain it. This is the work of my masters. It is the greatest work of power since the beginning of creation! It will bring the realms together, all of the realms. And this is how it will grow.)* He drew the web reaching deep into the darkness of the sky, penetrating the very stuff that formed the foundations of the sky, of other realms, of other universes. He showed it flashing with deep, violent power, reaching out to embrace Jael's own universe with its strength and its beauty.

(NOOOOOOOO—!)

(What? Jael—?)

Her inner voice had failed, but she was shaking with grief—and rage, upwelling like a volcano. Her fear reverberated like a drum in the binding spell. He tried to draw the image clearer, but that just made her cry out again, softly: *(No . . . no . . . never! . . . I swear, never . . . !)*

Jarvorus could not comprehend her reaction. Why did this not move her to joy? She seemed appalled by the violent forces that flickered through the web, giving it strength—the strength of pain and death. She remembered the vision from the pool, of dragons dying in battle. And it was true: violent deaths would pass before the structure was complete. But wasn't that life—contests separating the strong from the weak? And even the weak were given their part: the intensity of their emotion, their despair and their shame, was woven into the very fiber of the work. Without the violence and the despair, none of the beauty was possible.

(Never!) she whispered. *(I will not be a part—!)*

(But there is no other way!)

He realized, as he spoke, that the other riggers in the net were able to see the image, as well; and they were as frightened by it as Jael. What was wrong, that he could not persuade them of the beauty and the truth?

(You have imprisoned me for THIS?) she cried, her thoughts aflame with anger and hatred. *(For this abomination?)*

He fell back from her in dismay, stunned by her anger. He'd thought that she would see. *(I have imprisoned you for what must be,)* he whispered sadly. *(And now that it is done, there really is no other way out for you.)*

No way out, he thought silently, as she wept inwardly. No way except death. You have been trapped by Rent's magic, and unless the Master himself frees you, nothing but death can release you from this prison. I grieve for you, Jael, my captive.

The thought of the Master brought him back to the present with a start. It was time he reported back to Rent on his success. Gathering himself silently, and regretfully, he sank into the underrealm away from the Cavern of Spirits.

Once the false-iffling was gone, the true-iffling stirred from its hiding place. There were still servants of the Enemy around, but they appeared to be keeping watch from a distance. The iffling didn't know what, if anything, it could do. It could not release Jael; the weaving had solidified around her like rock-hard ice. Obviously, though the spell had been triggered by the false-one, it was the work of someone far more powerful. That was hardly surprising; both the iffling and the false-one were servants of greater powers. But what was that *uncertainty* that the iffling had observed in the false-one, just before its departure? It almost looked like *doubt*.

The false-one was gone now, probably to visit its master. But where, the true one wondered, were *its* masters, its iffling-parents? Was it alone in the world, alone in the realm? The iffling probed outward from the cavern, stretching its senses along certain layers of the underrealm where perhaps only ifflings could reach. It felt *something* . . . a distant glimmer of life. That touch sent a shiver of recognition through the iffling. Was someone out there? Someone who would recognize an iffling, and welcome it home?

With the false-one gone, perhaps it was time to seek help—for Jael, and for itself. It had not dared to try earlier, both for fear of the false-one and for fear of losing Jael. But Jael was bound now, and would not be moving.

The iffling gently touched the glowing surface of Jael's mind, and found her agitated and despairing. *(Remember,)* it whispered. *(Remember. And keep hope. Always keep hope.)*

(How can I hope?) Jael cried back to it, perhaps recognizing it and perhaps not.

The iffling probed helplessly at the sorcery that bound her—and found no weakness, no hope. But the false-one had leaked one thought, one possibility, one inkling of a way in which Jael's cry for freedom might be fulfilled. The iffling didn't dare voice the possibility; it was too drastic, too uncertain. But it might be the only way.

To Jael, it said, *(You must. The realm needs you.)* And in afterthought, it added, *(Your friend needs you. Windrush.)* It was aware of Jael's sharp intake of breath, but there was nothing more that it could say. It drew apart from her.

The sorcery could hold the riggers—but not the iffling. It was time.

The iffling slipped out of the riggers' presence, slipped away down the long, rippling silence of the place where only its kind might tread . . . slipped away, whispering and crying for anyone who might know its voice, and answer in kind. For anyone who might help.

Chapter 34
GATHERING STORM

LUMENIS CRACKLED and exploded, raining light through the night sky. The dragons thundered, their fever for battle rising like boiling clouds of steam. Windrush watched from one end of the Valley of Fallen Light, as the last of the lumenis disappeared into the jaws of his fellow dragons. Like many of the others, he had not fed, and would not. Those dragons feeding now were the ones who had gone hungry the longest. He would feed in flight, as best he could, if there was any lumenis dust left in the air.

Windrush had far more on his mind now than feeding. The challenge before them was so difficult, the odds so staggering, that he had to steel himself against a mood of desperation. He trusted his leaders to lead well; but when the battle came, they must all be driven by instinct and by fierce, blinding determination.

By tomorrow, the dragon realm could be restored to freedom and majesty . . . or it could be gone.

SearSky had bullied the younger warriors through dozens of mock duels, almost to the point of exhaustion, before Windrush had called for a rest. They had perhaps not rested enough, but SearSky had assured him that the warriors were braver now and more determined for his bullying. Farsight had organized all of the patrols into large attack groups. All the dragons were flying, even the wounded; there was nothing left to protect here. They would fly when the feeding was done. The Enemy, he assumed, knew very well how desperate their situation was; but Windrush hoped to surprise him with the sheer audacity of their attack. The dragons would be at their peak after the feeding; and if they were wild from the lumenis intoxication, perhaps that would make them fight all the more ferociously. He remembered how SearSky had fought in the Deep Caverns, and imagined an entire army of lumenis-drunk dragons fighting like that.

Windrush thought of his cavern, which he might never see again, and of the iffling's last visit, and of the sweepers' tiny but valiant effort to point the way for him. He still didn't understand the meaning of that last underrealm window, but he knew this: whatever help he had hoped to receive from the ifflings he now had to put out of his mind. He could not delay the attack any longer. He could not spend any more time searching the underrealm. He wanted to hope that Jael, somehow, would have a role to play, but it was hard to see how. His search parties to the south had found nothing. If she was a captive of the Enemy, his only hope was that some unimagined magic might free her for the coming battle. It was a faint hope, indeed.

Several dozen dragons thundered and hooted and blasted the air in front of him. Only tiny shards of lumenis remained on the ground, glinting in the starlight—seed for the future. The hungry dragons were snatching up even those fragments of seed.

"Enough!" Windrush bellowed, launching himself into the air. "Leave the seed! *Leave the seed!* Gather now for flight!"

Cries of protest reached his ears, but he had no time for it. Some of them would have to fight hungry. *He* would have to fight hungry. "ENOUGH!" he thundered. "Gather behind me! Prevail against the Enemy, and we'll have all the lumenis we desire!"

A rumble of assent rose around him like the sound of an approaching storm, followed by the dragons themselves, orbiting around him, their cries echoing in a great roar. Windrush vented a flame into the air and cried, "Fly, now! Fly to the camp and gather the others! Fly!"

Like a frenzied armada, the flight of dragons abandoned the Valley of Fallen Light and churned through the night sky to join the rest of the patrols, already waiting at the encampment. Those who had fed were bright with fire, and lusting for battle; the unfed flew just as fast, hardened by hunger and anger.

As they passed over the encampment, Farsight rose to join them, followed by wave after wave of dragons, roaring and fuming, until it seemed that the sky could hold no more. Even Rockclaw came, and Windrush called out to him, "Are you ready to fly so far?" The gnarled dragon, pumping his wings, called back, "You lead, and I'll get there! Someone has to remember this properly for the next younglings!" Windrush chuckled, his spirits lifted despite his worries. *"For the draconae!"* he bellowed to the growing force.

The responses echoed in the sky:

"For the lumenis!"

"For Treegrower and the egg!"

"For the fallen!"

"For the realm!"

Soon, with over a hundred dragons circling in the air, several dozen more came in from the north and south, from the smaller camps. The night air was alight with the flicker of dragon flames, despite Windrush's warnings to save their fire for the fight.

"TO BATTLE!" he thundered at last.

"TO BATTLE! TO THE ENEMY!" came the answering cry, reverberating from the mountainsides.

Windrush flew westward, climbing to crest the Scarred Mount Ridge. Following him were nearly two hundred dragons, their eyes afire with battle fever. Almost a hundred more had set out earlier under Stronghold and Longtouch, splitting far to the south and north to enter the Enemy's realm from flanking directions. Windrush's flight would not divide; they were crossing the Valley Between as one, and all going over the top of the Borderland Mountains together. It was a dangerous approach, and it would take them close to the Enemy's east camp; but Windrush hoped that the core of his flight would make it through to strike at the Enemy's heart in the Dark Vale, far to the west. What would happen then, only tomorrow would tell.

Windrush's blood burned hotter as they flew; he burned

with a growing lust to meet the Enemy and destroy him. High and fast the dragons flew, and if those who had not fed were laboring harder than those who had, it didn't show when Windrush glanced back. All he saw in the sky behind him was a night full of fiery, battle-hungry eyes. He nodded in approval and pounded the air harder than ever before.

* * *

The realm shall tremble
when dragons assemble
to strike out of fear,
with hope nowhere near.

The One comes,
the end comes,
and who shall prevail?

Who knows where a friend
Shall be found close and dear?

The Words reverberated in FullSky's mind.

His presence in the Dream Mountain was becoming more strained, as forces in the underrealm shifted about with growing turbulence. Powers were gathering everywhere. FullSky knew he could not remain here much longer. But surely his role had not yet ended! The draconae were busy strengthening their defenses against the Enemy's inevitable assault upon the dreamfires, upon the binding and creative force that sustained all the life in the realm. But what was *he* to do?

With the draconae, FullSky had watched helplessly as the Enemy had stolen the power of the Deep Caverns; as he'd snatched the remaining lumenis—and the Grotto Garden, with Treegrower and the egg; as he'd captured Jael at the Pool of Visions. Now they watched as the dragons launched their desperate attack—an attack with no hope of success, against a foe who was now aware of every move that they made.

The Enemy must have delighted in letting the draconae witness his victories. FullSky knew, as did the draconae, that their despair only fed the Enemy's dark sorcery; but being aware of it was not enough to save them from it. Jael's capture had discouraged them most of all. Even they, with their prophecy, hadn't expected her to fall to the Enemy before the final battle had even begun.

It's not over yet, he'd told them. But his words had seemed hollow even to him.

FullSky felt the underrealm quiver with the approach of battle, and he drew his kuutekka close about him. Even if his presence here went unnoticed by the Enemy, he had very little time left in which to do anything useful. His strength was already drawn thin. His body, imprisoned in the Dark Vale, was battered and tortured beyond healing; and while he could draw some strength here from the draconae's power, he could not be wholly divorced from the state of his physical body. He had never expected to emerge from this struggle alive. But as long as he still had some power to act, he was determined to make his presence count for something.

Jael. He felt certain that his actions were meant to involve her. But how? It did not seem that he could do anything more for Windrush. His last underrealm window for his brother had been a failed attempt to show how the Dream Mountain had been captured, and how it might be freed. But who had been missing from that picture? Jael. And she was beyond help now.

Except, perhaps, through the underrealm . . .

Bending his thought toward the draconae's underrealm window, FullSky probed delicately, quietly, toward the place where he thought the rigger had been taken. If he was to do anything for her at all, he would have to be watchful and shrewd indeed.

And he would have to be ready to give up to her the very last of his own strength. . . .

For WingTouch, in captivity, the pain was a constant, a sheet of fire within his body. He had learned, to some extent, to ignore it; but he could not do so altogether. The servants of the Enemy saw to that. At irregular intervals, they came and taunted him, or changed the binding spell in some new and devilish way. They did not have to increase the pain, only to *alter* it, to make it fresh and new as it blazed up his nerves.

His feet remained entombed in stone, and his inability to move or stretch was driving him mad. His legs were fearsomely cramped, and the immobility weighed terribly upon his spirit. Not content with that, the drahls had attacked his eyes with their freezing fire, so that he could see only dimly now; they had torn away at his scales, and pierced him with sharpened stones; they had starved him, and denied him a view of the sky and the sun.

In his heart, he tried to believe that the pain was meaningless, that the suffering was worthwhile if only he could remain adamant in his resistance to the Enemy. In truth, he probably would have succumbed to despair by now, if it had not been for the dreamlike memory of his brother's voice, speaking somehow into his mind, urging him to keep hope. *The Enemy is lying,* FullSky had said. *I will help you if I can.*

Maybe it was only a dream. But if a dream was all that he had to cling to, then that was what he would do.

Someone, or something, was walking toward him. He felt, and heard, the human's footsteps and voice before the creature came into his shadowy sight.

"I pity you, dragon," Rent said, his footsteps a clink of steel on stone as he approached. "You won't even see it happen, in the end. You'll just feel it—as the world closes in around you. As everyone you know *dies.*"

"Away from me, demon!" WingTouch hissed, or tried to.

"There's nothing that can change it now," Rent continued, with feigned sympathy. "But it's a shame you won't even be able to watch those pitiful brothers of yours die." He laughed mockingly. "Or perhaps I could arrange for you to watch it—to *feel* it, as they suffer."

WingTouch trembled, from both weakness and rage. He longed to step out of this stone prison, to destroy this being, but that power was not his. There was no power that was his anymore. He knew it, and his captors knew it—and they knew how deeply it frustrated and infuriated him to have to stand here and listen to his tormentor, without hope of escape. But as he heard the wretched creature's words, he realized something—and he felt an abrupt, astonishing burst of joy. He barked laughter into the face of the monster Rent.

The human drew back, stuttering with anger. "You *laugh* at the deaths of your brothers?" he hissed.

No, WingTouch thought, shuddering with the physical pain caused by his own laughter. No, I don't laugh at their deaths. I laugh to hear that they are *alive*, that in all this time you have not been able to kill them! I laugh that, even now, they still fight you!

To Rent, he said nothing. The blush of hope passed quickly enough, and Rent seemed to sense that. The human danced before him, howling with mockery, "Laugh if you can, because soon you will laugh no more. There will be nothing more in your life to amuse you. *Nothing!*" He paused and stabbed a finger in WingTouch's direction, his eyes full of hatred. "And I guarantee you this: I will keep you alive long enough to suffer to the end. I'm going to leave you now—I'm going to *walk away*! But I will be back, WingTouch! I will be back to watch you suffer, as all of your brothers and all of the dragons die!"

Rent placed his hands on his midsection and bounced from foot to foot, and capered wildly, undoubtedly to remind WingTouch of his own immobility. As if he needed reminding. The pain in his legs was excruciating; and yet he dared not give in to it. If he lost his balance and fell sideways, it could break his legs—and that might kill him, or might just magnify the pain.

There is always hope, FullSky—or FullSky's spirit—had said. Was FullSky really still alive somewhere, somehow? Rent had not spoken of him lately, and Rent had been quite gleeful once in proclaiming FullSky a traitor. Was it possible that FullSky had escaped? Or was it all in his imagination?

WingTouch could answer none of his own questions.

But the more Rent gloated, the more determined he was to resist to the end. He might despair inwardly, as the pain shimmered around him. But never would he let this demon know. This was his only remaining weapon: to not let this miserable human prevail.

There is always hope.

Thank you, FullSky, he thought as he laughed out loud at the departing human. And when he saw the human tighten in fury, he laughed again—heedless of the pain, the meaningless pain.

Chapter 35
FRIEND OR FOE?

THE WARRIOR-SPIRIT had to wait an unusually long time for Rent to appear. It was unnerving to hover alone at the edge of Rent's underrealm abode, waiting to report to his master. Jarvorus was jittery, without quite knowing why. Perhaps it was because he didn't know precisely what instructions his master would have for him next. He knew that his capture of the rigger was a crucial milestone, and that he ought to be proud of it. He knew that much was at stake in what happened to Jael.

And in that, he was troubled. He was disturbed by what he had experienced with Jael and her companions, in the Cavern of Spirits. He found himself brooding about the way in which his master was going to lead Jael to her death—an important and significant event. He couldn't keep from dwelling upon it. Perhaps it was just as well that Rent wasn't here now, because Jarvorus had some thinking to do—and he knew that his feelings on the matter had changed, significantly. How was this possible?

It had started with a grudging respect for his adversary, and a trace of sympathy for what she must suffer. For all that, she was still the target, the enemy, the One. But now he had shared her thoughts and her feelings, now he knew what she had been through in this realm, what she had experienced, and done. The trouble was, Jarvorus knew now that he liked Jael far better than he liked his own master.

It might mean nothing in the end, and yet it was a staggering thought, one that charged him with fear. His master was brimming with power and cruelty, qualities that Jarvorus had once admired, and even emulated. But they were qualities that seemed absent in Jael, and he found now that he admired their absence more than their presence. He'd once thought that Jael wasn't strong, because she was not the master over others, like Rent. But that glimpse into her soul had shown him another sort of strength, and he was beginning to wonder if maybe Jael wasn't the stronger—strong enough to risk her life for someone else's. Jarvorus wondered if Rent would do that. He recalled her vision of the dragon Windrush risking his life to save Highwing, and he wondered if Rent would do that.

He recalled his own memory of the cavern sprite dying, saving several younger sprites, and he found himself wondering—what if *he* had been among those who had been saved?

He was aware, as he waited for his master, that none of this meant that anything would change. It was too late for that. Nevertheless, he could not help quivering with unease.

Rent's cavern, in the underrealm, was a glowing place of shimmering heat and pulsing energy. It was a place that spoke of power. Unlike Hodakai's spirit jar, this cave of the spirit was no prison, but rather a base from which Rent sallied forth in his work for the Ultimate Master. The powers that throbbed in this cave filled Jarvorus with a fear of Rent—and an even greater awe of the power of the Ultimate Master, if the power of Rent, a lesser one, gave any measure.

He caught his own thought, and trembled at the possibility of Rent hearing himself referred to as *less* than anyone—even the Ultimate Master. Such thoughts would not be pleasing to Master Rent.

Jarvorus floated at the edge of the cave, trying to gather himself into a calmer state. It would not do to be found this way. He started suddenly, sensing movement in the underrealm. There was a flicker, then a sharp brightening of the glow in the walls. A shadowy black figure strode through the walls, and stood, hands on hips, glaring around the cave, radiating waves of indignation. Jarvorus drew himself into a smaller flame.

STATE YOUR BUSINESS! thundered the owner of the cave, pointing an angry finger at the warrior-spirit.

Jarvorus found himself trembling with fear—and a certain shock of recognition. Rent's form was human, just like Jael's. Had he seen this before? He guessed he had—but not so starkly. Never had he really stopped to think that, perhaps, Rent *was* a human, like Jael.

JARVORUS? SPEAK UP! Rent commanded. *I can see it is you. Why do you hang there in silence?*

I . . . have come to report on . . . the rigger Jael, Jarvorus stammered. Had he done anything to deserve his master's anger? He didn't think so.

Rent's human figure dissolved into a bright flame of light, far brighter than his cavern. The fire of his presence flew rapidly around the cave, circling along the wall, almost too fast for Jarvorus to follow. *Report, then! And quickly! I have just come from dealing with dragons who were slow to obey! If you want gentler treatment, I had better not catch you resting!* It was clear that he was furious about something. Jarvorus wondered what the dragons had done to make him so angry.

Jarvorus could not help hesitating, before delivering his report. *I have taken the rigger . . . to the Cavern of Spirits. I have encased her in the spell-shroud. As you commanded.*

Rent's fire slowed and drifted to the center of the cavern. Jarvorus felt himself the object of a penetrating gaze. He was starting to feel angry in turn. Rent had no right to be cruel to him; he had done exactly as ordered. Jarvorus kept his anger concealed, as best he could.

Rent spoke in a measured tone. *Very well. Now, tell me: have they admitted defeat yet? Does the rigger know that she has reached her end? And what of Hodakai? Does he remain bound to our side?*

Jarvorus hesitated again. A multitude of possible answers rose in his mind, and it took him a moment to choose among them. When he spoke, he was not aware of a conscious decision to lie to his master. Nevertheless, he did, saying, *Yes. They have admitted defeat. They are ours.*

Ours? hissed Rent. *Ours?*

Yes, Jarvorus whispered. *They are ours.*

Rent erupted like a volcano. OURS? he thundered. *You presumptuous sprite! Do you know how I deal with servants who make presumptions?* A flower of light erupted from somewhere, blazed into Jarvorus, and knocked him senseless.

It took him a few moments to realize that he was still alive. Jarvorus struggled back to full consciousness, struggled to regain his dignity. That blow had almost killed him. Ours? he thought. How could he have been so stupid? *They are . . . yours!* he whispered contritely. *Yours. Yes. You need not worry about what they might do. They are quite secure.*

There was another burst of light, but this one only flashed through him and made him tremble a little. *Very good, Jarvorus,* Rent crooned. *You required a little reminder; that's all. Remember that it was I who gave you the breath of life. It would be a shame if you forgot.* Rent's voice was soft, threatening.

Jarvorus made himself as small as he could. He wasn't sure why he had lied to Rent; it was a stupid and foolish thing to do. But now he had just heard Rent lie to him in return: "It was *I* who gave you the breath of life." But Rent had not given Jarvorus life. Jarvorus might have believed so, before some of those memories had returned. Rent had *changed* him from a sprite, but that was not the same as *creating* him. The master lying to his servant. Though Jarvorus didn't know what to do about it, he knew that he no longer trusted Rent. He preferred his prisoners to his master. And that was a perilous situation.

Did Rent still trust him? Had Rent *ever* really trusted him?

Is that all you have to report? the master asked, his voice still silkily threatening.

Jarvorus dimmed and brightened deferentially. *Yes.*

Then why do you remain? Tend to your prisoners!

Yes, master, Jarvorus whispered.

Good, Rent answered darkly. *I will come soon to see this one in person, and deal with her myself. The end approaches, even now. A great battle is beginning. See that you keep her secure until I come. Now, begone with you!*

Jarvorus dimmed and slipped back out of Rent's cave, leaving his master muttering to himself. Jarvorus did not pause to listen. But he was thinking furiously, and making a decision, as he sped back through the underrealm to his captives.

He found them quiet and gloomy in Hodakai's cavern. They seemed to understand instinctively just how close they were to the time when Jael must fall to her enemy. Jarvorus shared their mournfulness, observing from a distance. He delayed making contact while he considered how to proceed.

Jael was going to die anyway, and her death would be the final link in the Ultimate Master's plan, Tar-skel's web of sorcery. Jarvorus no longer found that plan such a beautiful thing as he had so recently believed it. *Jael* did not find it beautiful; she abhorred it. And Jael had never lied to him, or deceived him, unlike his master. And if he no longer believed in his masters, why should he believe in their plan? He preferred Jael's way. And he wished that he could do something about it. He wished that he could undo the spell in which he had captured her; he wished he could send her to her friend the dragon.

But Jarvorus did not have that power.

But there was one way in which he might free her. It would require Jael's agreement and cooperation, and perhaps that of her friends. And he would have to act quickly, before Rent came to stop him.

Rent, he knew, would be very angry—far angrier than he had been just now. If Jarvorus did what he was contemplating, Rent would surely kill him. That thought made him hesitate. But he remembered what Jael had done, which was the very thing that so made him want to take her side. She had shown herself willing to give her life. And he would be asking her to do it again.

Before he could reconsider again, Jarvorus ordered all of the warrior-sprites to retreat to the outside of the cavern, and to remain quiet, and not to interfere. Then he slipped through the seal of sorcery and into his captive's mind.

* * *

(There is one way you might yet have a chance,) he said, without preamble. A sense of urgency was upon him. He noted that the iffling was gone, which was just as well. He didn't need to contest for Jael's attention.

She burst back with indignation, *(GET OUT OF MY MIND!)* Her resentment boiled around him with fierce heat.

Perhaps he had been too abrupt, he realized, pulling away hastily. He studied Jael, her underrealm presence shimmering darkly. How could he do this? Finally, he allowed himself to become visible again in the cavern, in his animal form—so that all of them, including Hodakai and the other riggers, could see and hear him. He hoped this appearance would seem less threatening. He padded across the cavern floor to Jael, who was peering out of her cell of ice in lonely desperation. Her spaceship glimmered, half visible, behind her; and nearby, in the fractured rigger-net, Jarvorus could just make out the forms of the tall rigger, Ar, and the strange little green rigger that was called Ed.

He raised his head to meet Jael's eyes. *I've changed my intentions,* he murmured. *I'm . . . on your side now.* Ignoring her sputtering of disbelief and the outcries from all of them, he continued quickly, *You must believe me. Time is very short.*

Believe you? Jael answered. *Never!*

Jarvorus hissed and shook his head. *You must! My master plans to kill you—and not just that, but to do it in the presence of the dragons. That will complete the prophecy—and the sorcery. But I think I can help you.*

Help? She laughed bitterly. *Are you going to save me?*

I—I can't stop you from dying, Jael. But . . . if you would choose another time, and another way, I can help you do that. It would be better for you—and for your side!

Jael was unmoved. *You want me to step into another of your traps!*

Even as she made her sarcastic reply, Jarvorus was wondering when Rent would be coming. If he did not convince her and perform the deed before Rent came, he could do nothing. Instead of answering her sarcasm, he plunged ahead to explain.

You are the key, Jael—key to the Master's final victory. The dragons are to be kept from reuniting with the Dream Mountain and their draconae—and the despair of the dragons is his most powerful weapon. The one you call the Nail knows that the dragons' only hope is your appearance, as the One of the prophecy.

Jael whispered, *Then, damn you, why don't you let me go to help them?*

I wish I could! Jarvorus cried. *But this spell is not my spell. I haven't the power to unlock it. The Words say that you must fall, and the Master has already planned how that will happen—in a great battle that is even now taking shape. A battle which the dragons cannot hope to win without you.*

Jael stared at him in silence, and so did Hodakai and the other riggers. The small green rigger was making futile rasping sounds. They all seemed equally incredulous.

He continued nevertheless. *When the dragons see you die in battle, they will lose all hope. They know the Words: "The One will fall as the battle is fought . . ."*

And Jael whispered, finishing the words for him: *"Upon her death is the ending wrought."*

Yes, Jarvorus answered. *And then the dragons and the Dream Mountain will be severed forever. They will die. The ifflings will die. And neither the Dream Mountain nor the draconae will be able to stop the completion of the Master's web of power.*

Touching the rigger-net, he again showed Jael, and her shipmates, a visible image of what would happen. He showed them the despair of the dragons and draconae transforming the living energy of the Dream Mountain so that it would strengthen, rather than oppose, the Nail's sorcery. And then he said, as the riggers began to protest, *I cannot free you in your present form. But I think I can free you from your life.* That startled them into silence. He added quickly, *I can free you from your part in the sorcery.*

There was a moment's hesitation—and then the rigger

Ar answered furiously, *What do you mean, you can free her from her life? Do you mean, KILL her?*

Jarvorus paused. *That's right,* he said softly.

The hatred that poured out from Ar was an almost physical force. From Jael, there was still a puzzled, angry silence—she might not have been able to hear Ar's words. Jarvorus spoke again. *You would have to help me . . . by allowing it. If you choose to die, it may be that you can thwart the sorcery. The Words do not say how the One is to die. But my Master's plan calls for your unwilling death, for your defeat. If you give yourself, at a time of your choosing, you may not be defeated. I do not know what the prophecies say about this, but . . .* He hesitated. There was much he did not know. He was making many guesses, and hoping that Jael would agree with them, and that they would be right.

He continued haltingly, *It may even be that . . . you can be saved, in death. If you can reach out . . . if you can find Dream Mountain as the ifflings once found it, as the dragons find the Final Dream Mountain . . . perhaps you will be able to reach your friends the dragons . . . then.*

Perhaps? hissed Ar. *Perhaps?*

Jarvorus walked slowly around the imprisoned riggers, gazing at Jael in her cell; and studying Ar, half concealed within the net, along with the fluttering green rigger; and turning at last to Hodakai. *I did not speak truth to you, when first we met,* he said to Hodakai. *Especially regarding myself, and Rent.* The rigger-spirit flickered in his jar, but said nothing. He turned back to Jael and said, *Here is truth. I can promise nothing—except freedom.*

Death, said Ar; and from the spark in Jael's eye, it seemed that she'd heard him.

Death, Jarvorus agreed. *But perhaps not in vain.* Jarvorus paused. *Jael . . . it is because I have shared in your thoughts, and known you . . . that I have decided to offer this. You have shown me a way I did not know before.* He peered into Jael's thoughts. He saw fear there, and distrust. But also a willingness to listen.

I do not blame you for distrusting me. But there is no other escape from what Rent and the Nail have planned.

Ar interrupted, his voice echoing strangely. Jarvorus shifted the underweb slightly so that Ar could be heard more easily. *—you say not in vain. You offer vague promises. Why should we believe you?*

Because you have no other hope. I offer no promises, except freedom for Jael. It may be the final release—the final death. Jarvorus hesitated, trying to find certainty among all the uncertainties in what he was suggesting. *The Masters, the Nail and Rent, will kill her anyway. That is certain. But her death now, at her choosing, not theirs, will strike a blow against their plans. Against their sorcery. As, I believe, you struck a blow once before.*

The others stared at him.

They have not forgotten the Black Peak! Not at all. Yes, I heard you tell of it. And I wish to help you defeat them again.

Why? Jael whispered.

Jarvorus sat up, gazing at her. He said, in a deep, throaty voice, *I do not like them. I do not like what they do. I wish to . . . hurt them.*

Ar answered in slow, soft words. *By deceiving her, as you deceived her once already? How do we know this isn't precisely the way the Enemy plans to kill her?*

Jarvorus pondered that. He looked at Hodakai, whose nervous dance had stopped. He looked at Ar, who was studying him with fierce, purplish eyes. He looked at the small green rigger, who had quieted and was peering intently back at him. And he looked at Jael, who was not looking at him at all, but staring into space. And he said, *Hodakai, you know something of the Nail's plans. You know that they plan to take her into battle, and to kill her there, against her will.* He paused, but Hodakai was silent.

He turned back to Jael and pressed his paws to the ice, gazing in at her. *I will open my thoughts to you. All there is to see. Study me, and judge.*

Jael, behind her prison wall of ice, slowly turned her eyes to his.

IT WAS already going wrong. Windrush realized it from the time the dragons crossed over the towering, icy summits of the Borderland Mountains, into the Enemy's territory. The air had been empty of lumenis dust. There was a silence all about the land, a darkness that belied the dawn that was growing behind the dragons. Far off to the right, beyond the end of the Borderland range, the Black Peak flickered—its open wound, where the Enemy's sorcery had once been broken, glaring across the distance with an angry red fire. Everything Windrush saw made him feel that they were about to be met by an Enemy who not only expected them, but had prepared a special sorcery in their honor.

The Nail of Strength did not disappoint him. By the time they had drawn abreast of the Enemy's eastern camps—the one they had attacked before was a dirty smudge to the south, and a smaller one was just out of sight to the north— they had not met a single enemy warrior. But ominous cloud formations were gathering around and behind them, darkly coiling clouds looming over the shadowy landscape; and Windrush knew that once more the Enemy had commandeered the very elements to his side. From the camps of drahls, there was no sign of activity, which Windrush found unsettling. It was not that he *wanted* drahls to appear; but the absence of opposition was another sign of Tar-skel's treachery lying in wait. It was possible, of course, that the drahls were busy laying waste the territory the dragons had left behind, but Windrush doubted it; more likely, he thought, the Enemy was hoping to gather in all the dragons and destroy them in a single, crushing blow. But what form would the blow take?

Farsight drew in close from the right, murmuring, "I think there are drahls in those clouds, Windrush. They'll be shadowing us until we're hemmed in on all sides. That's my guess. Be prepared for attack all around." SearSky sped in from the left and muttered his opinion. "They're all gathered ahead of us, Windrush. They know our strength, and they're gathered like cowards over the Dark Vale. We can sweep them from the sky. Maybe we'll get that traitor, Stonebinder, while we're at it." He glanced with approval back at the skyful of dragons following them.

Windrush acknowledged both opinions, but made no pronouncement. He suspected that neither guess was altogether correct. The Enemy had gone to much trouble to prepare a welcome, he thought, and he doubted that the drahls were overly fearful of their approach. The towering storm clouds that were chasing and flanking them seemed utterly opaque, and yet now they were beginning to flash with pulses of purple and green lightning. Ahead, a reddish glow that did not seem of the dawn beckoned them onward toward the Dark Vale. He guessed that the Nail was planning something more dramatic than merely engulfing them in swarms of drahls. But as to what that might be, his undersense gave no clue. No ifflings had appeared in midair to mutter enigmatic advice, and no rigger had arrived, flying her silver ship.

Windrush waited until Farsight and SearSky were back at the heads of their flights; then he drew a deep breath of cold dawn air and urged the dragons on with greater speed than ever. They would learn the answers soon.

The Dark Vale appeared ahead of them in the grey dawn like a vast crater cloaked in shadow. No detail was visible. The red glow that had been beckoning them was now glaring down from clouds high overhead, reflected from some invisible source. Windrush scanned the area. Even as they drew close to the vale, its details remained hidden beneath an eye-twisting interplay of erupting fires and light-snatching shadow, almost as if a blanket of sorcery lay across its top. Around the dragons and behind them, the storm clouds were crowding inward like marching columns of smoke, funneling the dragons into the vale. Windrush thought he glimpsed, and cries from the flank-scouts confirmed, the dark flecks of Stronghold's and Longtouch's flights approaching from south and north. Those flights, too, looked as though they were being driven by the storms.

Enough of being driven!

"Dragons!" Windrush called, with a long breath of flame. *"Downward, into the vale of the Enemy! Beware treachery! But strike boldly, for the life of the realm!"* And with a final thought that he should somehow have been more stirring in his cry, he banked into a steep dive. *"FOR THE REALM!"* he screamed into the wind as he sliced downward through the air, followed by two hundred bellowing dragons.

The Dark Vale loomed beneath him, light and shadow flickering. Suddenly the curtain of sorcery parted, revealing the land below. But what he saw lit by the overhead fire was not a valley swarming with enemy warriors, but instead a great, dark abyss. There was no land at all, but only dense, grey cloud, parting to form the vast shaft of a chasm. The dragons above him rumbled in confusion and dismay, but there was nothing to be done; they were already diving into the gaping emptiness where they had expected to find the Enemy's fortress. "Stay behind me!" he shouted to those who began to surge ahead, and though his words seemed swallowed up by the cottony greyness all around, the other dragons slowed, as though instinctively understanding the need to stay together.

What was this treachery? A camouflage surrounding Tarskel's fortress? Or a fantastic maw in the land itself, about to swallow the entire dragon armada in a single gulp? Was this the path to the Final Dream Mountain?

"Windrush! Where are we going?" shouted SearSky, from his left.

He didn't answer. Slowing his descent, he began a sweeping turn, looking for anything solid. The others followed, but the formation was now stretching out above him in a ragged spiral shape. It was impossible to maintain tight grouping in the crowded space between the clouds. Battle cries were giving way to rumbles of alarm, and the beating of wings, as fear and uncertainty gripped the dragons.

Windrush glanced around for Farsight and the other leaders. SearSky was veering away from the formation and flying perilously close to the walls of the shaft, blowing long tongues of flame into the cloud. His flames seemed at first to pass through without effect. Then there was a flicker of light coming back—and a high, keening cry.

The sweep of his turn had taken Windrush away from the spot, and he had to crane his neck to look back at what SearSky had discovered. But he needn't have turned. That first piercing cry was echoed—once, a dozen, a hundred times—until the very walls of cloud shrieked inward upon the dragons. Windrush felt a sudden, wrenching change in the air, a shudder of sorcery passing through the sky, and an instant later, it seemed that the whole world had turned into a maze of broken lenses, making it impossible to see clearly.

But above and below and all around, Windrush heard the screams of drahls and enemy dragons closing for battle.

The iffling felt the presence of the others before it saw them. It had nearly abandoned hope, but had continued streaking on through the silence in desperate determination to find someone who could help. The underrealm here was a great rarefied hollowness of distant mists and light, and strange tricks of perception that made the iffling wonder if it had left the realm of iffling and dragon altogether. Could it even find its way back to Jael now, if it tried? It didn't dare look to see.

And then there came that feeling again across the emptiness, drawing it on with a sudden new hope. There *was* someone, yes—and now the iffling began to sense a flickering light—no, a *series* of lights, and beyond the flickers, nearly obscured by mists, the dim glow of a much greater, but distant fire. The iffling sped recklessly, heedlessly, joyfully toward the lights and toward the source of the feeling.

What it felt was the unmistakable pull of familiarity, of *family*. It shouted and pleaded to the emptiness, and it heard faintly the answering cry:

—*Our child*—
—*returned at last!*—
—*but the need grows!*—
—*do not stop*—
—*we long to see you, to speak*—
—*but do not stop!*—
—*fly onward*—
—*to one reaching out from the mountain*—
—*one reaching toward you*—

The iffling was bewildered by the cries, but propelled by their urgency. The voices sounded so tired . . . and yet they were the voices of its own kind, perhaps the very ones who had given it life. As it drew closer to the flames, it perceived that they were weak indeed, like tiny candles flickering in a wind. The iffling called out to them: —*I have come home! I need help, and quickly!*—

The iffling wanted desperately to fly to them, but a force like a wind seemed to deflect it away, and it heard a single voice commanding: —*Fly onward!*—

So great was its desire to unite with its parents that instinctively it fought the change in direction; but the memory of Jael, waiting to die, was enough to send it onward in obedience. As it passed the flickering ones, the iffling sensed a great longing carried on the wind; and it realized that those tiny flames were joined to the distant fire ahead, or should have been.

They wanted to be joined to it again. Instead of being able to give their child the help it needed, they were saying to it: Your work is not yet done.

The iffling sped onward.

It seemed to take forever . . . but in time the iffling felt something new reaching out to it, something that was unlike any presence it had ever felt before. And yet, it seemed to resonate within the iffling, as though it were a kind of presence that it had long been prepared to meet. For an instant, it feared: Was it the Enemy?

The presence coiled around the iffling like a tiny whirl-wind, and touched the iffling's thoughts with a remarkable gentleness and what seemed fear and astonishment. And the iffling heard a voice in its thoughts that it somehow recognized as dragon.

My name is FullSky, the dragon whispered urgently. *Can you help me?*

For the dragon, reaching with dwindling strength toward the region where he *hoped* Jael might be, the appearance of the iffling-child was a breathtaking surprise. He had felt some force drawing him that way, but it wasn't until he touched the tiny, frightened being that he recognized it for what it was.

The iffling was even more surprised than he was, but the need in its thoughts was so clear that there was no time to lose. FullSky opened his thoughts to it, crying out for news of Jael. The iffling shared its knowledge in a bewildering cascade, and then he knew with terrifying certainty what the task was for which he had been guarding his last strength.

He already felt unutterably weary. His kuutekka was stretched out through the underrealm, from his tortured body to the Dream Mountain, and then out to this strange plane where the iffling-child wandered. It seemed impossible for him to accomplish what had been given to him to do. But he already felt the realm groaning with battle in the Dark Vale, and he heard, as though across a vast sea, the cries of the outnumbered and terrified dragons; and he knew that he had no choice at all.

Help me, draconae, if you have any strength to lend! he cried silently back along the thread, not imagining that anyone might hear. And he cried aloud to the iffling: *Take me to her! Show me the way to Jael!*

Chapter 37
A CHOICE OF DEATH

FACING JARVORUS the animal, Jael was almost afraid to look into his thoughts. Afraid that he might be telling the truth. His words were terrifying, so terrifying she could hardly think straight. And yet . . . she had been willing to die once before, for Highwing. Why not now—for Windrush, for the realm?

In truth, death no longer seemed as horrifying a prospect as it once might have. She felt no other hope. She was imprisoned, paralyzed, and unable to help herself or her friends. Could death be any worse?

She felt the creature's thoughts touching hers, and she shrank from it—but she could no more avoid the touch now than before. There was a difference this time, though. Jarvorus was allowing her to see beneath the rippling surface, to the hidden labyrinth of thoughts deeper within. Jarvorus was allowing her to see him as he really was.

It was an astounding revelation. She was peering into the heart of a warrior-spirit, an iffling-imitator who had embarked upon a mission of blind obedience. It owed its allegiance to the one who had created it, or claimed to have—who had transformed it from a sprite and instilled in it intelligence and a warrior's instinct, through the sorcery of Tar-skel. But the sorcery had been administered by the one called Rent. Jael was horrified to realize how completely Rent, a former rigger, had succumbed to the seductive power of the Nail.

Jael saw Jarvorus' flickering memories of his past life as a simple sprite, and his capture and transformation in Rent's forge of sorcery. She saw him awakening in the static realm, where he had been sent to subvert the ifflings' plan to bring the One back to the realm. She saw battle with the iffling-children, and shuddered as she saw them extinguished, all but one. She saw Jarvorus taking control in the dragon realm—and she felt a fresh wave of hopelessness, and anger, as she relived the springing of the trap.

And then . . . she saw Jarvorus changing, against his own will. He began both to understand and to empathize with his adversaries. She felt his confusion as he listened—first casually, then more closely—to *her* story, told in quiet desperation to Hodakai. Jarvorus found himself unexpectedly moved by her words and her memories—moved by her friendship with a dragon, a friendship that would lead her to risk her life for him. And Jael glimpsed, with astonishment, Jarvorus' impulsive lie to his master, and his decision to set her free.

She felt his tension, his urgency. Jarvorus feared that he would not have the courage to take Jael's life, even if she offered it; he feared that Rent would come to take her before he could set her free. Jael's heart tightened, as she glimpsed Rent's plan to take her and destroy her in the presence of the dragons.

With a shiver, she felt the link with Jarvorus dissolve. She stared once more through the wall of her icy cell into the eyes of the strange animal form that Jarvorus had taken on—an awkward imitation of the ifflings' animal form, a creature with large eyes and sleek grey fur, and powerful jaws. The form was more frightening than reassuring; this was the creature who had betrayed her, tricked her into a spell that could not be broken except by the Enemy, or by death.

She was stunned to realize that she believed him—believed that he was trying to offer her a way out that was better. But was it, really? It was clear that it had to be done quickly, if at all.

Through the fragmented net, she heard Ar muttering darkly—and nearby, she heard Ed rustling his wings and whispering incomprehensibly to himself. Outside the net, Hodakai was flickering, apparently trying to decide what he thought about it all. No one seemed certain, except Jarvorus. And . . . perhaps . . . her.

I believe you, she whispered to Jarvorus. *But what you ask is hard.*

Yes. But it is the only way.

But the way to do what? You spoke of the Dream Mountain—of meeting the dragons—but you do not say how. She imagined herself leaving her body, dead but not dead, and floating out over the mountains, lost forever. She remembered Mogurn's death, when she had forced him out the airlock into the Flux, and she shuddered.

The creature bowed its head. *I cannot tell you, or show you. You are human, I am not. I do not know what is possible. You must be ready for the final death. But be certain—there is no life for you here. Not any longer.*

She nodded, frowning. She wanted to turn again to Ar and Ed for help—but forced herself not to. If she thought too hard about her friends, she would never be able to say yes, even if it was the right thing to say.

Rigger Jael, whispered Jarvorus. *Time grows short. Rent is coming. And I believe that the battle with the dragons may be commencing, even now. If you wish to choose your own time and place, and not the Nail's . . .*

Jael did not listen to the rest of his words. She closed her eyes, remembering something Kan-Kon had said to her: "You're a rigger! You can *change things!*" She realized that she was weeping—for Kan-Kon, for her friends, for herself. She forced herself to stop trembling. *Can you guarantee,* she whispered, *that it will be a blow against the enemies of Windrush—even if I die the final death?*

Jarvorus bobbed his head. He seemed to grin joylessly. *I guarantee that it will make them very, very angry.*

Jael stared at him and laughed out loud, through her tears. *All right,* she murmured, her voice trembling. *Then tell me what you want me to do. How are you going to get me out of this ice?*

No—!

Ar's shout echoed and faded into the labyrinth of the

twisted remnants of the net. If Jael heard him, she didn't answer. He wasn't sure it would have mattered. When she made up her mind to do something, he didn't know any way of stopping her. But he couldn't just let her agree to die.

Jael! His voice sharpened to a tight, metallic shriek. *Don't let him do it! Please!*

I have to, she whispered. *There's no other way.*

Her voice filled him with dread. *You don't know that!* he pleaded, but already she had turned her attention elsewhere. *Jael!*

Several heartbeats passed, and he heard another voice floating to him, trying urgently to get his attention. It was Hodakai. *You—what's your name?—Ar! Can you hear me?*

Yes! he answered.

The spirit was dancing urgently. *You must listen. Listen carefully. She is right—it may be the only way.*

Not you too! I don't believe it!

You do not know these weavings of power as I do. Jarvorus is right—I see no way out of the spell except to interrupt it at its source. And that source is her life. It is woven into the very fabric of the spell.

But SOMEONE could stop it! What about this Rent?

Hodakai's voice was low and bitter. *Don't be a fool! They're keeping her alive for one reason, and that is to wilt the hearts of the dragons in the final battle. She is—forgive me, Jael, friend of Kan-Kon!—she is as dead to your world now as I am.*

Ar struggled for words.

And if you want her death to mean anything, to give any hope—

No, no, he wanted to cry. He didn't care about hope or meaning. He just wanted his friend to be free! And alive!

He became aware of the voice of the only one who had not spoken. *Scrawwwww—Arrr—must do it—must give her the chance!*

Ed, please don't—not you, too!

Melt the ice, rawwww! It's the only way, scrawwk-k-k, it can work!

His confusion was turning to anger. *How do you know it can?*

The parrot fluttered his wings violently. *We're riggers! Rig-g-g-gers! Melt the ice! Hawwwwk-k-k! Must give her the chance—melt the ice!*

Yes, that's it! Hodakai cried. *Maybe we can do that for her! Jarvorus!*

The false-iffling's head flashed one way, then another. Suddenly it rose up on its hind legs. *Yes!* it hissed. *I must have your help! We must remove the ice barrier! You must soften it, to let me in! Use your powers! Are you willing, Jael?*

Through the twisted net, Ar could see Jael staring wide-eyed, and nodding her head, and speaking so softly that he could not hear. But her lips seemed to be saying, *Yes, you must . . .*

Ar could not speak. Everyone else was set upon this insane course. But perhaps if he went along with them . . . if they could soften the barrier . . . melt the ice . . .

Perhaps they could free her. Not for death, but for life.

Surround her with heat, Hodakai said, glowing brighter.

Ar studied the effects of their efforts so far. *We haven't the strength for that. But if we focus heat on the weak points, on the fracture lines . . .*

Jael, on the inside, looked frightened but determined.

There was a brief interplay between Hodakai's shadow-figure and the inner glow of his spirit jar, then a thin beam of light shot out, striking the surface of the ice. Hodakai retained his rigger's ability to craft images—but was it enough to help?

Jael, you must try to melt it from within, Ar whispered, formulating his own image—a fine plane of fire cutting like a scalpel at a flaw in the ice. But it was hard to distinguish the ice of the binding from the fracture zones in the net. Carefully, he thought. Carefully!

His words were punctuated by the sound of Ed tapping with his beak, testing other points in the ice. *Ruck-k-k . . . ruck-k-k . . .*

The false-iffling scurried around the barrier, hissing, as it watched their efforts. It was growing frantic. *You must hurry!*

Rent will be coming! More heat! You must melt it all! Use your anger! Use your anger for heat!

Suddenly Ar understood what Jarvorus was talking about. He was full of anger—rage at Tar-skel, who had threatened the realm in the first place—and rage at Jarvorus, who had tricked Jael into a death sentence—and rage at himself, for allowing it to happen!

A sullen glow radiated from his fragment of the net, fueled by his anger. Outside the net, he could see Jarvorus prompting Hodakai, until a similar glow emerged from the captured rigger-spirit. *Damn you!* he whispered to himself. *Melt—damn you!* If he had to burn out the rigger-net to free her, that's what he would do.

It's working! Jarvorus hissed, dancing close. The ice was shrinking, growing thinner around Jael. The false-iffling was quivering with excitement. *It's working!*

Jael—if you can, spring, when we've melted through! he whispered silently. *Be ready, Jael!* She was peering out at Jarvorus now, eyes wide with fear. *Be ready!* Ar cried inwardly, not wanting to say it aloud, not wanting Jarvorus to know that he was hoping to free her alive.

Almost, Jarvorus whispered. The ice flashed and evaporated from her face and head.

More! she gasped. *I'm almost out!*

Ar couldn't contain himself any longer. The ice broke away from her shoulders and arms with great clouds of steam. *JAEL!* he screamed. *BE READY TO BREAK OUT! BE READY TO FLY!*

He could see her struggling to move; but her arms, though free of ice, moved as though she were caught in a thick liquid. *I can't, Ar! Don't try—please! Just let me—!*

She cannot! cried the false-iffling, seeing what Ar was intending. *She will be caught by Rent! You must let me—ah, there!*

The last of the ice vanished with a sudden sparkle of heat. But there remained a glimmering light surrounding her like a forcefield, and Ar realized with a shock that they had only broken through one outer barrier. She remained bound in the spell; her eyes caught his, and in them he saw her despair and her desperation. She could move her limbs only a little; she could not flee, or move the ship at all.

That's enough, Jarvorus said throatily. For a moment, his form seemed to flicker, now an animal, now an iffling-flame. *Jael, it is time . . . if you would have me do this!*

Ar felt his breath explode in helpless protest: NO—!

As the last of the ice melted, doubt suddenly rose up like a towering wave in Jarvorus' mind. He heard Rent's voice, with the force of a howling typhoon. KEEP THIS ONE UNTIL I ARRIVE! It felt as though his master's hand were pressing down upon him, forcing him to abide by his instructions. But he no longer wanted to please Rent. He had already decided. *I have made up my mind. I will not do what Rent wants. I cannot. I must not . . .*

Only one thing enabled him to persevere, and that was the sight of Jael, the ice barrier gone, her eyes filled with fear and with a longing for freedom. Jarvorus pressed his thoughts to hers, felt her quiet desperation, and her doubt. It was killing her to wait, while her friends cried out their grief . . . and she was starting to wonder: Was Ar right? Could she escape?

Jarvorus grieved for her. *Jael,* he whispered, *Rent is surely on his way. You cannot move, you cannot escape him any other way.*

The heat of Ar's and Hodakai's efforts flashed around him, sheets of fire on his body. He instinctively began slipping back into nonphysical form, but he needed the animal form to do what he must do. He flickered between the two forms, as he bounded through the softening protective layer of the binding. Ar was trying to free her physically, but there was no hope of that, and Jarvorus had no time to expain.

At last he faced Jael within the glimmering confines of the inner spell. *It is time,* he whispered, from his solid form. *Are you ready?* She nodded, and her eyes seemed terribly bright as she turned her head, presenting her neck to him. *I will be quick. Farewell, my new friend!* he hissed.

Baring his teeth, he sprang.

* * *

The world was on fire. Jael could make out nothing, except the heat pummeling the icy prison that held her. Ar had come to agree with her after all, then—and Ed, and Hoda-kai. She was nearly overcome with terror—she did not want to die—but even in the midst of the fire, she knew it was the only way. Hurry! she thought to the others. Before I lose my courage! Oh, Windrush—Ar—Ed—!

As the ice vanished, she felt an instant of hope—then felt the molasses resistance of the spell, and heard Jarvorus' words: Rent is coming! And she knew there was no other hope. She heard the others calling out to each other, but her ears were pounding and she could scarcely make out a word. Jarvorus' shadowy animal shape was bounding through the barrier. It was shimmering, now shadow now flame now shadow. And its voice was whispering in her thoughts . . .

Bow your head . . . I will be quick . . .

The tears came even as she obeyed. She averted her eyes so that she would not have to see him strike. She felt another sudden movement, and a rustling presence ballooning into her mind, crying out urgently, Jayyyyyyyllll, awwwwk, come with youuuu . . . ! She could do nothing to stop Ed's sudden flashing movement, joining himself to her, and she couldn't help weeping with joy . . . and with grief for Ar . . .

His voice rang through the net, a terrible cry: Jael—NOOO!

She felt a moment of terrible doubt. Ed was wailing softly within her . . .

Jarvorus sprang, and she glimpsed a flash of shadow-fire: Jarvorus' fangs, as they plunged into her throat. The pain was instantaneous, a searing fire—and the realization that it was done—then a shock of ice, and a great wave of dizziness. After the first moment, she no longer felt pain, but only the dizziness of consciousness beginning to slip away.

There were voices calling to her, but failing . . . growing inaudible. The binding spell was dissolving, fading against the sky like stars against a dawn; the ship slung to her back was falling away, drifting free; the tortured and fractured net no longer surrounded her. She was drifting away . . . the pain was gone, but so were her friends . . . she cried out to them, but they were receding . . .

She thought dimly that there must be something more to it than this . . . some way to reach to her friends *Windrush!* some way to help *Ar!* some way to help, *some way not to die!* . . . but now she could no longer even see the cavern, it was not so much like rising, as she had always imagined it, but rather *expanding*, growing thinner, thinner . . . so this was what it was like to die, whispered a voice like a faint breath of wind.

There was a vague sense of mountains around her, and beneath her, and above her, and nowhere to go, nothing and no one to save her. . . .

Chapter 38
DEATH AND FREEDOM

THE LIFE-MONITOR alarms clamored in the net.

Ar watched Jarvorus strike—felt Jael's passing, like a flame through his heart. He screamed, *NOOO!* But it was too late. In his effort to free her, he had only opened the way to her death.

As the binding spell dissolved, she began to grow transparent in the net. Ar cried out, helpless to stop what was happening. She wavered and vanished from the net. For an instant, she seemed to take form again on the outside, adrift in the Flux; then she flickered like a ghost, and was gone. *Jael . . . Jael . . . Jael . . . !* When he finally managed to stop shouting her name, not just aloud, but in his mind, he knew that it was over. Had he heard her crying out to him at the end? He wasn't sure.

An internal indicator flared red in the net, warning of critical life-signs in rigger-station number two. Auto-resuscitation had switched on, but was cycling without effect. Ar cursed the alarm and shut it off. He couldn't get out of the net to go to her physical aid, even if he knew of anything he could do that the auto-unit couldn't. He was helpless.

He had no chance to think about it further. The tensions in the net were shifting drastically. Jael's side of the net fluttered and closed down, like a bubble collapsing. Ar's side expanded abruptly into the space; he gasped with the sudden power rushing into the net, and realized that he had been frozen in various vectors of movement, like a wrestler caught in mid-struggle, a dozen muscles pulling in different directions. With the sudden release of power, the ship began spinning and tumbling, and he had to act frantically to neutralize his control inputs and damp down the movements.

He had control of the ship again, at least—however damaged the net. The interference between his station and Jael's was now gone, along with Jael herself. He recognized the cause of his new freedom, and shuddered with grief, which rocked the ship yet again. He knew he had to control his thoughts, and discover what forces were acting upon the ship, and understand them.

He stretched his hands into the Flux and felt the air shaking violently. It was not just his internal struggle, then; the whole cavern was shaking, and Hodakai had contracted in his jar to a tiny, dark shadow. Ar could no longer see the false-iffling. *Ed, are you with me? Hodakai? Jarvorus? WHAT'S HAPPENING?*

It was all he could do to keep the ship from careening sideways into the cavern walls. There seemed to be an earthquake shaking the mountain, and he had no idea how to protect himself and the ship. He didn't know how to get out of the cavern, and anyway, he was loath to leave the place where Jael had vanished. How could he be sure she was gone for good? How could he know she was . . . dead?

Enough! he snapped aloud. *You have a ship to bring in— control your thoughts!* And his voice caught, because what did he care about bringing in the ship, if it meant leaving his friend behind?

STOP—THINKING—! he shouted to himself, until his voice echoed from the walls of the cavern.

Against the din, he at last heard a small voice calling out to him: *Ar! Ar, friend of Jael! The realm trembles! The One has come, and given her life! The sorcery has been shaken! Can you feel it?*

Who was that? Jarvorus? Ar scanned the area and finally saw the false-iffling, crouching low in its animal form. Its eyes were wild with fear and excitement.

Is this what you intended? Ar shouted.

It has begun! cried the false-iffling. *She has torn the sorcery! Even the Nail of Strength cannot undo it now. But the danger is not passed!*

Flee! cried another voice, quaking with fright. *Warn the people! Go home!* It was Hodakai, dashing violently from one side of his containment to the other. *Take word! Take warning! Go!*

Ar stared at him. Take warning? To whom? How? But there was no waiting for an answer, because at that moment a tremendous crack appeared in the cavern walls, forward and back, and through the floor. *My sacred word,* Ar whispered. The cavern was splitting open like an eggshell, and through the opening he could see only a roiling darkness. *Hodakai, do you know what's happening—?*

But he had no chance to finish, because he and his ship were suddenly falling. . . .

Hodakai watched in astonishment as the rigger-ship, a distorted silvery shadow with the ghostly shape of a Clendornan at its prow, tumbled through the crevasse that gaped open in his cavern. It vanished, twinkling, into the abyss. The realm was shaking and he feared for his own survival, oh yes—but somehow the thing that hurt the worst was watching the only rigger-ship that he had seen in half a lifetime vanish from sight. Where was it falling to? Back to the static realm? Or to somewhere else in the Flux? It hardly mattered. Ar and the ship were gone.

And so was Jael. He had seen her spirit gather and vanish like smoke, and whether her role was done now, he couldn't guess, but one thing he knew, and that was that Rent was going to be angry. Oh yes, he would be angry. And for once, Hodakai felt no ambivalence about it. He was thrilled—and terrified, yes, but ecstatic that they had subverted the Enemy's plan. Yes, the Enemy. His enemy. There was no going back on that now.

He wished that Windrush would come, so that he could tell the dragon what he had done. But of course that was impossible. The dragons were battling for their lives at this very moment, and the fact that he and Jael and the others had just double-crossed Tar-skel here didn't mean that the dragons were going to prevail. They were all still very much in danger.

Jarvorus! he called across the shaking cavern, across the abyss, looking for the false-iffling. *Jarvorus, what do you see? Have we struck a good blow? Is she—?*

And there his voice failed him, because he could not bring himself to say the words, to ask, is she dead?

The false-iffling didn't answer, anyway.

Turning restlessly, Hodakai probed a short way into the underrealm, looking for any sign of Jael. The only thing he could really do was to reach out to Rent, and to crow about what they'd done here. But though he was exultant, he was not *that* exultant. He would keep his triumph to himself just a little longer.

And anyway, things were shaking terribly down in the underrealm: the familiar channels and pathways were buried or swept away by earthquake, wind and storm, and fire. He pulled out, gasping, and clung to his existence in the spirit jar, in the cavern. It was like clinging to the surface of an avalanche; the spell that kept him alive here was holding, but for how much longer?

Jarvorus, talk to me! he cried, searching the cavern with his gaze.

But Jarvorus seemed to have vanished.

The warrior-spirit huddled in a pocket of the underrealm, stunned by the cataclysm that they seemed to have unleashed. Were the Words so powerful? He knew, of course, that they were something that caused his former masters both tremendous hope and tremendous fear. But were they so deeply woven into the sorcery that they could cause all this to happen?

Jarvorus knew that he had tampered with powers greater than he could ever understand. Rent would be here soon, was almost certainly on his way here at this instant; and if Jarvorus was lucky, if he was very lucky, his death would be quick. He was not sorry, he did not think that he was sorry, but he was very, very frightened. The sprite-warriors that he commanded had all fled in terror. He wasn't sure why he stayed himself, except that he had nowhere to go. This cavern was the closest thing he had to a home—here, where he had shared in Jael's momentous death. And here he would live or die in consequence of that act.

These forces shaking the cavern were, he perceived, only echoes of far greater powers that were cascading through the distant reaches of the underrealm. He hoped he would be able to detect Rent coming, in the confusion.

Not that it mattered in the end. He had done what he had been born to do, and *that* was what mattered.

As *Seneca* tumbled through the violently shifting currents in the Flux, Ar fought to regain control. Was he alone now? Was Ed gone, too? He couldn't see where he was going, and had no outside references; but it felt as though something was *pulling* the ship onward, something that was disturbing the whole fabric of the Flux here. More of Tar-skel's sorcery?

Even as he fought back spatial disorientation, his mind was wheeling through useless lines of thought. Hodakai had urged him to go warn the home universe. What was he supposed to do? Return to Cargeeling and announce that the universe was in peril from a terrible, invisible evil somewhere in the Flux?

Please, he whispered to the darkness, *this cannot be real, cannot be happening. Jael, speak to me! Ed!* But he had sensed Ed diving into Jael's consciousness, just before she had died. Could he have survived?

He felt the answer before he heard it, a nudge at the front of the net, a snapping of wings. *Ed!* he gasped. He tried to bring light into the net, just a faint instrument-glow of light, so as not to dazzle himself against the darkness outside.

The parrot was flying to and fro, almost drunkenly. He was trying to orient himself, trying to find up and down. His green feathers gleamed in the light Ar had created. *Ed,* Ar whispered. *I thought I felt you go over to Jael! I thought you went with her!*

The rasp of the parrot's voice was a balm to his spirit. *Rrrrawk. Did go. Did.* Ed wheeled and flew straight into Ar's gaze. He could feel the parrot's thoughts collide with his, then spin away, trying to help him wrestle the ship back under control. *Ed split. Hawwwwk—went both ways! Ed dizzy. What happening, Arrr? What-t-t-t?*

Ar took a sharp breath. Ed had split? But of course, he was a cyberparrot, all pattern and artificial intelligence. Of course he could duplicate himself.

Fly, Ar—awwwk! What happening?

I don't know, Ar murmured. *Jael's gone, Ed—gone! We killed her, Jarvorus killed her.* He tried to find purchase in the currents with a set of short, stubby wings. There was something ahead . . . something drawing them closer . . . something that made him fearful.

Hawwwwk-k! Gone yes! Ed squawked, joining him in the effort. *Maybe not killed! Maybe not! Scrawwww!*

Ed, it won't help to deny it. Ar saw something ahead now, a dull reddish glow in the far distance. He was regaining control over the ship, at least enough to ride through the shuddering changes in the flow; and that glowing thing, whatever it was, gave him a reference to fix upon. *Jael, where are you?* he cried, deep in his heart, amazed that a Clendornan could so hurt for a human. *Where have you gone? Did you find Windrush before you died? Did we kill you for anything good?*

Don't know she died, Ed insisted, chopping his beak in Ar's direction.

Ed, there's just no way—look at the monitors in the rigger-stations. His voice caught as he looked himself. *Life-signs in her station have ceased,* he whispered. And he realized that he had just pronounced the evidence against any remaining hope he might have had.

Aawwrrrrr, Ed growled, gargling. *Does Ed live? DOES HE? Ed taken from his body! And Ed WENT with Jayyyl!* Flapping his wings angrily, Ed shot back to the front of the net and stretched it as far as it would go, scanning ahead toward the red thing that was drawing them on.

Ar stared dumbly at the parrot. Ed lived in the net with him, through cyberchip technology, though his body was long since gone. *Could* Jael have somehow survived? And Ed had sent his memories and personality with Jael. Ar wondered if Ed was so angry right now because he wasn't with her—this half of him wasn't with her. *Ed, do you really think she . . . could have survived, somehow?*

Hawwwww, don't . . . KNOWWWW! Ed wailed, flapping from side to side ahead of him.

Then hope, Ed! Ar thought silently. And help me hope.

The thing ahead of them was beginning to loom like an object of substantial mass and size. It appeared that this was the object that was drawing them forward. It was a sullen red thing, surrounded by a spiraling veil of gas and dust.

Sacred word, Ed—is that a black hole ahead of us? Ar whispered in shock, realizing that he should have recognized the danger long ago.

Rawk-k-k? Hawww? Ed asked, casting a frightened glance back at him.

Ed clearly did not know what a black hole was, and Ar didn't have time to explain. If that's what it was, he needed to act at once, or they would be following Jael in death a lot sooner than he'd thought. There was a very strong current carrying them, and up to now, he had not tried to steer out of it. He was completely lost, navigationally, and wasn't even sure that they were in a charted layer of the Flux. But a quick check of the instruments revealed that, indeed, the object out there was distorting space on a cosmic scale. It was a singularity of some sort, and though he couldn't be sure that it was a normal-space black hole, the readings indicated that they were fast approaching the epicenter of a cataclysmic disturbance.

Ed, shear off! If we fall into that thing ahead, we'll be crushed! Ar made a fast judgment as to which direction offered them the best hope of veering free—and kicking the ship over sharply on its stubby wings, he began a slow crawl across the main current.

The parrot saw what he was doing, and bent his wings to help him. It was like crossing a turbulent sea on a raft, fighting their way across a water roiling with cross-chop. Ar tried, for the sake of clarity, to remake the image that way; but either the net was too badly damaged or Ar was too exhausted from his uninterrupted time in the net, because his efforts were futile. The current was dark and invisible, and they had to fight ceaselessly to keep the ship from tumbling out of control.

Ar realized, as he stared at the glowing thing, just how weary he was. But he could not let up, he could not even pause to mourn his lost friend and shipmate, he could only fight to cross the increasingly powerful currents, fight to save his ship. And not just that, he realized with a flash of horror. Once they escaped this—*if* they escaped it—they needed to discover if this terrible thing was the beginning of Tar-skel's breakthrough into the static realm, into Ar's own universe.

With a glance at Ed, laboring in his small way to help steer the ship, Ar realized that he *had* to keep hoping, had to do whatever he could to ensure that Jael had not given her life in vain.

The singularity before them glowed ever brighter as they drew closer to it. Gradually its light, scattering through the gas and dust around them, began to illuminate the actual currents—and Ar began to hope, for the first time, that he might indeed be able to fly his way out.

Chapter 39
TO THE DREAM MOUNTAIN

IT WAS the most difficult challenge of his life. As FullSky stretched farther and farther into the underrealm, following the speeding iffling, he felt that at any moment he would stretch past the limit, and his kuutekka would part from his body forever, and this was where he would die. The underrealm here seemed a hollow void; but he felt the chaos of battle in the Dark Vale booming like a distant drum. He knew that time was growing short.

Somehow he did not reach the limit of his strength. As the small, fiery iffling vanished into a nest of underrealm spells deep within a mountain, FullSky felt a sudden renewal of his energy, and he knew that somehow the draconae were lending him strength through the underrealm connection. He plunged into the mountain, and found himself peering with astonishment at a place he recognized—Hodakai's cavern.

Floating in the cavern near the spirit jar was a strange gathering of beings: the iffling, a false-iffling, and several unfamiliar creatures existing within a gleaming vessel that he imagined to be a rigger-ship. He realized at once that one of them, caught in a web of sorcery, was Jael. The iffling streaked back to him, whispering, *Hurry, dragon—if you can do anything to help!*

It took FullSky a long heartbeat to understand what was happening. And by then, Jael was dying. Suddenly FullSky knew that a staggering betrayal had just occurred—not against the riggers, but against the Enemy. The cavern had begun to shake, and many of the spells woven around it were unraveling.

But Jael was dying. Had he come only to watch her pass to the Final Dream Mountain?

HELP HER! screamed the iffling, its voice a torn whistle of wind.

It took FullSky a fraction of an instant, which was almost longer than he had, to come to his senses and begin crafting a weaving through the threads of the underrealm. It was his fastest and most perilous weaving yet; he cast it breathlessly around the dying spirit of the rigger. Her kuutekka was already expanding, stretching, thinning, searching in desperation for that which she could not see or find . . .

Not yet, Jael! FullSky whispered, pouring his remaining strength into the spell. I will not let you go to the Final Dream Mountain. Not yet. We need you too much here . . . !

The tides of space and time seemed to sway her this way and that in the fuzzy strangeness that was death. She knew she was no longer a part of the world, that she was caught up and carried by forces beyond her reckoning; but the strangest thing, as she came to be aware of it, was that she was aware of anything at all.

I have died.

I am not dead.

Nor am I alive.

Is this the life that lies beyond life?

There was a murmuring presence around her, and she thought she heard a voice answer, No, you are not going to the Final Dream Mountain, not yet. But before she could even wonder what that meant, she felt threads of power coming out of nowhere to gather around her—and she felt a surge, then a whistling, dizzying movement, spinning her like a whirlwind in the net. But she was not in the net; she was not anywhere; she felt no awareness of body, or sight or sound, or smell or taste or touch.

And yet . . .

She felt herself riding a fantastic, invisible thread of power through a sky that had no height or depth or substance. There was a booming presence of life around her, but distant; and closer to her was another presence, and something about it spoke the word *dragon* in her heart.

We are almost there, whispered the voice she had heard before. *And there we shall be gathered in, and perhaps you can find again the life you have lost* . . .

And then the voice, once more, was lost on the wind.

But she knew now that it had been a dragon voice—not Windrush, but perhaps someone close to him. It all felt exceedingly odd to her, and again she said, *I have died, haven't I? Is this where dragons go when they die?*

There was no answer, but only that rushing sensation that was neither sound-sense nor touch-sense, but something deeper within her. And then she felt everything slowing, and regathering . . . and she suddenly felt an astounding sense of safety and enclosure. And then the voice said, *You have died, and yet not died. There is little time to explain. We need you more urgently now than ever.*

And another, more melodious, voice said, *Welcome, Jael, to the Dream Mountain.*

Her sense of sight came slowly back to her, though she had no idea how. She found she could only gaze in amazement and wonder. This was the Dream Mountain, of which Windrush had spoken so long ago? It was like a great cathedral of translucent glass . . . and in its center, a darkness, within which burned a fire like a hot forge. The fire was enclosed by powerfully woven threads of underrealm magic, which she could see but not comprehend. The fire, the magic, and the darkness were all contained within the Mountain, the outlines of which were sketched by a vast shadow-presence of stone.

It took her a little while to realize that she was inhabiting several layers of the Flux at once. She was inside a mountain, but in the underrealm; and in this place there was a sharp boundary point in the continuum, and that boundary was something extraordinary to behold.

There is much to make clear, sang a low voice which she at once knew was a female dragon.

But we cannot take the time, or the Forge of Dreams may fall to the Enemy, cried another.

The voices were a distraction. She was fascinated by that ghostly fire in the center; it created in her a strange and irrational mix of fear and wonderment. The fire, she perceived, did not exist just in one particular layer of the Flux; it penetrated *through* the layers, and within its woven enclosure, it seemed to warp and twist the space that immediately surrounded it. It gave off tremendous energy, which was somehow being channeled by the draconae's weaving of magic here in the Dream Mountain.

It was, she realized, a space-time singularity. At the heart of the Dream Mountain. The Forge of Dreams.

Even as she considered the name of the singularity-fire, she realized that she was connected to it now; it was the powers of the dreamfire that gave her life.

Her thoughts and memories were expanding into the darkness like little puffs of air into a vacuum. She saw memories gleaming around her like raindrops in the sun: memories of her father, helping her and cursing her; of her mother, trying and failing to shield her from the darkly mercurial person her father had become; of friends in rigger-school who could never quite gain her trust; of Mogurn, who enslaved her; of Highwing, who freed her; of Ar, who befriended her; of Ed . . .

In this strange realm of energy and darkness, surrounded by voices that were trying to gain her attention, she wept silently for all those people who had been a part of her life. Especially, she wept for Ar, and for Ed.

It was Ed's voice that brought her back, away from those glittering memories: *(Hawwww, Jayyyl . . . very, scrawww, interes-s-s-s-ting place here, awwwwk? How do you lik-k-ke being f-f-f-freee like a bird-d-d, hawwww?)*

(Ed?) she whispered in astonishment. And then she remembered, Ed had joined himself to her in her passage to . . . death, or whatever this was, if not death. How did she like being free? She remembered a memory of Ed's she had witnessed once, when she had "rescued" him from a recreational cyberbank: the parrot's own recollection of being

captured, his memories and personality being siphoned out of his physical body. Now she understood what a terrible shock it must have been to him.

(Hawwww, yes . . .)

But Ed was not the only one speaking. The draconae were becoming more insistent.

You have come, and the realm is trembling.

But it may yet fall.

Help us, Jael, friend of Highwing . . .

With a great rush, the urgency of the struggle closed back in upon her, and she was aware now not just of voices, but of the quick, shimmering movements of glassy beings within this mountain. What she saw were the ghostly presences of the draconae in the underrealm. They were singing desperately, *Will you trust us, friend of Highwing?*

And at last she managed to answer, *I trust any friend of Highwing. Is he . . . here among you?*

She felt a surge of energy, as though by speaking she had somehow loosed a reservoir of powers. *His spirit lives in the Final Dream Mountain,* sighed one of the voices. *But not precisely among us, though we have often felt his presence.*

Jael tried not to show her disappointment. *Are you his friends? I am . . . Jael, friend of Highwing.*

The answer was a rippling choir of voices.

Lavafire, friend of Highwing—

Cooltouch, friend of Highwing—

Gentlesong, friend of Highwing—

Starchime, friend of Highwing—

Strongthought, friend of Highwing—

Starfire, friend of Highwing—

Deeprock, friend of Highwing—

The names streamed by in a torrent, more than she could count. With each one she glimpsed the sparkling presence of a dracona, and felt the surge of a fiery soul. Finally she heard a different voice, the one that had come with her from the Cavern of Spirits. *I am FullSky, brother of Windrush,* it whispered, speaking with difficulty. *Highwing was my father.* And she felt something different about that one, not just that he was a male, one of the draconi, but that he was present here in a more tenuous and perilous fashion. She recognized great pain and weariness in him, and glimpsed the sacrifice of strength that he had made to bring her here. And even now, he was laboring, crafting a final spell for her.

That realization made her tremble. But she knew that, whatever it was he was preparing, it was something she could not refuse.

Then, my friends, she whispered, *tell me what it is you want me to do.*

Chapter 40
WINDOW IN THE BATTLE

IN THE smoke and confusion of battle, Windrush dropped away from a trio of drahls that were pursuing him—or seemed to be. The Enemy's sorcery was endlessly confusing, not just to him, but to all of the dragons. The air was full of smoke and mirrors; everything was twisted and doubled and tripled, and nothing was as it seemed. Drahls and Tar-skel dragons had attacked in great numbers. But sometimes they were where they seemed to be, and sometimes they weren't. Many true dragons had already fallen, defeated as much by confusion as by the invincibility of the foe.

The dragon flights were in disarray, and Windrush could smell the discouragement in the air. The leaders shouted orders and encouragement, but their words were lost in the tumult. The dragons were losing confidence, and the illusion spells cast by the Enemy were growing stronger.

Windrush blew angry fire as he dove, and a cluster of drahls below him scattered in alarm. But above him, four others were still bearing down. Windrush veered and climbed sharply, then fell sideways into another dive. That seemed to shake the drahls; but he was even deeper now in the abyss of smoke, and it felt as if he would never climb out. Help us! he cried silently to the emptiness of the world, to the father who was gone, to the rigger who had not gotten through.

An instant later, he felt a violent shudder like a wind shear pass through the air, and he thought he heard a voice cry out to him. He nearly succumbed to a sudden dizziness and an unaccountable grief welling up out of his heart. He felt certain that a great power had just passed through the underrealm. The air was still shaking. But far from feeling like a Tar-skel sorcery, it felt like a sorcery coming unwoven.

He felt a great rush of wind, and the smoke that had coiled everywhere, enclosing the world, was suddenly torn away like a great curtain, revealing the land below. Windrush pulled up with a startled gasp; he was very low in the Dark Vale, speeding perilously close to dark pinnacles of stone and sharp-edged rock walls. The air overhead was filled with the swarming figures of dragons and drahls, vapor and flames, cries and screams. For the first time since the battle had begun, he could see his enemies clearly. And there were many of them, but not so many as he had thought.

He climbed to rejoin the fight; but even as he did so, he found himself distracted. Whatever had just happened, he knew that someone or something had touched *him* in that moment, touched his heart as it fled through the underrealm. But what—or who? Keeping a wary eye on the fight, he focused back on the sensation. What he had felt was a whisper of death, the passing of someone to the Final Dream Mountain.

Farsight? he thought, with a sudden dread. But no, no dragon's death would have shaken the underrealm so. But whose death would?

Jael! he whispered silently to the air. Jael, no!

He had heard the fleeting cry, but not recognized it. And now it was gone, and so was the presence that had touched him. He felt a new and burning emptiness in his soul. As surely as he rode the winds of battle in the Dark Vale, he knew that Jael had just died. And if Jael was gone, so was any hope for the realm.

He drew a breath and thundered his rage and anguish into the air: "NOOOOOOOO—!" So loud was his cry that a group of drahls scattered, and several dragons veered in mid-maneuver. "NOOOOOOO!" he cried again. "JAE-E-E-L-L-L-L!"

His cry echoed back from the floor of the Dark Vale, reverberating from one wall to the other. It seemed to still the battle for a moment. Windrush realized, too late, that it had been a cry of despair, and that it had been heard by all of the other dragons. He knew he should bellow something, some encouragement, to keep his brothers from losing heart, but he found no words of hope in him as he climbed to rejoin the battle.

A shriek rose in the air from the drahls—a sound of triumph, as if they too had sensed the passing of Jael. But it was a confused and wavering call, as if they were a little unsure of their triumph. Nevertheless, they wheeled in the air and attacked with renewed fury.

Windrush fought alongside his companions, but his fighting spirit was gone. He glanced down into the shadows of the vale, wondering if Jael had died in that grim place; and he wondered where down there the real Enemy, Tarskel, was hiding. It hardly mattered now. This battle was the last for dragonkind.

Angry and sullen, he lashed out against a Tar-skel dragon, raking it spinning through the air. But his vigor gave out quickly. A blast of freezing drahl fire caught the top of his left wing, and he swooped dizzyingly and knocked the drahl from the sky even as he reeled from the pain. At the same time, he saw two of his brothers, set upon by traitor-dragons, tumble out of the air and vanish. The true-dragon force was dwindling. Windrush veered and swooped, weeping inwardly at the approaching end of his kind.

He was roused from his misery by an angry outcry: "STONEBINDER! YOU LYING TRAITOR!" Startled, Windrush banked and flew toward the source of the shout. He saw SearSky ahead, circling in a tight dueling orbit with the dragon who had betrayed them all, before their failed attack on the east camp. Even from a distance, Windrush could see the fury in SearSky's eyes, and the fear in Stonebinder's. "I hope you're ready to die, you betrayer of friends!" SearSky snarled.

Stonebinder squawked unsteadily, fire hissing from his mouth, "You're already beaten, SearSky! Can't you see it? It's hopeless!"

The two circled, glaring at each other.

Windrush saw two drahls dropping toward the black warrior's back. *"SearSky! Drahls behind!"* he shouted, increasing his speed.

SearSky turned sharply, raking Stonebinder with flame; then he pitched up and over to meet the drahls. One was fast, and caught him with freezing flame on the right wing. SearSky faltered for an instant, then burned the other drahl from the sky. The first was almost back upon him, when Hailfar swept down past it, knocking it away with an angry shout.

Stonebinder emerged from SearSky's flame and saw the diversion that the drahls had given him. Before any other dragon could intervene, Stonebinder shot past SearSky and clawed him, once, before fleeing. That was Stonebinder's final mistake. SearSky roared in pursuit, with Windrush finally pulling up to flank him.

The cries of other dragons filled the air as they plunged through the tumult of the battle. "STONEBINDER— TRAITOR!" "KILL HIM, SEARSKY!" "FOR THE LUMENS!" No one got in the way as SearSky caught the traitor's wingtip, spun him in the air, and seized him with both hind and foreclaws. They began falling, together. SearSky bellowed his rage into Stonebinder's face, then blasted him with the full force of his fire. Stonebinder writhed helplessly as they fell through the air. Then he turned to glass in SearSky's grip and vanished. SearSky broke out of the fall, favoring his right wing, but rumbling in satisfaction.

"Well done, SearSky!" Windrush called, then turned, sweeping the area, in momentary respite from the battle. In that instant, he felt something new in his undersense. *What now?* he whispered, dizzy with exhaustion.

Come see . . . she lives . . . he thought he heard.

What? he cried silently, afraid that he was going mad.

Jael lives . . . a voice called, from very far away.

Windrush felt hope and rage burn together in his heart. Who was this, calling to him in the heat of battle?

The voice struggled to be heard. *It is FullSky! There is no time to lose! Let me show you, in the underrealm!*

Stunned, Windrush broke farther from the battle, seeking a place of relative quiet. There was a fractured pinnacle rising up below him. He spiraled down and landed, aware of the risk he was taking. But he had no choice. *Farsight!* he hissed in his undervoice, not wanting to draw attention to himself. *I am landing to seek FullSky in the underrealm. Guard me if you can!*

Without waiting for an answer, he closed his eyes and sank into the underweb of the world.

He passed at once into a window of silence. He felt FullSky's presence, invisibly accompanying him. *My brother!* he thought, but had no time for more. He was drawn instantly down a fine-stranded connection, and his kuutekka materialized in a place he had visited once before—flying fast and low over verdant lowlands, toward a sunset over the sea. And high over the sea, floating on a cloud, was the Dream Mountain, a white fire blazing within its glass vastness.

I have already seen this, he rumbled impatiently, wondering why it mattered now.

We haven't much time! See what has happened! Speak with her!

Stunned, Windrush flew higher in the underrealm, trying to reach the floating Mountain. *Speak with—?*

With Jael! Look! She has struck a magnificent blow! FullSky cried, and his voice sounded as if he were nearing the last of his strength. *Look in the Mountain, Windrush!*

He peered, straining to see. Though he was still far from the Mountain, he could just make out the figure of one who seemed to move through the Mountain like rippling light. He was suddenly weak with joy. *JAEL!* he cried, his voice tearing. *Can you hear me? Is she alive, FullSky?*

FullSky's voice sighed like a fading wind. *She has died—and yet she lives! In the Dream Mountain, Windrush! She is WITH us . . . she has given her life . . . and struck a great blow against the sorcery!*

Windrush struggled to comprehend. Struck a blow—by dying?

Look at the Enemy's web, FullSky whispered.

Behind the Mountain, Windrush saw the web of power glowing against the sky. It had grown stronger than ever— but it also had loose strands fluttering, in the beginning of what looked like a *tear* in the web. And the light that glowed from it was flickering with a slight unsteadiness. How was this possible?

Don't let this be in vain. FullSky's voice was fading. *She needs your help!*

Windrush gazed at Jael, and cried out in his heart to her. He thought he could sense her answering the cry; but she seemed terribly, terribly intent upon something.

Her voice seemed to whisper across the gulf of space: *Windrush, my friend—be ready for me! Be ready to fly! Above all, believe! The Enemy can still be broken!*

Jael—what can I do?

Her voice, answering, was drowned out by a much louder cry echoing from the emptiness around him. It was a cry of alarm filtering in from the outer world—a scream of urgency, calling him back. With a gasped, *I'll be ready! Call for me!* he blinked backward through FullSky's window and emerged from the underrealm.

Around him was chaos: dragon wings beating, flames thundering, and the chilling breath of drahls in the air. Windrush looked around in confusion. He was under attack—still perched on a pinnacle of rock! Half a dozen dragons had come to his defense, but the air was filled with enemy warriors. A cluster of drahls had just evaded his guardians and were diving straight toward him.

With an explosion of energy, Windrush leaped from the pinnacle and dove under the attacking drahls, forcing them to turn in a tight, fast bank. Windrush doubled back and beat upward, gaining altitude. "SHE LIVES!" he bellowed to the other dragons. "JAEL HAS REACHED THE DREAM MOUNTAIN! SHE LIVES TO FIGHT THE ENEMY!"

From the dragons rose a murmur of confusion. As a few of the dragons repeated his cry, the encouragement spread in a slow ripple. But the shout had cost Windrush energy that might have gone into speed—and now the drahls were hard on his tail, moving fast. Two shot past him, belching their chill fire; and though he managed to veer away from those two, he could not evade two others who caught him from behind, one landing on his shoulders and the other seizing his hindquarters. He roared out as their talons gripped him. He knew in an instant that he was caught, and he could feel their claws probing for entry. "Damn you!" he hissed, shaking violently—and through the pain, he bellowed out: "FOLLOW JAEL WHEN SHE CALLS! YOU MUST BELIEVE—!" and then his breath gasped out as the drahls' talons found a nerve.

He heard a shattering battle cry, and a wave of heat hit him from above. He nearly lost consciousness as dragon flame billowed over his head. But the two drahls fell away, burning, and as he veered to freedom, he struggled to clear his mind from the pain and heat, and he peered back up through the smoke to see who had saved him. "Sear-Sky—!" he cried raggedly, seeing the black dragon emerge from a ring of fire. Windrush tried to cry out his thanks, but he could scarcely breathe.

He realized with sudden horror that SearSky was battling for his own life now, with a cluster of drahls fastened to his back. SearSky must have dived straight through those drahls to save Windrush. Now he bellowed with pain, his flame crackling uselessly, unable to reach the drahls.

"SearSky . . . *help SearSky!* Needs . . . help!" Windrush gasped, trying to wheel and climb to the warrior's aid. But he could not move fast enough; he was still afire with pain.

SearSky's coal-red eyes blazed through the flurry of wings and freezing fire, and he roared out, his voice razor-sharp with agony, *"Windrush, you cannot—you must—lead the others! Find—your friend Jael—and—!"*

Two other dragons had broken to SearSky's aid—but they were too late, all of them. The light in SearSky's eyes flickered and went out, and the black dragon fell from among the drahls, turning from obsidian to clear glass and vanishing before he hit the rocks below. "SearSky!" Windrush cried hoarsely, circling in disbelief.

"Windrush, talk to me!" he heard, as another dragon sped to his side, silver eyes gleaming.

"Farsight! SearSky just saved—"

"I saw! I could not come in time." Farsight's eyes blazed with regret. "What did you say about Jael? We heard you cry out!"

Windrush exhaled a sharp-tongued flame as he felt a rush of hope again. "She lives!" he gasped. "In the Dream Mountain! Let all the dragons know—we are not alone— we are not fighting alone!"

Farsight's cry was a trumpet blast that echoed across the vale. *"DRAGONS! THE RIGGER JAEL LIVES AND FIGHTS IN THE DREAM MOUNTAIN! DO NOT DESERT HER, OR THE DRACONAE! PRESS THE BATTLE!"* The effect of his cry was like a bolt of lightning. The dragons who had not heard earlier shouted out with a clamor that rose above the sound of battle.

"And now, brother," Farsight said, his clear-faceted eyes blazing into Windrush's, "you must tell me what we are to do to help Jael!"

Windrush's breath went out in a great sigh of bewilderment. "We must hold against the Enemy until she reaches out to us! That's all I know, Farsight—that's all we can do!"

Chapter 41
A TEAR IN THE DARK WEB

RENT WAS just casting a thread of sorcery out toward the Cavern of Spirits, to gather in his prisoner, when he felt the quake in the underrealm. For an instant, he believed he was imagining it. After all, it could not be . . . no, it was just that he was still upset over that cursed dragon's defiance. And then he felt it, without question—not just a background trembling in the underrealm, but something far more profound.

He did not at first realize that he felt a life passing. But even at this distance, he felt the sorcery of binding dissolving like smoke through his fingers. And the only thing that could break that binding was the death of the one it held. The rigger Jael.

Rent felt it like a stab through his heart.

Jarvorus! he shrieked, speeding down the pathway to the cavern. What he found was a place that had been torn apart by an earthquake in the underrealm. An abyss yawned in the cavern floor, emptying into space. The impregnable weaving he had spun around his prisoner lay empty. The prisoner, the rigger, the One, was nowhere to be found. Nor was his servant Jarvorus, nor the ship in which the riggers had traveled. Only Hodakai was visible, quailing like a moth in his spirit jar.

With a rage such as he had not felt in a lifetime of rage, Rent flew like a flashing sun around the cavern. He hovered over the rift in the floor and glared down into the darkness of the abyss, and there, almost out of sight, he glimpsed the rigger-ship tumbling away into the distance. He felt a hot-blooded urge to pursue it, to destroy it. But it didn't hold the one he wanted; there was no presence of Jael on the ship.

Of course not—he had just felt her die.

Jarvorus! he screamed. He sensed that the sprite was around somewhere, but there was no answer.

He spun again, a spinning flame in midair, and hurled his anger at Hodakai. *What has happened here, traitor? Tell me what has happened, before I destroy you!*

Hodakai flickered once, twice, then suddenly burned bright in the underrealm presence of his spirit jar. His voice was low and trembling, but there was a shocking passion in it. *Do you think that you have the only power in this world? She is gone, Rent. She has died—by HER choice, not by yours!* Though Hodakai did not actually laugh, he sounded as though he wanted to.

Rent burned with fury. *Fool! Traitor!* His fury burned inwardly at himself, as well as at Hodakai. He had been far too complacent! He had trusted the sorcery! He groped for a way to express the magnitude of his rage.

Before he could find the words, he was interrupted by another voice—one that only he could hear. It was a voice that whispered through the underrealm, and thundered in his heart.

* Rent, I would have words with you. *

If the mountain itself had seized Rent and spoken to him, it could not have shaken him more. There was no question why his master was calling. Rent's anger vanished, in the face of terrifying guilt. *Yes,* he whispered. *Of course.*

* Leave that place and come to me. *

But I must— Rent hesitated. *Yes—of course. At once.* With a last, venomous glance at Hodakai, he sped away.

He sank through the underrealm, stunned by the turbulence he met, even in places that had been made strong and fast by the workings of the Nail. Rent grew increasingly fearful as he slipped through the weavings of power that lay between him and his master. He passed through a region of smoke and fire, and felt the underpinnings of the Nail's power shaking, like tremendous concrete pillars, deep in the underrealm of the Dark Vale. Rent came at last to a darkened place, and hovered over a pool of something resembling molten steel afire. Its surface shone like a mirror, blazing with a reflection of his kuutekka, a shadow-figure in the shape of a man.

Rent tried, trembling, to draw himself into full human form, but found he could not. At last he gave up and called out: *I am here, Nail of Strength.*

The pool grew still—then quivered and collapsed into a shaft of fire, opening deep into the underrealm. A voice spoke from the shaft, deep and reverberating. * **You have failed me, Rent. Do you not hear the battle rage in my vale? The time for the final victory is upon us, and you have failed me.** *

But I—

The voice thundered, * **Why did you allow her to die?** *

I didn't, I—

* **Do you not feel the realm trembling with her passing?** *

But I—Rent choked—*was on my way to see to her, when she—*

* **What? What did she do?** *

Rent struggled to find words. *She—took her own life. Somehow. I am not certain how. But I believe I was—betrayed by Jarvorus—and by Hodakai—*

His words strangled off into silence. Prolonged silence. He did not sense in the silence any forgiveness. When the next words came from his Master, it was in a voice that he had to strain to hear, though it seemed to shake the realm as deeply as the thundering of a few moments ago.

* **She has not died, you fool. She has passed to the Mountain of Fire. Everything has changed now. Everything. And you, my failed servant, must atone for your failure.** *

Yes, he whispered. *Of course—whatever—*

* **Go to my vale. As a man. Walk among the dragons. See for yourself the fire and struggle. SEE FOR YOURSELF THE SPIRIT OF THE DRAGONS!** *

The—spirit—?

* See for yourself how they rejoice! THEY KNOW THAT SHE LIVES! *

The dragons know? Rent thought in astonishment. But how?

* I will destroy those who betrayed me to do this. But you will FINISH the job I gave you to do in the Vale! You will CRUSH the spirit of the dragons. CRUSH the captives. *

Rent bobbed in acquiescence. He struggled to speak. *The . . . victory . . . remains certain, does it not? The preparations, and the One . . .* He gasped, struggling to form his plea for reassurance. *She has fallen, as the Words say . . . even if . . . early. Is that not . . . true?*

There was another silence, and this time he felt first a profoundly deep chill, and then the sudden fierce heat of the Nail's anger. * Do not question me, servant! You have your instructions! *

Yes, Rent whispered, as the shaft of fire abruptly closed, restoring the reflective molten pool. Yes, he thought. I will do that. I will make the dragons suffer, and despair.

I will not despair.

Jael was caught between joy at the fleeting touch of Windrush's presence, and fearful concentration as she tried to understand what FullSky was saying. *Must fly—join Windrush—probe the Nail's strengths, find his weakness—*

But how? she whispered, from the fluttering curtains of dracona-light.

Not sure. I—aahhhhh—! FullSky's words choked off, turning to a throaty cry of distress. Jael was stunned to realize that his presence, his kuutekka, was wavering and growing insubstantial.

FullSky! murmured the dracona Lavafire, from the shadows. *What is it?*

Under—attack, FullSky groaned, billowing a ghostly flame. *I—cannot stay!*

Wait! Jael cried. *I don't know what to do! I need your help!*

I—cannot—stay! FullSky gasped. *Jael—do what you must! Never doubt!* He was less dragon than a formless light now.

Draconae—you must help her! he whispered. Then he was gone.

FullSky! Jael cried. *You can't! Not after—!* Not after saving my life, bringing me here . . . but to do what? she whispered desperately, in the silence of her heart.

There was no answer.

But from the draconae there came a loud murmuring, and she found her mind filled with an image of FullSky's underrealm presence: stretched like a spiderweb thread from the Enemy's dungeon to the Dream Mountain, and she understood suddenly his shocking vulnerability, and the risk he had taken in reaching out to the Mountain, much less to the place where he had found her. The draconae had given him strength where they could, but they were helpless to protect him at his source, the body from which his kuutekka had sprung.

And yet the draconae kept hope, and their hope was in Jael. Why me? she whispered silently. And she knew that it was because of the Words, because she was the outsider who had come and befriended a dragon. And now her life was in their hands, and theirs in hers.

(Urrrk . . . fly, Jael? Fly?)

(I don't know, Ed—I just don't know.)

Jael felt a curtain of fear closing around her, and struggled to resist it. She focused upon her own kuutekka, and made herself as real, and yet as insubstantial, as if she were still in a rigger-net. Only now she was standing in the draconae's cavern of translucent glass, parrot on her shoulder, staring at the almost apparitional sight of the Forge of Dreams, where the draconae labored to draw their skeins of protective magic about the fire. She heard them sing a fragment of the Words:

> The One will fall
> and the realm shall tremble.
> And the fires will flicker and bend . . .

And she suddenly understood something . . . that perhaps the way to save the dreamfire was not to protect it, but to use it. If the Enemy had his weaknesses, Jael thought she knew what one of them might be. Tar-skel's greatest sorcery was the web of power that was strangling the realm, holding the Dream Mountain and the lumenis groves captive. She had torn the web a little, with her death. But she needed to tear it a lot more, and she thought she knew where she might do that—in a place where a rigger had once before defeated the Nail of Strength.

(*Awwwk, yes—try, Jael—try!*)

(*We can't do it alone, Ed,*) she murmured, but she was already making her plan. *Help me reach out!* she whispered to the draconae. And she felt the helping, strengthening touch of Deeplife, and Waterflow, and Starchime, showing her the way through the underrealm.

(*Scrawwwww, yes! Now!*) cried Ed in the back of her thoughts. And she nodded, and human and parrot together, they slipped into the underrealm and reached out toward the Black Peak.

Rent strode through the chasms of the Dark Vale, heedless of the battle raging overhead. His form was human—but what human had ever wielded such barehanded power? Lightning flashed from his fingertips—darted and blazed and drew screams of agony from the imprisoned dragons. Rent had been given the one task that could restore his own pride to him: make the dragons suffer, make them despair.

He held at least a hundred captives in his power—not just dragons, but shadow-cats and sprites, and guardian-spirits, pressed into his service. From all of them came the stink of fear—fear of the carnage in the air, and fear of a human demigod bringing his wrath upon them. He wasn't trying to kill them, not yet; but if some died, he would hardly worry. The death of a few would be a fine stimulus to despair.

Rent flicked a spike of flame at a young dragon impaled upon a lance of stone, and he crowed to himself as the creature writhed. Hearing a groan of outrage, he whirled upon a larger dragon, an old and nearly broken beast. With a scornful toss of his hands, he flung fresh bolts of pain at the groaning creature.

"*You will die, demon!*" the dragon gasped angrily, and vented a failing breath of flame at him.

Rent jumped back, startled by the blast of heat as the flame singed his face. He'd felt *pain*. What was this! He probed back through the sorcery that formed his body, and discovered that it had been altered at its source. He was no longer wearing his human form like a cloak; his life and breath and kuutekka were now contained *within* his human form. He felt a clammy chill of fear. He was vulnerable now, just like the others. He had never been vulnerable, as the Nail's most powerful servant. He felt a tingle around him at the thought, and he wondered in horror, was even *his* fear being tapped into the web of power?

Just the thought made him tremble; he felt a sudden weakness in his stomach and groin.

He felt the tingle about him grow stronger.

Tar-skel, he thought desperately, *you aren't leaving me to the fate of your prisoners! No!*

Though he heard no audible answer, he imagined the voice of the Nail thundering in the back of his mind: * **If you prove your worth, all of the power you can ask for will be yours. But if you do not—** *

As he stood before the old dragon, battling his own fear, the dragon hissed at him through the pain that Rent had inflicted. "You will not live, demon! You can kill us, but you cannot defeat us!"

"*SILENCE!*" Rent screamed. He drew forth a new bolt of fire, and a second, and held the crackling thunderbolts aloft on his fingertips. Then he hurled them one after another into the dragon's eyes. Fire erupted from the dragon's head, and it screamed, and a moment later crumpled to the ground. As Rent stood triumphant over it, the dragon turned transparent and vanished.

"DOES ANYONE ELSE HAVE SOMETHING TO SAY?" he bellowed as he strode through the blasted maze of the dungeons. He passed one broken prisoner after another, but none answered his challenge. He didn't expect them to.

But there was one dragon whom he thought might talk back to him. He had been saving this one for last, but perhaps now was the time. Perhaps now he would make the thing suffer and suffer, and finally die.

"WingTouch, I am coming to you!" he snarled, as he strode across the blackened floor of the Dark Vale.

The attack had come as a sharp spasm of pain, deep in his kuutekka. FullSky knew at once that he had been discovered. It was all he could do to hold fast to the Dream Mountain long enough to cry out a farewell; then he let go and fell back through the underrealm, a spark fleeing from a fire into darkness.

The underrealm was a thunderstorm exploding with battling furies of wind and fire, blackness and light. He glimpsed the eye of Tar-skel in the storm and streaked past it, a speck driven by the wind. The eye was flashing in every direction, and FullSky felt the razor-sharpness of its vision, taking in all of the world. FullSky felt a burst of hope, because the Enemy's angry searching spoke not just of arrogance and power, but of worry, and—could it be?—of *fear*.

And then the eye flashed upon *him*, and FullSky knew that the Enemy had identified him as the one who had saved Jael, who had transported her to the Dream Mountain, out of reach. *You!* that flash of recognition seemed to cry. *Yes!* he whispered back, fleeing even faster down the thread of the underrealm. For a terrifying moment, he thought that the eye would strike him down right here in the midst of the storm. Instead, he felt the eye suddenly shift *away*—drawn perhaps by something more urgent. The Enemy had greater concerns than a single dragon kuutekka, even one who had angered him. Jael, perhaps? Was she doing as FullSky had urged?

He was not free of the Enemy's wrath, however. The underrealm was full of the Nail's servants, and FullSky felt a searing blast following him down the thread. A watcher, probably summoned by the Nail, was in pursuit. He dodged frantically, jumping from one thread to another. As he approached the lower clouds, he saw two other watchers speeding across the clouds to intercept him. A heartbeat later he reached the clouds, and skipped across two threads, shifting through the pathways of the web, fleeing for his life through the turbulent concealment of the clouds. He knew he could not escape for long, but for the moment, he was still free. FullSky streaked inward toward his own body, lying broken in the dungeons of the Dark Vale.

Fire erupted around him as he reentered the underwebbing of the dungeons. The place reverberated with the screams of aroused prisoners, and he darted frantically through the glowing caverns of fire, hoping for just a little more time, struggling against the inner pull drawing him inexorably back to his body. Nothing awaited him there except pain and death, but perhaps there was yet something he could do here.

Though weary beyond belief, he continued through the undercaverns, searching for his brother. Everything looked different now; fires blazed in all directions, and he sensed a growing intensity in the torment, and he sensed the presence of the human enemy, Rent. There was terrible suffering here—even more terrible than before. He felt the captives' desperation and pain feeding the flames of the sorcery. He felt their awareness of the battle in the sky, and of the appalling losses of the dragons.

If only he could bring them hope!

But perhaps he could. How many of them knew that Jael was alive and powerful, and that the Enemy had suffered his own losses today? He prayed that there was one being still alive who had kept the spark of hope burning even here. *WingTouch!* he called. *WingTouch! Are you alive?*

If only his brother had even a speck of underhearing!

And then he heard the answer, crying out through pain: *FullSky? Is it you?*

He spun and saw him—a shadow-thing flashing and shuddering. His brother was so close, he could almost reach out and touch him now; and yet, without that answering cry he might have missed him altogether, so chaotic was this place of fire and misery. *WingTouch!* he cried, and then realized that his brother was not alone. The underweb around his brother shook with flashes of rage, and that rage wasn't from a dragon, but from a human. Rent was attacking his brother!

FullSky darted close, hoping that Rent's attention was drawn away from the underrealm. He examined the binding spell that held his brother cruelly captive—twists in the very earth, holding him immobile. But FullSky saw that the weavings were somewhat weakened, as the great web had been weakened. FullSky had little strength left, but it was enough to reach into the weaving and loosen the bonds holding his brother prisoner. The spell seared his kuutekka, and he knew that a cry of alarm was going up somewhere as his efforts were felt. *WingTouch, you are almost free! Be ready to leap!*

FullSky? whispered his brother.

Jael lives in the Dream Mountain! Jael lives! Tell the captives! Tell them they must hope! FullSky gasped, the fire in the binding nearly killing him. And then it was torn loose, spinning away from WingTouch with its flaring heat. *WingTouch, go! You are free!*

WingTouch had been shaking with such rage at his tormentor that he could not even speak. Even the earth was quaking. Rent's hands wielded lightning like a whip, lashing it across WingTouch's back. He shuddered each time, yet each blow strengthened his resolve not to surrender. He knew he could not survive much more of this. Above him, the dragons battled drahls and sorcery. Before him, Rent shrieked with laughter as he hurled lightning, crying, "They die, dragon! Your brothers die!" *Crack-k-k!* "All of them, one after another, they die!" *Crack-k-k!* "There is no hope for any of them now! Their efforts are useless, futile, stupid!" *Crack-k-k!*

So desperately did WingTouch want to be free and at his brothers' side, even if in death, that he almost did not hear the voice that cried out from within his own mind. It was the voice of his other brother, the voice of FullSky! *Wing-Touch, you are almost free——!*

Crack-k-k!

It seemed impossible that this was anything but a nightmare—and yet when he heard FullSky cry out again, *Jael lives!* and *Go! You are free!* he felt an astonishing release that almost made him forget the agony of Rent's punishment. The rock had melted away from his feet, and the sudden freedom was almost more painful than the imprisonment—and he sagged for a moment, unable to move. He glared up at Rent, who was prancing about on the rim of the chasm, and he hoped that Rent would not notice his release.

He was astounded to see the human spin away with a shout of anger.

Trembling, WingTouch bent and stretched his legs—slowly, to avoid attracting notice—and then flexed his wings a little. Every fiber of his body screamed with pain; but if FullSky had freed him, he could not let mere pain keep him here. And where was FullSky? He tried to reach down into the underrealm to search for his brother, but it was beyond him; all he could make out was a hazily glowing place full of shadows. *FullSky?* he whispered. There was no answer.

FullSky felt his brother's astonished disbelief, and the shuddering movement of WingTouch stirring from his shackles. Then a blast of fire hit him, knocking him brutally away from his brother. FullSky felt a moment of triumph, even in the pain and disorientation. A guardian appeared before him, striking furiously, then another. He was surrounded by fire. He felt his kuutekka slip back into his broken body, his strength gone at last. But he had freed his brother . . .

The underrealm shimmered and faded, and he opened his eyes with a gasp of pain. He peered up blurrily from the scorched crater in which he was chained—into the eyes of two drahls who were hissing their freezing breath at him, who had already torn and bludgeoned his body near to the point of death. As he struggled for breath, he heard a bellow of rage—human rage—and he heard the voice of Rent, screaming, *"He is the one who did it! He is the one!"*

For an instant, FullSky thought that Rent was enraged because he had freed WingTouch. Then he saw the blazing fire in the eyes of the drahls and he knew, somehow, that he had been condemned by Tar-skel for a far greater crime. Rent appeared over the rim of the crater and screamed: *"He took her to the Mountain of Fire! He's the one! KILLLLL HIMMMM!"*

There was nowhere for him to flee now, and no strength left to resist. And yet, as the freezing fire blossomed over his helpless body, he felt an astonishing upwelling of joy. It carried away the pain like a stream of cool water; and when he felt his body shudder and die, he knew that the pain was ending forever.

His last thought as his awareness slipped from him was how welcoming was that stream of water, bearing him away to the Final Dream Mountain.

WingTouch heard Rent's scream—*"He's the one! Killll himmm!"*—and realized at once whom the demon meant.

WingTouch threw himself into the air, beating his aching wings. He did not quite become airborne, but he made it to the outcropping where Rent had stood just moments ago, and he clambered toward the sound. Deep in his throat, his own fire was burning to life. A dozen stumbling steps brought him to a sight that made him halt in horror: Rent bellowing down at the mangled form of a dragon, frozen where two drahls were still blowing their killing breaths upon it. In the instant that WingTouch recognized the dragon as his brother, FullSky turned to clear glass and vanished. Rent crowed in savage triumph. Then he turned and saw WingTouch.

Motionless, WingTouch met the human's gaze with cold fury. "You have killed my brother!" he whispered, and drew a deep breath around the fire in his throat.

"You!" Rent screamed. *"How did you—"*

WingTouch exhaled. His breath caught the human in a

splash of fire and smoke, flames gouting around the demon's head and body. The human stood wreathed in flame, and his last agonized cry, "—get freeee—?" was a screech that rose into the air like the fire and smoke that were consuming him. It took only one breath. When the smoke cleared, the human's charred corpse remained crouched in its position of surprise and fear.

The ground shook with another quake, and the two drahls that had just ended his brother's life stared up at him with eyes suddenly full of fear. Were they afraid of him because he had just destroyed their master? Did they know how wounded he was? He incinerated them with one long breath.

WingTouch turned around slowly, gazing in astonishment over the ruins of the earth that were the dungeons of the Dark Vale. Overhead, he could hear the sounds of battle. He could hear the cries of dragons here in the dungeons, and he felt their hopelessness like a weight upon the air. He could not free the others as FullSky had freed him, but perhaps he could give them something to rejoice about. What was it FullSky had told him before he died?

Jael is alive in the Dream Mountain . . .

Yes.

Lurching into the air, heedless of the screaming protests of his body, WingTouch began flying low over the dungeons, bellowing out the news.

"ALIVE IN THE DREAM MOUNTAIN! JAEL IS ALIVE!"

Chapter 42
DRAGON RIGGER

The one shall fall and the realm shall tremble.
And the beginning begins anew.

But the beginning would be, *must be*, for the Nail of Strength.

In the place where darkness coiled about itself in patterns of masterful deception and power, he who was called Nail of Strength noted the passing of his servant Rent. The human had been useful enough; but his pride had grown too great—and his desire, not just to serve, but to *be* the Nail of Strength, had become all too evident. And still he had failed in the task to which he'd been entrusted. And so the Nail had changed the terms of his gift of body to his servant, and withdrawn the shield of invulnerability that Rent had grown to take for granted.

The manner of Rent's death was left to chance, and chance had wasted no time. Rent's terror, and the pain of his passing, were as useful as any dragon's in fueling the fire of the web-sorcery.

And the web was growing.

The web was strong.

The web *would* pierce the boundaries between the worlds and draw them all, all of the universes, into the power of the one called the Nail.

The darkness coiled about its center of power, and brooded. The darkness, even in its certainty, felt fear. There was still the problem of "the one."

How often had the Nail tried to convince himself that the prophecy was meaningless! But he knew; he had seen the ancient vision himself, through the eyes of a servant; he knew the window into space-time that the draconae had seen. He knew the truthfulness of the vision and the words that had sprung from it. And he knew, most of all, how diabolically ambiguous those words were! And so he had woven his web of power carefully, with *exquisite* care, around such portions of the vision as could be clearly understood.

And yet, even now, as the Words unfolded, so much was unclear.

Plotting in his place of strength, the one called Strength had built his plan around the fall of the rigger. But by *giving* her life rather than having it struck from her, she had sidestepped his plan. And for all that, she yet lived, reborn in the Dream Mountain, thanks to the infuriating treachery of the dragons! But the Nail of Strength remained the Nail of Strength, and the dragons fought their losing battle, isolated from their sustenance of lumenis, and from their mates in the Mountain of Fire. The prophecy might be muddied, but the victory would still be his.

Now, however, the plan must be changed. It angered him not to wield the power of the Mountain of Fire; but since the draconae, with their petty defenses, continued to resist, he would crush them. The power of the Deep Caverns ran strong in him now; and once he had reached out beyond this realm, there would be no limits to the new sources of power.

He had been pleased to use the dragons' despair to strengthen his plan. But that time was past, and a new time had come. Time not just to humiliate the dragons, but to destroy them.

As Jael reached out from the Dream Mountain, she felt perilously exposed, even with the power of the draconae helping to keep her kuutekka tight and strong. She felt as if she were stepping off into space from a dizzyingly high mountain, with untested wings. She could see the structure of the Enemy's web with greater clarity than ever—a vast glistening spiderweb enclosing the sky. She could see its power surging from the Dark Vale where the Enemy kept his prisoners and servants in thrall, and from another place called the Deep Caverns.

It was hard to envision how such power could be defeated. And yet, in places, it was somewhat weakened— even in the Dark Vale, where the dragons' spirit had been bolstered by the news that *she* was here. Her very presence strengthened the dragons and weakened the sorcery! She felt awed and humbled; she could only trust that she could find a way to complete the task. She had unraveled a small part of the Enemy's skein of sorcery; she must somehow unravel the rest of it.

In the Dark Vale, the dragons continued to fight a desperate battle; and yet, perhaps not so desperate as they believed. Could the dragons see what she did—that the Enemy's illusions made his forces seem far greater than they were? They could still be defeated; but first she must collapse the illusion of invincibility in Tar-skel's sorcery. First she must join together the power of the draconi and the draconae.

Riggers can change things, Kan-Kon had reminded her. And who knew it better than she who had defeated Tar-skel once before, at the Black Peak—where she had undone the Nail's plans to hurl Highwing to his death in the static realm, where she had broken his terror by joining rigger and dragon together? Even now, that tear in the sorcery remained unrepaired. She meant to strike there, at the Enemy's weakness; she meant to join once more with a dragon.

(Hawww, yessss!) hissed Ed, urging her on.

Come to meet me, Windrush! Come to the Black Peak! she whispered again and again into the winds of the underrealm, as she flew toward that place of smoldering magic.

Surprise twisted through the center of the darkness like a draft of cold air, fanning the inner flame to a dark, angry heat. **✳ She dares, then, to challenge me where she fancies she won a great victory! Let her do so. Let her flaunt**

her pride and her arrogance. The victory is mine. It is already mine. *

The Dark Vale was a place of chaos and noise and the stink of death. The dragons fought with renewed spirit and determination, but always the Enemy seemed to have the greater numbers and strength, as though he had a limitless army of drahls to expend in the killing of dragons. Still, the fury of battle did not keep Windrush's heart from leaping when he heard Jael's voice in his underthoughts. *Come to the Black Peak! Join me there, with all the dragons you can bring!*

He was astonished and overjoyed—and dismayed, as well. How could he take dragons from the battle now, to fly all the way to the Black Peak? The air was shaking with currents that threatened to knock all of them out of the sky. He himself was weary and wounded, though he'd been fighting as though he were neither.

But he dared not fail her. Whatever else he lost today, he must not fail Jael, when she needed him.

He blew a crackling flame and called out: "WINDRUSH FLIGHT! WINDRUSH FLIGHT! TO THE BLACK PEAK! FARSIGHT, TAKE COMMAND HERE!" He circled tightly and watched as those in his wing, the alarmingly few left who could answer him, broke from the battle to join him. "TO THE BLACK PEAK, TO JOIN JAEL!" he cried.

Somewhere, he heard Farsight's call of acknowledgment, taking over leadership of the main battle group. Then he broke away and flew northward and eastward, out over the desolate plains of the Enemy's realm.

He flew as though consumed by madness—with Jael's voice echoing in his thoughts. The warriors of his wing, confused and uncertain, had nevertheless fallen in behind him. Together, battle weary and yet putting aside their need for rest, they flew. They flew as though time and distance had no meaning. They crossed back over the desolation of the Enemy's realm, and flew northward to the end of the Black Mountain range and the tallest of all the mountains, the Black Peak.

The red glare of the peak drew them on. Windrush half expected to find another battle raging, or an army of drahls waiting to assail them. Instead, he found the place deserted, as though all of the Enemy's forces had been drawn to the Dark Vale. Nonetheless, it was a brooding and frightening place, perhaps even more frightening in its emptiness—an enormous mountain shrouded in thunderclouds, with the blood-red light of another world's sun glaring out through its upper slopes. It was a vast and terrible tower riddled on the inside with old and sorcerous caverns of the Enemy. Here his father had been imprisoned through treachery and betrayal, and sentenced to exile. And here Jael had challenged the Enemy and won, and brought Highwing back; and the smoldering wound in the mountain's side remained as a testament to that victory.

Remember that victory, he whispered through the haze of fatigue. It is certain that the Enemy remembers. And that thought gave him renewed strength. And for a moment, he thought he felt his father's spirit touching and supporting him, even here, even now.

But to do what? With his flight of dragons, he soared around the grim peak, searching for signs of either Jael or Tar-skel. He smelled the Enemy's presence, and there was a strong and troubling turbulence in the air. *Jael?* he whispered, trying to find some sign with his undersenses. *Jael, are you here?* He heard no answer, and wondered, had he imagined her call? Had he been deceived by the Enemy, at last? Had he brought his brothers here for nothing?

Finally he called out to the others, "You must guard me once more, while I search the underrealm! Whatever happens, my life is yours!" Overhead, the sky flashed and shook. But Windrush ignored that and found a place to land, high on the slopes of the peak. And with only a glance back at his circling companions, he sank into the shadowy world of the underrealm.

It was no easy stretch to the Black Peak for Jael. The underrealm was a place of shifting and treacherous winds. But FullSky had given her skills and shown her the path well enough, and Ed murmured and encouraged her the whole way.

What she found was a gaping wound in the underrealm, surrounded by a frayed fabric of sorcery. She knew what the place looked like in the outer world: the image of the towering black mountain, its summit erupting with the light of a red sun, was emblazoned in her memory. In the underrealm, though, it was a net of spun sorcery torn and half patched, with the light of the distant sun leaking through like a sunbeam slanting into a dusty attic.

It looked like a good place to make a stand, she thought.

At that instant, she felt two new forces burst into the underrealm around her. One was the Enemy's power, exploding through the torn web like electricity through a splintered cable, sparks shooting off to form tendrils of new sorcery. Tar-skel knew she was here. The other was Windrush, his presence a shadow whispering through the gloom.

Windrush! she cried. *Join with me and show me how to be a dragon! Join with me now!*

From the dragon she heard a gasp of astonishment and joy, and then the shadow-ghost of the dragon's presence turned and swooped to approach her. *Jael!* he cried. *Jael, is it really you?* He seemed to grow stronger and more solid as he drew close, searching for her.

Yes, Windrush! Jael found the strength to make her kuutekka more visible, flying toward his, until at last she materialized, astride the dragon's neck. Her heart leaped as she felt Windrush become solid in this strange place, or at least as solid as if he were a partner in the rigger-net. *Windrush—yes!* she cried, hugging his neck fiercely. *I'm here—and I need your help!* As she spoke, the underrealm was flashing like the heart of a thunderstorm.

Jael! Windrush blew a great flame of greeting. *My help is yours! But what can we do? The Enemy is strong here!*

Not as strong as we can be! she shouted, realizing how foolish that sounded, her small voice defiant in the storm. She was only a human rigger, and he was only a dragon. But she felt the strength of the draconae moving within her, as they flew among the strands of the Enemy's webbing, and she cried out: *I am a rigger! WE are riggers!*

(Hawwww—yes! Graggon riggers!) cried Ed.

Yes! she thought. Who could better take hold of the Flux and shape it than a rigger? A dragon rigger. She must become more than a rigger, and Windrush more than a dragon. And Ed had shown her the way—Ed, who was more than parrot and more than rigger. *I am Jael, friend of Highwing, friend of Windrush!* she whispered, and she hiked her kuutekka-self up over Windrush's shoulder and peered into his spirit-eyes. She peered through those glowing facets and sank spinning into the depths of his eyes, of his soul.

She shuddered with the power and joy of the union, and her mind overflowed with dragon hopes and griefs and questions, and she was almost swept away on the stream of the dragon's innermost thoughts. But she forced herself to hold aloft the image she wanted, sharing it with Windrush—an image of riggers transforming the underrealm together, transforming themselves—and she felt the underrealm tremble as she merged with her friend's kuutekka and became one body with him, dragon rigger.

(Hawww, yes! Graggon!)

(Yes, Ed! Dragon!) They were dragon, three joined as one. She felt her wings beat the air with dragon strength, astonishing strength, even through the terrible fatigue. She clenched her talons, sharp and hard and strong. And she felt Windrush marveling, as she marveled, at the union—and she felt an almost overpowering desire to soar and wheel and plunge through the air for the pure joy of dragon flight. It seemed impossible that such joy could be interrupted by the darkness of a war.

But the shuddering power of the Enemy quaked around her, an angry power, and she knew there was no time for rejoicing. *(See the webbing!)* she murmured to her other selves, and even as she spoke, they banked and turned toward the fiery, arcing web of the Enemy. *(That is the source of the storm, and the illusions.)* And she reached out their claws and hurtled straight for the place where it was torn.

Hawwwwwwwwwwwwwww! screeched the parrot.

FOR THE REALM! thundered Windrush in amazement, flying with all of his strength.

For all the friends of Highwing! whispered Jael.

They struck the web and it exploded with lightning and fire, hurling them back with stunning force. The concussion from the blast echoed from the Black Peak like hideous laughter. But heedless of the laughter, heedless of the pain, they turned and dove again—and it was like attacking a high-voltage wire, but this time, through the billowing sparks and fire, they caught the webbing in their dragon claws. And they didn't let go, but tore at the web and dove and tore and dove, Jael and Windrush and Ed screaming with determination.

And through the madness of fire and electricity and earthquake, the web began to stretch, to give, to tear. But they needed more strength; they needed more help. And Jael knew where it had to come from.

Deeplife, Waterflow, Starchime! she cried back through the underrealm. *DRACONAE, HELP US!*

Chapter 43
THE WORDS MADE REAL

FROM THE Dream Mountain, whiskers of strength flashed this way and that, as the draconae strove to help the One in whom all hope rested. From the heart of the mountain, Lavafire and all the others poured as much light into the One's kuutekka as it could stand. Without the strength of the dreamfire coursing into that one's being, she could not have lasted even this long. And yet it was not enough.

Starchime sent out a sunburst of thought in the opposite direction. *Riggers! If you can hear us, we need you! Jael needs you!*

Ed, it's no good! We can't control it! The current is too strong! Ar's cry came out as a gasp in the midst of his labors. No matter how they tried to steer or skate the ship away from the singularity, it kept turning and tumbling, pulled by forces Ar could not see clearly enough to understand or counter. The singularity blazed diamond-white before them, drawing them inward along its throbbing currents.

What, rawk, that? gasped the parrot.

What's what—? And then Ar saw it: a tiny thread of fire twisting out across the Flux, toward them. He instinctively looked for a way to evade it; then he realized that it seemed to be seeking them, and instead of evading, he braced for its arrival.

It grew, brightened, and flashed into the net. Ar trembled as he felt a connection open suddenly—and a thought touched his, and it was an alien touch. *Who—?* he whispered.

Graggon! croaked Ed, suddenly fluttering from side to side. *What graggon here, hawww?*

I don't know, Ar whispered. He shivered as he recalled the connection he had once shared with Windrush, when they'd met for the first time and the dragon had searched his thoughts. But this was different. There was something lyrical and musical and . . . female . . . about this one.

The alien touch slowly shaped itself into words. *We need you . . . Jael needs you . . .*

In utter astonishment, Ar felt the connection altering, expanding, telescoping outward in a way that he could sense but not comprehend. And then he felt a new presence touch him, and this one was different; it was a raging dragon crying out in battle. *Windrush?* Ar whispered, stunned.

Ar, help me . . . ! cried a voice that was torn by pain and need—and it took him a heartbeat, two heartbeats, to believe who was calling to him.

JAEL! he screamed.

Jayyyyllllll!

Over the parrot's cry, and the echoing cry of a second parrot, and the thunder of a dragon's rage, he realized that he was touching not just one being, but three. But it was Jael, most of all, who cried out to him, and her cry was laden with desperation and hope. *Jael! Jael, what can I do?* he cried out, heedless now of the starship's headlong fall toward the singularity.

In answer, he did not so much hear her voice as feel her thought, and her need. Ed shrieked in surprise—and he realized that an image had appeared in the net—far ahead of them, in the very heart of the singularity. A tiny window had opened there, and within it he saw the figure of a dragon—and he knew that it was not just Windrush, but Jael and Ed, as well. A terrible fire flashed around the dragon, and he struggled to make out what it was. The dragon was tearing at a blazing web, stretching it and trying to destroy it, and the web was flashing back with killing fire.

Help me, Ar! Help me, Ed! Jael gasped.

What . . . how?

Come through from the other side . . . come through the Dream Mountain! Break a path, Ar, break a path!

Hawww, yes! Break a path! shrieked one Ed.

Break a path! shrieked the other.

Ar stared in fear and awe at the singularity. *Is THAT the Dream Mountain?*

YES, Ar—come! cried Jael, her voice thinning.

With a clap of thunder, the window closed. Ar sensed that the Enemy had done that, and that he had only moments to react before the ship itself would be under attack. An explosive wave flashed out from the singularity. Frightened, Ar shrank the net. *Hold tight, Ed!* The shock wave hit the ship like a hammer, shaking the net with terrible power. But it held. *Ed—straight in! With everything we've got!* Ar bellowed in fury.

Hawwww! Straight through, straight through! screamed the parrot, rocketing to the front of the net and helping Ar stretch them out like a long, shiny needle plunging straight for the blazing singularity that was the Dream Mountain.

Another wave hit them, but Ar was no longer afraid of that, and they flashed through it with only a single hard *thump,* and the fire of the singularity grew and brightened and blossomed before them. And if he had taken the time to think about it, he might have been terrified; but he felt a tremendous and unreasoning hope burning in his veins now, as they approached the singularity that by all rights ought to destroy them.

Damn the torpedoes, hawwwwwwwwwwwwww! shouted Ed.

And Ar changed their shape from a needle to a forcefield scalpel as the singularity exploded around them.

It was Lavafire who first understood, but even then it took a choir of draconae voices to persuade her to take the terrible risk. The Forge of Dreams was secured in a weaving of protection that even the Enemy could not break through—or if he did, all of that power would be released in a conflagration that would destroy the realm with the Dream Mountain itself.

But with all of their foresight, they had never imagined the One doing something like *this.* With Jael attacking the web at the Black Peak, and Ar diving headlong through the underrealm in a terrifying plunge that would take him straight through the dream forge, they had no choice if Jael was to succeed, if Ar was to survive.

Loose the bonds—!

Open the fires—!

Let him not die for our fear—!

Our last hope—!

—came the cascade of voices, and with that affirmation, Lavafire and the others bent all of their thought to undoing everything they had just done.

The weaving came loose, was stripped away . . .

And the heart of the Dream Mountain lay open to all who had the power to reach it.

The darkness coiled with outrage at the forces rising against it—far more than it had expected. But it did not for an instant consider drawing back. Though its web was under attack, it still had the dragons in a state of disarray. As long as the Mountain of Fire was kept from their sight, they could never regain their full measure of strength.

The Nail's attention was divided now. Part was focused on the Vale of Darkness, maintaining the sorcery, where the last of the dragon strength battled a foe that was half illusion. The Nail's servants were fewer now than before. He didn't mind the deaths of the drahls and Tar-skel dragons, but the loss of numbers hampered the illusion-sorcery that kept the dragons afraid. Another part of his attention was on the Black Peak, where the rigger-spirit had somehow bound itself to a dragon, and where its attack against the web was more troublesome than expected. Still, with the power from the Deep Caverns, the web could withstand the attack there.

And now the draconae had brought forth another irritation, calling the fleeing riggers in their rigger-ship toward the Mountain of Fire. It wasn't clear why they wanted the riggers, but as the Nail peered through the underrealm at the imprisoned Mountain, he laughed with sudden, pure, naked delight as he saw the foolish draconae make their fatal mistake.

* The time has come! Time for the promised ending! *

The keepers of the Mountain had opened their defenses, and the time had come to claim control of that place, as the Words had promised. No longer was there any reason to hold his power in reserve. The flame and the darkness coiled, and the Nail of Strength laughed with infinite satisfaction as he prepared his final blow.

The Nail drew together *all* of his power—from the Deep Caverns, from the vale, from his own inner reservoirs—and funneled it into the grand weaving. It was a torrent of power, a tidal wave, a tsunami—all of it directed toward seizing the Mountain of Fire. And once it had those fires of creation, it would flower outward without pause—leaving this realm a cinder perhaps, but flowering outward, with unstoppable force, into the universes beyond.

Jael, plunging through the web with all of the strength of a dragon-spirit, was blasted back by a stupendous arc of lightning. She felt Ed and Windrush both shuddering and gasping from the blow. *(What was that?)* she whispered. *(What has Tar-skel done?)*

The web crackled, and waves of energy flashed from somewhere behind her, across the web, toward the Dream Mountain. She saw the peril that she had created: the draconae had opened the heart of the Dream Mountain for Ar to pass through . . . and opened it to the Enemy, as well. In a terrible, sudden insight, she realized that if the Enemy succeeded, he could have his victory and move on, though the realm would lie in smoking ruins behind him.

HE MUST NOT! she screamed, her voice the voice of Windrush and Ed and Jael, and she hurled herself again at the web, and again and again, each time clawing harder at the binding force that held it together, each time knowing that she could not break through it alone.

HELP US! she screamed into the tumult of the underrealm. *HELP US—ANYONE—PLEASE—!*

In the Cavern of Spirits, the underrealm rang like a tremendous bell gonging in the depths of an infinite sea. Hodakai listened, wondering, wishing he could see what was happening. All of the ordinary paths of vision were obscured. At one point, he'd felt a sharp twinge, and thought of Rent, and wondered why he'd thought of death at the same time. He was dizzy with everything that had happened; but he felt bereft now, and alone. Even the cavern sprites seemed to have left him.

Jarvorus! he cried into the gloom of the cavern where the rift yawned. *Why have you left me alone here?*

To his astonishment, he heard an answering whisper: *I've not left you, Hodakai.* The false-iffling slipped like a flame out of a fold in the underrealm and murmured, *He is gone now, isn't he? I think he has died.*

Hodakai danced with relief at having someone here for company. *Who has died? Rent? Maybe so! But who cares? Jarvorus, isn't there something we can DO?*

At that moment, the ringing in the underrealm changed suddenly. There was a strange kind of silence, and then a voice echoed distantly out of the rift. *Rigger, we need you! Jael needs you!*

Hodakai stared at Jarvorus, frozen in astonishment. Was that a *dracona* voice? Calling to him? Or to Ar?

A few moments later, from another part of the underrealm, he heard another voice. *Help us—anyone—!*

Hodakai cried out silently, recognizing that voice. *Jael!* he cried weakly.

He heard Jarvorus whisper in amazement, *She lives! Maybe we can do something, maybe we can! We must try! Hodakai, I must find the ifflings! And you must find a way to help! Use every spell you know!*

And then Jarvorus was gone, leaving Hodakai staring in disbelief.

The iffling-child was the first to hear the cry of the false-iffling, and there was something in its voice that made the iffling-child listen, and believe, and finally carry the cry back to the flickering, dying powers of the iffling-parents. Hearing, they seemed to burn just a little brighter, a little stronger.

—*When the One breaks through*—

—*The change will come*—
—*For the Enemy*—
—*Or for us*—
—*And when the Mountain is opened*—
—*Comes our time*—
—*Our hope*—
—*The last*—

And thus began the journey of the flames through the underrealm—a slow parade of guttering candle-flames, moving toward the place where they hoped the Dream Mountain would appear, and where at last they would die, if it did not.

Hodakai began, hesitantly at first, to probe outward with the spells of communication that he had never used to reach anyone except Rent. But he was a *rigger*, by God; he could do this! The underrealm was a place of frightful chaos, but he found that he could, in fact, probe open small pathways. With increasing boldness, he searched farther and farther from the Cavern of Spirits, to see if he could find a window, a way to see, to call, to hear news, to find out what Jael was doing.

He heard Jael, but could not see her. But one thing he did see, opening up to his view as if through a long telescope lens, was the vale where the dragons were battling. He listened to the cries and chaos of battle, and was appalled to realize that the dragons were being deceived by the same spells of illusion that he had used right here!

If he could shout loudly enough to make himself heard, perhaps he could help just a little, after all.

In the Dark Vale, Farsight paused in his struggle against the airborne enemies, too many of which had turned out to be ghostly apparitions, rather than living drahls. He thought he had heard a shout, through the noise of battle—a shout that had a peculiar familiarity to it, a cry for help. A . . . human voice . . . in his undersense. *Jael?*

He listened intently, to see if he could catch it again, thinking how very odd it was to be underhearing a voice that was not his brother Windrush's. He didn't hear Jael's voice again; but a short time later, he heard a different voice—also human!—a little louder. *You are being deceived! Go below and free the others! You are wasting time! Go into the dungeons!*

Farsight was dumbstruck by the voice. Go below, to the dungeons? Wasting time? Who was saying that? And he suddenly realized, with the terrifying power of a revelation, how right the voice was. They had become so entangled in their fight here in the sky that they had forgotten the purpose of their attack: to strike at the Enemy's heart.

"You three!" he cried to a trio of dragons who had just burst through an exploding illusion of enemy warriors. "Fly with me! Downward to the dungeons!"

They were not that far above the ground to begin with, but Farsight realized, as he leveled off over the chasms, that in the crevasses of the vale right below him, creatures were stirring in the shadows. Many of them were dragons!

Yes! called the voice at the edges of his thought. *You can free them! The bindings are weakening! You can break them!*

"Spread out! Search the dungeons for our brothers!" Farsight shouted to the three flying with him. He slowed, peering and listening over the chasms. He heard a dragon cry, off to his left—a familiar cry. He drew a breath of astonishment and turned to find its source.

He heard the voice again, bellowing: "SHE LIVES! THE ONE LIVES IN THE DREAM MOUNTAIN!" And at last he spotted a grey-green dragon laboring to fly low over the dungeons, shouting down to the captives.

Farsight was so astonished that he could not speak until he had flown to the other's side and gazed at him in disbelief. His brother looked terrible—battered and wounded, and struggling just to stay airborne. "WINGTOUCH!" Farsight roared. "YOU'RE ALIVE!"

His younger brother wheeled in the air and regarded him with equal amazement. Against the smoke and the gloom, WingTouch's sea-green eyes glowed, tired but undimmed. However badly hurt, WingTouch was more triumphant than beaten, by far. "Welcome to the dungeons of the

Enemy!" WingTouch cried, wobbling as he swerved to avoid a wall.

"You're wounded! Are you able to fight?"

"Fight?" WingTouch muttered. "I AM fighting! We have lost FullSky—but he freed me before he died, and I have slain his killer! Come, help me free the others! The bindings of fear are breaking!" The battered dragon beckoned Farsight downward into the gloom of the dungeons.

Indeed, Farsight thought. The Enemy had been stalling them overhead, distracting them from their purpose! What better way to strike at the Enemy than to free his prisoners? "Wait, WingTouch!" he cried, and turned his voice skyward, booming, "ALL DRAGONS—DOWN TO THE DUNGEONS! OUR BROTHERS LIVE! WINGTOUCH LIVES! LEAVE THE SKY TO THE GHOSTS AND COME FREE THE PRISONERS!"

Following WingTouch, he plunged downward into the chasms, bellowing a cry of freedom to his imprisoned brothers.

Jael felt the change from the dungeons like a whisper of cool air reviving her in the heat of battle. Though she couldn't see what was happening in the Dark Vale, she could feel the dragons' defiance and joy, and could see its effects on the web. The Enemy's explosion of power was mutating, in a way she didn't think the Enemy had intended.

She and Ed and Windrush continued to attack the web, but not alone. Rippling waves of shadow were passing through the fiery network, each wave a burst of defiance or hope or freedom somewhere in the realm. Each wave weakened the web just a little, and the next a little more. The Enemy had channeled all of his power toward the Dream Mountain, thinking he no longer needed it elsewhere—but the web that carried it was weakening with every defeat he suffered, in the underrealm or the outer world. The web, incandescent with power, was brightening and stretching where it had once been strongest, like a filament about to burst.

Now was the time . . .

(*Windrush, Ed—DRACONAE!—all of your strength—NOW!*) Jael cried. Their answer came in the heady rush of adrenaline to her limbs, the strength to her wings, and she turned and hurtled with suicidal abandon toward the most blazingly bright strands of the overburdened web.

This time, when her claws connected, she felt not just the explosion of fire, she felt the strands stretch and then tear—in a great long rip, as the web parted from its own inner stresses, spewing incandescent fire into the deep darkness beyond.

And the dragon rigger flew headlong toward the distant, hazy form of the Dream Mountain, the filaments of power bursting against her claws like shears tearing through fabric—in a long, exploding stream of fire.

* TREACHERY! TREACHERY! *

The center of darkness was shocked into disbelief that such defiance and irrational hope could be springing forth from every corner of the realm—challenging his structure of power!—surging into the tiniest tears in his web!—ripping at its fiber!—draining its unquenchable strength—!

* This cannot be! *

Exploding with bottomless fury, the Nail erupted with every ounce of his strength toward the Mountain of Fire, focusing only on channeling his power into the web that streamed toward those fires of creation.

He barely even noticed his own rising desperation. He was too preoccupied to swat at the dragon rigger that was hurtling through his web.

* It *will* be mine! It *will* be! *

Yawwwwwwwwwww! screamed Ed as the spaceship plunged, shimmering and twisting, through the singularity. The parrot's voice quavered and turned deep and then booming-bass and then shrill as the abrupt spatial-transformation flashed through the net. It sounded as if there were two voices screaming at once, and Ar realized that one of them was his.

He had been shaking, and now he bellowed with joy as the singularity flashed away behind them, and their scalpel-prowed ship plunged into a new layer of the Flux, plunged into the underrealm, into the outstretched web-structure of Tar-skel, parting it in their wake like so many fraying strands of thread. It exploded around them with a terrifying electrical discharge, but they were moving like light itself now; and as they flew, it almost seemed that the web was tearing open *before* them, spilling its energy in a great cascade of fire.

Something ponderous was giving way in the web. Before he could begin to understand it, there was a tremendous shaking convulsion in the Flux, as though the bottom had just dropped out of a vast ocean. The web was disintegrating before them. It was dumping an incredible fountain of power into a yawning emptiness, an even deeper layer in the Flux.

Eeeeeeeeeeiiiiiiiiiiii! Ar screamed to Ed, to Jael if she could hear, to the universe. He didn't even know why; it was a scream that just erupted, an exhilaration out of nowhere, an explosion of such joy that he almost didn't see what was ahead of them in their path—until Ed's frantic cry, *Look-k-k! Hawwwwwwww! Look-k-k!* made him squint ahead through the exploding light.

It was the distant, silvery shape of a dragon, raking open the web in a plume of fire as it hurtled toward them.

* Impossible! It cannot be happening! *

The error was too great, too profound. He could not have made such an error! Somehow it had all turned wrong, wrong, in his stroke of triumph. His final blast of power was destroying the very structure that it was supposed to be completing.

This was not how it was supposed to happen!

In the Dark Vale, the prisoners' bonds were falling away. His own servants were weakening, his hold on them slipping; some of them were blinking through newly opened eyes, turning and freeing the very ones they'd been holding prisoner!

This was not how it was supposed to end . . .

The Mountain of Fire was slipping out of his grasp, and all of the power in his sorcery was pouring into a great emptiness, streaming away, dissipating into nothingness . . .

* NO-O-O-O-O-O-O-O-O-O—! *

He was losing it all . . . but he would not lose without taking the Damned One with him!

At first, all she could see was the explosion racing before them, the web spilling its power with tremendous, jarring bursts of energy. But it was not just the web they were tearing; the web was interwoven with the fabric of the underrealm itself, and it was impossible to tear one without the other. A bottomless blackness was yawning open beneath them, and it was into that abyss that the lightning-fire of the web was emptying.

(My God, where is it going, where is all that power going?) she breathed.

From Windrush she sensed amazement and bewilderment. (Out of the realm,) the dragon whispered. (Out of the realm. Jael! Look!)

(Hawwww!)

Above the abyss, a curious tableau was forming, as though focused through a very strange lens. Ahead, the Dream Mountain was emerging from a mist, radiant in its translucence, a diamond-white fire burning in its center, with a shining speck streaking out of it. Something made Jael glance behind her at the Black Peak. The wound in the Flux there was closing, the glowering sun vanishing. Between the two mountains, illuminated in a strange dawnlike light, was a vision of a blasted valley that could only have been the Dark Vale. Above it, Jael saw tiny tongues of dragon fire and heard shouts of hope and joy. And farther beyond, across a distant plain that seemed to lie in another realm altogether, she glimpsed marching toward the Dream Mountain a tiny parade of flickering flames, which looked as though the slightest breeze might extinguish them. (Ifflings,) she whispered.

But in the heart of the Dark Vale, something was happening that made her clench with fear. Something was spiraling open in the fabric of the underrealm, a window opening, and through it she glimpsed darkness and flames. This was not the nothingness of the abyss below, but a writhing, coiling darkness filled with a living malevolence. She felt a moment of stark revulsion as she glimpsed that *thing*; but the darkness and flame were flattening and twisting, and coiling out into the web . . . coiling out into the rift and the nothingness beyond.

She began to feel a rising wave of relief. In a moment, it would be gone, forever. She raised her sights to the Dream Mountain.

(*JAEL!*)

The dragon's voice shocked Jael alert with terror. (*What—?*)

(*Uurrrrrrrruk-k-k-k—*)

Above the rift, the flaming darkness had suddenly turned and snaked out a whip of light-devouring fire. It was streaking through the underrealm, coiling toward Jael. She could not speak or act. She could only watch, frozen, as it sped toward her, curling out in a great arc to ensnare her, and Windrush, and Ed.

If she was paralyzed, the dragon within her was not. They banked and dove, fleeing.

* You cannot flee. *

The voice thundered deafeningly, soundlessly, in her heart.

* You are mine. The One is damned. The One shall die. *

Windrush sped through the underrealm, but the whip of dark fire was faster, and it arched up and around and behind them and spiraled with dizzying speed, spinning a coil of itself around them, a coil of darkness that blocked off the rest of the underrealm. (*Windrush?*) she whispered. (*Turn, Windrush, we must turn!*)

They swept in a frantic turn—and Jael screamed.

An enormous face filled the darkness before them, and it was the face of Mogurn, and the face of her father, and the face of a young terrified rigger who had no hope in the world, no hope at all. *No!* she whispered to the face. *That's all in my past! It's all over!* The captain who had terrorized her was dead, her father was dead, she herself was dead.

The mouth of Mogurn opened, and through rotting teeth he boomed out a laughter of triumph. His hand reached toward her, with his cursed pallisp to enslave her.

YOU CAN'T! she screamed. *I broke it! It's gone!*

The coil of dark fire was tightening around her like a noose, and at the other end of it, she could see it still streaming into the abyss, and she could feel it pulling *her* toward the abyss now. She raked her talons at the face of Mogurn, and she blew flame at him, but that just made him laugh all the harder; and her father sneered with disgust at his weakling daughter.

(*Jaylll, awwwk-k-k—*) she heard, but it was a distant, plaintive cry, and it couldn't help her.

(*Jael, remember who you are,*) she heard, and it was a soft voice, dragon she thought, but she couldn't quite tell anymore who was who. (*Jael, remember!*) insisted the voice. (*Believe and remember!*) Who was that, Highwing? But Highwing was dead. Tar-skel had killed him, as he was about to kill her. She couldn't quite think anymore.

(*You must believe—!*) urged the fading voice. There were a host of voices clamoring around her, and within her, and she could understand none of them now. She was icy cold, with fear.

The snake of devouring fire was tightening around her neck now, and it was pulling her faster toward the abyss, down, downward toward blackness . . . there was no way to escape from it now.

And then something made it jerk suddenly . . . and loosen just a little . . .

Jael, we're here! We see it! IT CAN'T HURT YOU IF YOU DON'T LET IT! A voice was reverberating through the darkness. *You're a rigger, Jael—remember! You're a rigger!*

The coil lurched as it lashed angrily at the offending source of the voice. A spaceship, silver and ghostly, flashed through the flame, flashed across in front of her. *Jayyyyylll—hawwwww!* screamed a voice from the ship.

The distraction was enough to give her a moment to remember. She was a rigger. She had defeated Mogurn, she had forgiven her father, she had grown out of that weakling, and she had helped to defeat Tar-skel. *(Believe,)* she heard again, and that time it was a chiming dracona voice. She glimpsed the distant light of the Dream Mountain, and felt the power of the Mountain flowing through her, and remembered that that was where she lived now, and the power of the Mountain was greater than the power of a defeated enemy.

She shifted her gaze to the whipping dark flame, the devouring flame that had flailed ineffectually at the spaceship and was now turning back for a final strike at her. She remembered that she was unafraid, remembered that she had *already* defeated it.

No! she said to it. She said it coldly and clearly. But she was not cold on the inside anymore, she was burning bright and hot with dreamfire, and with dragon blood, and the fearless anger of a parrot, and most of all with the certainty that she was Jael and she *lived* in the dreamfire, and that fire was forever denied this dark one.

No! she said, and she punctuated the word with a short blast of dragon flame. She raised her head and gazed back at the coil of darkness, and she knew that she had defeated a creature like this once before, but as dragon, not woman; and she felt her dragon eyes blazing with the light of the dreamfires, blazing bright, brighter, her entire dragon body blazing with light.

The snake of darkness rose against the light—and fell back from it with a wail. The underrealm was visible again, and Jael saw now that the web of sorcery was in tatters, and the last of the flaming darkness was streaming out of the window of the Dark Vale into the rift of emptiness. A voice groaned from the darkness, unutterably deep and angry. It spoke no words she could understand, but it shook the underrealm with its hatred. Jael shuddered at the voice, but Windrush kept them flying, blazing, streaking like a beam of light toward the Dream Mountain. The voice suddenly cut off into silence, and the last of the flame of darkness vanished into the rift in the underrealm, and the silence of its parting shook the realm and the underrealm with a tremendous, soundless, shattering earthquake.

The concussion reverberated for a long time. As it slowly subsided, the window in the Dark Vale faded, leaving only the valley in which it had appeared. The last remaining shreds of the web fell like feathery ashes into the abyss of emptiness.

Something was flying toward Jael and Windrush and Ed.

Ar! she cried. *Ar, you came! You made it through!* And after a moment, she added tearfully, *And you saved me, you saved my life!*

The answering cry was just as triumphant: *Jael, I can't believe you're alive, you're alive!*

In the curious ringing space of the underrealm, before the Dream Mountain, they spun into a dizzying orbit around one another, the dragon and the spaceship; and then with a shriek, two parrot shapes flickered out into space, one from the dragon and one from the spaceship, and they danced in space around one another, not quite able to join and not willing to be parted.

Chapter 44
RIGGERS IN THE REALM

BEFORE THE two Eds, or Jael and Ar, could say another word, they were stunned into silence by what was happening around them.

The underrealm space was shimmering and changing colors, first reddening, then shifting up through the spectrum: orange, yellow, green, blue, violet—and finally turning clear. The cloud upon which the Dream Mountain was floating slowly dissolved, and the Mountain emerged, now rising solidly from the ground, some distance beyond the Dark Vale. The fire in its heart seemed brighter, steadier, and the voices of the draconae could be heard ringing out like distant chimes. Jael's center was still with the draconae, of course; but her presence was stretched halfway across the underrealm and back, and she could hear their choir of joy from both sides of her being.

Do you hear them, Ar? Do you hear the draconae? she whispered.

Cawww—graggons!

Yes, Jael—it's beautiful!

Graggons, glizzards, all around Ed, awwwwk!

I'm with the draconae, Ar. I'm a part of them—or they're a part of me—and the Mountain—

The spaceship floated closer, Ar's ghostly wedge-headed countenance just visible on its prow. His eyes glittered purple. *I thought you were with Windrush, Jael. For a moment, I thought I saw you on his back. Now, I can't quite tell.*

I am with Windrush, Ar. My kuutekka is joined with his— from the Dream Mountain. It's hard to explain.

But Jael, I thought—

Ar's words were interrupted as great shafts of light burst

out of the Mountain and fanned slowly over the landscape of the underrealm, illuminating places that had been lost in shadow. The Dark Vale was caught in a prolonged light, and it seemed to flicker, until it began to shine as though with its own inner source. Dragon flames were still visible there, but they seemed to be flames of jubilation, not battle. Though she could not quite discern what was happening, Jael sensed that the struggle in that place was ending. She could make out the movements of hundreds of tiny shapes, rising from the floor of the vale. *Ar, the prisoners are rising from the Dark Vale! Look!*

Ar was staring in wonder. Did he understand that this was a different view from what they'd been accustomed to, that this was the world of the underrealm? What did it look like on the outside? Jael wondered, and wished that she could see.

She was about to ask Windrush, when another sight caught her eye, out beyond the Dark Vale: the procession of tiny flames that she had glimpsed before, bobbing across a distant plain like hand torches borne by invisible marchers. Her breath escaped—or was it Windrush's? The dragon's voice rumbled, almost reverently: *It is the ifflings, returning to the Dream Mountain!*

Returning home? she whispered.

Returning home, answered the dragon.

And that, Ar said slowly, *is where we shall have to be bound before much longer. We are tired, and our ship is damaged. Jael is there no way that you can return to the ship—to us?* Even as he said it, his tone made clear that he knew the answer.

My friend Ar, she sighed—and with an effort, she separated her kuutekka from its direct union with Windrush's, parting with a shudder—and made herself visible again on the dragon's back. *I have no life in that realm anymore, Ar. I've passed through that door. I don't even know how long I can live on like this in the Dream Mountain. Do you know, Windrush?*

Jael, rumbled the dragon, *I am astonished and overjoyed to have you here at all! It is truly rakhandroh! Who knows what the power of the draconae can do? It is beyond my knowledge. But*

Jael, I too must return to the outer world! I must see it with my own eyes! And I hear the call of those who guard me! I must return!

Jael felt a rush of sadness. She reached back in thought to the draconae, wondering if it was possible for her to accompany the dragon into the outer world. She heard murmurs of regret, and knew that this was beyond the power of the draconae; she could be with Windrush in the underrealm, and only there. *Windrush,* she said softly, *I must leave you when you go. But you may find me in the Dream Mountain, and I will be calling your name in the underrealm.*

The dragon answered, *I wish you could remain with me, Jael. But look for me soon, in the Dream Mountain!* He bobbed his great, ghostly head at Ar. *Perhaps you can steer your ship up through the underrealm with me, and join us in flight to the Dark Vale, to see our victory?*

Ar hesitated. *We will try,* he said. *But we have suffered damage. I don't know how well we can manage.*

Then let us fly back through the underrealm, and I will lead you and help, as in the past, said Windrush. He turned in a great sweep. One Ed scrambled to rejoin Jael, and the other fluttered back to the prow of the ship; and Windrush, with Jael still on his back, sent his kuutekka fleeing back toward the Black Peak, where his dragon companions were calling for his return. Jael glanced backward and saw the silver starship trailing behind, trying to keep up.

The Black Peak was dark and silent now. The shadows of Windrush's flight of dragons were clustered there, waiting. *Jael—farewell for now!* Windrush cried softly. *Ar—follow me, if you can!*

Jael, will I see you again? called Ar.

Fly to the Dream Mountain. I will be waiting, Jael answered. *Let Windrush bring you. Come soon—!* Her words were interrupted by a series of squawks as the two parrots spun around one another a last time, then separated.

Awwwk—Ed!

Ed—rawwwwk!

G'bye—!

G'bye—!

And Jael's Ed soared back into her eyes and landed fluttering among her thoughts, while the other Ed circled Ar in the ship's net. Everything shrank then, and her friends vanished, and Jael felt her kuutekka moving with dizzying speed back through the underrealm. In an eyeblink she felt the reassuring presence of the Dream Mountain surrounding her again; and her thoughts were filled with the chiming choir of the draconae, sharing with her the joy of victory.

Windrush emerged, lightheaded, from the underrealm to find his fellow dragons clustered on the slope around him, rumbling with questions. "It is astonishing!" he cried, blinking and twisting his head about.

"Windrush, what happened?"

"Tell us!"

"We felt the air shaking—"

"The Enemy has fallen!" Windrush cried. "Tar-skel has fallen!"

"Windrush, *are you all right*? WHAT HAPPENED?"

It took him a few moments to catch his breath and look around to see that the other dragons and he were alone here. The Black Peak was dark and silent; the glowing window from Tar-skel's old sorcery was gone. "My brothers," he began. "It is not easy to say—"

"Windrush! What is that?" cried Fleetwing, to his left.

Windrush turned his head. A silver spaceship was shimmering into view in the air, and he blew a tongue of flame in greeting. "Welcome, Ar—and Ed—friends of Jael, of Windrush, and Highwing!" he called. To the bewildered dragons, he explained, "They came to help us defeat the Enemy—in the underrealm, with Jael! Riggers, if you would, come ride on my back."

Windrush launched himself from the mountain slope. The other dragons murmured with amazement as the spaceship approached Windrush, then disappeared, as a humanlike rigger and a parrot materialized upon the dragon's shoulders.

"Awwwk! Again we ride!" squawked the parrot.

"Indeed," said Windrush. "And now, my friends, let us

return to the Dark Vale and join the others! I must see with my own eyes what has happened! Quickly, now—quickly as the wind, let us fly!"

And as they gathered and sped from the Black Peak toward the Dark Vale, Windrush blew joyous tongues of flame and realized that he hardly felt weary at all.

"Rakhandroh!" the dragon whispered, over and over, as they approached the Dark Vale. It was not just the sight of the vale itself that was astonishing—the air filled with shouting, triumphant dragons, and the floor below swarming with dragons, flyers, and shadow-cats who were staggering up from craters, caverns, and crevices, blinking at their newfound freedom. Looming over that sight was something even more astonishing, more rakhandroh, rising above the horizon far beyond the vale: it was a great, shimmering glass mountain, freed at last from the sorcery that had kept it hidden. The Dream Mountain!

All of the dragons wheeling in the air were drawn to the sight, gazing at it with great curiosity and desire.

Windrush bellowed out his joy. He called out to his leaders to report. He was answered instead by shouted questions: "Windrush, what happened?" "What did you do?" "The sorceries have vanished!" "How did you bring back the Dream Mountain?"

"I? I did nothing!" Windrush rumbled, laughing. He tried to explain, but his words came out in a hopeless jumble, and made no sense even to him. "Just say this!" he cried at last. *"Tar-skel has fallen! He is gone from the realm! The riggers Jael and Ar and Ed and the ifflings and FullSky and all of you helped to defeat him!"*

"Windrush!" cried a familiar voice. Farsight was climbing from below to greet him, and another dragon was limping behind him. "Don't forget WingTouch!"

"WingTouch!" cried Windrush in amazement, spiraling down to join the two in a dance of joy. "You're alive, WingTouch, you're still with us!"

"Indeed, thanks to FullSky," answered his youngest

brother. "May he live long in the Final Dream Mountain! I had the privilege of destroying his killer."

"FullSky!" sighed Windrush at the reminder of who was *not* among them, at the reminder that many brave dragons had fallen here today, and one of them was their brother who had done so much to bring them this victory. "May all our dragon brothers live long in the Final Dream Mountain," he said finally. And for a moment, he felt an urge to fly a flight of grief for those they had lost. But now was not the time; they could grieve later.

Farsight and WingTouch greeted Ar and Ed on Windrush's back; then the dragons exchanged reports. "After you were gone, there was a great upheaval that shook both the sky *and* the earth," Farsight said. "When it passed, I felt that a great power had gone out of the realm. The sky and the earth became quiet. The drahls lost all spirit for battle. They began to take their own lives, or to surrender, or to flee. The prisons fell open. And the Dream Mountain—reappearing, like a ghost, out of the air! Truly rakhandroh! And there have already been reports of lumenis groves sighted out beyond the vale!"

"Indeed," said Windrush, and on his shoulder the small, noisy parrot-rigger hooted and cawed in loud approval. "When we have restored some order here—and perhaps when we have fed—some of us must fly on to the Dream Mountain. There the spirit of Jael awaits us."

Those words sent ripples of excitement through the dragons flying nearby. "To the Dream Mountain," they whispered and rumbled. And slowly the rumble grew to a chant that filled the air. "To the Dream Mountain! To the Dream Mountain . . . !"

Chapter 45
THE REALM RETURNS

FOR THE ifflings, it was a return to their source of being. Born of the dreamfire, they at last saw a true path out of their exile, a true path home. The Mountain beckoned, calling them in across the gulf that had divided them.

One iffling-child accompanied them, the one who might have been the last. And one other came with them: a strange one, a changeling sprite, who had once been their foe and now insisted upon being their friend. They accepted that one with a kind of weary puzzlement, as they made the long march home across the underrealm.

—*Draconae!*—

—*We glimpse you!*—

—*Open your hearth!*—

—*Give us your fire!*—

Visions of strength, of new iffling-children, of freedom to wander the realm, to visit the draconi, to grow and blossom . . . the visions loomed before them like mirages on a desert, but mirages that now could grow into reality. The vision gave hope, and in that hope they found the strength to move forward across the bleak plain where at last their underrealm met that of the dragons.

A chasm broke the plain, a black rift in the underrealm where the power of the Enemy had fallen, and had streamed away out of the realm. When the ifflings reached that place, they floated across it as though riding on a warm updraft of air. At first it seemed as though the air currents would snuff them out like so many dying candle-flames; but across the emptiness a beacon flared and then paused, its beam touching them and strengthening their fires. It was the touch of the draconae-tended dreamfire, and it drew them onward in a rippling coruscation, across the chasm and the plain, in a great cascade of light flashing in circlets over them, pulling them, drawing them in.

And then the Mountain was around them, and the chiming voices of the draconae greeted them, and the regenerative fire of the Forge of Dreams in which they had been born blazed forth with a white heat that filled them, and consumed them in a welcoming embrace . . .

—*And in this place*—
—*All things begin*—
—*Anew*—

In the gloom and the emptiness, after the reverberations had passed and the distant cries had faded to a background mutter in the underrealm, Hodakai drew himself down into a small, silent bundle in the Cavern of Spirits. He felt lonelier than he had felt in a long, long time. He missed Jarvorus. He missed Ar and Ed. He missed Windrush, and even, in a way, he missed Rent. Most of all, he missed Jael.

He knew now that she had survived her death, and not only that, but had, astonishingly, toppled the vast empire of power that belonged to Tar-skel. Hodakai was glad of that, really he was. But just now in the silence and emptiness of this warren, he was finding it a little hard to enjoy the victory.

Sprites! he sighed. *Won't even you come out to keep me company? Where are you all?* But there was no answer, no taunt, no teasing, from the hidden corners of the cavern. It seemed that even the sprites had gone away. Perhaps they too had fled to the Dream Mountain, as the ifflings had. As Jael had. As the dragons all probably wanted to do.

For a while there, he had felt useful. It wasn't that he had done much—he'd just shouted some helpful encouragement through the underrealm to the Dark Vale—but it was a lot more than he had ever dared to do before. And maybe it really had helped in the battle.

Kan-Kon, he thought wistfully, peering out of his silent jar into the cold silence of the cavern, *I think you would have* been proud of me at the end. I hope that fellow Ar makes it back to tell you about it.

Truthfully, there didn't seem much else to do, think, or say. There was just the silence. He had thought briefly of his rigger fantasies; but whatever escape they might offer now seemed empty and meaningless against the memory of what he had just been through. He supposed he could try to reach out again through the underrealm, but it was all changed now, all stirred up like a lake after a storm, and he didn't have the skill to see through it.

He huddled, and waited—but for what, he didn't know.

When it came, he was so absorbed in the silence that he didn't really even notice at first. It was a voice, calling softly. But from where? Outside the cavern, that was for sure. Perhaps it was drifting up through the crack in the floor that marked where the rift had gaped, before the shaking of the realm had closed it again. It seemed to be calling his name.

Hello? he whispered, his voice quavering. He was half afraid that he was talking to himself.

Hodakai? Can you hear me?

Yes, he whispered, even more softly. Was that the voice of—?

There you are! said Jael, her voice growing stronger. Suddenly her kuutekka appeared in the underrealm beside his spirit jar. It was just her face—but how good it was to see a human face! *I've been trying to find you!* she said. *I wanted to see if you're all right.*

Hodakai laughed convulsively, with churning emotions. *See if I'M all right? YOU'RE the one we killed, don't you remember?*

Jael laughed with him, but she seemed to have noticed the melancholy tone underlying his answer. *I remember, all right. Hodakai, a lot has happened since then. I don't know how much you were able to see or hear . . .*

Well, I . . . I saw some. I felt it happen, in the end. I know you won. Congratulations.

Don't just congratulate me, Hodakai. I understand you were helping out at the end, too. And you helped me get to where I am now.

Er—yes, Hodakai said, *And you are, I assume—*

Her voice seemed full of music as she said, *In the Dream Mountain, Hodakai, the Dream Mountain.* And the joy in her voice sent a spike of sadness through him, sharpening his loneliness—until she added, *I've been trying to think if there's some way I might be able to help you, Hodakai. Some way to bring you here.*

Hawwww! said a parrot, its tiny head visible in the pupil of her eye. *Yessss!*

If you'd like to come, I mean . . .

Hodakai seemed to go blind and deaf as her words echoed like gongs in his mind; and she had to call out to him again, before he finally was able to stammer, *Yes . . . I . . . I think I might like that. Since you ask. If it's not too much trouble. But only if it's not too much trouble—!*

And when she went on to explain that he might have to wait a little while before she could work out a way to do it, he hardly heard, hardly cared. He could wait as long as she wanted him to. He could wait very nearly forever, as long as he knew that he was not forgotten, as long as his time in this lonely cavern was at last coming to an end.

The ship's bridge was terribly silent, as Ar rose at last from his rigger-station. Even Ed was gone, sleeping in the data-memory until he returned, or perhaps holopresent in the ship's commons. Ar had never in his life felt such physical exhaustion; he had no idea how long he had been in the net, but it was many times longer than his longest previous stint. He could scarcely focus his eyes, and every muscle and joint in his Clendornan body seemed on the verge of spasm. But he was alive, freed at last from the net by the collapse of Jael's section.

Never in his life had he felt such grief, and such joy. He stood for a few moments beside the second rigger-station, gazing down at the still form that had been his crewmate and friend. *No,* he reminded himself sternly, *that body was not my friend. My friend is alive still, alive . . . out there . . .*

But he could not complete the thought. Instead, he broke down at last, kneeling and raising his face to the ceiling, crying out his grief with open, shuddering gasps of pain. The ceiling sparkled with scintillations of grief-light from the backs of his eyes. He remained in that posture until the explosions of light in his eyes faded, and his cries gave out, and then he was silent for a time in the gloom of the bridge, mourning the sight of his friend who had given her life for the dragons.

At last he rose and opened Jael's rigger-station. There was, he thought, an expression of peace on her face. Slipping his arms under her, he lifted her from the station and bore her at last from the bridge. She would complete her journey in a stasis box, cold and silent, until he could bring her to a final resting place. Which ought to be . . .

He had no idea, he realized. He would have to ask her when he saw her.

Ar went to the galley and ate, not even noticing the taste of his food. Reluctantly, he went to his quarters and lay down to rest. But he knew he could not sleep, not thinking about Jael. Besides, he needed to perform a thorough check on the ship's systems, without much more delay. And in truth, he wanted to return to the net as soon as possible. Windrush was looking after their safety on the outside, but it would not do to be away too long.

The dragons would soon be flying to the Dream Mountain, and he didn't want to miss a moment of it.

The process of healing had already begun, Windrush noted as he gazed over the land from the air. Even here, in this devastated land that had been the stronghold of the Enemy, the effects of Tar-skel's sorceries were fading. Trees and lumenis had returned to view, and the dragons had wasted no time in feeding on the latter. It was the first lumenis feeding in a long time that was full of joy and not desperation. Quite a number of drahls and other altered beings had been found, struggling to adjust to the crippled bodies that were left when Tar-skel's spells of distortion had fallen away. They were being gathered together, their fate to be determined in due time.

In one respect, the land had been sharply altered by the final battle, and as Windrush flew over it, flanked by his brothers and bearing the ghostly rigger-ship on his back, he thought that the change looked permanent. The rift in the underrealm through which Tar-skel had disappeared was mirrored in the outer world, a long dark chasm that was somehow impossible to look into with a probing eye. It deflected the gaze somehow, or drew it away to a confused nothingness.

Windrush felt, looking down upon it and perceiving only blackness and depth, that it was not a simple physical abyss like the drop-off of the Amethyst Cliffs, staggering though that drop was. This seemed more like an opening from this realm to some other, to some lightless place that might be another universe, or might be something else altogether. He wondered if Tar-skel lived, still, somewhere beyond that empty darkness. Windrush shivered at the thought, and hoped that the answer was no.

Maybe someone, someday, would explore the depths of that rift to assure them that Tar-skel was gone forever. But he didn't think it would be dragons. That was not a dragon place. It smelled alien, cold and distant.

He had ordered a guard along the length of the rift, and thought that they would be wise to keep it guarded forever, or for as long as the race of dragons lived, anyway. Who knew what might come up through this opening in the weave of their realm, one day? He had an unsettling feeling that the dragons might never again be quite so isolated in their own realm as they once had been.

He kept these thoughts to himself, for now. The others had enough to think about already. As they flew on toward the Mountain, leaving the rift behind, he felt his heart lightening. At that moment, Ar and Ed rematerialized on his shoulders. *You were not gone long*, he said to Ar, noting that the parrot was asleep on Ar's shoulder. *Are you sure you would not like to rest a little more, while you can? Were you not very tired?*

The tall rigger's eyes glinted with purple light. *Perhaps I will, after we've reached the Dream Mountain, Windrush. Perhaps I'll be able to rest then. Just now I don't think I can. I don't want to miss a thing. And I—* His voice broke sharply, and he seemed unable to finish his thought.

You long to speak with Jael again? Windrush murmured. The rigger nodded.

Yes, said the dragon. *Yes,* he whispered again, to himself. And he found himself flying just a little faster, without meaning to, just a little higher and faster toward the vast, translucent peak that was steadily growing before them.

In the continuing musical presence of the draconae, Jael found a kind of silence, a solitude of peace among those who bore so much knowledge and so much passion. She wasn't sure yet what she thought of life in the Dream Mountain; it would take a long time to explore it fully. She hoped that the weavings of power that gave her life here would give her the time to do so.

With the final fulfillment of the Words, the tone of the draconae's music had changed—had become not just joyous and uplifting, but filled with a fury of creative energy. The Forge of Dreams had been opened to the realm once more, by Lavafire and the others. But now, instead of being tightly woven into protective magic, the light and power were being spun out into the realm, restoring and healing the land. Somewhere within that forge, the ifflings were finding renewal, and were preparing to create another generation of iffling-children, ifflings who would know a freedom of the realm that had almost been forgotten by the present generation. And within the slopes of the Mountain, dragon eggs once held frozen by the Enemy's sorcery, neither living nor dead, were again pulsing and glowing with life.

A flight of draconi was en route to the Mountain now, led by Windrush. Many of the draconae were clustered on the outer slopes, eagerly awaiting their arrival. How long had it been since they had flown freely together, fearlessly in communion, flying the skies, powerful dragons soaring and glassy draconae blazing in the sun? It seemed an age ago. Many of the draconae had not flown in so long, they were reluctant to venture far at all from the slopes of the Mountain, though Starchime had expressed her hope that that feeling would change, once the draconi had joined them.

Jael was eager for the arrival of the dragons. But more than anything else, she awaited the arrival of Ar.

(*Rawwk! And Ed!*)

(*And Ed,*) she mused, jostling the parrot affectionately in her thoughts. (*Yes, indeed. It's going to be hard to say good-bye to them, in the end—when they go, and we stay.*)

(*Gwarrrkk. Ed knows. They'll come back, though—awwwwk, yes?*)

Will they? Jael thought. She hoped so, certainly, but there was no way to know. There was also no point in worrying now about the future. They had not even said good-bye yet. There would be time enough for those worries later.

A chiming voice caught her attention, from the outside of the Mountain. *Dragons! Draconi! Crossing the plain!*

And soon someone else called, *Welcome Windrush! Welcome Windrush and the draconi!*

The cry was echoed, until it rang over and over throughout the Mountain. But Jael had her own cry as she formed her kuutekka in the underrealm fires. *Ar, are you there? Ed? Windrush—?*

Rawwwwwk—!

Come quickly!

Epilogue:
NEW BEGINNINGS

THE ACTIVITY in the Mountain seemed unceasing, *was* unceasing. It was not just the draconae flying out across the realm with their new freedom, or the draconi flying with them, asking them endless questions, courting them, renewing relationships long forgotten. It was also the ifflings appearing at intervals from the dreamfires, each time looking brighter and more numerous. And it was the long talks with Ar, his spaceship parked on the outer slopes, Jael speaking through the underrealm to his shimmering presence.

And it was the dragon eggs, glowing back to life in the inner slopes of the Mountain—the next generation of dragons!—bathed on one side by the radiance of the sun shining through the glass slopes of the Mountain, and on the other by the warmth of the Mountain itself, flowing out from the Forge of Dreams. It seemed that there were always glasswinged draconae fluttering over them now, sheltering and nurturing them—and even a few curious draconi, spending an unusual amount of time watching and listening to the unborn dragons.

Nor had they forgotten the egg in the Grotto Garden—which, like much of the lumenis, had been imprisoned by Tar-skel, but not destroyed. Sheltered against the long darkness by Treegrower, that solitary egg had survived. And so had the aging dracona, refusing to admit of any possibility of flight to the Final Dream Mountain until she saw that egg hatched. At first, the talk had been of bringing them both to the Dream Mountain; but the egg was fragile and thin-shelled, and the draconae had decided to weave their spells of growing, and to release the power of the Mountain directly to the Grotto Garden itself.

Who would that young dragonling be? Jael wondered—that lone dragon-to-be, protected against the Enemy for so long, and cherished by a dying dracona to be raised in a new day? She was as eager as any of the draconae to meet the dragon when it hatched.

So much was happening in the realm, and in the Mountain, that time had almost ceased to have meaning for her. To Jael, it was not so much that time was flying by, as that it was standing still. She wasn't sure, really, what time *meant*, in this existence, so different from anything she had known before. She wondered if this was a taste of what it felt like to live in the soulfires of the Final Dream Mountain. Would she have a chance to speak again with Highwing, when she had passed through that last door? More than once, she had thought that she had heard his voice whispering to her, in the near silence of secluded moments in the Mountain. Was it real? Almost anything seemed possible in the dreamfires, in that strange and marvelous singularity that lay at the heart of the Mountain.

She had already asked Lavafire if the singularity could be focused somehow, to help Ar and Ed and the damaged spaceship *Seneca* find safe passage out of the realm to a starport in the static realm. It was an idea that fascinated the draconae, and they were working on it.

But it was an idea that saddened her, as well. It was a reminder that Ar and his Ed would soon have to leave. To Jael, it seemed as if they had just arrived, but they had been here on the Mountain now for many shipdays of their time. They could not linger here forever; they still had a mission contract to fulfill, and news to take back to Kan-Kon, and in truth she thought it was hard on Ar to see her here as a . . . living ghost, probably, from his perspective. The friend he had known, as he'd known her, was gone. No longer could they relax in the ship's commons, around the stondai tree, with Ed flitting about. He could talk to her only through the net, and then only to her kuutekka-presence, because that was all she had now. She knew he didn't find it easy.

One way or another, we will return, Ar assured her, for at least the twentieth time, stretching out his hands from the ghostly prow of the ship. It was parked in the outer world, but he and Ed had their heads stuck into the underrealm, as though peering underwater, to speak with her. *But who can say how long it will take—or what that will turn out to be in your time? We do have to earn a living. And I'm not sure how many clients will want us to be passing this way.*

Awwwwwwk-k-k. Safe now! crowed Ed, Jael's Ed, fluttering out from her kuutekka. *Mountain realm safe!*

Ar chuckled. *Maybe so. But I can't help noticing that every time we come this way, we end up limping back home to the repair docks.*

Ed cackled. *Good for business—hawwww!*

Jael smiled, knowing that there was no real answer to Ar's concerns. *Maybe you can persuade Kan-Kon to visit. Starshime tells me that they're almost ready to bring Hodakai here—as soon as they tighten the transport spell just a little more. They're being very careful.*

More careful than FullSky was when he brought you here, it sounds like, said Ar.

Jael nodded. Of course, the situation was different now; they could take all the time they needed. And the truth was that even the draconae were astonished at some of the things that FullSky had managed to do, all while a prisoner in Tar-skel's dungeon. *Is Windrush going to help you fly out, when the time comes?*

Haww, yes! cried the parrot in the ship's net.

He said he'd fly us right up to the singularity and fling us through, if that was what we wanted, Ar said. *Not exactly in those words, I guess. But yes—he'll see us off. Here he is now.* Ar pointed off into the shimmering, glassy distance of the underrealm.

The dragon was approaching, his kuutekka glowing silver. *Windrush!* Jael called. *How is the new garden coming?*

The dragon emitted a happy tongue of fire that shone like a dancing ghost in the underweb of the Mountain. *I've*

*found a spot, and Starchime is almost ready to sing it into being
with me. It will be a good place to raise . . . younglings, I think.
I may have to ask the ifflings to ask the sweepers if they would
come create some sculptures for me.*

Highwing's spot? Jael asked softly.

The dragon's eyes glowed brightly. *Just downstream from
it. I wanted to leave his old garden alone for now—the spot
where it was, I mean. I don't want to intrude. After all, it
wouldn't surprise me if his spirit still visited there from time to
time.* Windrush paused thoughtfully. *Even now, I often feel
as though he is still with me, somehow.*

Perhaps it was Jael's imagination, or perhaps it was just
the fluttering of Ed in her thoughts, but she could have
sworn she felt a silent whispering presence pass by her, like
a breeze stirring a curtain in a window. And a moment
later, she was absolutely certain she heard a voice say, very
softly, *(Of course I am with you—all of you. I have never left,
and never will.)* And she felt the presence moving again, and
realized that Ed—her Ed—had cocked his head at her, as
though listening for something.

Well, she said to Windrush, and saw a similar expression
on his face. His eyes, even in their kuutekka form, glowed
bright and emerald and deep as a clear-crystal sea, and she
knew that he had heard the same voice.

Somehow I don't think you have to worry about intruding, she
said to Windrush. With a wink at Ar, she added, *Why don't
you go sing that garden into being, and take Ar with you to see
it happen?*

Windrush nodded and puffed another bright flame. *I
would be pleased if you would come join us,* he said. *And—*

Ed! squawked Ar's parrot. *Don't forget Ed!*

Not in an age! the dragon chuckled. *And we'll see that the
draconae don't forget you, either. Would you like to be remembered in a song, my rigger-friend?*

The parrot cocked his head, but before he could speak,
the question seemed to be answered for him by a soft,
distant choir of draconae voices, chiming in the heart of the
Dream Mountain.

ABOUT THE AUTH

Jeffrey A. Carver is the author of a number of t
provoking, popular science fiction novels, includir
Infinity Link and *The Rapture Effect*. His books con
hard-SF concepts, deeply humanistic concerns, and a s
of humor, making them both compellingly suspenseful a
emotionally satisfying.

Carver first wrote in his "star-rigger" universe that is th
setting for *Dragon Rigger* in the novels *Star Rigger's Way*
(1978) and *Panglor* (1980), both of which will be reissued
soon in Tor Books editions, and more recently *Dragons in
the Stars*, published in 1992. He currently lives with his
family in the Boston area.

hought
g The
bine
nse
nd